5/16

-A-
Perfect
Life

-A-
Perfect
Life

A Novel

Eileen Pollack

An Imprint of HarperCollins*Publishers*

HarperCollins books may be purchased for educational, business, or sales promotional use. For information, please e-mail the Special Markets Department at SPsales@harpercollins.com.

FIRST EDITION

Designed by Ashley Tucker

Library of Congress Cataloging-in-Publication Data has been applied for.

ISBN 978-0-06-241917-0

16 17 18 19 20   OV/RRD   10 9 8 7 6 5 4 3 2 1

For Tom

-A-
Perfect
Life

1

In another few minutes, I will need to climb the stairs and explain to my daughter why her father and I gave her life when we knew she would need to live it watching the clock, watching herself. Maybe Lila won't hold her fate against me any more than I held my fate against my parents. But then, I was older. I knew they had acted out of ignorance. And how could I condemn the very people to whom I owed my existence, enthralled as I was with the mystery, the miracle, of being Jane Weiss?

Maybe we are divided into those of us who think that our parents' choice in giving birth needs to be explained, and those for whom such a demand would seem incredible. *We fell in love. We got married. We had a child—we had you.* We are divided, too, I think, into those of us who live with a clock ticking in our heads, and those of us who don't. I have heard my own clock ticking since my earliest years, a decade before I learned that the word "Valentine's" means more to our family than a holiday of love.

The story I am about to tell begins with such a clock. Or more accurately, with a timer, the cheap plastic kind you use to cook eggs. I was working in my lab. Not the lab I work in now. This was my lab at MIT, when I was only a postdoc. It was a Friday, at six P.M., and I could hear the timer ticking backward toward zero. I was due to meet my father across the bridge in Boston in less than fifteen minutes, but first I had to extract the DNA from one last blood sample. In my right hand I held a sterile pipette, in my left hand a test tube. The iron-heavy red cells had sunk to the bottom. White cells floated in the middle. A faint yellow serum lay spread across the top. It reminded me of the "tropical" Jell-O parfaits my mother used to serve before she stopped cooking.

I started to work the rubber cork from the test tube with the thumb and index finger of the same hand that held it. I had done this a million times. It was one of those small acts of competence that helps us to believe we are what we claim to be, we know what we are doing. The mistake I made this time was watching my hand, thinking about my clumsiness, worrying. I foresaw what would happen. I would be left holding the cap while my other three fingers let the tube of blood fall. I tried to prevent this, but my hand wouldn't respond. The tube dropped to the linoleum.

Flora Drury, the woman from whose veins this blood had come, was thirty-four years old, one year older than I was, but she looked at least fifty. When I had entered the Drurys' trailer earlier that day, she had been sitting in the kitchen with her eyes rolled toward the light, head swiveled, fingers clutching the edge of her red vinyl chair. She vibrated as if that chair were electrified. Her teeth chattered—*click, click, click*. Flora's husband, Mac, a jut-toothed man in overalls, had given his consent for the procedure. But I insisted on making clear to every new donor why we needed his or her blood. As I pronounced the words "a cure for Valentine's chorea," Flora's shaking grew frenzied. The metal legs of her chair danced across the floor. Flora's head, which was covered with dry reddish tufts, like the petals on a marigold, rattled on her neck. I knew what was coming. But knowing what is coming doesn't always calm us. The more a person knows, the more her nerves tighten. When Flora barked, "Yes!," my heart catapulted around my chest. I tried a trick I had perfected: eyes closed, I inhaled, imagining the air to be liquid concrete, filling my body, hardening. By the time I had let my breath out, the trembling had nearly stopped.

"All right then," I said. I pried Flora's hands from the chair, then held her fragile arm while Rita Nichols, our nurse, tied a length of rubber tubing around Flora's bicep, pinched the wax-paper skin to locate a vein, and plunged a needle deep in the crook of Flora's elbow. After a few moments, Rita yanked the needle out. A bright drop of blood rose from Flora's skin, and Rita slapped it with a gauze pad. She was always brusque with donors. ("You tell that husband of yours he'd better keep you clean or I'll report him to the authorities," she had told Flora earlier, with her husband looking on.) I was brusque, but for a different reason. If I had opened my mouth to tell Flora I was sorry for any pain we might cause, I wouldn't have been able to stop apologizing.

The tube of Flora's blood was as foamy and warm as freshly cooked jam. I slipped it in the rack beside the other samples we had drawn from Flora's family. (Not even the youngest child, a boy of six, had made a fuss or cried. His father loomed above us, snapping one of Rita's used tourniquets, and I hoped the boy's obedience came from love and not fear.) I was disposing of the syringes when Flora leaped from her chair and spun about the room, arms flailing, chin tucked against her chest.

"Shit on Valentine's!" she screamed. Then she froze where she stood. Speechless, immobile, arms overhead, she looked like a tuning fork still humming from the hammer's last blow.

IIIIIIIIIIIIIIIIIIIIIIIIIIIIIIIIIIII

Now, in the lab, I knelt beside my bench trying to accept that I would need to drive back to the Drurys' trailer in Pittsfield and ask for more blood. Not that I would admit I had spilled the first sample. Flora's husband wouldn't ask. At worst, I could lie and say I needed more of Flora's blood because her genes were so interesting, so vital for determining the cause of the illness that threatened us all. None of this calmed me. The drive to New Hampshire and back would consume half a day. I could see myself sitting in Rita's rusty Chevette, urging it on. The car would go slower the harder I wished, until, by the time we arrived at Flora's trailer, I would be clutching the dash and struggling to draw a breath.

What I dreaded wasn't seeing Flora Drury so much as becoming her. One day, I, too, might be sitting in a kitchen chair, shaking and shaking, until I shot up and flung myself about the room shouting obscenities, as my mother had done that interminable year before she died of Valentine's. A fifty-fifty chance. Heads, I was healthy. Tails, I had inherited the disease that killed my mother, her two brothers, and their father before them. Of the twenty-three pairs of chromosomes in each of my mother's cells, one pair contained a good and a bad gene. The egg from which I had developed might have contained a copy of the good gene, or maybe it contained the bad. Whichever it was, that gene was hidden among the two hundred thousand other genes that were strung along my chromosomes, imperceptible pearls on a necklace too tiny to be worn by a flea. Even with all the donors I had bled and all the DNA I had studied, I didn't have the slightest clue where to look.

The earliest sign of Valentine's is clumsiness. And I was nothing if I wasn't clumsy. Never mind that the prospect of seeing my father, even on time, made me so nervous I could have dropped a dozen test tubes. There always were *reasons*. Rushing to the sink for a wad of paper towels to wipe up Flora's blood, I bumped into Susan Bate. The accident was her fault. Susan was always scurrying here and there in her big plastic goggles, chattering, *"Shit-shit-shit-shit,"* like a squirrel that suspects its nuts have been stolen. Even scientists less frenzied than Susan Bate and I bumped into each other in the course of a day. Knowing why we had collided didn't comfort me, any more than it comforted me to know why I was always tripping across the threshold (the tiles there were warped). Excuses meant nothing.

Or rather, they meant I was acting the way my mother had acted whenever I asked why she had cut her hand yet again, or why she had forgotten to pick me up after science club, or why she had taken to cursing—foul, shocking oaths that even my father wouldn't have said to a man. Always, she had excuses. And these excuses made sense. Hadn't I believed them? And even if my own excuses were true, even if they let me reassure myself that I wasn't sick (yet), by the time I had contrived them, my heart had lost its rhythm. Already I had made myself so hyperconscious about not dropping anything, I was sure to drop the next object I touched.

I made it to the street. I was unlocking my bike when Vic O'Connell, the biologist who ran my lab, pulled up in a taxi. Vic is very tall, with sorrowful, downcast eyes and a question-mark slouch. He's the kind of man who thinks that if only he bows his head and shuffles, no one will figure out that he is taller and smarter than they are. He unfolded from the taxi and stood looking me up and down. "Are you leaving already?" he said. (Only a scientist would ask why someone was going home at six fifteen on a Friday night.) You could see he was disappointed. He had been in Amsterdam all week. Slung across his shoulder was the scuffed vinyl bag in which he carried his only suit. He asked if I wanted to grab dinner and talk about some probes he had brought back from the conference.

"I wish I could," I said. And believe it or not, I did. There was nothing romantic between us. But we shared the tender appreciation that grows between any two people who care about each other's work more than anyone else cares. Vic's wife, Dianne, cared only about their kids. I had no boyfriend to care at all. I wanted nothing more than to sit across from Vic at Legal Sea Foods, eating a bowl of clam chili and listening to his soft, too-earnest voice discuss those probes he had brought back from Amsterdam. But my father was in town, and he had arranged another of his fundraisers at Tommie's Pierside. How could Vic try to keep me? Money from my father's fundraisers helped to pay his bills.

"Of course!" Vic said. "How could I forget? Look at you, all dressed up!"

I was wearing a khaki skirt and a once-white blouse that bloomed with so many chemical stains it might have been a floral print. Back then, I hardly cared about my appearance. I equated dressing up with growing old. Old enough to become my mother.

I told Vic I would stop by later and we could discuss the conference then.

He nodded. He would like that. In the meantime, I should give his best to my father. He turned and waved good-bye.

I climbed on my bike and pedaled off. I was late. I had to rush. Even when I wasn't late, I had to rush. My mother had come down with Valentine's when she wasn't much older than I was now. I biked across the Charles. A pair of elegant sculls skimmed beneath the bridge. The masts of slender dinghies leaned this way, then that, like a troupe of ballerinas trailing white scarves. The State House dome shimmered on Beacon Hill. Farther west, the Citgo sign kept pointing, pointing at the sun, which was as round and red as the drop of blood on Flora Drury's arm.

I might have stopped to watch, but one of the telltale symptoms of Valentine's disease is the urge to stop and stare. I sped across the bridge, then darted past the cars circling the rotary at the other end. I stood on my pedals to make the hill.

"Nice ass!" a truck driver called. "Keep it moving, sweetheart!"

Boyishly small, with short hair and no hips, I rarely was the target of comments like these. I was so startled I didn't see the car door fly open ahead of me.

I swerved just in time. If I had fallen and gotten hurt, I couldn't have explained my injuries to my father. He hated that his daughter, a woman in her thirties, should still be riding a bike. *You're not a child,* he would have said. *Here, I'll write a check. Go and buy a good used Chevy.* I would have protested that I didn't need a car. This was Boston, after all. Everyone here rode bikes, even Harvard professors with silver hair and red bow-ties. But my father was right. I liked feeling childish. A child didn't need to confront the possibility that she might come down with Valentine's. Or that she might marry and have a child who came down with Valentine's. Or that she might grow too old to marry and have a child before she could figure out if she did or did not have the gene for Valentine's. On a smooth downhill stretch, I would sometimes ride with my arms out. How could anyone whose balance was so acute and who could pedal so quickly, even uphill, let death overtake her?

Distracted, I missed the turnoff to the pier. The shops were all closed; there was no one to ask directions. I rode furiously up and down narrow one-way streets that met at odd angles. The harbor lay east, but I couldn't get my bearings. No matter which way I turned, I saw the same open manhole, the same iron-barred jeweler's. My mind raced around those streets, but I couldn't seem to move. That happened all the time. I would find myself standing in the lab planning what to do next. *Develop those blots. Ask Lew for more reagent. Check to see the mice haven't eaten their babies.* In my mind, I would be doing all these things at once, in ever smaller circles. That was how my mother had described her trances: *I was spinning so fast, I seemed to stand still.*

I pedaled down an alley and emerged on a well-lit road. Just beyond lay the harbor. A green neon fish kept flashing TOMMIE'S PIERSIDE. I told myself that even native Bostonians had trouble finding Tommie's. The ocean breeze was chilly. I was too lightly dressed. Anyone, even a person who stood absolutely no chance of inheriting the gene for Valentine's, would be shaking this hard.

2

Tommie's was a tourist trap, but the tourists it trapped were far better dressed than I was. I slipped past the maître d', who kept watch from behind a podium that had a ship's steering wheel on the back and a bosomy figurehead of a woman nailed to the front, then ducked inside the ladies' room, hoping to make myself more presentable. I combed my hair with my fingers, the helmet having flattened it. I wasn't unattractive. But whenever I looked in a mirror, I saw my father's humped nose. I was his daughter, after all. Or so the family myth had it. I was plain, clever, and ambitious, while my younger sister, Laurel, was blessed with our mother's beauty and charm but doomed to die young.

I glanced in the mirror, then took a scallop of soap from a clamshell dish and used it to scrub the flecks of Flora's blood from beneath my eye.

⠀⠀⠀⠀⠀⠀⠀⠀⠀⠀⠀⠀

My father raised a wineglass. Then he saw me come in. "Doll!" he said. "Jane!" as if I were the object of the toast he had intended to propose all along.

My admiration for my father always overwhelmed me, it seemed so out of proportion to what a short, unsophisticated man he was. He had never gone to college. His diction was coarse. But he had used his native shrewdness to amass a small fortune—from a single army-navy warehouse in our hometown of Mule's Neck, New York, he had built a chain of small department stores that stretched across several counties. Then, after my mother died, he had funneled every penny he had ever earned into establishing a foundation to find a cure for Valentine's. He had browbeaten scientists into joining his cause, although most of them would have preferred working on diseases whose symptoms were clear—a lump in the breast, too much fat in the heart. Diseases that could strike a senator's wife or a taxpayer's child instead of those few unfortunate souls who had been born to a family with terrible genes. (Even Merriwether Valentine, who had first identified the syndrome in the mid-1800s among his patients in rural Georgia, had mistaken its cause to be vice.)

As long as my mother was well, my father hoarded. Then he hacked down the dam he had built around his money and out it all poured. He established two trust funds—one for Laurel, and one for me. How could he die knowing that his daughters might be consigned to a state institution, tied to their chairs and reeking of piss? How could he live knowing that he hadn't done everything to find a cure for our illness? He was doing this for my sake. And for Laurel's sake. And his own.

He stubbed out his cigar and wrapped his arm around me. "You look good," he said. "Too skinny, but good."

I didn't bother to thank him, any more than I had thanked him for all those other inspections I had had to endure in high school. *Baby, can't you do something with those eyebrows? What's it called, tweeze them? You never heard of lipstick? You'd really be some dish if you'd only dress up.* Later, when my mother began her decline, he grew even angrier to see me unkempt, as if her beauty were a religion whose rituals I had profaned. After she died, I got by with the barest attention to appearance hygiene would allow. But by then, my father was inspecting me less for stray hairs than for reassurance that I didn't tremble or twitch, didn't fall into trances or curse without cause. He reluctantly approved anything that would allow me to spend more time in the lab. If I found a cure for Valentine's, I could get married and stay at home, primping and tweezing for the rest of my life.

I apologized for being late but told him that I'd had an experiment I needed to finish. He shrugged—this excused me, as I had been hoping it would. "Come on," he said. "Let me introduce you." He led me around the table. My father was a man who only felt complete leading a woman around a room, and it made me happy to think I could be that woman, although it also made me sad, knowing that he would rather have been leading my mother.

One of the few guests I already knew was Sumner Butterworth, a Harvard neurologist my father had persuaded to look for "our" gene. Sumner's approach involved dissecting the brains of people who had been killed by Valentine's. Although my father raved against anyone too sentimental to leave his loved one's brain to science, I couldn't help but wonder what he would have done if some doctor had asked permission to hack my mother's brain from its stem and freeze it in a Ziploc bag. I respected Sumner's work, but his methods struck me as crude. I had switched from medical school to research in the hope of finding a more elegant cure for Valentine's. But I hadn't had much luck, and for now, we needed Sumner.

He stopped shucking the clams before him and shook my hand limply. In the world of science, Sumner Butterworth commanded far more respect than I did. But my father's foundation funded Sumner's lab. I almost wished that he would ignore me, as he would have ignored any other scientist who wasn't tenured Harvard faculty.

"Doll," my father said, "I'd like you to meet Franklin DeWitt. Of DeWitt Pharmaceuticals."

I forced some warmth into my voice. "Hello, Mr. De-Witt. Thank you very much for coming." Like most of the guests, Franklin DeWitt wore a well-tailored suit, a silk tie, and a fancy watch. I had to fight my instinct to distrust him. If a stranger showed up in a lab wearing a suit and tie, we figured he was there to sell us supplies. The last thing a scientist wants to be taken for is a salesman. If your theories are true, if your results can be verified, you don't need to *sell* them. Being a fluent speaker is fine, but only if you have something important to say.

I greeted the other guests, then stood nibbling a pack of oyster crackers and watching my father glad-hand the room. He had this habit of draping one arm across the person to whom he was speaking and whispering confidences to the man. Every few minutes, he would pull his victim closer, as if he were trying to wad him in a ball and tuck him in the inner pocket of his suit. Sometimes, he frowned and jerked his thumb in my direction.

The only woman I recognized I had met a dozen years earlier, when she and my father had gone before Congress begging for funds to cure the disease that had widowed them both. Honey Land's late husband, Dusty, had been a moderately famous actor. Once, on a sick day from school, I had sat beside my mother watching one of Dusty Land's earliest films. He was tall and thick-bodied, with a jaw so square it might have been a block glued to his chin. I wasn't sure he was handsome until I heard my mother comment, "Dusty Land can park his boots under my bed anytime he wants," a remark that shocked me, given how infrequently she talked about sex before she fell ill. I can't recall much else about that movie. Back then, I didn't know or care who Dusty Land was. I didn't yet understand how our lives would be linked.

"Good!" my father boomed. He was crushing the shoulders of a man even shorter than he was, as round and tan as an acorn. "I knew you'd come through, Syd. Honey, get over here."

Honey excused herself from the knot of men around her. Years before, as Hannah Nathaniels, she had been a Rockette, and even now, in her early sixties, she wouldn't have seemed out of place onstage at Radio City Music Hall.

"Syd here's decided to make a real contribution. A man gives away that much money, he ought to get a kiss from a beautiful dame."

Honey pecked the man's forehead. "I only wish I could do a little something more to show you how much I appreciate your generosity."

"Don't get ideas, Syd. For 'a little something more' we're talking six figures."

"You mustn't listen to a word this man says," Honey scolded. "Not one single word."

Despite this feigned fight, I could guess what my father and Honey had in common. Although our family's trials had been nearly unendurable, the Lands had suffered even more. While my mother had confined her lewdness to comments only we heard ("I bet he's well hung," she had said of Henry Kissinger as he was addressing a phalanx of reporters on TV), Dusty Land had been arrested for stopping a teenage girl on the street, unzipping his fly, and asking if she wanted to lick his all-day sucker. The doctors were so certain that Dusty had the DTs they consigned him to Bellevue. Several months later, when an intern informed Honey that her husband wasn't actually a sex-crazed lush but rather a victim of an obscure disease called Valentine's chorea, she was seized with remorse. After he died, she flew around the country starting support groups for anyone whose relatives suffered from the disease. She joined my father in trying to raise money to find a cure.

Now, at Tommie's Pierside, Honey put her hand on my arm. It startled me to see those scarlet nails against my skin. "Oh, Janie," she said. "You aren't thinking of leaving already, are you? I want you to meet my son, Willie." She crossed the room, and I tried to think why she would want me to meet her son. She couldn't possibly be trying to fix us up. Of all people, Honey ought to know that any son of her late husband had to be the worst choice for me to date.

"Jane," she said, "this is Willie. Willie, this is Herb's daughter, Jane."

Even then, Willie was no one's idea of thin. He had his father's cleft jaw, although on him it looked less glamorous than reassuring. In those days, he wore his hair scraggly and long. Men with long hair usually struck me as vain. But Willie seemed simply to have forgotten to cut his. Maybe that was his allure. He defied the usual categories by which I judged whom I did or did not like.

"Hey," he said.

"Hey," I said back.

"Jane, Willie . . ." Honey seemed uncomfortable. "You two . . . you have a lot in common. You're going to be . . . Let's just say it's high time you got to know each other." Then she rushed off to greet more guests.

I couldn't figure out what she meant. From what I knew, Honey's son spent most of his time on some hill in New Hampshire, consulting his swami and eating brown rice. We had nothing in common other than having watched a parent die of Valentine's. In those days, friends often fixed me up with men who had diseases. One of my college roommates had introduced me to a lawyer who was legally blind; a classmate from graduate school had given my number to a Vietnam vet with one leg. The one-legged vet in particular was a sweet guy. But why did everyone assume that an illness gave two people more in common than any other trait?

"I've sure heard a lot about you," Willie said. I could hear the twang in his voice, but I couldn't place the accent. His father had been born in Oklahoma, but as far as I knew, Willie had been raised in Manhattan. As fast as most New Yorkers crammed their words together, that's how slowly he spoke. "Pretty great news, don't you think? Although, I guess it's still hush-hush."

I smiled, unwilling to admit that I didn't know what secret he assumed we shared. One by one, the donors left. A busboy in a ruffled shirt cleared away the dishes. I expected my father would want to spend some time alone with me. But he startled me by kissing me on the cheek and telling me he had to go. "Honey got us tickets for some show," he said. "What's it called, *A Cage of Faygelehs?*"

"Shhhhh!" Honey looked around the room. "What can you do with him?" she asked me. I shrugged. I couldn't imagine how she had convinced my father to pay a hundred dollars to see a show. Even before my mother fell ill, my parents rarely went out.

"Sorry, doll." My father squeezed my arm. "We'll have brunch Sunday, right?"

I had never heard my father use that word, "brunch."

"Nine o'clock," Honey said. "The early bird gets the worm." Then she actually added: "I don't think the Ritz-Carlton *really* serves worms."

They started to leave. But Honey stopped at the threshold. "Herb, wait. Janie hasn't eaten." Her hand fluttered to her waist, which was smaller than mine. "Call the waitress back and make her order something."

I waited for my father to say, *She's thirty-three years old. If she's going to show up late, she can find her own dinner.* Instead, he stood with his arm linked in Honey's, both of them staring.

"I've been busy," I said. "I haven't been sleeping." But I knew why they were staring. In my mother's last year, she had trembled so hard she had burned away her flesh at an alarming rate. Sometimes, she had shaken so violently I thought her very bones would ignite. "It's not Valentine's," I said. "That isn't why I'm so thin." Except, indirectly, it was. Valentine's was the reason I so rarely took the time to sleep or eat. "I need to go back to the lab and feed some cells," I said. "I'll grab some dinner later."

"The lab!" Honey splayed a hand across her chest. "Willie, dear, drive her. And make sure she eats something."

He was studying a photo of the restaurant's owner, Tommie Anastasio, shaking the hand of a minor black celebrity whose name I didn't know.

"Thanks," I said. "I have my bike."

"At night? The way people drive in Boston?" Honey wrinkled her nose. "Willie, put this *bike* of hers in the back of that old *thing* you drive and make sure Janie gets where she is going."

"Oh no," I said. "I do this all the time. Really. Enjoy the show. I'll see you Sunday morning." I kissed my father, then edged out the door and left them standing together, Honey and Herb. Jesus, I thought, they sounded like a salad dressing.

"Hey," someone called. I turned and saw Willie standing beside a pyramid of lobster traps. There was something touching about his size. He was too big, the way Vic O'Connell was too big. But he wasn't awkward, the way Vic was. Vic carried his body the way he carried that suit— like something he was forced to wear on special occasions but otherwise would have preferred to leave hanging in his closet. Willie carried his body the way he might have supported a drunken friend—tenderly, with some compassion.

He asked if I was sure I was all right.

I assumed he was asking: Was I sure I would be okay riding my bike at night? "I'm sure," I said. "Thanks."

He plucked at my blouse. "So then, what's all this red stuff?"

I dropped my head to see.

"Maybe it's ketchup." He drawled the word so slowly I could see the tilted bottle, the heavy red paste refusing to pour. "Then again, maybe it's not."

I couldn't understand how Flora's blood had splashed so high. He asked if I'd had an accident. Maybe I'd gotten hurt?

No, I said. I dropped a test tube.

"Don't you wear one of those white coats?" he asked.

No, I said. Only doctors wore white coats.

He cocked his head and raised his eyebrows, which were curly and lush. It wasn't fair that a woman couldn't get away with having eyebrows like that.

"You're not a doctor?" he said.

Some researchers were medical doctors, I explained. They saw patients most of the week, then messed around in the lab for a few hours on Friday afternoon and got in everyone's way. *They* wore white coats. Biologists—Ph.D.s.—did their research in jeans.

"So," he said, "lab coats are for sissies? Like cars? Like accepting rides from friends?"

I apologized. I hadn't meant to be rude. I just got nervous when people treated me like an invalid.

He snorted. "She treats everyone like that. She treated my dad like that, even before he got sick. Brushed his teeth for him, for Christ's sake. He loved it. Don't ask me, some people like to be treated like a baby. She treats me that way, and I'm forty years old! Anyway, I made my peace with it. Doesn't bother me anymore. I hardly pay attention."

"But my father . . ." I said. In the old days, he had acted more like my mother's father than like her husband. Surely not like her son.

"But I shouldn't let her talk for me," he said. "I *want* to give you a ride. You need something to eat, and I wouldn't mind getting the taste of that lobster pie I ordered out of my mouth. I don't mean to seem ungrateful, but that wasn't exactly the best dinner I ever ate." He thrust his hand in one of the traps. "I think I got the last poor sucker they pulled up in this thing." He tried to get his hand out, but it was tangled in the net. The hand was hairy, pale, soft. Definitely more a mammal than a crustacean. My heart twinged, as if a not-too-bright animal had blundered into danger and couldn't find its way out.

The maître d' looked up from his podium and regarded us suspiciously. Willie freed his hand. "I've never seen anyone feed her cells before."

"They're not *my* cells. They're cells from other people. Cancer cells. As long as they get fed, they'll keep dividing forever. I feed them fetal-calf serum. It's made by chopping up little fetal calves. Is that weird enough for you?"

"Weird enough?" He leaned toward me. I smelled a familiar smell, the same piney shampoo my sister, Laurel, used. His lips brushed my cheek—just below the spot where I had washed off Flora's blood. "Jane, darlin'," he said, "if you're going to be my new little sister, which, from what my mother just hinted, I'm pretty sure you will be, then you'd better get a whole lot weirder, real fast."

3

I unlocked my bike from the anchor in front of Tommie's and lifted it into the back of Willie's Jeep, which was old but immaculate. He tipped the valet with the offhand manner of a man lending a friend a dollar. A Jeep was its own affectation, I thought, but not as ostentatious as a sports car would have been. After all, he had to drive something.

We left the lot, then the pier. He didn't glance in my direction, and I wondered if I had offended him. But the longer I watched, the more I came to think that here was a man who could do only one thing at one time. Right now he was driving. He moved his head back and forth, monitoring each gauge and listening so intently to the engine he seemed to shift gears without using the clutch. I couldn't remember when I had last done one thing at one time. Even as a child, I had kept a book on my lap and read it while the teacher lectured up front. I chose friends for this same quality, this impatience with the limits of what a person could accomplish in a normal life. My first lover enjoyed teaching me about biology almost as much as he enjoyed teaching me about sex. *Do you know, Jane,* he had asked, guiding my hand up his leg, *if you stretched out the seminiferous tubules in a man's testes, they would be sixteen hundred feet long?*

Willie drove so slowly it took me a while to realize he had stopped in the middle of the bridge. Cars rushed up behind and, honking, surged past.

"Look at it all," he said, motioning back toward Boston. "How often do I get to see this? I never smell the sea." He inhaled so deeply I could feel the sky drained of air. "Go on. Try it. You haven't taken one good breath since we met. You pant, you know? Like this?" He panted like a puppy, his fleshy tongue hanging out.

I hated when people told me I was too serious. Besides, telling someone to relax is the least effective way of ensuring she will. I told him if he hadn't stopped in the middle of the bridge, I might be more mellow.

"Just look back," he said. "You won't get turned to salt."

To humor him, I glanced at the row of brownstones bordering Storrow Drive, and the skyscrapers behind them, glittering against the sky. Maybe he had a point. What could be more spectacular than the Boston skyline at night? And Willie . . . there was something of that outsize quality about him, too. Maybe, if our parents got married, I would be able to lean on him a little, instead of always taking care of everyone else.

It was a great view, I admitted. But maybe we could go now, before someone plowed into us?

"Trust me," he said. "I'm a very careful driver." And really, he was. He turned on his blinker and resumed inching across the bridge. We reached the opposite shore. We weren't far from my lab, but we needed twenty minutes to find a spot to park. Until the late seventies, the area behind MIT had been a wasteland. Now, in the early eighties, offices and labs were springing up like wild, mutant flora. The streets were pocked by craters. Entire blocks were cordoned off.

Willie whistled through his teeth. "How can they put up these suckers so fast? I was in town a few months ago and none of this was here."

Everyone thought this. Skyscraper skeletons grew concrete skins overnight. Only for me did the changes come too slowly. When my second-grade teacher had asked us what we would want to be if we couldn't be ourselves, one of my classmates had said "a bird," another had said "a brontosaurus," another had said "a horse," and I had said "a mountain." I didn't want to miss a thing. I wanted to live long enough to know how the human race turned out.

Willie tapped my arm. "Where does a person get some chow around here?"

Even with all the offices going up, there were still surprisingly few restaurants—most people from MIT grabbed a sandwich from a pushcart or a packet of peanut butter crackers from a vending machine. I motioned in the direction of a nearly empty block that until recently had been the site of a florist, a delicatessen, and a shoe repair shop. Only the deli still stood, stripped now of neighbors, braced on either side by wooden struts. The restaurant seemed doomed, but the new Center for Biomedical Research would simply engulf it. The B&B Deli would survive as a symbiont, feeding its host, the way human mitochondria once lived on their own before moving in and becoming part of our cells.

The deli was dark and smoky, with scarred booths and paneled walls. The initials in the name stood for Barney and Bob, but MIT students used to joke that "B&B" stood for "Bed and Breakfast" since so many lab rats ate their dinners there at midnight, then stretched out in the booths and slept until dawn, when the B&B served delicious waffles and eggs.

"What'll it be tonight, Professor?" asked the man behind the counter (both owners wore bushy beards and Red Sox caps, so I never could identify which one was Barney and which one Bob). I flushed with the pride of being called "professor," even though I knew he called me that only because I looked so much like a kid. I ordered a pastrami sandwich and a knish, then tried to decide between rice pudding and chocolate cake.

"That's great," Willie said. "I love that. A pastrami sandwich. A knish!" All he took on his own tray were two cartons of chocolate milk.

"I forget to eat sometimes," I said. "But then I make up for it."

He nodded. "Sure. Got to build it up. Need that extra layer of fat. Although really, there's no sense trying to stockpile it. How long do you think it would take for you to shake off an extra twenty pounds? My dad could have done it in a week."

It was like discovering that another person could monitor your thoughts. I didn't know whether to be horrified or relieved. I led him to a booth, trying not to drop my tray or slosh my Coke.

"You think about it all the time, don't you?" he asked.

He had said aloud the most important fact about me, the fact I kept most hidden. Every moment I was alive, I thought about dying. "And you don't?" I said.

"Sure." He shook a carton of chocolate milk, then pried open the seam. "Every few weeks."

I told him that I didn't believe him. How could he avoid thinking he might have Valentine's?

"Zen," he said. "I used to think about it a lot. Then I went to Japan and became a Buddhist."

I must have rolled my eyes.

"That's a little arrogant, isn't it? Dismissing a philosophy that's been around for a couple of thousand years just because a few flakes in California took it up?"

The last thing I needed was a stepbrother who thought meditating on the sound of one hand clapping would cure my problems. I finished my pastrami sandwich and started on the cake. Willie kept staring at my mouth. I thought he wanted a bite of cake; I held out a forkful.

"What?" he said. "Thanks, why not."

He reached across the table, and his hand swallowed mine. That's when I knew I wasn't safe. No one can predict this, who might cause you to recall you don't live only in your mind. You know that old cliché about how people use only a fraction of their brains? In my case, it was my body I barely used.

He guided my hand toward his mouth and ate the cake. His tongue scoured his teeth for chocolate. They were such big, square, white teeth. And there was that long vertical crease that ran down his forehead, continued beneath his nose, then cleft his chin in two. I liked that face. I would have stopped in a museum and stood before it, staring.

I asked if our parents were really getting married. When did all this happen?

"You're not serious," he said. "They've been seeing each other for years."

"I know," I said. "The president of the Institute for Valentine's Research and the chairwoman of the Valentine's Disease Society getting together to plan their strategy." That my father was marrying Honey Land as a business arrangement seemed easier to accept than that he had proposed to her for the same reason he had proposed to my mother. "Do they love each other?" I asked stupidly.

He seemed puzzled. "Why would two people get married if they didn't love each other?"

My eyes began to well. I plucked a napkin from the dispenser. After so many years of being widowed, my father would finally have a woman to keep him company. A woman he could love.

"That's what this brunch thing is about," Willie said. "They want to announce their engagement. But your sister can't make it until Sunday morning. She's, what, a dancer? Modern? Ballet? She any good?"

I didn't know how to answer. I had never understood my sister's dancing, although her take on it was that a dance wasn't something that needed to be "understood." Still, I loved my sister more than anyone else. I thought she was the prettiest woman in the world. Her hair was so black and thick it hung around her shoulders like a living shawl. She had the same full lips and broad-toothed smile that had made our mother so attractive, and the same Kirghiz eyes—green and slanted, like a cat's. Willie, I was sure, would fall in love with my sister. Everyone did. She was beautiful. And tragic. Like me, she had reacted to the possibility that she might be carrying the gene for Valentine's by swearing never to have a family. But that didn't mean she lived alone. She slept with a great many men, but only men she couldn't love, or men who couldn't love her. I hoped she would see how kind Willie was and spare his feelings. But sometimes she gave in to softhearted suitors she couldn't bear to hurt, at least at the beginning.

I asked when Willie thought our parents might get married.

"This summer," he said. "Maybe August."

It was nearly the end of May!

He pried open the second carton of chocolate milk. I loved watching men's hands. A good biologist's hands are like acrobats, flicking the tiny caps from Eppendorf tubes, squeezing pipette bulbs, flaming metal loops over Bunsen burners. Willie's hands were too ungainly to be graceful, but they knew what they were doing. "That still leaves three months," he said. "In three months, my mom could have arranged Chuck and Di's wedding."

I couldn't believe that Honey would hold her wedding in Mule's Neck. But I also couldn't see my father wasting money on a fancy New York affair. A Valentine's benefit was scheduled for that July. Maybe he and Honey were planning to combine the events. It bothered me that they derived all the advantages of Valentine's—the excitement and purpose it gave to a life—with none of the risks.

"Doesn't it upset you?" I asked Willie. "The way they seem to get off on it. On Valentine's."

"Why?" he said. "Don't you?"

I pushed away my tray.

"Wait," he said. "Why is it all right to get wrapped up in your own disease, but not in someone else's? It doesn't take much imagination, does it, feeling sympathy for yourself?"

I had to admit he had a point. All of us had grown obsessed with studying who we were. If you were black, you studied being black. If you were a woman or Jewish or gay, you studied being that. Even scientists fell prey to self-obsession. Except my friend Maureen. She had been crippled as a child by rheumatoid arthritis and people expected she would work to find a cure. *I could, but I don't* was all Maureen would say. Instead, she was searching for the cause of a rare form of blindness that afflicted a few remote families in Peru. Her disabled friends acted as if arthritis were a nationality or a religion she had abandoned from shame. But now, listening to Willie, I thought she might be right. What would science be if doctors tried to cure only those diseases they themselves were prone to? I hadn't intended to study Valentine's. I had grown up wanting to figure out how an egg became a chick. I had only switched to medicine, and then to genetics, after my mother got sick and I came to understand the threat that hung over my family.

I asked Willie what he did with his time.

He took his last sip of milk and licked his lips. "Truth be told, I don't *do* a whole lot." He had a fair amount of money from his father's estate, he said. He had bought a little land in New Hampshire, back when hippies like him were doing that kind of thing. He had put up what you might call a house. In the seventies, there was a revival of interest in his father's movies, and the royalties started piling up. He had quite a bit of moolah to play around with, he said. He invested in new companies, and then, if he made a profit, he found a cause he liked and gave most of it away.

"You play the stock market?" I said. "Are you serious?" Dusty Land had made his reputation portraying working stiffs whose allegiance was to the poor rather than to the fat cats who owned the factories.

"I know," he said. "Farmer Sinclair's son growing up to be a venture capitalist scumbag." His accent grew thicker, as if he felt guilty about being rich. My father did the same thing. Whenever he felt self-conscious about being well off, he ladled on the inflections of a poor Brooklyn Jew.

"You make money," I said, "then you give it away?"

"Why?" he asked. "You need some?"

The lab always needed money. Enzymes cost a hundred dollars a drop. An ultracentrifuge cost as much as a Cadillac. But my father was the only member of the family who knew how to beg. "Valentine's is a good cause, isn't it?"

"Didn't used to seem that way. More like a lost cause." He stretched his tongue and coaxed another drop of milk from his glass. "Maybe you could convince me I'm wrong."

I pretended I didn't know what he wanted me to do—I hated explaining my work to laymen, if only because I found it so hard.

"I'm not such a dumb guy," Willie said. "I read the newspaper. But I usually can't make heads or tails of this genetics stuff. Every other morning you see some head-line that says something like, 'Revolutionary Breakthrough, Scientists Discover Secret of Life.' You read it, but you can't figure out what the hell the reporters are talking about. It's *still* a secret, as far as you're concerned. Here I have a real, live geneticist, and I'm not letting you go until you give me some answers."

I told him there weren't any answers. Not short ones, at any rate.

"I didn't ask for a short answer. Just give me a second." He gestured toward the men's room. "When I get back, I want you to explain what you do in that lab of yours all day."

I slid to the edge of the booth. Once, at a party, I had met a painter who claimed to be enthralled by my doctoral thesis on the cell-by-cell development of a worm called *C. elegans.* Spurred by his interest, I reached a height of elo-quence I had never before attained. *Maybe,* I thought. *Just this once.* But later, in his loft, he lit a cigarette and told me he had a question. "Here's my question," he said. "Were you saying 'D *and* A,' or 'DNA'? It's always kind of bugged me, not knowing which it is." I was aware that other women didn't require their lovers to understand the subjects they were studying. Foreign students at MIT courted American women without either one knowing how to say much more than "I love you" in the other's language. They married on trust, believing love to be a matter of emotions rather than of ideas. But what if you had nothing in common with the man you married? What if he cared nothing about what you did?

Willie returned from the men's room. "Hey," he said. "You know what someone wrote on the wall in there? 'The only women at MIT are the men who've worked their balls off.'"

I felt raw and exposed, the way I had felt when that truck driver shouted his obscenities. "Well, I have to go work my balls off, if you'll excuse me."

"Wait." He took my wrist. If anyone else had done that, I would have shaken him off. I was unsettled by how much I wanted that hand around my wrist. "This disease killed my dad," he said. "I'm not going to drive myself nuts over it. But that doesn't mean I'm not, you know, curious. I like to understand things. Come on. Sit back down." He leaned across the table with those bushy eyebrows raised. And I had to give in. At that moment, he seemed the only person on the planet to whom my research mattered.

"Do you know how genes work?" I asked.

Now he rolled his eyes. "What do you think? You think I believe these tiny little people come ready-made, all curled up inside a guy's sperm?"

I started to apologize.

"You know," he said, "according to the Buddha, there are only twenty truly difficult things in this world. Number eleven is: 'It is difficult to be thorough in learning and exhaustive in investigation.' You're doing a heck of a job with number eleven. Number thirteen, though, number thirteen is how difficult it is not to feel contempt toward the unlearned."

"I don't feel—"

"Yeah. It never crossed your mind that I didn't finish college. You never thought, Oh, jeez, I've got to sit here and explain the secret of life to an ignorant old hippie who's got seaweed for brains."

It surprised me how much I regretted losing the good opinion of a man I had just met.

"Come on," he said. "Even little kids today know about genes. Go ahead and just talk. If I don't understand something, I'll ask."

Every table in the deli came equipped with a soup can filled with pencils. By the end of most meals, the deli's patrons had scribbled formulae and graphs on every square inch of their place mats. I took one of those stubby pencils and drew a chain of DNA. Willie reached in his shirt pocket and took out the kind of reading glasses you buy at a dime store. His pair had heavy black frames and narrow lenses; they made him look like a kid who was pretending to be a grown-up.

"Let's assume this is part of your DNA," I said. I tried not to put on the professorial voice that annoyed my sister. "Most of the bases on your chromosome will be exactly the same as the bases on my chromosome, because they code for genes we share. They code for the basic stuff that makes us human. But a few of our genes won't be the same. You have curly hair; my hair is straight. Your eyes are blue and mine are brown." I was afraid he would think I was fishing for a compliment, or maybe giving him one. But he stared at the place mat as if the only thing he cared about was the chain of DNA that I had drawn there.

Encouraged, I explained that there were these other stretches of DNA, and no one knew what they coded for. It wasn't eye color, or hair color, or anything that obvious. Maybe some piece of his DNA read AGCC*G*TC, and my chromosome at that same spot read AGCC*C*TC. At that one spot, that one letter, our chromosomes were different. The useful thing was, there were a lot more of these random differences than the kinds that coded for, say, eye color. Scientists didn't used to know this. Now, suddenly, we had all these new markers to work with. It was the difference between giving someone directions on how to get around a desert, and giving someone an address in New York.

"Cool," he said. "I get it."

I had the impulse to kiss him. Startled, I told myself this was only because he had understood what I'd said. "Now," I went on, "suppose we could sort out all the bits of my DNA and compare them to all the bits of your DNA. The patterns your DNA would make would be a little different from the patterns my DNA made."

His glasses slid down his nose. He left them there, preferring to peer above the tops.

"I won't give you the gory details," I said, afraid I would lose even him. "But that's a fairly easy thing to do. You chop up a person's chromosomes and let the pieces migrate along a gel. You take the gel and make something called a radioactive blot, and you develop it so you can see all the different pieces of DNA. One person's blot doesn't look like anyone else's. So, suppose we study all the blots for one family. A family where some of the people have Valentine's and some of them don't. Suppose everyone who has the disease shows a certain pattern of DNA, and everybody who doesn't have the disease shows a slightly different pattern. Then we would know—"

"You would know that the Valentine's gene is hooked up in some way to this pattern?" He took the pencil and sketched a stick-figure man, a stick-figure wife, and three stick-figure kids. I was overcome by an irrational tenderness toward these figures, as if one of them were Willie and another were me. He laid a finger beside the stick man. "Say the dad and one of his sons have the pattern. But not, say, the daughters? Like, the dad passes along the pattern *and* the gene for Valentine's to his son? Is that it? But he doesn't pass either one to his daughters? If one of his daughters doesn't have the pattern, she doesn't have the gene?"

"What do you do up there in your cabin all day?" I asked. "Do you lie around reading genetics textbooks?"

He sat taller and beamed. "These blot things? These patterns? Do they correspond to anything you would notice about a person? Like, the two people in a family who've both got Valentine's might look like each other?"

I thought he was asking this because Laurel and our mother looked so much alike—that same full smile, those same green, catlike eyes, both of them so tall, while my father and I were barely five feet two, with dark eyes and strong noses. But there was nothing to support the notion that Laurel had inherited the Valentine's gene from my mother. On more than one occasion, I had attempted to explain this. *Just because you're pretty doesn't mean you have any more chance of getting it than I do.* But my sister always smiled that sad smile of hers, as if what I had said were nonsense. I was about to ask Willie where he had seen my sister when I realized he hadn't. He was asking because he and his father shared that cleft chin. "If the pattern were so obvious," I said, "someone would have spotted it by now. It can't be that easy."

"No?" he said. "Things can't ever be easy?"

"You never know. But it's not likely."

He stretched his legs beneath the table. His knee brushed my calf. "How many of these blots do you need to make before you find the right one? The one that means a person has the gene for Valentine's?"

That was the question my colleagues always asked. *You're crazy,* they said. *You don't even know which chromosome to look on. It could take you ten years.* I explained this to Willie, downplaying how long it might take me to find the right probe—if the project seemed futile, he wouldn't give us money.

He tapped his teeth with the pencil. "Remember that TV show when we were kids? The one with all those great toys in that big treasure chest, and that enormous pile of keys? And some kid had, what, thirty minutes to try all the keys he could before the buzzer went off?"

I was stunned he had mentioned this. Every time my gaze wandered to the list of probes taped to my wall, an image of those keys flashed through my mind. I kept this to myself, not wanting Willie to know how frightened I was that I would never find the key. "If you want to know whether a certain marker travels with a gene, you need to do blots for a really big family. Otherwise, you won't have enough clues to figure out who's inherited what from whom. There's this one pedigree, the Drurys—" I thought with a pang about driving back to Pittsfield. "We've got blood from two of the grandparents, and the mother and the father, all four kids, two cousins, and an uncle. That's the biggest genealogy anyone's found. If we're incredibly lucky, some pattern will show up. But mostly we're using them for practice. We've sent out letters to neurologists on three continents, asking for bigger pedigrees."

"Okay," he said, "suppose you find this big family. You try a whole bunch of keys, and the right one turns up. What happens then? What's inside that treasure chest?"

"If we find a marker for the gene—"

"You can tell some guy he's going to die this terrible death and there's not a thing he can do about it. Finding the gene doesn't mean diddly. Am I right?"

I felt my face flush. "Some people are going to find out they're positive for the gene. But what about all the people who find out they don't have it? They can get married and have kids and stop worrying every time they trip or drop something. They can tell if the fetus they're carrying is affected. If everybody did that, we could wipe out this disease in one generation."

He slapped his palms on the table and leaned forward, leering over his glasses like LBJ. "Yes, sir, my fellow Americans, we can wipe out a whole generation to save it. Heck, if they'd had this little handy-dandy test a generation ago, they could have wiped out you and me. Is that how you feel? You'd rather not have been born?"

The more I heard such questions, the less I believed them. The fact that people had become intelligent enough to shape their own evolution frightened me less than leaving my fate to chance.

He asked again if I would have wanted to be wiped out as a fetus.

Yes, I said. If it meant wiping out Valentine's. Although as soon as I said this, I wondered if I meant it.

"Whew. At least you're consistent. Got to hand you that. So you'd take this test?"

"Wouldn't you?"

"What if you found out you had it?"

"It couldn't be worse than this."

"No? A zero chance is better than fifty-fifty?" He gnawed the pencil. "Call me a jackass, but so long as there's nothing you can do about it, then no thanks, I'd rather not know. I'd rather just go on telling myself I probably don't have it."

"Then why do you care about all this?" I gestured toward the place mat. "Why do you want to see my lab?"

He removed his glasses and slipped them in his shirt pocket. "I didn't say I never think about it. Besides, I have a kid. My son, Ted. I wouldn't have *not* had my kid just because he might get sick. But I wouldn't mind knowing he wasn't going to have to go through what my father went through. I don't much care for this test of yours. But maybe if you find the gene, you can figure out what it does. What causes all that weird stuff to happen. The shaking and the cursing. You could keep that from happening to Ted."

That was the first I had heard about Willie having a son. He must have been married before, I realized. I might have asked if he still was married, but a colleague of mine stopped by and interrupted. Yosef and I hadn't known each other long, and I still had my doubts about whether I could trust him. Or maybe it was only that Yosef didn't trust anyone else. He suspected that everyone in the lab was plotting his downfall. Biologists talk all the time about collaborating on experiments, but to Yosef the word "collaborate" carried the connotation of betraying your neighbor to the KGB. He leaned against our booth in his ratty leather jacket, sucking on a Camel and straining to see what was written on the place mat. When he had taken in how simple the diagram was, he smiled at me and winked.

"Hi there," he said, giving the *h* that guttural rasp, so the word came out *chai*. He nodded to Willie. "You got to be some helluva guy, this one leaves the lab for you." Yosef was one of those people who rebuked me for being too serious. "I can understand a person doesn't drink," he had told me once. "Even not sleeping. But not making love? You think some guy would not marry you because you have this sickness? Pretty girl like you? You Americans think everybody has to be perfect. In Russia, you wait around for someone who doesn't have some kind of disease, or crooked teeth, or this big red birthmark on the head, you end up mighty lonely Russkie."

But Yosef dated only women who had no visible flaws. Waiting beside him was a postdoc named Monique. She wore short skirts and high heels—even though, like the rest of us, she stood on her feet ten hours a day. She and Yosef seemed unutterably foreign to me then, not because they were Russian and French, but because they could spend a Friday night at the deli, flirting and cursing and gossiping about who had stolen ideas from whom, then go out to a club, make love, and sleep until noon.

"Sweetheart," Yosef said, "I just came over to tell you. Those two researchers in Utah, the Polish guys who are studying that big Mormon family? Well—" He tried so hard not to let his *w*'s come out as *v*'s that "well" came out *whhhhel*. "This friend of mine, he saw the paper they sent to *Genome*. And those two Polish guys in Utah, they think they found a polymorphic locus on chromosome five that is linked to your gene. Maybe it is nothing. They have this very little family, this very shitty linkage. It is probably a wishful thought. But when that paper comes out, everybody is going to be all over chromosome five like flies on a piece of you-know-what."

Yosef was supposed to be working on Valentine's, too. In reality, he scorned the project as hopeless and spent most of his time working on experiments whose nature he never divulged, even to Vic. Every few days, Yosef would stop by my bench and ask, "So, sweetheart, how is it going?" If the Valentine's project started to move, he would hop on the bandwagon. In the meantime, he had his secret research to occupy his time.

He swirled smoke through his nose. "This news doesn't mean anything? You don't care if you get scooped?"

I knew those Poles in Utah. Their work was sloppy and rushed. If their data had been stronger, the paper would have been accepted by *Nature* or *Cell*. And how sad could I be if someone else found the gene for Valentine's?

"Yosef." I patted his sandpapery cheek. "If you spent as much time worrying about your experiments as you worry about getting scooped, you would have your own lab by now." I slid from the booth and stood.

Yosef called, "Sweetheart!," assuming, no doubt, his news had upset me. Willie followed me outside, asked me to wait, then ran back to get the place mat. "Please," he said. "I really do want to see your lab. I've been trying to avoid thinking about any of this for a long time. But now, well, I want to know all about it." He folded the place mat, then folded it again, then slipped it into his shirt pocket with his glasses, patting it as if it truly did hold the secret of life.

4

Most people who take a tour of a genetics lab aren't that impressed. I had a friend who taught English, and when I showed her my lab at MIT, she said it wasn't Gothic enough; I think she was hoping to find Dr. Frankenstein and Igor creating new life. The businessmen my father brought there for tours expected to find a machine that could manufacture a child. Bunsen burners and test tubes—how could anything important be discovered with those? I wished I could have said: *That's what I love about being a biologist. You don't need telescopes in space or supercolliders to study a cell.* Vic sent our technicians to Star Market to buy rolls of Saran Wrap to mummify our gels, paper towels to wick them, toothpicks with which to transfer bacteria from one plate to the next. We ordered Seal-a-Meal bags from the company that made them for the Jolly Green Giant. Every six months, the labs on our floor held a Tupperware party, at which we badgered the hostess about whether her trays were resistant to formamide and whether or not they would buckle when autoclaved at 120 degrees.

But I couldn't tell a potential donor his money would be used to buy Tupperware and Saran Wrap. I might mention that the numbers clicking on a centrifuge didn't represent one rotation per second, but rather one thousand. But this rarely fazed anyone. What was a centrifuge except a big spinning drum? *This microscope allows us to isolate a single egg from a mouse ovary, pierce the wall with a needle as thin as a hair, and insert DNA right inside its genes.* But a microscope was only a microscope, it seemed. And what was so hard about poking an egg with a needle? Any housewife could do it, if her hands were steady enough.

Even my father showed surprisingly little patience for what went on in that lab. *When?* he would ask. Rarely, *How?* Never, *Why?* He liked to find out how many pipette tips the lab used in a year, how many rubber gloves. Later, when he dropped these statistics, I was amazed to see the businessmen take notes, as if the numbers were proverbs they could quote later on.

Only my mother appreciated what she saw. She died three years before I started my postdoc at MIT, but I managed to show her the lab in Harvard Yard where I studied for my doctorate. I was forced to wheel her through a service door near the Dumpster. The iron-grilled cage that carried us up was so small it scraped the armrests of her wheelchair. She was trembling too violently to put her eye to a microscope, but I explained what I had done, how I had figured out the paths by which each of this tiny worm's two hundred cells had grown and divided from that first single egg. My mother's powers of speech already had decayed, but she managed to bark, "Oh! Yes!" I would have felt proud, but she was blinking back tears. How could I take satisfaction in accomplishing what she hadn't been allowed to accomplish, first because she was a woman, and later because she had fallen ill with Valentine's?

The night I met Willie, we rode the elevator to the fifth floor of my building, and I was surprised by how much I hoped he would find what I did to be interesting and important. I noticed him staring at the poster above the buttons (SEMINAR TODAY: MATING HABITS IN YEAST), and I cringed with embarrassment. The halls were lined with bikes. I leaned mine beside the rest, hoping he would think I wasn't so odd for riding one.

He pointed to a sign: BICYCLES MAY NOT BE LEFT IN HALLWAYS, BY ORDER OF CAMBRIDGE FIRE MARSHAL. "Glad to see you people take safety rules so seriously."

I understood that he was only teasing me. He couldn't have known what it had felt like a few years earlier when the Cambridge City Council held meetings to debate the dangers posed by scientists like me—the mutant microbes we might unleash through the sewers, the plague for which no cure could be found. I had stopped attending parties to avoid the hush that fell over the room when someone asked me what I did. The council had passed a moratorium on any research involving recombinant DNA, which had forced us to abandon years' worth of progress and switch to other projects. Then, just as suddenly, the council revoked the ban and we raced to catch up with geneticists in other cities. But we knew from then on we would always be suspect, like criminals who have been frisked and tossed in jail, then released with the warning they will be tossed in jail again at the merest hint of wrongdoing.

"We're careful about things that matter," I said, then led Willie inside the lab.

Achiro, our postdoc from Japan, was slicing mouse brains as thin as a butterfly's wings and using chopsticks to mount the samples on glass slides. Some of the world's most ambitious biologists worked on that floor, but Achiro and I put in the longest hours. He had arrived from Tokyo the year before, leaving behind a wife and two daughters. If he didn't produce a result important enough to secure him a position at a Japanese university, he would spend the rest of his life working at a company that made artificial sweeteners or deodorants. He wore a surgical mask and didn't raise his eyes when we came in. But I could tell he was pleased that I had come back. Even if we didn't talk to each other much, we enjoyed each other's presence, the way two deaf, lonely widows might knit side by side on a nursing home porch.

"Hey," Willie said. He stood above Achiro, peering down at the mouse brains. Achiro's shoulders went rigid, as if he feared Willie might thump him on his back. But all Willie did was murmur, "Oh, man, if that isn't Zen, what is."

Achiro looked startled by the word "Zen." Once, when I told him that Vic had dropped out of graduate school to study at a seminary before returning to complete his degree, Achiro had asked, "This means Christian?" I nodded, it did. "And you?" he said. "You also are a Christian?" No, I said,

I was Jewish, at which Achiro stared blankly. "And you?" I asked. "What religion are you?" "Ahh," Achiro said. "Since little boy, I think all religion is, how you say, nonsense?"

Now, with Willie behind him, Achiro let his eyebrows rise above his mask. He sucked in air, which dimpled the cotton mask. "Ahh," he said. "I forget to tell you. Someone call, mmm, two, maybe three time. She says she wants to talk to you about Valentine disease. I tell her you be back soon." He rubbed his mouth beneath the mask, as if the exertion of speaking all those English words had left his lips sore. Then he motioned with his eyes. On a pink Post-it by the phone he had written "MIRM BURN" and a ten-digit number. I wasn't in a hurry to return the call. People phoned the lab all the time, hoping to find some miracle to save a relative's life. Whatever Vic told them in that soothing, overly sincere voice of his left them feeling less hopeless. Often, he would persuade them to donate their DNA. I couldn't bring myself to confess that I didn't have some elixir or pill to give them, that their relative would be dead before a cure could be found.

Vic wasn't in his office, but his Boston Marathon windbreaker was hanging from his chair and his ratty backpack crouched beside his desk like a faithful dog.

"Your boss," Willie said. "He's supposed to be a big deal. I'll tell you, folks in Hollywood may have swelled heads, but there aren't many of them as puffed up as these scientists my mother introduced me to. Like that one at Harvard, Summer . . . Sumner . . . ?"

No, I said, Vic wasn't like Sumner Butterworth. The only time Vic let his ego peek through was once a year, in

October, when the Nobel Prizes were announced. On those days, he would show up later than usual, eyes bleary, face drawn, as if he had been sitting up all night waiting for the phone to ring. Then he would summon us for a pep talk. "We've been worrying too much about what other labs are doing. Prizes are fine, but the important thing is whether or not you're doing good science." And I loved him for that, for thinking what we did was a calling and not a race. "All right," he would say, "let's start everything fresh," and he would order a cleanup. We would spend the rest of the day kneeling in the cold room, throwing out plates of moldy bacteria and bottles of reagents left by grad students who had cracked up and gone home to Louisiana or Darjeeling. And this made us feel pure, as if those fuzzy orange spores had been rotting our souls.

Hundreds of people clamored to talk to Vic O'Connell. And yet he spent hours talking to me. He would come into the lab on a Saturday afternoon, pause beside my bench to ask about the gel I was running, and the next thing I knew, it would be Saturday night. People like Susan Bate hinted that Vic's interest wasn't platonic. But Vic was the last person at the university who would have hit on a post-doc. If he had felt those feelings toward me, he would have been painfully shy. Besides, he had hinted to me once that he owed his wife his loyalty for taking him in as an awkward young man with a nerve-racking fear of the opposite sex and supporting him as a nurse while he studied for his degree. So even if she had grown colder and more remote, even if she was concerned with matters of interior decor and social standing, even if she cared about genetics only enough to ask if their sons would inherit their father's height and thinning hair, he would never divorce her.

No, what caused Vic O'Connell to devote so much of his time to me was the understanding that if I failed at my research, I not only wouldn't get my own lab, I might die a particularly slow and agonizing death. When I had tried to find an adviser for my postdoc, no one would take me in. The approach I was advocating to find a marker was so unpromising that no one wanted to be responsible for my failure. For Vic, the very impossibility of my quest kindled his compassion.

Then again, not many postdocs wanted to work for Vic. Once, when we were at a conference, he told me about the time he had taken a much-needed vacation from graduate school and gone hiking in Yosemite. There, he said, he had been so overcome by the sublimity of what he saw that he had fallen to his knees in gratitude. Science, he thought, couldn't explain how the universe came to be, how such an intricate web of physical laws governed chemistry or evolution, or how the cells in his brain interacted in such a way as to render him conscious of his own existence. The next day, wandering the park in this rapturous awe, he heard a hiker scream that he was drowning, and even though Vic could barely swim, he jumped in to save the man. Luckily, a ranger pulled the drowning hiker to safety before Vic could be swept away by the currents, too. But he had needed to ask himself how evolution could account for his willingness to throw away his DNA to save a man who was even weaker than he was, even less fit for life. Sitting on that rock, warmed by the sun, he felt a connection to God he couldn't deny. He left graduate school to attend divinity school, but he soon realized he didn't have the temperament to become a minister. No, his calling was to help his fellow humans understand the beauty and complexity of the science by which God's creation worked. Not long afterward, he had made a name for himself developing a brilliant new approach to cloning. And yet, even those scientists who respected his results regarded their discoverer as somehow soft in the head. They were suspicious that at any moment he might stand up and make a case for intelligent design, or claim that God had planted the fossils to test our faith.

Initially, I had been suspicious, too. My parents blamed my mother's disease on genetics, and no amount of prayer could cure her. Better to put my faith in my earthly father and the money he was raising for his foundation, or my own ability to find the gene. And yet, working for Vic, I came to feel I benefited from a double layer of protection. I had Vic's power to provide the equipment and material I needed to conduct my work. And maybe, just maybe, his extra powers of intercession would provide a miracle.

Now, with Willie hovering behind Achiro, I slid my petri dishes out of the incubator and carried them to the tissue-culture hood. After all that talk about feeding my cells, I was embarrassed that Willie should see how simple the task really was. All I had to do was siphon off the old media, then squirt on fresh stock, bright as pink Kool-Aid.

"That's it?" he said.

I slid the dishes back into the incubator. We went out in the hall. "Not quite," I said. "A few of my mice are ready to deliver. If you don't catch them right away, the mothers eat the pups. The mutants, that is. And they're the ones we're interested in."

We were standing in a corridor so narrow that if Willie had stretched out his arms, he could have laid his palms on opposite walls. "Why would the mothers eat their babies?" he asked.

For some reason, I felt the need to pretend the mothers' cannibalism didn't bother me. "They probably don't want to waste all that good protein."

"Nah," he said. "You give them mouse kibble. I think they're just ashamed." He stuffed his shirttail in his trousers. "Were you ever ashamed of your mother?"

People hardly ever asked me about my mother. My friends seemed to avoid the word "mother" altogether. And my family didn't feel compelled to reminisce. Still, the question Willie had just asked had haunted me for years. It was a terrible thing to watch your once-fastidious mother drool juice on her blouse, or roll her eyes backward in her head until the capillaries showed, or tremble so incessantly she stripped her scalp raw against her pillow.

"I wasn't ashamed of her," I said. "She was a very attractive woman. But after she got sick, we couldn't keep taking all those wool skirts and silk blouses to the cleaners. She couldn't manage buttons, so my father brought home these double-knit pants from his store, and these polyester tent-dresses. I would try to replace the buttons with Velcro. The pamphlets make it sound so easy, but I can't sew. She had to wear these awful nurses' shoes, because it was so hard for her to walk. I wanted to tell people, 'She wasn't always like this. She started college at forty and she would have earned her doctorate in biology if she hadn't gotten sick.' But I don't think you could say I was ashamed of her. It was just that I knew she would have been ashamed of herself."

Cesar, the janitor, was mopping the floors. The sooner he finished, the sooner he could go home. But Willie was planted in the middle of the hall, and I knew he wouldn't move until I had asked him the same question he had asked me. "Were you ashamed? Of your father, I mean. Of Dusty."

He stroked his big chin. "I don't know," he said. "We would be out somewhere, and I'd see all these people staring. I thought it was because he was so famous. You know, 'There goes Dusty Land and his son.' Then I realized they didn't have the faintest idea who this old geezer was. They thought he was a drunk. So yeah, I guess I was a little embarrassed. But my mother—"

"You talk someplace else." Cesar shook his mop in our direction. I always got in his way. I would wait outside the lab while he worked, but I was usually so impatient I came back in too early and tracked up his shiny tiles.

Cesar swabbed his mop between us and carried on down the hall, leaving us stranded on two islands of dirt. Willie laughed. "My mom's just like that guy. She'll be sweeping the crumbs off the tablecloth while you're still eating." He tucked his hair behind his ears. "That's part of why she married my dad. When they met, he was, you know, this shabby cowboy. Sometimes he'd go off on these benders, thumb his way to L.A. or Alaska. Then he'd show up on her doorstep. He'd have this six-week-old beard. Calluses. Lice. She'd carry on, but she was enjoying herself. You could tell by the way she'd get him in a tub and soap him. She'd take a razor to his face. She'd kneel down and cut away the dead skin on his heels."

I wondered what it was like to be on such intimate terms with a man's body. In the year I had nursed my mother, I had grown maddeningly familiar with the mole on her left buttock, the bramble of hairs reforesting her thighs, the puckered skin around her nipples. But I had never been that familiar with a man. Not even the bodies of the few men I had slept with.

Willie seemed to regret having spoken at length on such a gloomy subject. "So where's the maternity ward?" He cupped his hands around his mouth. "Paging Dr. Weiss, paging Dr. Weiss, mouse in labor on four."

It occurred to me that I would be an idiot to show Willie our mouse room. Buddhists were so squeamish they avoided stepping on ants. Or maybe that was Hindus. All I knew was he wasn't going to like what he saw. "This isn't for people with faint hearts," I warned him.

"Faint hearts? You're talking to a man who helped his wife give birth in a cabin with no running water."

Again I felt a pang of jealousy, although I couldn't figure out if I was jealous because I had vowed to remain single, or because Willie had been married to a woman who wasn't me. "Well," I said, "don't complain," although already I could tell he wasn't the type to complain.

"Look," he said, "if you really don't want me to come, I won't."

But the idea of him leaving saddened me. "All right. Just don't give me a hard time," I warned him.

He followed me to the mouse room. The odor was strangely appealing—pungent and sweet—even as it made you want to throw up. I flicked on the light, and the mice rustled in their shavings.

"Which of the poor bastards have Valentine's?" Willie asked.

I could see he pitied these mice. His father had died of Valentine's, yet he considered me cruel to breed these mice and study them. I yanked a cage from a shelf. In one corner, an emaciated white mouse stood with its head cocked and its hind legs rooted to the floor. Every part of it trembled. The mouse kept wringing its paws.

Then, as we watched, it sprang up in the air. The other mice shrieked. It leaped about, flailing. Then it froze in midtwirl. I waited to see how Willie would react. Some people were offended to share a disease with a mouse, to watch it parody an illness that had killed someone they loved. I felt that way myself. But mostly I regarded these mice as a gift.

He set the mouse on his huge palm and stroked it. The mouse seemed to thaw. It took a few tentative steps. To keep it from falling off, Willie pinched its tail. But by then, the mouse had frozen again.

"If they're so messed up," he asked, "how do you force them to breed?"

"We don't force them," I said. "The mice that are just coming down with symptoms, they'll jump on anything."

He laughed that awful bray of his. The mice skittered in their cages. "Yup," he said. "That sounds like my dad."

I was appalled that he could joke about his father's illness, although I might have been better off if I could have joked about my mother's. "Actually," I said, "we're not sure what these mice have. The symptoms look like Valentine's, but we're only guessing it's a mouse version of the disease."

Willie patted the mouse. "Are two Valentine's genes worse than one?"

Again, I felt the urge to kiss him. "That's it," I said. "That's the million-dollar question. If the mouse gets two shots of the gene, maybe the symptoms will be so bad we'll be able to see what's going on, what's responsible for killing all those brain cells. The thing is, most of the homozygotes are so screwed up they die at birth."

"Pardon me if this is a stupid question," he said, and that made me doubt it would be. "The holes in the brain? The way a person's speech slows down?" I knew what he was going to ask. Even in his earliest movies, his father had chewed each word as deliberately as he chewed his cigarette. "Was the way my dad talked part of who he was? Or was it part of his sickness?"

I didn't know what to say. My mother had slipped gradually from not talking much to not talking at all. Her tendency to be withdrawn might have been a part of who she was—she had grown up watching her family die. Or her withdrawal had been a warning. To think about the brain—all those tangled neurons, the neurotransmitters carrying messages across all those synaptic clefts, the enzymes breaking down those transmitters, over and over, so the cells wouldn't keep firing—gave me such vertigo I could barely keep from reeling. What was a human soul if it could be so radically changed by a minuscule stretch of DNA? And how could this one protein make a once-polite woman spout such horrifying invectives, obsess over sex, and lose interest in her own daughters?

"It probably takes more than a single gene to make a person who she is," I said. I pulled down another cage and rubbed the swollen belly of the pregnant mouse inside. Given the laws of probability, a quarter of her pups ought to be born with two normal copies of the gene for Valentine's. Half would inherit one copy of the good gene and one copy of the bad. And a quarter of the pups ought to inherit two bad copies. If we could save these homozygotes before their mother ate them, we would drop them in preservative and give them to Achiro to dissect.

"So," Willie asked, "who kills the poor suckers?"

I wanted to say that I hated killing mice. One of our postdocs, Lew Schiff, was an Orthodox Jew who had written a prayer—in Hebrew, no less—which he murmured each time he sacrificed a victim, "sacrificed" being the word we all used, maybe as a euphemism, or maybe because it was the perfect word to describe the solemnity a person felt in performing such an act. I wanted to say that a mouse grew from nothing in a mere nineteen days. Each whisker was a tube with a single nerve cell that allowed the mouse to feel its way in the dark. The fibers in its tongue were a net of fine muscle running this way and that so the mouse could move its tongue in two directions instead of one.

I lifted a mouse by its neck. "You yank them by the tail. The spinal cord snaps. Then you pickle the brain in picric acid. You soak it in wax. That makes it easier for Achiro to slice."

He clucked his tongue. "You're one tough cookie, aren't you."

No, I thought, I wasn't. The question was why I wanted him to think I was. I switched off the light. "I just hope they don't deliver while I'm brunching at the Ritz."

"So," he asked, "what's your sister like? You never did get around to telling me."

Laurel, I thought. I was so looking forward to her visit. A friend was lending us his sailboat, and I wanted nothing more than to be with my sister in the middle of the Charles, alone. To watch her hands loop a knot. To see her smile that brilliant smile and reveal the little bridge of flesh from her upper lip to her gum, which Laurel thought was repulsive but I thought was so charming it brought a catch to my heart. There wasn't anyone else I would have allowed to interfere with my work. But if taking my sister sailing meant some mouse pups got eaten, I would need to run that risk.

"She can be a real pain in the ass," I admitted. "But I love her more than just about anyone else on this planet."

"Sounds like my son," he said, then rubbed his eyes like a sleepy child.

"There's one more thing I need to do," I said. "You can leave, if you want to."

No, he said, he intended to stick around to the bitter end.

Well, I said, if he was sure. And then I surprised myself by telling him that it was nice to have the company.

The entrance to the darkroom was a cylindrical booth with a revolving door. Only one person was meant to go through at a time, but Willie squeezed in behind me. Even in the darkroom, we kept brushing against each other. I busied myself developing a blot. I had chopped up the DNA of a family with Valentine's—not the Drurys, but an Irish family of five who lived in East Boston. If all the diseased siblings showed the same arrangement of lines on their films, but not the same pattern as their healthy sister, I would have a candidate for a probe. The odds that this would happen were one in eight. Still, as I slipped the film in the developer, hope pricked my scalp. We stood there and waited. Willie smelled of chocolate milk. Finally, I slid the blot in a tank of fixative, pulled the string dangling from the bulb, and saw that the film was black. Maybe someone had exposed the paper. Or I had accidentally left out a step. Once before, I had forgotten to tag the DNA with radioactivity.

"I take it that's not the way a blot is supposed to look," he said.

It was all I could do to keep from crying.

"Did it ever occur to you things might go a little easier if you'd get some sleep?" He drew a breath. "You know, you could come to my place in New Hampshire. I'll be driving after brunch. It's not that far. And, well, it's beautiful out there. Think of it as a little R and R. I could drive you back Monday morning."

"Oh, I can't," I said. "I'm taking my sister sailing. And there's this blot . . . I'm going to need to try it again before I go home."

"I get the idea." He sounded less angry than sad. "Me, I'm only human. I'm about to fall asleep." He stepped into the revolving door. "Thanks for showing me around. It's been interesting. I mean that." Then he spun the door behind him and, like a magician twirling his cape, he disappeared.

The darkroom seemed too big. I went out to the lounge to make myself some coffee, but the grounds missed the filter. My hands weren't steady enough to pour a new gel. Vic's office was dark. Even Cesar had gone home.

Only Achiro remained in the lab. He was talking on the phone in a soft, mournful voice, punctuated now and then by a shrill *hai!*, as if he had been punched in the stomach. The mask hung around his neck, but he was cupping his eyes with one hand. Tears coursed down his cheeks, more tears than I had ever seen a man weep, even at my mother's funeral. Someone in Achiro's family must be dying, I thought. But I didn't want to ask who it was, forcing him to simplify his grief by expressing it in English. I backed out of the room, then wheeled my bike through the harshly lit corridors, the gears clicking hollowly, the tires marking a line down Cesar's clean floor.

5

I had been disappointed when my father said he planned to spend the next day, Saturday, at a meeting with Honey. "Sorry, doll," he said. "This merger's a tricky business. Got to get all the IVR board members in the same room as the VDS gals and hammer out the details. This thing isn't done right, there're going to be a lot of ruffled feathers. You understand? You okay with all this?"

I told him I was fine. Do what you need to do, I said. *What you want to do,* I might have added, knowing my father would do what he wanted only if it coincided with what needed to be done.

"You going into the lab today?" he asked, and I told him I was, because it comforted him to hear this. In fact, I stopped by for only a minute to check on my mice. They hadn't given birth, so I climbed on my bike and rode to the open-air produce stalls at the Haymarket. I wandered from one stand to the next, picking the wispiest asparagus, the most densely leafed artichokes, sniffing peaches and melons, choosing cherries one by one and sifting through the green beans to make sure the vendor hadn't slipped in brown ones at the bottom. I knew all the tricks. The summer I turned ten, I had sat on our lawn in Mule's Neck selling surplus corn and tomatoes from my mother's garden. Nothing pleased me more than my father stopping by on his way home from work. "How much you rake in today?" he would ask, and I would count out the profits, piling cent upon cent and smiling at our secret—that vegetables weren't only something to eat, but merchandise to sell.

Now, in Boston, I ran a thumb along the silky skins of red and yellow peppers in a way that had little to do with mere buying. I spent half a week's stipend on flowers. "My sister loves flowers," I told the bent Vietnamese grandmother who sold me the bouquets. She wrapped my purchases in paper and I slipped them in my backpack, the blooms bursting from its mouth, then pedaled to a grocery in the cobbled North End.

"My sister is coming to dinner tomorrow night," I told the woman behind the counter. I chose a thick chunk of milky mozzarella. A pound of Parmesan. Those black olives. That oil.

She wiped her hands on her bosom. "Your sister. That's good. Most Americans, they don't know what it is to have a sister." She ladled out the cheese—it floated in its tub like the softest white island. She slid the olives and jar of oil in a bag, then tossed in a handful of powdery white cookies. "For your sister," she said. "She'll like them."

I rode along the river, avoiding the cracks and bumps so my fruit wouldn't bruise, then stopped at the MIT boathouse to make sure I could borrow my friend's boat the next day. "My sister won a regatta her freshman year at Cornell," I told the sunburned young man minding the dock. "She had never even seen a sailboat before she went away to school."

He helped an overweight older man in a neon pink life preserver climb up from his boat. "Me and my buddy Bosco over there could give you two girls a run for your money. We could have ourselves our own little regatta."

"Oh no," I told him. "Thanks. My sister and I haven't seen each other in a very long time. We just want to, you know, drift."

Back at my apartment, I arranged the bouquets in beakers from the lab. Then I started cooking. In those days, I often cooked dinner for my friend Maureen, who would never admit how much trouble it required for someone in a wheelchair to cook a good meal. Today, I planned to cook fresh fettuccini in my own marinara, made with basil and oregano clipped from the plants I grew on my fire escape. If the recipe was successful, I would serve the same meal to my sister the following night.

For the rest of that afternoon I chopped, peeled, and stirred, glad this one day to be able to see my ingredients, to be reasonably sure that if I followed all the steps the procedure would work. I thought of nothing more profound than the way the seeds spilled from a just-cut tomato or the poignant, bitter taste of garlic when my finger touched my lips. Just as the sauce was thickening, the intercom buzzed. My apartment could be reached only by a steep set of stairs. I loved the privacy and the view, but whenever Maureen came to visit, I felt selfish for living in such an inaccessible place.

I raced down the two flights.

"Hi," she said, "what's cooking?"

"Spaghetti," I said, though that wasn't what she meant. I scooped her from her chair and carried her up the steps. It wasn't hard—she weighed thirty pounds less than my mother had weighed when I used to carry her. But unlike my mother, who was stricken mute by her illness, Maureen kept up a constant chatter, pretending that being carried by a friend was an everyday thing. Which, for her, it was.

"So tell me," Maureen said. "Yosef saw you in the B and B with some hunk no one knows. I called you at one in the morning and you didn't answer. Isn't this something I should know about? Don't I tell you everything?"

The fact was, she did. Maureen talked about sex more than any woman I had ever met. Her hair was spiky and short, the color of a goldfish. She was the first person I knew who wore more than one earring in each ear. She collected glitzy shoes—the pair she had on that night were ruby red, like Dorothy's. I set her in a chair beside my table, hoping the stuffed artichokes would divert her from asking more questions. But all that happened was she asked those same questions with her mouth full of crabmeat. "Didn't I predict this? All that crazy talk about never getting involved with anyone."

I told her that the man Yosef had seen me with was going to be my new stepbrother.

"Stepbrother?" Maureen said. "Oh, sweetie. There are plenty of real brothers I wouldn't trust as far as I could throw them. You think this stepbrother of yours asked to see the lab because he's interested in fruit flies?"

I didn't want to believe her. I thought—I knew—Willie's interest in my work was sincere. Besides, didn't she realize that with our combined chances of carrying the gene for Valentine's, Willie Land was absolutely the worst possible choice for any man I could get involved with?

"You're not going to tell me anything?" Maureen pouted. "I guess you won't be needing these." She took out a pair of fishnet stockings and laid these across her lap. Then she lifted her wineglass. The arthritis had gnarled her knuckles and her wrists, but she had learned to get by, to accomplish what she had to. In the lab, she lifted beakers by cradling them between her in-turned hands. This gesture seemed exotic, the way a movie star might smoke a cigarette in a more sophisticated manner than an ordinary woman. She held her fountain pen slanted awkwardly between her thumb and first finger, but the script in her lab journal was elegant and precise. She lifted her glass and took a sip, then asked me when I was going to be seeing this stepbrother of mine again.

The next morning, I said. For brunch.

"*Brunch?*" The word must have sounded as strange from my own lips as it had from my father's. "I hope I'm not standing in the way of your plans for tonight." Maureen sniffed. "I mean, if you'd rather go dancing with your stepbrother."

Maureen and I went dancing all the time. The first time she had asked me to go with her, I had assumed she needed company. The nightclub might have some stairs, or the bathroom might be inaccessible. But later I came to think she was using her disability to force me to leave the lab.

"Don't be silly. Of course we're going dancing. Just wait here and I'll go in and change."

"Nothing too risqué!" Maureen shouted from the kitchen.

She made the same joke every week. "Aren't you ever going to give up?" I shouted back.

"I'll give up when you start having sex on a regular basis."

"What's the point of having sex if it can't lead to anything?" I yelled. I knew I was putting her at a disadvantage by making her shout, but I stayed in my room.

"You don't have to marry every guy you sleep with!"

I went back to the kitchen.

"Why, jeans and a T-shirt, what a surprise."

"Listen," I said, "it's not so weird the way I act. A lot of people at risk for Valentine's decide not to get married."

"That doesn't mean they have to give up sex. It isn't healthy." Maureen fiddled with an earring, which she always did when she talked about sex.

I reminded her that she was a biologist. What did she think was going to happen if I didn't have sex? Would all those sex juices get bottled up inside me and explode? What I didn't admit was that my own theory was equally bizarre: the less often a person had sex, the more she thought about having sex, and, since sexual obsession was one symptom of Valentine's, it was best for a woman in my position to have sex with someone she didn't really care about every few months. "Besides," I said, "the last thing I need is to get pregnant."

"Ever hear of birth control?"

I reminded her it didn't always work.

"Ever hear about abortions?"

That's all I needed, I said. To have an abortion.

"So have a kid!" she said.

Have a kid. I nearly cried. From the moment I had learned that every baby mammal grew inside its mother, I was amazed by the prospect that one day I, too, would be granted this privilege. Once, when I was young, I had glimpsed my mother nursing my newborn sister, and I couldn't take away my eyes. I couldn't stop thinking about the miraculous idea of feeding someone from my own body. I never lost that image. Sitting in a classroom, studying in the library, running blots in a lab, I would slip into a daydream in which I was sitting in a field nursing a newborn. I imagined taking a toddler for a walk, listening to all the strange, garbled ideas he or she thought to say. The truth was, I had loved taking care of my baby sister, and I wanted more than anything to have a child.

Well, Maureen said, why didn't I just assume that I didn't have the disease and get on with my life? It was a gamble, she said. Like whether God exists. If you led your life being good and then found out God didn't exist, you would kick yourself for having missed all those exciting times.

"You call that logic?" I said, then started to explain why her argument made no sense.

"It's Saturday night," she said. "I am not going to sit here listening to a lecture on logic."

But I wouldn't give up that easily. "Here's an analogy," I said, although I usually hated when scientists used analogies. Nothing was enough like anything else to warrant such comparisons. Nothing important, at any rate. I asked Maureen what she would do if her doctor said she had cancer. You would go nuts, I said, wouldn't you? But eventually you would come to terms with it. You would get on with your life. Now, imagine if you felt perfectly fine, but you knew that any minute someone was going to jump out from behind a bush and kill you. Wouldn't you think about dying all the time?"

"No! I would just make sure I didn't walk by any bushes!"

I glared. She stuck out her tongue. "What am I going to do with you?" I asked.

She batted her eyelashes. "You could take me dancing."

The tights she had brought me lay crumpled beside our plates. I stretched them across my hands. The silk was thin and webbed, with fake pearls sewn into the pattern like dewdrops.

"Oh, all right," I said. I went back in my room and found a denim miniskirt I hadn't worn since high school—I could swear it still smelled of pot—and a stretchy black top puckered with elastic. Rolling around in my desk was a tube of lipstick Laurel had left behind; I smoothed some on my lips and rubbed the rest on my cheeks. Then I slipped on a pair of platform sandals I had bought for my college graduation eleven years earlier.

"Wow," Maureen said. "Madame Curie meets the Mod Squad."

"I told you it was no use."

"I was kidding," she said. "You look great."

I didn't believe her, but I couldn't face the thought of

putting on those jeans and that T-shirt again. I carried her down the stairs, taking every step carefully, uncertain in those sandals, and set her back in her wheelchair. The motorized lift on her van levitated us noisily inside. Maureen couldn't turn her head, so I sat in the passenger seat and warned her of approaching cars. The way people drove in Boston, I was afraid she might get killed. But I couldn't go everywhere with her, could I?

We found a handicapped spot just outside the club, then got in the line and waited. The bouncer didn't seem to notice us, even when Maureen was sitting right in front of his beery gut. The club was in a basement, and Maureen told him that we would need his help getting down the stairs.

He shook his head no.

"No?" Maureen said. "What do you mean no?"

"No wheelchairs." He stamped the next couple's hands.

"You have a law against wheelchairs?"

"No law," he said. "I just don't want to get a hernia."

The couple behind us pushed past us. I wanted to seize the wheelchair and carry it down myself, but I had tried this once, at an entrance to the T, and nearly dropped Maureen down the longest flight of stairs in Boston. Most of all, I wanted to punch the bouncer. What a relief it would be to get angry on someone else's behalf. For all her feistiness, Maureen rarely showed anger. "How can I?" she told me once. "I never know whose help I might need." This was true of my own life as well. I couldn't show anger toward my father, or Susan Bate, or Yosef or Vic. If Laurel came down with the disease, I would regret any harsh words I had ever said to her.

I told the bouncer that if he didn't help me carry my friend's chair down the steps, I would report him.

"Yeah?" he said. "To who?"

"Just tell me this," Maureen said. "If I were inside the club, and I drank too much, and I picked a fight with someone, you would throw me out, wouldn't you?"

The bouncer shrugged. "I guess so."

"Okay, so why not throw me *in*."

He narrowed his eyes. Then he grabbed the wheelchair, spun it roughly backward, and bumped it down the steps as if Maureen were a load of beer.

"You creep!" I yelled, wishing I'd had more practice cursing. I ran down and yanked his vest.

He turned and raised his fist. "Fuck you *and* your ugly friend," he said. He plucked his vest from my hand and lumbered back up the steps.

"Don't you want a kiss?" Maureen shouted up to him.

He shot us both the finger.

"That does it," I told Maureen.

Never mind, she said. She had gotten us in, hadn't she? She tried to straighten her stockings, but her hands were shaking.

"He shouldn't be able to get away with that," I said.

"Jane," she said, "if I stopped to report everyone who was a jerk to me in the course of a day, I would never have any fun. Let's go in. I'd rather spend my time dancing."

Reluctantly, I held the door while she wheeled through.

The club was more crowded than usual, probably because spring had finally come. No matter how many times Maureen said "Excuse me," the people in front of her wouldn't clear a path. Her only view was of crotches and rears. *I could barely see, even when I stood on my toes.*

A bearded man in a flowered shirt stopped beside Maureen. "Need a drink?" he said. "I'm on my way to the bar."

She had met many such men at clubs, just as she had met them at record stores and shoe shops. Often, she dated the same man for six months or a year. But most of these men tended to vanish at the critical point, perhaps for the reasons most men don't ask the women they date to marry them. Or they didn't have the courage to ask Maureen.

"Hi." A boy tapped my arm, then jerked his thumb toward the band. "Want to dance?" His hair was shaved short. He had a delicate skull, light brown skin, and a goatee.

"Sure," I said. We found an empty space. The music was so loud that all I had to do was move my body with the beat. I hadn't danced much in high school. Dancing was something my sister did, not me. But now it seemed the perfect way to exorcise the temptation I felt to twitch or drop things or move in unpredictable ways. Since I had started coming to these clubs, I had found that I looked forward to dancing all week. I felt blissfully limp. From the corner of my eye, I saw the bearded man steering Maureen's wheelchair toward the door.

"Bye," she mouthed. "Good luck," as if, despite knowing me, she assumed I was hoping to go home with this boy.

He opened his eyes and smiled. He had a pleasant face and a lithe body. "Want to leave?" he asked.

I suddenly felt so alone, abandoned not only by Maureen but also, strangely, Willie, that I smiled and said, *Why not.* The cold air made me shiver. "I'm Ché," he said. "And you're—?"

"Jane," I said. He asked where I went to school. I'm a biologist, I said. I'm older than I look.

"Biology?" he said. "That's cool. I studied anatomy once. And a semester of botany. To help me, you know, paint." He asked if I wanted to get coffee and a doughnut.

"I can't," I said. "I'm sorry." A trolley clattered past. "My sister is coming tomorrow."

"Your sister," he said. "That's cool. You can hang out with me tonight. Then I'll go to my studio and you can hang out with your sister."

"No," I said. "She's coming very early. I need to get some sleep."

"You make her sound like a test." The boy snapped his fingers. "Never mind the doughnuts. I have this really amazing almond cake my mom sent. And there's a pint of Steve's mint chip in my freezer."

Ice cream and cake. He seemed so harmless, so young. The light changed, and the trolley rattled up the hill. I said I guessed some ice cream and cake couldn't hurt.

His apartment was only a few blocks away. He lived in one room, with a hot plate on the floor, a single bed, and a refrigerator the size of a safe. Most of his artwork was at his studio, but a dozen frameless paintings hung on the walls. Each painting showed a fragment of a body. One painting showed a hand—I could almost make out each of the nineteen bones beneath the skin. Another showed a shoulder blade and a knee. Another, a woman's ear. Each image was composed of a few brushstrokes, as evanescent as the cross sections of tissue that Achiro mounted on his slides.

"I like these," I said, and Ché leaned over and kissed me. I stroked his boyish cheek. He got down on his knees and slid a foil-wrapped box from under the bed, then went to the sink and rinsed two plates. The freezer was just large enough to hold the ice cream. He sliced the cake with a palette knife and served out two portions. Ché talked about the teachers he liked at art school, and those other teachers, the ones who seemed to find pleasure in destroying kids' souls. Another trolley rattled past. I felt I had gotten off a train in some city whose name I didn't know and the train had continued on without me.

"Guess I'm kind of sleepy," Ché said. "Afternoons, I work this shit job at a furniture store out in Newton." He stripped off his shirt. I was welcome to stay, he said. His body, the color of tea, looked beautiful against the sheets. The pulse in his scalp throbbed. I pressed my lips to the spot.

"You're nice," he said. "Jane." He closed his eyes, and I propped my head on one hand and studied him as though I might need to paint him later. He was finely made and hairless. I brushed some cake crumbs from the mattress and curled up beside him. But it was Willie I was thinking of. Those big hands and big teeth. The way he had tipped back his head and stretched his tongue to catch the last drop of chocolate milk.

6

The next morning, when I arrived at the Ritz, my father was waiting with a mangled *Wall Street Journal* beneath his arm and a pile of crushed cigarettes blotting the marble floor by his heel. Even on a Sunday morning, he was doing his job, giving his two unreliable daughters a glowing Lucky Strike at which to aim their arrival, safe and on time.

Honey towered above him, stiff and straight as a hat pin. She took my father's arm and, for a moment, I thought I saw my mother hovering behind them, looking the way she used to look when she was young, her face alert, her hair neatly cut and styled. It occurred to me that for the rest of my life, I would need to try not to hate my stepmother, which was so unfair to Honey that I already loved her.

Willie had dressed up for the occasion—he wore a decent pair of khakis and a pink-and-white-striped shirt. The day was so warm he had pushed the sleeves above his elbows; the muscles in his arms seemed incongruous on a man with such a soft face. He was grinning down at Laurel with a soppy expression I took to be love, or at least infatuation. She was smiling up at him and tossing her hair in that flirtatious way she'd always had, even as a kid. But then I thought no, they could never be a couple. They looked too much alike. If you had seen them walking down the street, you would have thought they were *too much*. All that hair, his and hers. The way they smiled so broadly, with those wide, full-lipped mouths. Most people don't smile much. Some, not at all. For my sister and Willie, a smile seemed the normal shape of their mouths.

Oddly enough, my sister preferred spending time with men who looked pained. Her boyfriend, a young stock-broker named Chuck, stood a little way off, grimacing and checking his watch. A shank of dark hair hung over his eyes; he wore chinos, Top-Siders, and a light blue cardigan. This stranger was the first to notice I had come. He nudged Laurel, glad, no doubt, to have this excuse to divert her from Willie. They turned to me then, and their expressions reflected just how tired I must have looked.

I hadn't been able to fall asleep. Ché's bed had been too narrow, and I was too excited about seeing Laurel. When I finally did doze off, I heard Laurel call my name. *Jane!* I heard, *Jane!*, although I knew she couldn't have been there. I jumped up—and saw that it was after nine. Miraculously, the stockings I had been wearing the night before hadn't ripped. But what would people think when I showed up at the Ritz in that puckered top and miniskirt?

Honey reached out and traced the shadows beneath my eyes. "Willie," she scolded, "you promised you would look after her."

Laurel extended her arms. She wore a lacy white shawl, which hung like a tattered sail. She wrapped those arms around me. "You know," she said so quietly only I could hear, "I miss you so much sometimes, I think, 'If only Jane could see this, if only Jane could be here.' The next time I go to Europe, I'm taking you with me." She was doling out just enough of what I needed to hear so I wouldn't finally give up and stop loving her. "You look wonderful," she said. "You always do. You're one of those people who can jump out of bed and throw on anything and look terrific." She liked giving me compliments. And maybe she still saw me through a younger sister's eyes. "Jane, this is Chuck. Chuck, this is Jane. My brilliant sister, Jane."

Laurel's date took his hand from his pocket and extended it like a gift. "We had other plans," he informed me. "But Laurel insisted we put them off. I finally gave in. I mean, how often do I get the chance to meet a genius?"

"Man," Willie said, "who invented this brunch thing? If you eat when you wake up, then a few hours later you're sitting in front of this big old omelet, and you can't force down more than a few bites. If you *don't* eat, you're cranky as a bear." He put on those dime-store glasses and peered at the menu. We ordered and made small talk. I tried not to watch my sister the way other people watched me. Was she tossing her head more than usual? Why did the marmalade slip from her knife before it reached her croissant? And why had she stopped playing the cello, as she mentioned she had, after practicing it so many years?

"I didn't give it up." Laurel smiled and revealed that little bridge of flesh. "I just got busy with other things."

I couldn't bear the thought of that beautiful cello going unplayed. How many hours had I sat in our living room studying while the cello's mournful voice drifted down from upstairs? Once, on a shadowy October afternoon, I was lying on the couch reading a book about the Pleistocene era—those colossal sheets of ice churning down from the North Pole, those half-human creatures about whom we know so little except the shape of their bones—and I looked up from the page, past the rippling silver spine of the radiator, to the backyard, where the dried cornstalks in my mother's garden quivered in the wind, and the sound of my sister's cello was the sound the wind made rustling through those cornstalks, the sound those Cro-Magnon men and women heard as they crouched shivering in their caves.

Laurel's music teachers had encouraged her to make the cello her career. But even then, in high school, she didn't have the patience. She wanted to learn to dance. She rode horses. She skied in Switzerland. She explored an underwater reef off Australia. "Don't you want to leave something behind?" I asked her once. And she answered: "Who cares? I won't be here to see it." Still, she had kept up her passion for dance. She had started ballet at six, and she kept taking lessons all through college, where she enrolled in a course called Physical Expression. She met some boys in that class, all of them beginners, and they worked up a routine. That being the early seventies, they took their friends' encouragement as a sign that they ought to drop out of school and start their own dance troupe, which they named Six Left Feet. The one time I saw them perform, they were so awkward and pretentious I slipped out before the end, to save myself from having to lie to Laurel.

My father wasn't pleased that his younger daughter was exhibiting her body on a stage. He gave her money to travel, and Laurel accepted it because he had plenty to spare and she thought she didn't have the time to earn it herself. No matter how often I reminded her that she had a fifty-fifty chance of escaping the disease, she remained certain that she would die even younger than our mother. I was working as much to save my sister, to prove she didn't have the gene for Valentine's so she could stop wasting her life, as I was to save myself.

Now, as we ate, Laurel told us about the time she had spent in Germany. She described what it had felt like to drive down the autobahn and see a sign for Bergen-Belsen, or to stand at the gates of Dachau. What she said was quite moving. But her life seemed a sort of scavenger hunt. She had brought back her knowledge of the Holocaust the way she had brought each of us souvenirs: a rare chardonnay for our father's birthday (I had been foolish enough to take him at his word that he didn't enjoy receiving expensive things he didn't need); an Hermès scarf for Honey (how had Laurel known to buy a gift for a woman whose engagement to our father hadn't yet been announced?); and a beautiful linen nightshirt from Belgium for me. When it came to Willie, Laurel rummaged through her handbag and pulled out a cassette, which, she explained, was one of only two copies of an original composition by a composer whose name I didn't recognize but caused Willie to nod his head. The composer had written this piece for Laurel. "We'll be giving a concert in Boston on Christmas Eve," she told us. "It's the first time I'll be choreographing my own pieces. I hope you all can come."

Willie slid the tape into the breast pocket of his shirt. *How could you?* I thought, as if I were the only woman who had a right to that spot. "Always on the lookout for an excuse to visit the big city."

Laurel smiled and said she hoped he wouldn't be disappointed. She described how difficult it was to choreograph a dance. Willie's face seemed a spotlight shining only on her. What could I expect? My sister had more interesting things to talk about than how to kill a mouse.

Only Honey seemed impatient. I saw her shuffle crumbs from the tablecloth to her palm, then hesitate, as if she weren't sure where she might deposit them. Glancing down, I was startled to discover she had taken off her shoes. Honey saw me staring and slipped them back on. Her hand fluttered to the vase and plucked a withered bloom. When the centerpiece was perfect, she raised her knife and tapped her glass.

"Everyone! Herb and I have an announcement. Don't we, Herb? You young people might think we're just a pair of old fools, but we've decided to take the big plunge." She looked around the table, but none of us responded.

"Ahh," my father said, "what she means is, when I hit sixty, she started to worry she'd been letting me *shtup* her for nothing. She was afraid I was going to drop dead without leaving her a dime."

I felt sorry for Honey. But maybe my father's jokes were like the calluses on Dusty's feet, something rough she could take satisfaction in smoothing away. "Herb!" she said. "The children know you're joking, but a visitor might believe the ridiculous things you say."

My father turned to Chuck, who was patting his lips to conceal a smirk. "Think it's funny? Think you're rich enough and handsome enough you're going to be shacking up with beautiful young girls forever? Girls you have no intention of marrying?"

Chuck began to stand, as if he intended to ask my father to settle their dispute outside.

"Chuck," Laurel said. "That's just my father. That's just the way he talks."

Since this was true, I wondered why she felt compelled to bring her boyfriends home to meet him. Chuck stared at her, as if reminding himself of what he would lose by disagreeing. He flipped the hair from his eyes, and our father made a face that conveyed his disappointment that Chuck hadn't thrown the first punch.

"Excuse me." Honey cleared her throat. "In my day, when a couple announced their engagement, someone wished them good luck."

Willie stood and raised his tomato juice. "To our parents," he said. "May you enjoy many years of joy," at which my father gave Honey such an unabashed kiss I felt happy for them both. After she got over being flustered, Honey told us her plans for the wedding. She would fix up the house in Mule's Neck to accommodate a "modest lunch." The reception would be held in the sunny backyard where my mother's garden used to be. Laurel smiled absently, as if when these events came to pass, she wouldn't be here to see them. Chuck whispered something in her ear, and Laurel pushed back her chair.

"I'm sorry, everyone," Laurel said. "One of Chuck's friends runs a skydiving school, and I'm supposed to take my first lesson in an hour."

I imagined her falling through the clouds, her hair flying in all directions. In place of a parachute, she wore only that tattered shawl. "But you promised," I said. "You told Mom you would never do it." Years before, Laurel had gotten it into her head to take skydiving lessons. When our father reminded her how much things like that cost, our mother interrupted. Laurel, she said, promise me you won't even think of jumping out of an airplane until after I'm dead.

"I kept my promise," Laurel told me now. "You know, Jane, I kept it."

I nearly slapped her for thinking she could get away with saying that. She had always been rash. With our mother so distracted, I had been the one to keep Laurel from getting hurt. With my help, she had survived a bout with a hornets' nest and a near kidnapping by a stranger whose car she climbed into because that seemed easier than giving the man directions. I had cared for our mother for that entire awful year before she died. Yet my sister never acknowledged how much she owed me. "I borrowed a sailboat," I said. "I wrote you. You said you were looking forward to being on the river again. To going sailing."

"Jane," she said, "I'm sorry. I forgot and made other plans."

Anyone else might have believed this version of events. But my sister cultivated this aura of being flighty to provide a cover for getting out of what she didn't want to do. I knew that she was avoiding me. I had always been the good one. The one who stayed in college. The one who was doing something useful. When our mother had grown too feeble for our father to take care of, Laurel had hitchhiked home to help. She spent one week in Mule's Neck, then called me at midnight, sobbing, and said: *Please, Jane, I can't. You're the responsible one. I'm not. I can't stand to see her dying.*

"I'll be back in Boston later this summer," Laurel said now. "We'll go sailing then, I promise. We'll do whatever you want to do."

I told her that it wasn't only a question of what *I* wanted. Didn't she think our father wanted to spend time with her? And what about Honey? Didn't Laurel think her new stepmother would want to get to know her?

My father waved away my anger. "Go on," he said. "Honey and I understand. We have to be starting back anyway."

I knew this was nonsense. My father wanted to be with Laurel as much as I did. But he never rebuked her. "You need some money?" he asked, and Laurel shook her head, although I knew he would send a check anyway, or slip it in her purse. "Be careful," he said. "That's all I ask." He jabbed a finger at Chuck. "And you. Anything happens to my girl, I'm pushing *you* out of a plane." Chuck started to defend himself, but Laurel shushed them both. She clasped her shawl to her chest, leaned forward, and kissed me. She rubbed her cheek to Honey's. Then she surprised me by brushing the hair from Willie's ear and whispering something until he laughed.

"Sure," he said. "Of course I will." Chuck led Laurel from the restaurant without even thanking our father for brunch.

I looked around the table, the shock and loss as visible as if a genial thief had lightened us of our wallets, then walked off without anyone attempting to stop him. I laid my napkin across my chair and ran after her.

Luckily, Chuck had gone to get his car and Laurel was still waiting inside the lobby. "Please," I said, "I don't care if you go sailing with me or not. But you can't jump out of an airplane. Who is this guy, anyway? You barely know him. How do you even trust him, let alone trust this friend of his who runs a skydiving school?"

She glanced out the door, no doubt hoping that Chuck would drive up and rescue her. "Listen, I'm really sorry I forgot about the sailing. It was sweet of you. Very thoughtful. But Chuck rented the plane. And it's not that dangerous. You make it sound as if I'm jumping without a parachute."

"That's exactly what you said that time you went climbing in Alaska. 'Dad,' you said, 'it's not as if we're not going to be wearing ropes.' And you know what it did to him when he got that call? Do you know what it must have cost him to pay for you to be airlifted off that mountain? You can't keep doing this. You can't keep living as if you're sure you're . . . Listen, I know, all we talk about is Valentine's. But we're doing it for you. We're doing it to—"

She cut me off. "Shh," she said. She put her finger to my lips. "I *know* why you're doing it. And I appreciate it. Really. But I wish you would stop. I didn't ask any of you to do any of this. Not you. Not Honey. Not Dad. You're wasting your life one way, Jane. And I'm wasting my life another way. But at least I'm having fun."

The trouble was, I didn't believe her. She didn't love Chuck. She didn't really care if she went skydiving, or climbed a mountain. She was sure that she had the gene, and she was determined to die young, before she could come down with the disease. As irrational as this was, I was equally sure that she didn't have the gene. I wanted to give my sister back her life while she was still young enough to stop throwing it away.

"I haven't seen you for nearly a year," I said. "And you're just going to run out on me? You don't care that Honey and Dad are getting married? You're all I have. I don't want to lose you, too."

"Oh, Janie." She spread her arms and wrapped me in that shawl. "You ought to know you can't keep from losing someone. This way, you'll only miss me less when I need to go."

I felt smothered in that shawl, as if she were wrapping me in the darkness of her thoughts, in death itself. A horn honked. She removed her arms. "Good-bye," she said. "I really do love you." And she hurried out so quickly the doorman had to rush to do his job.

When I got back to the dining room, my father was stubbing out his Lucky Strike and calling for the check.

Honey said something to console him. I couldn't make out what it was. If someone had said the wrong thing to me then—*Don't worry, she'll be all right*—I might have started crying. But Willie came up behind me and repeated his offer to drive me to New Hampshire for the weekend. Since he didn't pose this as a question, I didn't feel inclined to turn him down. I couldn't remember the last time I had taken a walk in the woods. "Sure," I said. "Why not." It occurred to me that his cabin wasn't very far from the Drurys' trailer in Pittsfield. "Do you mind if we stop at the lab?" I asked. "There's something I need to pick up."

"Of course," he said. We waited until our parents had checked out of their hotel, then he drove me back to MIT. We couldn't find a parking space, so he stayed in the Jeep. I could tell he was worried I might not come out. In truth, if he hadn't been sitting there, I wouldn't have gone in. I darted in the lab to fetch a few syringes and was startled to find that Achiro's bench was bare. I didn't dare ask what had happened to him, any more than the inmate of a nursing home asks why a friend hasn't come down to lunch.

"Hi, sweetie." Maureen pushed the lever on her wheelchair and spun it in my direction. "What happened with that cute boy I saw you dancing with last night?"

I collected some test tubes. If I told Maureen the truth, we would be there all afternoon arguing about why I hadn't told Ché I would see him again. "He asked me out for doughnuts," I said. "I told him I couldn't go because my sister was coming to town."

"Where is she?" Maureen turned her head stiffly. "I thought you were spending the day with her."

The tears came. "I was."

Maureen pressed her fingers to my hand. "Listen," she said. "Why don't you take *me* sailing? A few pointers and I'll be casting off the poop deck with the best of them."

I rubbed my eyes and laughed. "I don't know the first thing about sailing."

"Then we'll do something else. That guy I met last night, the one with the beard? He's a lawyer, but on weekends he takes people on these wilderness things. He said he could teach me to row a kayak down a waterfall. I'm sure he'd take you with us."

Why was everyone trying to throw away her life—or throw away *my* life? I told Maureen my stepbrother was downstairs waiting.

She cocked her head toward Vic's office. He was sitting at his desk, reading a journal, but I had the impression he had been staring at me. "Does Vic know about this stepbrother of yours?"

I kept telling Maureen there was nothing between me and Vic, but, like Susan Bate, she never quite believed me.

"Jane?" Vic called. "Do you have a minute?" He was standing in the door, holding out the latest issue of *Cell*. "Have you seen this yet? Fred Dike's thing on retinoblastoma?"

Maureen spun back to her bench. I grabbed a pack of needles and a tourniquet, then I told Vic I was sorry but I had found this new family and they were only around on weekends, so I had to hustle and draw some blood. If he left the paper on my bench, I would talk to him about it Monday morning after group meeting. Then I gathered my supplies and left.

Willie and I stopped at my apartment to pick up a toothbrush and a change of clothes. This time, he parked the Jeep and came upstairs. He looked around the room. "Nice flowers," he said.

I had forgotten they would be there, all those bouquets wilting in their beakers, the ripe tomatoes, the bunches of basil and thyme, the delicate white wafers the storekeeper had given me for Laurel. Once, when one of Maureen's dates stood her up, I told her that anyone who would stand her up wasn't worth crying over. But Laurel wasn't a boyfriend. If you broke up with a boyfriend, you could always find another.

Willie tossed a tomato in the air and caught it. "This reminds me of all the times my son, Ted, told me he would come to visit, then didn't show up. Or the times he would come, and after five minutes he would say, 'Jesus, Dad, isn't there anything except these dumb trees to look at?'"

"It's my fault," I said. "All of us, all we talk about is Valentine's."

He took a big bite of the tomato, then wiped the juice from his chin. "Doesn't mean she has to make you feel bad."

That thought had passed my mind. But it was another thing to hear someone outside the family criticize my sister. "She wouldn't be like this if it weren't for Valentine's.

She wouldn't have dropped out of college. She wouldn't be running around with all these awful men. She wouldn't be avoiding me."

"People are people."

No, I thought, they aren't. Knowing you might die from the terrible disease you watched your mother die from made you a different person from who you otherwise would have been. My sister would have been a flighty, narcissistic person no matter what. But she was talented, warm, and kind. If not for watching our mother die, if not for thinking she would die a miserable death herself, she might have been an accomplished musician, a loving, devoted wife, and a doting mother.

"You can't save someone." Willie licked his fingers. "You can fix them. The way my mother likes to fix them. But it's dangerous to think you can save anybody."

"So you're fixing me," I said, "not saving me?" I tried to smile, but I had never felt so serious.

He slipped the tomatoes in a bag to take with us. "You don't need saving," he said. "You're great the way you are. You just need to take a little time off and rest."

7

Even from this distance, I can't figure out why I let myself fall in love with the man who was statistically the worst possible choice I could make. Even for a scientist, numbers and statistics have less power, less reality, than another person's mouth pressed against your own. Or, like Vic experiencing that conversation with God, I got tired of believing I was on my own. Of calculating all the odds. Of controlling everything I did with science. Maybe, like someone who has a terrible fear of crossing bridges, I got so exhausted by my own terror of falling off that I found the highest bridge and jumped straight off. At least I would rid myself of my fear. I could relax and enjoy the fall. Or maybe what I did was to find the one person who feared bridges as much as I did so I could grasp his hand and we could take the great plunge together.

Then again, I might have fallen in love with Willie Land for the same reasons most women would have fallen in love with him. He was generous and strong, so solid I could lean against him, but not so well defended I had no room to crawl in. He was a handsome man. And famous—at least his father had been famous. He was rich, but not self-serving. He tried to do good. He cared about the same bizarre beauties of the world, in a way that made me feel they weren't bizarre at all. My intelligence didn't scare him off. It seemed to make him love me all the more.

And maybe every woman falls in love with the man who is both the worst and best for her. The worst provides the friction, the rub, the heat. Given a test to overcome, you feel twice as strong for winning. And maybe your heart refuses to fall in love with the person that your instinct—your very DNA—commands you to fall in love with. Maybe, as Vic believes, the rules of evolution don't quite explain as much as we think they do. Maybe our DNA commands us to do the opposite of what makes the most sense. Maybe, when we jump in a river to save a drowning man, what we are trying to do is to save ourselves.

As Willie drove me to New Hampshire, I tried not to think about any of the many reasons I shouldn't have accepted his invitation. All I knew was that being in his company allowed me to relax. For months, I had been tracing the same self-enclosed route from my lab bench to the tissue-culture hood, to the cold room, to Vic's office, to the mouse room, to the freezer, to the vending machines. Every few weeks, I would drive with Rita Nichols to western Massachusetts to collect a patient's blood. But these detours were brief. I could calm myself by thinking they were demanded by my work. Driving along the highway in Willie's open-topped Jeep, the wind beating against me, I was forced to remember how immense the world really was. The road curved, and curved again, slicing through jagged rock. I wanted to demand that he take me home. But returning to the lab seemed even more frightening. I would keep running my experiments, and those experiments would fail, as they had failed in the past.

The Jeep's tires hit a rhythmic *thuck thuck* against the road. I leaned back and closed my eyes. I barely remember waking when we parked and Willie led me up the trail to his cabin. We went in and climbed the stairs—the air was shadowy and cool—and I settled on the window seat while he went to the kitchen to fix some tea. Then I don't remember anything more until I woke to find myself nestled beneath a stack of quilts so musty they brought to mind the leaves in which I used to play with Laurel on our parents' lawn. I lay inhaling the smoky scent of the quilts and recalling the feel of Laurel squirming beneath me. A branch scratched a window. I willed myself to fall deeper into sleep. This was the reason I so seldom left the lab—I was frightened I wouldn't go back.

When I couldn't force myself to stay asleep any longer, I opened my eyes. In a corner of the room stood a red leather armchair with a kerosene lamp above it. I could hear the approach of a breeze—a faraway gathering of breath, a holding in, the presence of something as it passed, the shuddering of trees and leaves. I looked out the window and saw a bee crawl headfirst into a crab-apple blossom. A moment later, the bee crawled out. When it sprang from the pistil, the petals quivered.

On a chair beside the window seat stood a lopsided pitcher and a ceramic bowl some amateur potter—it turned out to be Willie's ex-wife, Peg—must have fashioned by hand. Beside the bowl lay a washcloth and a bar of soap. I pulled off my top—it smelled of almond cake and smoke—and rubbed my skin. I bent above the basin and washed my hair, then brushed it until it lay sleek against my scalp. I slipped on the shirt and jeans I had brought from home. Then, arrayed for new beginnings, I climbed the stairs.

There was only one room, a sort of loft. Sunlight filtered from the skylight and splashed the bed. On each wall hung a grainy black-and-white photo of a boy with a Cupid's bow mouth. In one photo, he toddled toward a woman's outstretched arms. In another, he puffed his cheeks to blow out the candles on a cake. In his teens, the same boy posed with Willie, their startled expressions leading me to think that the camera had been snapped by an automatic timer.

On the floor beneath this photo, Willie sat cross-legged, eyes shut, ankles hooked above his knees. I sighed and stepped back. Even if our genes hadn't made us incompatible, our temperaments would have. Why would anyone *meditate?*

He opened his eyes. "I was wondering if you were going to sleep through the weekend."

I imagined him plodding down the stairs and standing over me and staring in the hope I might wake up, as Laurel used to do when she wanted me to play. He glanced out the window. He wanted to take me on a tour, he said, but we had only a few hours of daylight left.

"I'd love to," I said. Then I followed him down the stairs and through the kitchen, with its pump-handled sink, past a second pump outdoors, and beyond it, the outhouse. The trail dropped toward the road, so laddered with roots I had to watch each step.

"Here we are," he said. "Central Operations." Beyond the Jeep stood a shed. It was connected by wires to a utility pole at the end of the gravel road. "That's as far as they would string the electricity when we moved here. If we had wanted to hook up the house, we would have had to pay a couple of thousand bucks. Peg and I, we didn't have that kind of money. Now I could afford to run the wires up the hill, but I prefer it this way. When I'm working, I'm working. When I'm not, I'm not."

Inside, on a plank laid across two stacks of milk crates, I saw a phone, a ticker-tape machine, a miniature copier, and a manual typewriter. Some annual reports were fanned out like a poker hand: Electrocar, Citizen's Assets, Sun Foods. He owned the kind of cheap fake-leather pen-and-pencil set you could buy in the gift shop at Weiss's Supply. In the center of the desk lay the blotter that came with the set. Tucked in one corner was a snapshot of a young man in a cowboy hat and boots—the same little boy I had seen on the walls of the bedroom, all grown up.

An ancient Frigidaire with a chrome grille stood behind the desk. When Willie opened it, I saw a bag of groceries and half a dozen quarts of chocolate milk. For a scientist, I had never been very good at making deductions. Startled to find myself making one now, I blurted out, "You used to drink."

He brayed that laugh of his, and I had to remind myself there was no one there to hear it. Yeah, he said. That was another thing he had learned from his father. He wasn't a stone-cold alcoholic, like his dad. But he used to drink. One night, while he was still married to Peg, he was so desperate for a beer or a jug of wine he started walking to town in the middle of a blizzard. When he got back, the cabin was empty. Peg had taken their son and left. Willie didn't blame her. There she was in the middle of nowhere with no phone and no electricity and not much in the way of food. She wrapped the baby in Willie's parka and hitch-hiked home to her parents on Long Island.

After he finished telling me this, Willie grabbed a carton of milk from the Frigidaire, tipped back his head, and gulped. "Come on," he said, "you can see copy machines in Boston." We left the shed, and I followed him through the woods, his hair swinging this way then that, haloed in gnats. The light at that hour was so expressive I felt something like love, not only for Willie, but for every living thing. As a child, I had spent a lot of time in the woods. I would leave the house early with an army-issued knapsack and a canteen from my father's store, the grape juice sloshing against my thigh. So many things perplexed me. How a maple tree unfolded from a seed. How feathers had evolved. Whether butterflies thought about where to fly next. All those billions and billions of years of evolution to produce a human being. To produce me, Jane Ellen Weiss.

Once, I took my sister for a walk. I lifted a rotting log and showed her the slime mold growing underneath, explaining how, after a rain, each tiny, dry spore absorbs moisture and swells until it splits open and expels a mass of cytoplasm—a "swarm cell," I said, as if I expected her to memorize the words. The cell wriggles away, I said, and when two of these swarm cells bump into each other, their nuclei fuse, then divide, and divide again, in unison at first, then in synchronous waves. Deprive it of moisture and a slime mold turns rubbery. Add water and it starts pulsing again, spreading across the forest.

"Is it a plant?" I asked my sister. "Or do you think it might be an animal? Can something be both?"

"It's a blob," she said, laughing. "Leave it to my sister to make a fuss about slime!"

Usually, I was ashamed to remember that day. But now I did something perverse. "Look," I said. "Down here." Willie turned and squatted beside me, balancing on his high-tops. I brushed the pinheads of mold so they burst and sprayed their spores. Then I flipped the log and explained everything I had explained to Laurel.

He looked at me as if he were about to tell me how peculiar I was. Instead, he leaned forward and kissed me. Our lips had barely met when he teetered backward on his heels and stood. He started walking off, which gave me the sense that none of it had happened.

Back at the shed, we stopped to pick up the groceries. Willie grabbed another carton of chocolate milk and brought that along, too. Not far from the cabin, I spotted a mushroom the size and color of a softball. "You can eat these," I said. "You slice them very thin, then you sauté them with garlic and salt." I was testing him, I guess. How many people will take your word that a mushroom is safe to eat?

He lifted the puffball to his nose and inhaled. "Mushrooms have such wonderful names," he said. "Angel's Wings. Wood Ear."

"Are you kidding?" I said. "Mushrooms have terrible names. Corpse Finder. Weeping Widow. Dead Man's Fingers."

"Say 'mushroom' again," he ordered.

Laughing, I shook my head no.

"Go ahead," he said. "Say 'mushroom.'"

"All right," I said. "Mushroom."

But even as he kissed the word from my lips, I was trying not to think *Trumpet of Death, Destroying Angel.*

llllllllllllllllllllllllllllllllllll

While Willie cooked dinner, I sat watching his hands peel potato after potato, the brown peel curving through the slot until the slick yellow flesh lay exposed in his palm. He talked about the year he and Peg had camped in these woods, building this house. I didn't know much about window frames or self-composting toilets, but I loved hearing his voice and watching the way the muscles in his back rippled beneath his shirt when he hacked the lamb for dinner.

Once the food was cooking, he set a few mismatched plates and pieces of silverware on the table. He filled both our plates with lamb chops—two for him and three for me—and dollops of something that turned out to be plum sauce. Precise as a chemist, he apportioned us each a scoop of mashed potatoes. Then lima beans. Biscuits. And slices of the puffball, which, to my relief, tasted ambrosial in its buttery broth. He had baked brownies the consistency of mud for dessert. He guzzled his milk. I sipped my tea. We talked about the giant fungus that recently had been discovered out west, an underground *thing* fifteen hundred years old, heavy as a redwood or a giant blue whale. And it seemed, as we discussed this fungus, some huge ancient thing was lurking beneath our table and we were pretending it wasn't there.

Finally, I found the courage to ask what my sister had whispered to him that morning. He carried our plates to the sink. "If a person whispers something," he said, "she probably wants to keep the information private."

I supposed that Laurel did. It wasn't Willie's fault if my sister felt compelled to give away to others what I wanted for myself. What did he think of her? I asked.

He scraped the leftovers in a pail. "She's beautiful," he said. "Self-absorbed. Nothing like you."

I would have been petty to take offense. The first and last items weren't meant to be linked.

We went up to the living room and sat beside the fireplace, staring at the logs. The silence was hard to bear. It was the loudest, most unendurable silence I had ever heard.

Then we started talking. It was the kind of conversation where both people jump in at once. He would talk about his father, and immediately I would echo with the same story about my mother. I wish now we had never had that talk. I wish we hadn't kissed. I wish we had been content with the affection and understanding between a brother and a sister. But, as Maureen had said, even real siblings sometimes can't control their love.

I was hoping Willie might start kissing me again, but someone pounded at the door. He cursed and went downstairs. I wondered if it might be some girlfriend he hadn't mentioned. But when I looked down, I saw a hairy little man so poorly clothed—the tie-dyed shirt he wore was little more than holes—I wondered if he had been hiding in these woods since the early sixties, like those Japanese soldiers who lived for decades in caves rather than emerge and learn their emperor had surrendered.

From where I stood, above the door, all I could see of Willie were his hands. "Hey," the guy said, "what gives? You pissed at me again?" He told Willie he intended to repay the bread he'd borrowed, but he needed another loan. There was some chick he had met in town—Willie knew the one. She worked at Frank's Spa? She wore those crazy rubber gloves with the fingertips cut off so she could handle the frozen food and still punch numbers on the register? She was coming to see his pad, but he hadn't scored any dope, and he had promised to turn her on.

Willie told him that he had a visitor.

"That's cool," the man said. "I can take a hint. I'll come back tomorrow morning. Have a groovy time."

Willie closed the door and trudged back upstairs. Even I could feel his sorrow. Of all the hopeful hippie kids who had built cabins in these woods, only these two remained.

By then, any chance I might have had of getting a kiss had vanished. Willie asked what time he should wake me the next morning. I said I didn't need to be back in Cambridge until the middle of the day, for group meeting, and I would just as soon miss that—I had been scheduled to give a talk for months, but I never had any new data, and I kept having to persuade Vic to let me skip my turn. I asked Willie if he would mind stopping at the Drurys' trailer.

The family didn't have a phone, but I guessed Flora would be there.

"You want to draw this woman's blood?" He seemed to suspect me of breaking some law. "I thought you weren't a doctor."

"I'm not," I said. But I had gone to medical school for a year before I dropped out and switched to research. And it wasn't as if you needed a license to stick a needle in someone's arm. At least, I didn't think you did. Then I realized it had been nearly a decade since I attended medical school, and the idea of sticking Flora's arm again and again while her husband and kids looked on began to distress me so much that I asked Willie if he would let me practice.

He needed a few moments to take this in. I wanted to draw his blood?

Instantly, I understood how crazy this sounded. I started to take back the request.

He cut me off. "I guess you can," he said. "Why not? I've got plenty to spare."

"You sure?"

He shrugged. "No. But you might as well do it anyway."

I laid out a clean syringe. A needle. A few vials. Some gauze. Willie pushed up his sleeve. I tied his arm with the rubber tube. His veins bulged—they were so thick, I could have stabbed him anywhere and been sure to strike blood. I laid his arm across my lap—it was heavy and warm—and swabbed a spot with alcohol. The needle pierced his skin. Our eyes met. He seemed frightened. I drew back the plunger and the syringe filled with blood. Reluctantly, I withdrew the needle from his arm, then jabbed it through the rubber cap of a test tube. The vacuum in the tube sucked blood from the syringe—I loved to see this happen, an invisible force performing work. Then I wrapped my hand around the vial and rocked it so the blood wouldn't clot. I had told him the truth—I had drawn the blood for practice. But holding it in my hand, I vaguely thought I might want it for something else. I started to put the tube in the Styrofoam container I had brought for Flora's blood.

Willie snatched it back. "Hey," he said. "Give that here." He wrenched my fingers open—not enough to hurt, just enough to free the vial. Then he walked to the window, pulled the stopper, and spilled the blood. He turned back to me then, and I didn't know if he was going to scold me or take me in his arms. "All right," he said, "sleep well." He handed me a flashlight and climbed the stairs to his room.

I lay back against the window seat and tried not to listen to the swish of his belt snaking through its loops, his trousers crumpling to the floor. I heard his quilt rustle, heard the mattress sigh and give way. To keep myself from climbing those spiral stairs I needed to remind myself that there was a three-in-four chance that within the next decade one of us, if not both of us, would be paralyzed in a wheelchair. I couldn't watch yet another person I loved die of that disease. All I could think about were the statistics. If I carried the gene for Valentine's, then any child I might conceive with a man who wasn't at risk ran a 50 percent chance of inheriting the disease. That was bad enough. But if Willie and I both carried the gene, any children we had would run a 75 percent chance of contracting Valentine's.

Maybe, if the child received two copies of the gene—that is, if it was a homozygote—it would develop the disease even earlier, in its twenties, or in its teens, with more severe symptoms. No one had studied a human homozygote. I saw an infant as small as a newborn mouse, saw that child twitch and moan.

I took the flashlight and went down the stairs and out through the kitchen. The mud beneath my feet felt yielding and cool. I stepped into the outhouse and leaned against the wall, inhaling the scent of cedar chips and excrement and trying to pretend that I wasn't falling in love with the worst possible man I might fall in love with.

8

The next morning, Willie seemed out of sorts. I couldn't figure out if I had overstayed my welcome, or if he wished I were staying longer. He served me pancakes and eggs, fried potatoes, and homemade bread and jam, as if he didn't trust me to eat after I left his care. If he had asked me to stay another day, I would have stayed. But he seemed to be having second thoughts about my being there.

I carried my belongings down to the Jeep. We took the back roads to Pittsfield. It was just after nine on a warm late-spring morning. If someone had asked me to choose the weather for the rest of my life, that was the day I would have picked. The trouble was, so few people got to choose anything important—the weather they enjoyed, the work they liked to do, the person they wished they might love and live with. Wanting to have a child didn't mean you got to have one.

The Drurys' trailer was set on a deserted road a mile beyond a former Dairy Queen turned "Indian Trading Post" and porn shop. Flora's husband's pickup wasn't there. I hoped Willie would wait in the Jeep, but he accompanied me up the steps. My knock echoed. The trailer looked so small, I expected Willie to lift it up and shake it.

One of Flora's daughters opened the door. She was eight or nine, wearing Santa Claus slippers, dirty white jeans, and a sweatshirt with John Travolta on the front. She had her mother's dull red hair, which she wore in a braid so tangled she must have braided it herself. *I'll do it for you,* I thought, aching to braid her hair the way I used to love braiding Laurel's.

"Booger, get down." An overweight chocolate Labrador with a bandanna around his neck was jumping on the girl. When she scolded him, he licked her face.

"Is your mother home?" I asked, wondering which daughter this was—Genevieve? Michelle? Or the youngest, whose name started with an *A*? There were dozens of questions I prayed the girl wouldn't ask, especially since Rita wasn't there to answer them. It wasn't that I felt out of place in the Drurys' trailer. If anything, I had more natural ties with the Drurys than I did with most people. But my sympathy choked me. That's why I usually let Rita do the talking. *This will just prick a bit. Here, hold this cotton. Now, don't get your hopes up. Just finding this gene won't be no cure.*

"She's in there," the girl said sullenly. She led me to the kitchen, then sat beside her mother and watched the small TV balanced beside the sink. Did this daughter stay home to watch her mother every day, or did all four children take turns? The year I spent nursing my own mother I found it nearly impossible not to resent my classmates in graduate school for leading normal lives. I tried not to resent my sister for saying, *I can't do it, Jane. I can't.* But Flora's daughter seemed glad for this chance to stay home and watch *Gilligan's Island*. I knew the theme song by heart, although the sound of it now, the thought of being stranded on that island with those people (had they ever been saved?) unsettled me so badly I wanted to leave. Before she got sick, my mother rarely had the patience to watch TV. But as her focus narrowed, she demanded that we keep it on all the time. She watched *As the World Turns*, *The Price Is Right*, and *Mister Rogers*. If someone switched off the set, she would thrash and shout obscenities. She spent the last days of her life watching game shows.

"Mrs. Drury?" I tried to sound cheerful. "I'm afraid I need to take more blood. If you would rather I didn't, try to let me know."

Flora sat with her hands clenched in the same position as the last time. She wore the same yellow shift. The only difference was that her gaze was fixed on an A&P calendar taped to the wall. It was a promotional gimmick, each day a coupon to be torn off and redeemed for paper towels, ground pork, or macaroni.

"All right then." I spread my packets across the table. The skipper smacked Gilligan. Flora's daughter kept her eyes on the screen.

"Hey, champ, it's okay." Willie patted Booger's head. Booger growled and bared his teeth.

I had forgotten he was there. "This is my colleague," I told Flora. "His name is William Land." I waited for Willie to expose this deception, but he kept crooning to the dog. He pretended not to watch, although I felt so self-conscious I could barely peel the wrapping from the needle.

I pried Flora's fingers loose and lay her arm across the table, where it quivered like a fish. This was nothing like taking Willie's blood—Flora's veins were thread thin. I leaned against the table to steady my hands. I tightened the rubber tourniquet, but Flora's veins didn't pop up. I held my breath and stabbed. Nothing. No blood. I pulled out the needle and stabbed another thread. On the fourth try, I struck blood, but the syringe filled so slowly I had to milk Flora's arm. My blouse clung to my back with sweat. The vial was full. I stoppered it.

Flora shot from her chair. "No more!" she screamed. Booger leaped from Willie's grip and barked so ferociously the walls rattled. He bounded to his mistress. As Flora spun in a circle, Booger rose to his hind legs, laid his paws on Flora's chest, and spun along with her. "Can't take!" Flora shouted. "Can't take! No more!" The girl's eyes flickered from her mother to me before returning to the TV. I could tell she would rather be anywhere—with her siblings at school, on that island with Gilligan—anywhere but in this kitchen, while her mother and her dog danced their duet.

Willie had wedged his fingers beneath the dog's bandanna and was pulling Booger back. The dog shuffled on its hind legs, straining toward Flora. I tried to speak quietly, so Flora's daughter wouldn't hear, but Booger's growling made this hard. I asked Willie if he wouldn't mind staying home with Flora while I took her daughter somewhere.

He yanked the bandanna with both hands. Booger slumped to his haunches. "Do you need the keys to the Jeep?" he asked.

I was only taking her for a short walk, I said. Maybe there was something I could buy her.

"Don't you think she's a bit young?" Willie asked.

I laughed and said I meant the trading post, not the porn shop.

Flora stood with her arms across her chest. Willie let go of Booger. He walked up behind Flora and wrapped himself around her like a coat. I had never seen anyone do that. Her body thawed enough so that Willie was able to fold her at the hips and ease her into her chair. Booger curled at Flora's feet.

"You girls have a nice time," Willie said. He picked up a deck of cards and shuffled it. "If you see anything interesting, be sure to bring me one."

I knelt and asked Flora's daughter if she could help me solve this problem I was having.

Staring at her mother, she shook her head no.

"Are you sure? Why don't you just let me tell you what the problem is and you can decide? You see, this very rich lady gave us money to buy toys for children whose parents have the same disease as your mom." I wasn't sure why I was lying. To save the girl's pride? What child would mind if someone bought her toys? "The problem is, I don't know what to buy. For these other children. What kind of toys they might like."

The girl sneered in a way that nearly made me weep. "Aren't any other kids in the world got a mother like mine."

"Not exactly like your mother. But the disease she's got, the sickness that makes her sit that way and shake, or jump around and say bad words? Sure, other parents have it." I swallowed. "My mother had it. I stayed home and took care of her, the way you're doing."

"I don't like when people make fun of me."

"I am not making fun of you. I know how hard it can be, staying home with your mom. And this lady I was telling you about—"

"The rich one?"

"She knows how hard it can be. She told me to go out and buy toys for the kids. As a reward. Of course, if you don't want to help—"

"Do I get one?" the girl said suddenly. "Because if it's for kids who take care of their mothers . . ."

I pretended to consider this. "Why, sure. I guess you'd qualify."

The girl looked around the trailer. "I'll go. If she won't get mad." She pointed to her mother, as if there might have been another "she" in the room.

Willie paused, one hand above the pack of cards, waiting to hear what I would say. "Why don't you ask her?" I suggested.

The girl opened her mouth, as astonished as if I had suggested that she ask Booger for advice. She scuffed across the linoleum in her Santa Claus slippers and put her mouth to her mother's ear. Then she stepped back and studied her mother's face. "She says it's okay." Then she raced out and came running back with a pair of see-through plastic sandals. "Let's go," she said.

"Okay," I said. "But I thought this could be sort of a special occasion. Why don't you let me braid your hair?"

The girl lowered her eyes. Cautiously, I asked if she had a comb.

"Of course I do!" She ran back to get it. Willie dealt himself a hand of solitaire. Flora's daughter knelt on a kitchen stool while I unraveled her twisted hair, pressed the side of one palm against her scalp, and tugged. I waited for her to scream, as Laurel used to do when I combed her hair, but Flora's daughter sat still. She let me make a braid and snap a rubber band at the end. She jumped from the stool, pulled open a drawer, and handed me a curly red ribbon someone must have saved from a gift. Once the bow was tied, she ran to the toaster and examined her reflection. "My mom used to do it nicer," she said.

"I'll bet she did."

She narrowed her eyes at Willie. "You sure this is all right?"

I said we wouldn't be gone long. She ran and kissed her mother, then pulled me out by the hand before anyone could stop us. The sun made her sneeze. In the middle of the yard, she looked up at me and said: "My dad said he'd whip me."

"If you left your mother alone?"

"Mmm-hmm."

"Well, she isn't alone. Dr. Land is in there with her, isn't he?"

She smiled so suddenly I blinked. Her plastic sandals scuffed the road. A woodchuck lifted its head, regarded us suspiciously, then waddled back through the ferns. The girl kicked a rock. Another few steps and she couldn't help but skip. "Do you know what they got there? At the store? There's this whole Indian village. It has Indian men, and Indian women, and Indian girls and boys. And dogs. These cute little Indian dogs? And these little cooking fires? And there's a canoe and two teepees." She put her hand to her mouth—these were too much to hope for. "It's wicked neat, even without the teepees and the canoe. It's six dollars. That isn't so much, is it? If this lady is really rich?"

We covered the distance to the store. The sign had been repainted to read INDIAN QUEEN, and, below this, TRADING POST SOUVENIRS TOYS MAPLE SYRUP. A lopsided addition around the back said ADULTS.

The girl glanced up and down the road. "We sneak in sometimes. My brother Ricky looks at that bad stuff. But the rest of us, we only look at the toys." She seemed stricken by regret. "You won't rat on us, will you?"

I raised my hand and swore I wouldn't, wondering if her father really did whip them. He seemed to love his children. He wasn't cruel. But how else could you keep your son from hanging around a porn shop? How could you prevent your daughters from deserting their mother? Maybe the entire family would have an easier time after Flora died. Maybe Mac would remarry. The kids' new mother might be kind.

When I opened the door, the building gave off the decadent smell of incense and marijuana. The proprietor, a heavyset man with a Fidel Castro beret and beard, was serving a customer in the adult section. This young man, who wore fatigues, wanted to buy a stack of movies, some magazines, and something wrapped in brown paper. The owner said he wouldn't accept the boy's check because it bore a different name from his license. The boy tried to explain how this was his real name and the license was the one he had been given in the air force, with the alias he had been assigned for secret work.

"What do I look like to you, a chump?" The owner pointed to a sign above the register that read NO CHECKS AND THIS MEANS YOU. Grumbling, the boy took forever to decide which two movies he could buy with the crumpled few dollars in his pants. After he had slinked off, the owner crossed the divide to the trading post and said in a softer voice, "What can I do for you two ladies?"

I gestured to the toy Flora's daughter had pointed out. The pieces were dusty, but the teepees seemed to be fashioned from real skins, and the canoe was sewn from bark. Each Indian wore a fringed dress or a loincloth made from real leather, with real feathers in his hair. The set, without the teepees or canoe, came to $6.99. I could sense Flora's daughter was afraid that I would be angry about the extra ninety-nine cents. "We'll take the whole set," I said.

The girl gasped, and it occurred to me that her father might resent the gift as charity. Well, too bad if he did. I bought a pair of beaded moccasins for Maureen, with a brave on the left shoe and an Indian maiden on the right, then watched the owner pack the pieces into a box labeled X-RATED BALLOONS. He seemed agitated, as if he wanted to tell me something. Or maybe he was just excited about making such a big sale. I tapped the label on the box. Startled, he replaced it with a carton stenciled PEZ.

The girl coughed. "You won't get mad at me if I tell you something?"

"Why would I get mad at you?"

"It's just, see, my sisters, and my brother . . ." The girl swung her braid to the front and chewed the tip.

"You want me to buy something for them, too? Because they help to take care of your mother?"

The girl nodded. I asked if she would happen to know what sorts of toys her siblings might want. She pointed to a bow-and-arrow set beneath the register. Then she pointed to a drum. "Is that okay? If it's too much money, we can all just play with the village."

With the moccasins and all the toys, the bill came to sixty dollars. I had thirty in my purse. "You don't take checks?" I asked the owner.

He peered down at Flora's daughter. "You live around here, don't you. I've seen you here before."

The girl neither denied nor affirmed the charge.

"This lady's check any good?"

She bent her head and shrugged. Did she even know what a check was?

The man drew his beard to a point, which made him look more like Burl Ives than Fidel Castro. "I don't take checks from lowlifes like that joker in here a minute ago. But two respectable ladies like you." He waited while I made out my check to "The Indian Queen," then handed Flora's daughter the box. I took the moccasins and turned to go, but he grabbed my arm and pulled me close. "He ain't a half-bad fella. He does the best he knows how to do."

He must have thought I was a social worker who was planning to take away the kids, or I was planning to marry Mac.

"Can we go now?" the girl asked. She felt like running, I could tell, but she forced herself to walk by my side the entire way home.

We found Willie at the table with the television turned off and some card game laid out as if Flora were playing the other hand. Booger jumped up and licked the girl's face. She pushed him down, then ran to her room and slammed the door. Willie looked at me as if I might tell him what was going on, but who knew what I had done wrong? Maybe it was just the idea of coming back that upset the girl.

We had said good-bye to Flora and were on our way out when the girl rushed back, clutching a grubby sheet of construction paper. The drawing, in crayon, showed a rectangular box, or maybe it was the trailer. Two adults and four children sat stiffly around a table, their plates piled with drumsticks. It reminded me of a primitive fresco of the Last Supper, although in Flora's daughter's drawing each disciple wore a smile as wide as his head. Even the dog was smiling. Beneath the trailer was scrawled: "THANK YOU ANNETE."

Of course. Annette Drury. Though she had omitted one *t*. How could a child misspell her own name?

I kissed her head, near the part. Willie and I went outside and got in the Jeep. We bumped along the road past the porn shop. I knew I would be embarrassed if he praised my good deed, but I still hoped he might.

He didn't say a word until we reached the highway. "That kiss last night," he started. We must have traveled ten miles before he finished this thought. "That wasn't the reason I got you out here."

"No," I said. "Of course it wasn't."

We drove another fifty miles in silence. The Jeep bumped along the potholes and reverse curves of Storrow Drive. The river shone to our right.

"Maybe this wasn't such a hot idea," he said.

I felt as if he had taken back some gift. What would Flora's daughter say if I took back the village? *Indian giver,* I thought, and tried to keep from laughing.

We pulled up outside my lab. "I'm taking a trip out west," he said. "To see Ted. You know, my son. I'll be gone a few weeks. I'll call you when I get back. Maybe we can go out for coffee?"

"Sure," I said. "Coffee." My arms were so full I had to bump the door shut with one hip. "Thanks," I said. "See you."

"Right," he said. "See you." As he drove away, I panicked, as if I might have left something important in the car. But no, I still had the moccasins, my duffel bag, the blood. I stood there expecting the Jeep to come back, though there was no reason it would.

I took the elevator up to the lab. Lew Schiff and Susan Bate were fighting. Susan, it seemed, had gone to use her stapler and discovered it missing. She had searched everyone's drawers and ransacked their benches before finding the stapler in a box of empty Coke cans under Lew's desk.

"I don't know how the damn stapler got there!" Lew shouted. "And you don't have the right to go rummaging through people's things!"

"Can't you read?" Susan screamed. She pointed to the stapler: THIS BELONGS TO S. BATE. In every lab I had worked in, there were two kinds of people: those who labeled every item with their name, and those who walked off with anything that wasn't nailed down. But Susan's reaction to the disappearance of her pens and inoculating loops exceeded all bounds. The first thing you did if you found a pen in your pocket labeled s. BATE was quickly to get rid of it. Maybe Lew was being blamed for someone else's theft, or he was afraid to confess. Susan crouched beside him, small, with fine hair, narrow eyes, and pointy ears, like a lynx. "Don't lie to me!" she shrieked. "I can't stand men who lie!"

She was one of those women who blame any man's fault on the gender as a whole. Because of this, her tantrums seemed to reflect as badly on me as they did on Susan. Apparently, she had been abused by her father, and she acted as if my own father were to blame for the gene that threatened me. She wasn't a bad scientist, but everyone knew why Vic kept her on, why he endured her rants and accusations. What upset me about Susan's tantrums was the possibility that I was also treated kindly, kept on year after year despite my lack of results, for the same reason—pity.

Most scientists of Vic's caliber chose only the brightest, most single-minded graduate students and postdocs to work in their labs, then goaded them with threats of getting kicked out if they didn't publish papers. Vic hired those applicants for whom he felt most sorry—Maureen, in her wheelchair; Yosef, who had arrived in America with the stubble on his cheeks and fifty dollars in his pocket; Lew Schiff, who had been hospitalized twice for manic depression and seemed so tightly wound he might spiral apart at the slightest wrong word; and Susan, whose only problem was a personality so disagreeable that she had been asked to leave two labs before this one. Other professors pushed their students to work weekends and nights, especially when their experiments had failed. Vic insisted a failure meant you take the afternoon off (everyone obeyed him except Achiro and me). He paid to install a lower workbench for Maureen. He gave Achiro permission to charge his long-distance calls to the lab. He let Susan pace furiously back and forth across his office—"the confession booth," we called it—and somehow convinced her that he wouldn't let her labmates steal her ideas. We worked hard to repay his kindness. But secretly we resented him for making our lab infamous as a warehouse for freaks. Not that other labs weren't filled with eccentrics. People who study sea-urchin sperm and fruit-fly wings aren't likely to be conventional. Getting in to MIT was a license to indulge the eccentricities that had gotten you teased in high school. But those of us who worked in Vic's lab weren't eccentric so much as flawed, and flaws weren't indulged at MIT.

"If you don't keep your grubby hands off my things . . ." Susan never completed her threats, whether because she couldn't think of a punishment severe enough, or because real violence scared her.

Lew had learned that the slightest word of defense would unleash a new tirade. He rubbed his fists against his wiry hair, then turned back to pouring his gel. Susan hurled the stapler. It hit the wall beside Lew's head, sprang open, and dropped heavily, like some broken-jawed bird. She stormed past me. "Watch out!"

I wondered if she had said this to excuse her behavior, or to warn me of the dangers awaiting me in the lab. No one was there except Achiro and Lew. The others were probably in the conference room, taking advantage of the free pizza and beer Vic bought every Monday afternoon for group meeting. I was surprised to see Achiro. But there he was, in a white polo shirt and striped slacks, bending over a notepad and writing something with a mechanical pencil. Beside him rose a stack of orange loose-leaf binders and the metal box containing his slide collection. I reminded myself not to ask what had happened. But he told me on his own, as smoothly as if he had been practicing.

"I am going back to Japan," he said. "My wife, she leave home. Our children are with my parents. They are, ahh, very old people."

I tried to make sense of this. Maybe Achiro's wife had grown tired of living with her in-laws and run away. Or she had had an affair.

"You take these." He waved his hand above the notebooks.

"Oh, no," I said. I couldn't. Not after all the work he had put in. And he would need the data in those journals when he found a new lab.

He shook his head violently. "Broken." He thumped his chest. "How you say, I no care?"

How was it possible to care as much as Achiro once had cared, then suddenly stop caring?

"Excuse me," he said. "Someone is waiting in this lounge." I thought he meant someone was waiting for him, to drive him to the airport. "But first, ahh, take these." He lifted the metal box. I had no choice but to take it. Achiro bowed. So did I. When he left I felt edgy, as if a comrade who had failed at some dangerous task had passed the mission on to me. I forced myself to walk down the hall to the meeting. As I passed the lounge, I saw a large, broad-cheeked woman leafing through a catalog of mice one could order from a breeding facility in Bar Harbor. The woman was middle-aged, with blunt-cut gray hair. It was a warm spring day, but she wore a long-sleeved flannel shirt, a wool skirt, and black woolen knee-highs.

"I'm Dr. Burns," she said. "Miriam Burns. I've got a family for you." Her voice was grating as a buzz saw. "I have a practice," she said. "In Maine. I see a lot of folks with Valentine's syndrome. I found Dr. O'Connell's name in a journal. I tried to get in touch with him." She lowered her voice, which made it sound like a buzz saw in a distant part of the woods. "Whenever I called I got this Asian man. Let's just say he didn't have a real good grip on the language. I could have written a letter. But I was coming to Boston anyway—I'm taking a refresher course in trauma—so I figured I would stop by in the flesh."

"You're treating a family with Valentine's?" I asked.

"Treating them?" she said. "There's no treatment for Valentine's. I tell them what they've got, then I stop around every now and then to make sure they're not rotting in their own filth. I make sure nobody puts a pillow to their face until there's no point not to." She removed a nail clipper from one of her many pockets, unfolded the file, and used the point to scrape the dirt from beneath her nails. She was exactly the sort of person you would want to show up if you had suffered from some trauma; she would stop the bleeding, then keep you from feeling too sorry for yourself.

"You live in Maine?" I asked. "Why do you have so many patients there with Valentine's?"

She refolded the clipper. "Let's just say somebody had it way back when, and that somebody married somebody else who had it, and they had lots of kids, and those kids had lots of kids, and everybody sort of married each other and had more kids."

"The family is big?" I said. "How big?" I prayed she would answer ten. Maybe, if I were incredibly lucky, twelve.

"The whole pedigree?" She counted on her fingers. "You have the Smiths. The Martingales. The Evergreens. The Fews. It's damn confusing—the head of the Smith clan way back when was a Few. The mayor made a chart. When he unrolls the damn thing, it stretches the length of town hall. With the distant relations, the count could run as high as three or three-fifty."

I allowed myself to think: *She means three hundred and fifty.* I waited for a sense of relief to set in. Instead, what I felt was a crushing compression, like a clock whose spring has been too tightly wound. *I'm not ready yet,* I thought. *Please, give me time.*

9

Strangely enough, I put off my trip to Maine as long as I could. It was one thing to theorize about the miracles we might accomplish if only we discovered a large enough family with Valentine's. It was another thing to find such a family, enlist the help of busy colleagues like Miriam Burns and Sumner Butterworth, then fail to find the gene.

Of course, there were also practical reasons to wait. Miriam Burns needed to prepare her patients. She couldn't get their hopes up. Donating blood wouldn't guarantee they would gain anything in return. Many of her patients had no telephones or cars. They lived miles from New Jerusalem and were tended by relatives nearly as infirm as they were. Some were squeamish. Some believed that giving blood would sap their manhood or strength. Many distrusted doctors. Those who lived in the village would be invited to a special bloodletting party, complete with cake and ice cream. Anyone too sick to attend would be visited at home. Later, I would go back and make a foray to the island offshore where the most inbred descendants of the original settlers with Valentine's lived. All in all, we would need to take blood from nearly three hundred people. What if none of them consented? What if they all did?

To pass the days until the trip—and to keep my mind off Willie—I spent most of my time reading about the Shakers who had settled in New Jerusalem a hundred years earlier and whose descendants still lived there, one tenth of them afflicted with Valentine's disease. The fact that genetics should be entwined with religion didn't strike me as strange. A person's faith is handed down from parent to child. The members of a given sect shun those outside their gene pool. Parents concerned with passing on their religion produce the largest families. They tend to keep track of who marries whom. Generation after generation, they voluntarily perform a series of matings no scientist but God would dare to carry out. The gene for Valentine's chorea might have existed in the human race since primitive times, but early *Homo sapiens* died too young to manifest its symptoms. Or the mutation arose later. Maybe it struck only once, so all recent sufferers trace their inheritance to that earliest source. If so, my mother's family must be related to those Shakers in Maine. More likely, the mutation arose several times independently, in various parts of the world, and our only link to whoever carried the gene came not from the past, but from the future we shared.

I had known before my research that the Shakers viewed intercourse as the root of all sin, but I hadn't been aware that the Shakers did shake. They clapped their hands, hooted, groaned, howled, and whirled in circles until their bonnets flew off. Such seizures were interpreted as a sign of God's will. A woman stomping her heels might be crushing snakes underfoot. A boy rushing from church and gobbling swill from a trough might be satisfying his secret hunger for sin. After such convulsions, a Shaker might freeze while his fellows interpreted the heavenly message. Hands up: *Mercy, life.* Hands down: *Judgment, death.* Hands thrown backward: *Leave the world of the body behind.*

In the late 1830s, a group of Shaker girls began to fall into trances. They sang songs in secret tongues and acted in ways that seemed drunken or obscene. Neat Shaker children wallowed in filth. They decried their elders' sins and sported fine clothes that would have been forbidden if these hadn't been "gifts" from Mother Ann, the founder of the religion. Most Shakers believed these fits to be inspired. Others doubted and scoffed. Eventually, the doubters and scoffers won out. Divine manifestations among the Shakers grew rare. Their chants came to resemble Methodist hymns. They learned their dances by rote. They turned to selling seeds and making furniture.

Then a widow named Elinor Smith came to live in New Jerusalem. What I could learn of the Smiths I had gleaned from a few references in books and voluminous letters from the mayor of New Jerusalem, a man named Paul Minot, who was also the town librarian, it seemed. His letters were written on onionskin paper, dry and frail as dead skin, and he used archaic locutions like "heretofore" and "mind you," which led me to picture a wiry old codger in plaid wool pants drawn up beneath his armpits. According to the mayor, Elinor Smith had sought shelter among the Shakers for herself, her two sons, and her three unmarried daughters. Soon after her arrival, she began to tremble at meetings, then she would burst from her bench and twirl about the room like the Shakers of old. Just as suddenly she would freeze, limbs locked in postures that pointed the way to heaven or hell. Even those elders who mocked the hysteria of an earlier age thought these seizures to be authentic. Two of Elinor's daughters began to throw fits. Then the younger son, Goodenough. Among the many documents the mayor sent that spring was a blurred photostat of a petition from Goodenough Smith to the elders of New Jerusalem dated 1881, when he must have been in his early thirties:

> *Seeing as Sister Elinor Smith is the Instrument by which the World has received a* Great Gift *from God, &, seeing as this* Gift *is clearly transmitted from parent to child by the will of the* Lord, *I petition you to grant that the Smith family is* Elect, *& entitled to enter into a* Lawful State of Carnal Union, *whose sole purpose is to engender more servants for* God. *I await your reply.*
>
> *Yours in the Spirit of* Jesus Christ
> *and* Mother Ann, *&c.*
> *Bro. Goodenough Smith.*

No answer is recorded. But several months later, Brother Smith left the village with his sisters, an older brother, and several friends. He sent a letter to his mother's family in Bath and informed them that they, too, were instruments of God. A cousin moved out to the farm Smith had bought on Spinsters Island. He married the cousin whose name was May Martingale. A dozen other lost souls joined them on the farm, among them a family from New Hampshire named Few. Except for Smith's claim that he and his relatives were entitled to breed servants for God, he lived as a Shaker, building cabinets and chairs for the fishermen's wives.

But within a few decades, the Shakers on Spinsters Island, like those celibate Shakers who had remained in New Jerusalem, declined and died out. Most of Smith's descendants slipped back to the mainland and tried to blend in. They might have refused to take part in our study, but the mayor had grown up in New Jerusalem. He wasn't related to the Smiths and was connected to the Martingales and Fews in the most roundabout way, but when he made his inquiries as to who had married whom and who had died from what, no one took the trouble to lie. I reread his stack of letters. The more intimately I was informed about the residents of New Jerusalem the easier it would be to convince them to give their blood. *Elisha Smith. Deliverance Martingale. Carrie Few. Belinda Hayes.* What sort of people would worship an illness? But then, didn't I worship it as well?

The commuter plane that serviced Bar Harbor carried no passengers that day except Rita Nichols, Yosef, Sumner Butterworth, and me. I was sure that my nervous energy could have powered it all the way to Maine.

"Okay, folks," the pilot said. "Buckle your seat belts. It's going to be a bumpy ride."

As the plane taxied toward the runway, Sumner pointed out various types of aircraft. He had never piloted a plane, but he enjoyed collecting information. He was one of those people who believe that collecting enough of one thing will reveal a great truth, the way fitting together the pieces of a jigsaw might reveal a covered bridge. He prided himself on knowing the function of every cell in the brain, but I had never heard him use the words "consciousness" or "soul." He leaned back against his seat and did a crossword. I peered between the clouds and tried to spot Willie's mountain in New Hampshire. A few days before, I had received a postcard from Montana, where he was visiting his son. On the back, in blockish capitals, he had printed: "I HOPE YOU FIND WHAT YOU'RE LOOKING FOR."

The plane started bucking, and Sumner put down his magazine. "Jane?" He dropped his voice. "There aren't any of these Shakers of yours still at it?"

I asked him what he meant, still at what?

"Making furniture," he said. "Or weaving baskets."

No, I said, I didn't think there were. The last Shaker in New Jerusalem had died the year before. The Shaker village lay in ruins; the mayor wanted to restore it, but no one had the money. "You know," I said, "I don't think you're going to have much time to go rooting around in people's attics." I tried to be tactful. He was fifteen years my senior and I was glad that he was treating me as something of an equal.

Yosef leaned across the aisle. "Tell the truth. You're not just a little bit worried what these goyim are going to think about us two Yids taking blood from their children? Maybe they think we're going to use the blood to make matzos?"

You're not worried they might think it's a plot by the Commies *and* the Yids and ride us out of town on a rail?"

Yosef loved to put on his thickest Russian accent and play up his origins as a "Commie" and a "Yid." Mostly, he enjoyed getting me to laugh. But he also believed some plot against Russians and Jews had denied him the success that should have been his. "Yosef," I said, "these people probably wouldn't recognize a matzo if they stepped on one. I swear, if you put on that Shylock act of yours—"

"Wouldn't you just know it?" Rita clicked shut her handbag. "When my James went off to camp, I was so sure he was going to forget to pack his inhaler that I put it in my purse. Then I forgot to take the damn thing *out* of my purse and give it to him. Soon as we land, I need to find a post office and mail it to him overnight. I've got to call the camp nurse and tell her to keep an eye on James and make sure he doesn't have an attack in the meantime." She glanced out the window. "Oh oh," she said. "I don't like the looks of *that*."

I leaned across Sumner so I could see out the window. The plane appeared not to move, embedded as it was in a thick block of clouds. I imagined my sister falling, her hair trailing like a comet, that filmy white shawl slowing her descent, though not enough to stop her.

"Okay, folks," the pilot said, "get back to your seats," though none of us had gotten up.

The plane dropped and pitched and rolled, then dropped again. If I had been annoyed at Sumner for considering this trip an opportunity to search for Shaker artifacts, seeing him now, gripping the armrests and grimacing, I was overcome by gratitude that he was taking so much trouble to try to cure an illness that posed no danger to him. And Rita, I thought. She had come on this trip to help cure a disease black people rarely got.

"All right," the pilot said. "I'm going to try to find the airport. Just sit back and hold on."

Despite the fog, we landed. We rented a car, which Sumner insisted on driving. We inched along the coast, unable to make out the cliffs to our right. When we reached New Jerusalem, it seemed like Brigadoon, a town that had been sleeping for a century and materialized, unchanged, from the mist on the moor. The shop windows were streaked with salt. The air reeked of bait. The few pedestrians seemed gloomy and suspicious.

"They're looking at me like I escaped from somewhere," Rita grumbled. She was a tall, statuesque woman who wore her hair in an elegantly braided bun atop her head. That day, she had on a red rayon business suit. Even in Boston, she would have stood out.

We weren't due to meet Miriam Burns for another hour. Rita went to mail her son's inhaler while the rest of us browsed in a five-and-dime store that smelled strongly of the parakeets and hamsters in the back. While Sumner searched for bargains, I examined a postcard that purported to show the world's largest moose. I knew Willie would have liked it. But I couldn't fit everything I had to say on a postcard.

The old man behind the counter rang up the Nixon inaugural plate and the Howdy Doody lunch box Sumner had picked out. "That'll be eight fifty," the old man said.

"Eight fifty?" Sumner marveled.

"I guess that is a bit steep for junk like this. What say we call it five, even?"

Sumner gave the man a five-dollar bill, scooped up his purchases, and hurried out before the owner could think better of their bargain. He locked his acquisitions in the rental car. Then we went to meet Rita.

"This is the spookiest place I ever been to," she said. "They got this dried-up old hag in that post office. I'm standing in front of her, oh, five minutes, she pretends she doesn't see me. Finally, I say, 'Lady, you going to sell me some stamps or is there some separate window for the colored?'"

I didn't want to tell her that the postmistress probably had an early case of Valentine's, as if the woman's behavior might reflect badly on me. I was surprised Rita hadn't made the diagnosis herself. But then, the Valentine's patients she had seen before had all been labeled.

For the rest of the day, everywhere I looked I saw someone with Valentine's. The residents of New Jerusalem were plagued by afflictions one rarely found in Boston— enormous goiters and growths, withered limbs and missing ears. But how could I mistake the man sitting rigid on the bench, fingers clutching the slats so tightly he seemed afraid he might otherwise float off into space? Or the woman who froze every few steps, until her rottweiler urged her on? I wondered what I would have done if I had stumbled into New Jerusalem a hundred years earlier. I wanted to believe that I would have drawn the right conclusions. But smarter scientists than I hadn't figured out how diseases might be passed from parent to child. When I first read the paper in which Merriwether Valentine identified the syndrome that bore his name—he had written his report in 1868, thirty-two years before Mendel's work on the gene was accepted—I had had the impression of a man trying to explain how a radio works without knowing the words "electromagnetism," "radiation," or "electricity."

> *There is some principle, some sort of* essential proto-plasm, *by which the disease is transmitted. To the un-tutored eye, the symptoms might easily be attributed to old age, bad nutrition, the effects of venereal diseases, or drink, especially since the latter symptoms tend to run in families. It was in this way that I myself first explained the trembling and profanity of certain men and women whom I happened to encounter on my travels through certain regions of Georgia before the late war.*

I found it difficult to believe that whatever had killed my mother—an attractive middle-class Jewish woman who lived in upstate New York in the middle of the twen-tieth century—had anything to do with those "certain men and women" Merriwether Valentine had found staggering around rural Georgia, or these descendants of the crazy Shakers I had discovered in New Jerusalem. But of course I knew it did.

"Excuse me. Dr. Weiss?"

I turned to see a bearded man on a bike.

"I'm Paul Minnow," he said. "I assumed you would be older." Beneath his beard, the man flushed.

Not "Minnow," I thought. *Paul Minot,* the name so carefully signed to the mayor's letters. But the man on the bike couldn't have been older than forty. He rode a sleek ten-speed, with clips around his cuffs. He was overwhelmingly handsome—he could have been the model for those portraits of a lumberjack in the backs of magazines: HOW WELL DO YOU DRAW?

"I can't tell you how glad I am you're here." I supposed he meant all of us, but the remark seemed addressed to me. "You must be on your way to Dr. Burns's office. You're still early, am I right? What do you say I show you around New Jerusalem?"

He wheeled his bike beside the curb, an incongruous escort that caused people to stare at us even more. "That's the library," the mayor said. He left his bike beside a rack. "My home away from home."

The library, like the mayor, showed an unsettling juxtaposition of the archaic and the new. Beside a bust of Plato sat Curious George. Beneath a gilt inscription of the Ten Commandments hung a sign urging residents to pass a referendum for a waste-treatment plant. And, like the mayor, the library seemed excessively earnest. A series of posters of Peoples of the World proclaimed ALL MEN ARE BROTHERS UNDER THE SKIN. Another sign explained: GIVEN THE LIBRARY'S BUDGETARY CONSTRAINTS WE HAVE BEEN FORCED TO DISCONTINUE OUR SUBSCRIPTIONS TO PERIODICALS WHOSE CONTENT HAS NO EDUCATIONAL VALUE.

The mayor told us that he had left New Jerusalem to study history at Brown. "There I was, fishing for a topic for my senior thesis, and I hit upon the idea of the New

Jerusalem Shakers. It dawned on me that no other part of the country was as rich in historical material as my own backyard. And, to make a long story short, here I am."

Yosef and Rita looked around to see what he had returned to.

"For instance, I'll bet you didn't know New Jerusalem was a stop on the Underground Railway." He directed this to Rita. "The basement of the Shaker laundry was the railway's last stop before Canada."

Rita snorted and said she wondered how happy the white folks would have been if those slaves had taken it in their heads to come up from that basement and stick around.

The mayor fiddled with his beard. "Got me there," he said. "I can't exactly claim New Jerusalem has been on the vanguard of what you might call cultural diversity. I'm afraid that your companion here, Dr.—?"

Yosef seemed unwilling to reveal his name.

"Dr. Horowitz," I said.

"Well, Dr. Horowitz, don't be surprised if the natives around these parts don't react all that cordially to your accent."

Yosef shot me another look.

"Your compatriots on the trawlers offshore have been overfishing their quotas. Our men often catch them poaching."

Yosef lifted his hands. "If I want fish, I go to the supermarket and buy Bumble Bee like everybody else."

The mayor looked at Yosef as if he couldn't comprehend that he might be making a joke. "Mind you," the mayor went on, "this isn't only the fault of the Soviets. Everyone is being shortsighted. That's one of my primary goals for this town—developing new ways to think about fish." He spent the next twenty minutes telling us about his plans to build a factory that processed "seafood by-products" into an odorless, colorless paste that could be shaped to resemble lobster meat or crabmeat and shipped anywhere in the world without spoiling. "I can't tell you how eager I am to cooperate with you on your project." He said this while directing his gaze at me. "How will this town ever be able to move forward if so many of its citizens are invalids? There's the strain on our medical resources. And the local welfare budget. Not to mention the strain on our human resources. I feel you've been sent to us by, oh, divine providence, why don't we call it." He ran his hand along a bookcase. "If you need help untangling anyone's genealogy, it's all here on these shelves. In the meantime, we still have a few minutes before Dr. Burns expects us. If you don't mind, there's something else you ought to see."

We followed him across the street to the town hall. After he had shown us the tax collector's office and the Department of Health, he led us to the basement. Two metal tables stood beside the flag. Another table, covered with a balloon-print tablecloth intended for a child's party, held stacks of plastic plates, Dixie cups, and forks. "Seventeen years of work," the mayor said, and I thought he meant it had taken him seventeen years to set up for the bloodletting party, but he stretched his arms to indicate a scroll of paper tacked to one wall. "You can imagine how a man feels when he learns that his labors haven't been in vain."

I leaned closer and saw that the chart detailed the pedigrees of New Jerusalem's inhabitants since the late 1600s. A small red *V* was inked beside many of the names. I touched *Judith Anne Howarth*, who in 1890 had married *Ebenezer Martingale*. Eleven names descended from their union: *Josiah Martingale 1894–1943; Emeline Martingale (m. John Harbridge) 1897–1931; Stephen Wade Martingale 1899–1951* . . . Of the eleven Martingale children, six had died young. Reading the chart was like walking through a graveyard in which you expected to find your own tombstone. I thought of the way Valentine's had brought Willie and me together, and how it would keep us apart. I felt like tearing down the scroll, with all its gold-headed pins, and ripping it to pieces.

"I would be glad to point out the most interesting branches," the mayor said.

I could see that he was hurt because I hadn't shown the proper gratitude. "Give me a few years and I'll have the whole thing memorized," I said, to be polite. Then it struck me what he had done. Without this chart, we would have no hope of understanding the pattern by which the gene had been inherited. What had prompted this man who didn't have Valentine's to devote so many years to a task he couldn't have known would be of use? *Divine providence,* he had said. I started crying.

"Now don't go getting all emotional on us." Rita squeezed my arm. "You get yourself together, girl, and get through this."

Get yourself together. Rita was right. I needed to bring together my two selves—the Jane Weiss who had spent so many years hoping she would never meet anyone who suffered from Valentine's disease and would therefore remind her of what her own family had suffered, what she stood to suffer herself, and the Jane Weiss who had devoted her entire professional career to finding other families who had fallen victim to the disease so she could study their blood.

The post-office clock chimed five. "We should go," the mayor said, and I wondered if he had had enough of our company; we must have made him realize that his life was odder than it seemed to him.

We walked along Front Street, where gulls scavenged among the rotted hulls and discarded appliances on the beach. The birds snatched clams from the tide, lifted them above the pier, and let them drop—the shells smashed and burst with startling thuds—then swooped down to collect the meat. At the end of the pier, a barrel-chested man was repairing a lobster trap. It made me think of Willie and his surprise at becoming entangled in that trap at Tommie's.

We reached Miriam Burns's office, a gingerbread Victorian which, according to the mayor, once belonged to the family that owned the shipyard. The sign on the right said MIRIAM BURNS, M.D., and the sign on the left said BARBARA LEWIS, VETERINARIAN. The mantel in Miriam's waiting room was carved with ornate schooners. A man sat beside the fireplace holding a bloody handkerchief against his cheek. He read a magazine, turning the pages with one hand.

Miriam emerged from a frosted door. "Oh, hello," she said. "I guess I got a little behind." She motioned for the bleeding man to step inside. "Won't be a minute."

And she wasn't. The patient came back out with his cheek neatly bandaged. "Thanks, Doc," he said, then handed her some cash and ducked out, as sheepish as if Miriam were the madam at a brothel.

She closed her surgery and showed us up the stairs. I thanked her for letting us stay.

"I couldn't very well let you sleep at the boardinghouse," she said.

Yes, I thought, she could have, just as she could have let someone else do the work of setting up the party.

Someone hammered at the door.

"I hope you don't mind," Miriam said. "I invited a friend to dinner."

Barbara Lewis, the vet, was a gangling redhead with a setter's friendly face. She dropped a paper bag on the table. The sides began to move. "Fresh off the boat." She yanked out a lobster, which waved its claws at us languidly. "Hope you like the local specialty. Can't say anyone around here eats much of it day to day."

Dinner turned out to be two lobsters apiece, steamed clams, and baked potatoes. Sumner paused to express the sentiment that crustaceans like these, plucked from cold waters, were sweeter than the kind caught closer to home.

"Think so?" Barbara Lewis sucked a claw. "Always thought the sweet ones were the females, no matter where they came from."

"The females?" Sumner said. "How on earth can you tell the difference?"

Barbara reached across the table and flipped Sumner's lobster on its back. "See these fins here? Where the body joins the tail? See how they're kind of feathery? That shows it's a female. See that coral stuff? That's the roe. The females stay tender even when you boil them. The roe gives the meat a salty-sweet taste. In the male lobsters—" She flipped her own dinner. "See, no feathers. The fins are bony. No roe. The meat's tough."

"I didn't know that," Sumner said, impressed that anyone knew more about anything than he did.

Over bread-and-raisin pudding, Miriam described the arrangements for the bloodletting party. The patients were scheduled to arrive at fifteen-minute intervals. Barbara and I would administer the questionnaires and keep the children occupied. Sumner would examine and classify each donor according to his or her symptoms. Yosef would label the vials of blood. The mayor would calm his constituents and serve the cake and ice cream.

"If anything doesn't suit you," Miriam said, "just speak up. I don't mean to horn in on your parade."

I assured her I couldn't have done better myself. And, what I didn't say: How could I ever repay this debt?

We helped clear the table, then Miriam came in with a Monopoly box and a tray of cookies. "We don't exactly have what you'd call an active night life around here," she apologized.

Only Rita declined to play; she had to call her family. Besides, she said, losing money made her nervous, even when the money wasn't real. Barbara set up the Monopoly board while Sumner explained the rules to Yosef.

"You think I just stepped off the boat?" Yosef said. "You watch. I make more monopoly than anyone else."

Paul volunteered to be the banker. "I always feel a bit offended when I play this game. It's as if all mayors are supposed to be portly buffoons in top hats."

Sumner laid out his deeds in rows and kept us apprised of interesting facts about Monopoly ("The closer a property is to Free Parking, the more likely a player will land there"). He bought everything he landed on, built houses and hotels. But he spread himself too thin and was the first to go bankrupt. After that, he kept himself amused by advising the remaining players. Not that Miriam or Barbara needed advice. They shared many private jokes ("I'm not in jail, I'm just visiting," "I'm the queen of Marvin Gardens!") and took pleasure in exacting exorbitant rents from each other ("That's eleven hundred dollars. Pay up, Barb, right now!"). The game went on for hours. Usually, I have no patience for board games. But I didn't want that round of Monopoly to ever end.

The other players went broke. Miriam landed on a railroad. I owned all four. I told her that she didn't have to pay. "Of course I do," she said and declared me the winner.

Barbara Lewis made an elaborate show of yawning. "I'd better be getting home. We've got a big day ahead of us tomorrow." All of us stretched and said good night. I brushed my teeth and lay down in the room I had been assigned. But I couldn't fall asleep. It was as if an enormous reunion were planned for the next morning. A reunion of my family. Except that I had never met a single member and had prepared nothing for their arrival. They wouldn't get along with each other. They would demand something I couldn't give them.

A bell clanged in the harbor. I pulled on a robe and went down the hall. At the back of the house, I found an empty room and sat in a love seat, watching the sea, which was very dark except for a light beyond the shore.

Across the hall, a door opened. Miriam came out in a nightgown. Then Barbara Lewis appeared, in the same sweatshirt and jeans she had been wearing at dinner. Miriam stroked Barbara's hair. They kissed—the sort of kiss that makes an observer wish she had a lover of her own—and Barbara walked out of sight. I heard another door open. Not the front door, downstairs, but a door down the hall—the two halves of the house connected. Miriam turned and saw me.

I hadn't meant to spy, I said. I just couldn't fall sleep.

"Of course you couldn't." She came in and settled beside me on the love seat. Her arms and shoulders were so white I longed to lay my head against them. "Everybody in town knows about Barbara and me. They don't mind a pair of dykes taking care of them and their mutts and cows, so long as they don't get their faces rubbed in it." She tugged up the straps of her nightgown. "The people here like me. As much as they like anyone. I've had my work all these years. And now this project of yours. This way to be of use. And there's Barbara, of course. Turns out, I've been given nearly everything."

Nearly, she had said. What hadn't she been given? But Miriam didn't reveal this, and I didn't want to pry. And we sat there on that love seat, watching the sun rise above the water, and the men on their boats, loading traps and winding nets.

10

The first family was scheduled to appear at eight A.M., the second at eight fifteen. Neither family showed up. I picked up a syringe and absentmindedly peeled it, then had to throw it out, certain this would be the only needle we used that day. Only the success stories in science get publicized. Few people outside our lab knew about the postdoc who had spent three years studying an extended family of Hasids, certain he had traced a correlation between a rare blood group they shared and an unusually high incidence of schizophrenia, only to learn one of his respondents was lying and her sons had been conceived by a non-Jewish father. When the postdoc learned the truth, he went home and tried to hang himself.

"They'll come," Paul Minot assured me. The post-office clock chimed the half hour. "See, there they are."

At the door stood the Manns. The mother seemed alert, and the daughter, who was thirty, had the sweet but apprehensive face of a child. The three eldest boys wore vacant expressions, but the youngest son seemed brutish. His sweatpants hung low to expose his hairy belly and the tops of his buttocks. In this he resembled his father, whose trousers wouldn't close; he held them up with knotted rope, as if this relieved him of the need to zip his fly.

"It's *her* fault," the father said, jabbing his chin toward his wife. "And her father's fault. And that bastid first husband of hers. They're the ones soured the blood in this family." He laid his arm protectively across his youngest son. "I said to her, you want to let them stick you and yours, fine. I don't see no reason to let them stick me and Little Jim."

His wife looked as if she hoped we would stick him with something more lethal than a needle. "No reason except I cook for you and clean for you. And my Debbie does the same. And even my boys go out now and then and earn a few dollars. If I ask a little something in return, that's reason enough. You do it or you can go live at the VA and let the nurses clean up your mess."

"And who's gonna clean your mess when you start shittin' on the floor, like your old dad did, eh?"

"That'll be the day, you cleaning any mess of mine."

Miriam Burns placed one hand on each of Mr. Mann's beefy shoulders and pushed him in a chair. "We'll need blood from all seven of you," she said, and jammed the needle in.

By the time Sumner finished examining all seven Manns it was a quarter past nine and the second family was waiting, as was the third. Everything took longer than expected. The complications of kinship were so intricate that, even with his chart, the mayor could barely untangle who was who. The simplest questions—How many siblings do you have? Are they living or dead?—might take a donor an hour to answer. To test the concentration of a fleshless old man, Sumner asked him to read a paragraph from the *New Jerusalem Post*. "You setting me up for a laugh?" the old man said. "Everyone knows I can't read." Sumner fared no better when he asked the old man to name the current president. "Don't know and don't care. Just a rotten gang of cocksuckers back to FDR, and him the biggest one."

This struck a blow to Sumner's pride. Many of the patients Vic referred to Sumner wrote back to say how compassionate they had found Dr. Butterworth. They had no way of knowing that even as they chatted, Sumner was observing them for symptoms—the twitch of a hand, the tendency to stop in midsentence—and he asked these same questions of every patient he saw, feigned the same interest, could pass that person on the street the next day and not know him.

"Can't stump you, can I." Sumner laid his pen across his clipboard and asked the old man how he felt.

"That's more like it. I'm ninety-three years old. I ain't got time for your bullshit questions. I feel lousy, is how I feel. Takes me till noon to unbend. Can't hardly take a piss. But when I think of my dad and granddad, dying of that chorea thing in their early forties, I thank my lucky stars. Now, you get that pretty young girl over there to take my blood, and I'll go on and get home."

It took me a while to realize *pretty young girl* meant me. Still, I couldn't be flattered. Either he had the sex-wrought brain of a Valentine's victim, or he was starved for love, as old men often are. I wrapped a length of tubing around his arm, which was as rubbery and thin as the tourniquet.

I swabbed his tattoo, so blurred by age I could barely make out the picture. "Hula dancer," he muttered slyly. "Sorry she ain't wearing no shirt."

Watching Sumner examine patients, I couldn't help but admire his insincerity and the power this gave him to alleviate people's fears. He praised children for their brilliance in counting by twos. When a woman couldn't touch her fingers to her nose, he assured her, "That's all right, dear, it doesn't matter," while I was too sad to do anything except murmur how sorry I was.

It was one of those days when the worst you've imagined truly does come to pass, along with disasters you hadn't been creative enough to predict. The room was so stuffy that three donors fainted. Children vomited and threw tantrums. The coolers that the mayor had bought to chill the ice cream couldn't contend with the heat. "You promised us refreshments," sneered a mother whose child was crying bitterly. "But there ain't anything here but crumbs and slop." This struck the mayor dumb. It was, he said, the first promise to a constituent he had ever been accused of breaking. I figured he must have seen a Valentine's seizure before, but not two in one morning—a man losing control of his bowels, a woman flailing so violently she knocked the flag to the floor. One moment I was elated that fate had chosen me to find the cause of all this suffering; the next moment, I was stricken by despair that I was torturing all these invalids for no purpose except my own misplaced hope.

Rita pumped up a blood-pressure cuff. "Who said helping your people ever comes easy?"

My people. What did I have in common with such a mean-spirited crowd? They shrank from Rita's touch and stared shamelessly at her braids. In return for this rudeness, Rita tied their tourniquets tighter and jabbed their needles deeper than I had ever seen her do. One disheveled woman brought a grandchild who had an earache. The girl wasn't prone to Valentine's but her grandmother thought it only fair that Miriam examine her. Miriam said she would be happy to see the girl at her office but didn't have the proper equipment here. The grandmother pointed to Miriam's bag. "Bet you got one of them ear things. I took the time off from work. Least you can do is take a look in her ear."

Miriam examined the child, who seemed listless and withdrawn. The ear was infected. Miriam wrote out a prescription.

"Hey, Doc," someone else called. "Got a lump in my neck I'm kinda worried about. Could you come and take a look?"

"Long as you're looking at his lump, you might give me your opinion on this welt on my shin. Damn thing won't heal."

By two that afternoon, the tension in the room was as stifling as the heat. A foul-smelling fisherman in a rush to get back to his boat flustered me so badly I stuck him with the same needle I had used on someone else. He jerked away, the syringe bobbing in his arm. "What are you trying to do, give me his cooties? I seen on the TV how there's this thing now in people's blood can make another person sick. That new thing, whatyoucallit."

"Who you saying has cooties?" asked the first man I had stuck.

"Ah, keep your fucking shirt on. All I'm saying is, you can't be too careful. These government doctors, they need some guinea pigs for some experiment, you think they're going to tell the likes of you what they're really up to?"

"Come now," the mayor said. "You don't actually believe—"

"Don't I? You heard that one over there open his mouth?" The fisherman waved a four-fingered hand at Yosef. "Tell me I don't know a fucking Commie when I hear one." He demanded Yosef's name. Yosef raised his arms, a vial of blood in each hand.

"That's Dr. Horowitz," I said, stepping between Yosef and the fisherman with a bravery I didn't really feel. "He's worked with me for years."

"Yeah? And why should we trust you? What kind of name is Weiss? Hundred to one Dr. *Weiss* here is making a little something off our blood." The crowd moved up behind him. "I was down to Boston once, sold a bag of my blood for twenty dollars. How come I ain't getting nothing for this blood?"

"If he's getting twenty dollars, we want twenty dollars," said a woman in a hairnet.

The mayor assured them that no one would profit from their blood.

"Easy enough for you to talk. You got a steady job. Don't got the sickness in your family."

The mayor looked so flustered that Rita rose to speak. Her braids were the highest thing in the room. "Do any of you fine ladies and gentlemen happen to know how much I'm getting paid for being up here with you today? Sixty-five dollars. Minus the two hundred dollars it's costing me to send my boys to camp." She tugged at her uniform. "How about you, Dr. Burns? You making anything here today?" Miriam said she wasn't. "And you, Dr. Lewis? Or you, Mr. Mayor? You earning any blood money here today?"

"The mayor's position is an honorary one," Paul said primly.

Rita asked if that meant he was doing this for free.

Yes, he said. It did.

Rita turned to Sumner. "And what about you, Dr. Butterworth? Could you give these fine folks an idea how much you would be making at that neurology clinic of yours at the Massachusetts General Hospital if you weren't here with us right now?"

"Actually," Sumner said, "doctors don't get paid an hourly wage."

"Just give us a general idea," Rita told him. "A ballpark figure. That's all the good people want."

Sumner estimated that his salary for a day would translate to eight hundred dollars.

"You're giving up eight hundred dollars a day to be doing this?" Rita said.

"Yes," he said, "I am." The crowd murmured its amazement that anyone would forgo eight hundred dollars to spend a day with them. Sumner looked modestly at his loafers, as if he hadn't understood until then how generous he really was.

"How about you, Dr. Weiss?" Rita went on. "Why don't you tell these people what you're hoping to gain from all of this."

I couldn't answer such a question. Nothing I was doing would help a single soul in that room. "I'm not earning anything," I said.

"You're not earning money. But if you find this gene you're after, you're going to write up a paper and publish it in some fancy journal. Isn't that why you're doing this? To get yourself famous?"

I had fantasized too often about seeing my name on such a paper to deny Rita's charge.

"Go on," she said. "Tell these people why you really need to find this gene."

Everyone stood there watching me, but I couldn't say a word.

"You want me to tell these people how it runs in your family? How your own mother died of this disease?" Rita grasped my wrist and pushed my sleeve above the elbow. I stared at the patch of skin she started swabbing. That patch of skin on which the alcohol dried was the only part of my body that wasn't hot. Rita jabbed in the needle. My muscles were so tense and the pain so startling, I gasped. I saw blood swirling in the syringe, and even though I had seen thousands of vials of blood, my head began to swim. Rita transferred the blood to a stoppered vial and held the tube aloft. I wanted to snatch it back. This must have been how Willie felt, angry that a stranger should steal a part of who he was.

Rita handed the vial to Yosef, who scribbled a code on the label to indicate the donor. "There now," Rita said. "You see anybody here getting paid for this blood?"

"How old was your mother when she passed on?" a woman asked me.

"Got the shakes yet?"

"I didn't think people on the outside came down with this thing."

"Hope you'll excuse us, Doc." The man who said this was excruciatingly thin, with a dirty gray ponytail straggling down his back. "We're used to doing for ourselves. Sometimes we have a hard time showing how we're grateful."

An enormous older woman took me around and squeezed me. She smelled like a large sea mammal—a walrus, or a manatee—and I grew faint in her embrace. Yosef pushed through the crowd and began to pass around Dixie cups full of warm Coke.

"Let's drink a toast," he suggested. "Like that sign in the library says, all of us here are brothers, get under same skin."

The fisherman who had demanded to be paid for his blood knocked his cup against Yosef's. "To the whole fucking lot of us," he said, then he knocked his cup to mine.

For the next several days, we visited the homes of donors who were too disabled to come see us. I kept thinking about Maureen and her trips to Peru to gather samples for her experiments. The mud had been so thick she couldn't use her wheelchair, so a crowd had raised it to their shoulders and carried her wherever she needed to go. They trusted her because she was forced to trust them. I showed up at the homes of the people I was studying with a large entourage. On my own, I couldn't have brought myself to knock on any door, not knowing if I would find a scene from my past—a child caring for a parent—or a scene from my future—a man my father's age spooning food in his daughter's mouth. I let the mayor introduce us. Outnumbered by experts, most donors were docile. They answered Rita's questions, revealing intimate facts about themselves they wouldn't have disclosed to their closest friends. I began to understand why Merriwether Valentine had assumed poverty to be the cause of the afflictions he observed rather than the other way around. On a solitary farm miles from New Jerusalem, Miriam and I found a woman whose husband had run off. The woman had never heard of Valentine's. Her son wore a helmet to keep him from injuring his head when he threw his fits. I spent an hour convincing the woman that his seizures weren't caused by the time she had dropped him from his crib twenty-seven years earlier.

"You're not just saying that? You promise?" She buried her face in the washrag she had been using to clean her son.

"It wasn't anyone's fault," I repeated, and she tried to kiss my hand.

In one house, we met a man who tied his sister to the bed because he couldn't afford a nurse to stay with her while he worked. We met a woman who supported her children by knitting sweaters for a company in Bath. Since her husband hadn't waited for his Valentine's to kill him but managed to shoot himself first, she hadn't been allowed to collect his insurance. Even Sumner seemed moved. He was childless and divorced, but he bought three sweaters from the woman, including a tiny red one with a reindeer on the front.

Among rich and poor, we found neglect. We found people who lied about their relatives ("He didn't really join them Shakers, they snatched him as a child"). But more than neglect or lies, we found the sort of self-sacrifice that is unimaginable for those who aren't called upon to make it. We met a woman in her seventies who cared for twin sons. Although each of "the boys" was taller than his mother and weighed fifty pounds more, she diapered and bathed them and rolled them in their beds so their skin wouldn't get sores. Miriam's suggestion that she send them to a nursing home was met by a puzzled stare. "Oh," the woman said, "that won't need to happen unless I die before them. But I'm hoping it will be the other way around." She took out a beaded purse. "I want you to have this," she said and handed me a ten-dollar bill. I tried to refuse but finally gave in and stuffed the money in my coat, making a mental note not to spend it on myself.

"Christ! Ma! Need you! Need you! Ma!"

The woman turned to go.

"I'll come back to visit you," I said.

"Of course you will," she said.

I tried to say, *Really, I promise I'll come back,* but the woman was already hobbling toward her sons.

On our last night in town, the mayor invited me to dinner. I tried to beg off. I was exhausted, I said. But I couldn't hurt the feelings of someone to whom I already owed so much. He sensed my hesitation. The fact was, he needed my opinion.

Couldn't I give it to him here?

No, he said, it wouldn't be nearly as convenient.

He wasn't the sort of man you could accuse of trying to seduce you. So what could I do but climb on the bike he must have borrowed from some child—it had pink-and-white streamers and a daisy-covered basket—and pedal along beside him.

We rode for fifteen minutes into the setting sun, the water lapping the rocks beside us. "There it is." He pointed to a cottage with lacy blue eaves and a white wicker swing creaking on the porch.

"It's beautiful," I said. And really, it was. I had never seen a prettier place to live. He held the door and we went in. The walls were china blue with cornflowers stenciled near the ceiling. A braided rug lay before the hearth. There were a china hutch, a wood trunk, and shelves and shelves of books. Paul went over to the stove, put on a pair of oven mitts, and took out a covered dish. Staring at his back, which was so much narrower than Willie's, I grew angry and sad.

He offered me a taste of whatever food was in the dish, but I turned away, repulsed by the sight of that spoon coming toward me. Long ago, I had vowed never to let anyone feed me. I took the spoon and fed myself. It was something chewy and bland.

"I was hoping you could help us think of a name for it," the mayor said.

"For what?" I asked.

"The product I was telling you about. We can't exactly market it as 'shaped and molded fish by-products.'" He offered me another bite, then waited so expectantly I had the crazy notion he would tie me to a chair and keep spooning this tasteless stuff in my mouth until I told him what he wanted.

"Why don't you just call it 'seafood'?" I suggested.

"*Sea Food,*" he repeated. "That's not bad. A housewife could say, 'Let's have Sea Food tonight,' and everyone would say, 'Sure! Let's have Sea Food. Everyone loves Sea Food.'" He was looking at me so adoringly you might have thought I had revealed the secret name of God. I was remarkable, he said. Sure, he admitted, he got lonely. The town wasn't exactly overflowing with women his age, not to say women who had gone to college. But he also didn't mind telling me that I was one of the bravest, most intelligent women he had ever met.

"You hardly know me," I said.

Well, he could *get* to know me, couldn't he? I would be returning to New Jerusalem. And he had a convention of New England mayors to attend in Boston the following month.

The idea of sitting in a restaurant discussing waterfront development and fish by-products with this man made me blurt out that I had a boyfriend, and even though I stumbled on the word, the lie felt truer than anything else I might have said.

He put the casserole on a trivet and stood there with the oven mitts on his hands. "I guess I do have a tendency to come on a bit strong."

Oh, no, I said, I should have told him earlier. About this boyfriend, I meant. We had only become involved a few weeks earlier.

"So it isn't that serious?" he asked me hopefully.

Oh, I said, but it was. Willie and I hadn't known each other for more than a few weeks, but we had such a lot in common. Both of us had had parents who had died of Valentine's.

That I had given this boyfriend a name made the lie more convincing. "I only hope he appreciates his luck," the mayor said.

I hoped he did, too.

The mayor set the casserole on the table. If the "seafood" had seemed rubbery and bland before, eating it now was like chewing on a hose. He offered little besides the casserole—soggy peas, a slice of bread, watery tapioca. We sat sipping a pot of coffee I suspected had been boiling since dawn when the telephone rang.

"Yes," the mayor said. "She's here, I'll put her on." He held out the receiver, assuming, I supposed, this must be my boyfriend, Willie.

"I hope I'm not interrupting anything." The voice was Vic's. "Miriam Burns told me where you were."

"It's fine," I said. "Don't worry. The mayor and I were finishing our dessert."

"I just got in from that meeting in California, and I had to find out how everything went. And, well, I wasn't sure what effect all this would have on you."

Hearing Vic's concern was like hearing someone inquire about a narrowly averted accident. Only then, thinking back on all the families we had seen with Valentine's, all the vials of blood we had drawn, did I grow shaky and need to sit.

"I should have flown up there to be with you. But I needed to write that grant. And there was that meeting in Palo Alto."

I told him that he could trust me.

"I do trust you," he said. "You've done a wonderful job with all this. But it's the most important work that's going on in my lab right now, and I feel as if I ought to be doing more." To someone in the background I heard him say: "Shh. Yes, it's her. No, I won't hang up." And then, back to me: "Just a second. It's Maureen."

I heard the clatter of the receiver being dropped, and I pictured Maureen lifting it between her wrists.

"Hi there. Vic'll fill me in on the science. I just wanted to make sure you weren't doing anything I wouldn't do."

"I'm being good," I said.

"That's what I was afraid of. Go out, okay? Enjoy the sights. Bring me a souvenir. You know, a seashell or a fisherman or something. Can't wait until you get back! Bye!"

"I miss you, too," I said and then hung up.

The mayor pulled off the oven mitts and bent his head like a defeated boxer. "I suppose I ought to ride you back over to Miriam's place."

Before he extinguished the candles I saw what he would return to—a house that was unbearable if you didn't have someone to live there with you. "I know a woman in Boston you should meet," I said. It occurred to me that the mayor might be offended by my efforts to fix him up. But he was right about New Jerusalem being short on eligible women my age. If he found my nearness to Valentine's disease romantic, if he was attracted to intelligent female scientists, maybe he would find a female scientist with arthritis to be romantic. "You'll like her," I said. And, as I said this, I decided that Maureen might also like Paul.

We walked out on the porch. A breeze from the ocean rocked the swing.

"Is she as interesting as you are?" he asked.

She was a biologist, I said. She was searching for the cause of a mysterious form of blindness that affected a small community of fishermen in Peru. This was particularly difficult, I said, because she was confined to a wheelchair.

"A wheelchair?" he said. "From what?"

As I went on describing Maureen's illness, Paul stroked his beard. Clearly, he found her interesting. "What sorts of things does she like to do in her spare time?"

I said she liked to go dancing.

"Dancing? In a wheelchair?" He frowned. "I don't dance much myself. Unless you count square dancing. I don't suppose that's the kind of dancing your friend likes to do?"

No, I said, it wasn't.

"Well," he said, with an eagerness to please I found endearing, now that it was no longer directed at me, "I've taught myself how to be a librarian. And how to be a mayor. And how to process fish. I don't suppose there's any reason I can't teach myself to dance."

11

All those racks of blood from which DNA had to be extracted. All those cells to immortalize. The months, if not years, of running gels and blots, hunting for a pattern that might betray the gene's hiding place. On those rare nights I got to sleep, I dreamed of dropping vials, misplacing them, contaminating a sample with bacteria. What if all this effort went for nothing? What if we never found the gene? What if we did?

None of my labmates wanted to help. They knew the project could drag on for years. Vic held a lab meeting at which he threatened to cut off people's salaries if they didn't spend at least half their time on the Valentine's project. A while later, I overheard Susan gripe to Vivian Gold, the lab technician, that Vic was ruining their careers because he was "head over heels in love with Little Miss Valentine." I wanted to step out from behind the P-3 partition and slap Susan's face. But I couldn't afford to lose what little support she and Vivian might be willing to give.

In the weeks that followed, I transformed and spun down nearly sixty vials of blood. Though tedious, this part of the project wasn't daunting. Its limits were well defined: so many vials done; so many left to do. The next part entailed slogging through an astronomical number of pairings of enzymes and probes. I could spend the rest of my life trying combinations, propelled by the thought that the next key, or the next, might finally yield the payoff.

In the middle of all this, Willie sent me another postcard. This one showed a famous New Hampshire rock formation called the Old Man of the Mountains, which looked remarkably like Willie's own profile, with that craggy nose and chin. All he had written on the back was "COME UP AND SEE ME SOMETIME." I thought about writing back. But what could I have written? After all the suffering I had seen in Maine, how could I imagine getting any more involved with a man who, like me, might carry the gene for Valentine's? I refused to marry anyone who stood a fifty-fifty chance of coming down with the disease himself. Bad enough if I ended up taking care of my sister. I couldn't take care of my husband, too.

On top of everything, the benefit was coming up. With all the new developments, Honey and my father expected to raise more donations than ever. My father's foundation was paying the expenses of everyone involved. This included Paul Minot, who had been calling Maureen twice a day from Maine and was escorting her to the dinner. Willie would be there, too. How would he react if Paul told him that he was lucky to have a girlfriend like me? I was tempted to ask Maureen to help me keep the two men apart, but that would have entailed admitting that Paul had propositioned me before I had passed him along to her.

I did allow her to take me shopping. I had agreed to give a speech outlining the technical aspects of the project, and I couldn't very well address such a gathering in jeans. "Don't worry," Maureen kept telling me. "When I'm through with you, this stepbrother of yours won't even know you."

From the display in the window of the funky boutique she took me to, I figured this was true. One mannequin wore a flowered plastic cape with nothing underneath. Her wrists were bound behind her, and her neck was provided with a leash.

When I yanked Maureen's wheelchair up and over the threshold and pushed her through the door, the salesgirls stopped chatting. "Hi," Maureen said. "I'm looking for a little something in a size two. I can't do zippers or buttons. So I'm looking for, I don't know, a tunic sort of thing? And leggings? And maybe a belt like this?" The belt she picked up was as wide as a tire, with pointy silver studs. "And shoes to go with it. I like yours, those are great." Maureen pointed to the Lucite sandals on which one of the salesgirls balanced, the heels thin as pipettes. "After I've found what I'm looking for, we can help my friend Jane find a little something, too."

With an energy born of relief, the salesgirls darted around the store, bringing Maureen various outfits to try on. The fitting room was too narrow for the wheelchair, so she changed in full view. The salesgirls cooed encouragement, flying back and forth with accessories. At last, Maureen decided on a silver lamé minidress, silver shoes, and silver earrings shaped like twin nudes, one female, one male.

"Do you think he'll like it?" she asked. "Maybe it's a bit too wild."

"He'll like it," I said.

She looked up at me suspiciously. "Jane," she said, "there's something you're not telling me about this guy." She stroked the male earring. "You slept with him. And he couldn't get it up. Or he's a born-again Christian who thinks anything except the missionary position is sick."

I assured her Paul was perfect. *Too perfect*, I thought, but I kept that to myself.

"I believe you!" she said. "I talked to the guy for an hour and a half last night. What I can't believe is that this is happening to me." She motioned me lower. "Don't tell a soul, but I think I've figured out something about my blindness gene." She looked around, as if one of her competitors might be hiding behind the rack of bustiers. "It's a gene that's not a gene."

A gene that wasn't a gene? I squatted so she wouldn't need to crane her neck.

"Look," she said. "This thing only acts like a gene. Because it runs in families. But other things run in families besides genetic weirdness."

"For instance?"

"The way a family acts. You know, whether they drink or smoke. Or the foods they eat. Or religious rituals. Maybe a certain family smokes some crazy herb. I haven't got it nailed yet. But I have some ideas." She clasped my hand. "You watch. This is going to be a terrific time for both of us. Me and Paul, and you and Willie. Both of us will get these really big papers in *Cell*." She flicked the lever on the armrest and spun her chair, flinging light from her minidress. "Okay, now it's your turn. Get in that fitting room and wait for your fairy godmother."

I did as I was told. I unbuttoned my blouse and jeans, then stood before the mirror and inspected what I saw. The Jane Weiss in the fitting room reached out to touch fingers with the Jane Weiss in the glass.

"Oh, sweetie," Maureen said. "Never mind those dresses. You want this Willie character to fall head over heels, go to the benefit just like that."

I crossed my arms.

"No. If I looked like you, I would sit in front of a mirror all day. Here, put this on." She handed me a dress so skimpy I needed the salesgirls' help to wriggle into it. One woman zipped up the back while the other salesgirl clasped a rhinestone choker to my throat.

"Wow." Maureen whistled. "That gown makes you look fifteen years older."

I tried not to flinch. Wearing a dress that made me look older wouldn't bring the disease any sooner. I turned and kept turning, my eyes fixed on the mirror, and for the longest time, I couldn't bring myself to take off that gown.

⁙⁙⁙⁙⁙⁙⁙⁙⁙⁙⁙⁙⁙⁙⁙⁙⁙⁙⁙⁙⁙⁙

In the end, I bought the gown, plus a blue cashmere suit to wear to my father's wedding. I maneuvered the wheelchair out the door, Maureen with a stack of boxes on her lap, me with plastic bags slung about my arms. It was a Saturday afternoon and Harvard Square was crowded. The cobblestones were quaint, but the uneven bricks kept catching

Maureen's wheels. Tourists had parked their cars in front of the curb cuts, and I struggled to lift her chair above the curb. A tide of Japanese schoolgirls flowed around Maureen; they made me think of Achiro and his daughters, and I wondered if their mother had come back home and, if she hadn't, who cared for the girls while Achiro worked at whatever company now employed him.

As I waited for the girls to pass, I noticed a store that sold travel guides and maps, solar-powered calculators, and, in the window above these items, a magnificent globe. I tried to figure out what the globe was made of. Porcelain? Ivory? The colors were rich yet subdued, the deserts a burnished gold, the forests a mossy green, the seas a heartbreaking blue. The dotted routes of explorers, with tiny hand-drawn ships, were labeled with the names *Vasco da Gama, Magellan, Admiral Byrd, Thor Heyerdahl, Columbus, Amerigo Vespucci.*

I knew the globe would make a perfect gift for my father's wedding. But the shop could be reached only by a flight of stairs, and the aisles were so crowded that Maureen wouldn't be able to maneuver through them. I asked if she would mind waiting on the street while I went in.

She puffed a wilted spike of hair from her eyes. Go on, she said. She needed to catch her breath.

Was she sure? I hated to leave her sitting there.

"Sweetie," she said, "sitting on street corners is one thing I'm good at. One way or another, I'll probably take in a few bucks."

I climbed the steps and approached the globe slowly. I pressed my palms to either side—the surface was surprisingly warm. A tag tied to the globe's North Pole said $800. That was half my entire savings, and I had just spent the other half on clothes. Still, how often did a person's father get married?

I found the manager and asked if he would keep the globe at the store until I had a better idea of when the wedding would be. Honey's renovations had become so elaborate the ceremony had been postponed until September. I bought them travel guides for Italy, England, France, and Israel, then wrote out a check for nearly nine hundred dollars, which left forty-seven dollars in my account.

The transaction took ten minutes, but when I went back outside and saw Maureen primping her hair and trying to look as if she hadn't been abandoned, I was overcome with guilt. I leaned down and kissed her. "I hope it all comes true," I said. "The blindness gene. And you and Paul." And right then, I wished I could have bought Maureen the world, too.

12

My father was a *macher*, a man who made things happen. And where was there, really, in a tiny town like Mule's Neck to make anything happen if not a restaurant? As cheap as he was, he liked eating dinner out: Mondays with the Lions at the Dew Drop Inn; Wednesdays with the Rotarians; Thursdays with a bunch of businessmen who played pinochle in the back of Goodie's Bar; and Saturdays with his family at King's Hong Kong Chinese, which, when I was a kid, we called the King Kong.

Back then, whenever we went out to dinner, my father would stop at all the tables. He even talked to tourists who were only passing through. "If you need anything," he would say, "go down to my store and tell them Herb sent you." All the while, my mother would stand beside him, smiling a smile that might have meant anything, or nothing at all. She held Laurel by the wrist to keep her from twirling across the dragons in the carpet, the sort of fidgety motion our mother couldn't bear. I stood perfectly still and listened. I needed to be prepared to say the right thing—

not the cute thing, or the sweet thing, but the truly clever answer that would make the men laugh.

By the time we reached our table, I was dying of starvation. But I tried never to complain. I didn't pile noodles on my plate and drench them with duck sauce, the way Laurel liked to do. "Stop that," I would hiss. "You'll make yourself sick."

"But it's good," she would say, holding out a spoonful of noodles in orange sauce.

Every week, our father ordered the same few items. The food arrived in minutes, just long enough for the county superintendent or president of the local bank to cup my father's shoulder and ask, "Hey, Herb, how's tricks?"

The pupu platter came first, a wondrous affair with blue china dishes swirling about the flame from a dragon's mouth. My father spun the lazy Susan and grabbed spare-ribs, doughy wontons, egg rolls, and reddish strips of garlic pork. When the waiter brought the entrées, my father mounded his plate with sweet and sour chicken, leaned forward, and *scooped*. (I never saw anyone use chopsticks, not even the Kings.) Though he wolfed down his food, those dinners would last for hours. Every few minutes, one of his cronies stopped by. As my father rose to shake the man's hand, the rice from his lap would flurry to the floor. I would sit trying to follow the men's debates—should the village approve a tax increase to improve the schools, was Cuba a threat or not—while my sister amused herself by pouring sugar in her tea. "That's disgusting," I would scold. "Sugar gives you worms. Every grain is an egg that hatches in your stomach," at which Laurel dipped her thumb in her cup, closed her eyes, and licked the syrup in an extravagant display of bliss.

Finally, my father spooned the last few mouthfuls of sauce from each silver dish. He pulled his napkin from his belt and offered his good-byes while Laurel and I waited by the door, tossing mints in each other's mouths and watching Mrs. King tote up that night's receipts.

I loved my father profoundly. His appetite, his very crudeness, signified a hunger for something I longed for myself. I already knew everything my teachers at school tried to teach me. From my father, I learned how to work a cash register, how to keep an account book, and how to judge the quality of fabrics, wheelbarrows, and women's hosiery. He knew *the right thing to say*: dirty jokes in Yiddish for his suppliers from New York, clean ones in English for the Reverend McCann, riddles for the children, slightly ribald stories about the husbands for their wives. If I observed him closely enough, one day I, too, would run Weiss's Supply.

When did I begin to see through his act? It must have been the evening he asked me to talk to Karl Prince about eggs. I had entered junior high and was very caught up in my first science-fair project. It was nothing original, really, just the standard "Egg to Chick: How an Embryo Grows." The project entailed little more than asking Mr. Prince, who ran a nearby chicken farm, to donate fertilized eggs. I set these in the incubator my father helped me build, and every day after school I tweezed a window in one shell and took notes on what I saw. My mother cleared a shelf in her Frigidaire and let me keep the eggs in a set of glass dessert-bowls she had been given for her wedding. At first, the exercise seemed pointless. I saw exactly what the textbook predicted I would see. Then I began to wonder why and how all this happened. At three days, the tiny heart lay beating in its dish. In twenty-one days, an entire living chick had grown from a single cell in a gooey yolk. How did each cell know which part of what organ it was destined to become? I was stunned to find out real scientists knew as little as I did. I decided to become whatever sort of biologist studied how an animal grew from an embryo or an egg.

I bought three sheets of oak tag and a box of Magic Markers. Carefully, I stenciled the title of my project. I retrieved the windowed eggs and sketched what I saw. The markers' inky smell, their squeak against the oak tag, made me dizzy with joy. My father brought home a dozen wire hangers, which I used to frame the posters so they would stand.

The night before the science fair, our family went to King's. On our way to our table, my father stopped to talk to Karl Prince about eggs. "Hey, Karl." He drew a drag of his Lucky Strike, which he held daintily between a circle of finger and thumb. "Those eggs you gave Jane? Seems she figured out a way to make chicks without the roosters. If you ask her nice enough, she might let you in on the secret. Won't you, doll?"

My father, I saw then, didn't consider an egg a mystery, a source of new life, but a product to be sold. An egg was a piece of merchandise. And my knowledge, my ability to make a good impression, *to say the right thing*, these were merchandise, too. So even though I knew the right thing to say to make Mr. Prince laugh, even though I knew it involved the words "I might, if he paid me," I couldn't bring myself to say it.

"Turning shy on me, doll? Happens to the best of them. Girls hit twelve and, *pfft*, they're useless for life."

Useless? Because I was a girl? Because I wouldn't let my father turn what I felt about those eggs into a joke, a product? I refused to say another word that night. I would never again take pleasure in saying just the right thing to make my father's friends laugh. I got over this, eventually. I started speaking again. But only when I had something important to say. I loved my father. I knew that he was putting on this benefit to raise money for the cause that might save my life. But I hated giving speeches. I hated dressing up. Performing.

And so, with some misgiving, I took the train to Manhattan. It dove beneath the city, and I grew more apprehensive. I caught a taxi to the hotel and checked in. As I lay soaking in the bath, and later, as I struggled to zip my dress, I tried to figure out how to act when I saw Willie.

I took the elevator to the ballroom, then stood beside the door and studied all the tall, slender, self-possessed women who, I was sure, wore fancy evening gowns and attended banquets every night. Across the room, my father looked up at me and smiled. I had begun to smile back when I realized that he didn't have the foggiest notion of who I was—he was smiling at some stranger in a slinky, revealing dress.

When he realized his mistake, he put one hand on the shoulder of the man he had been speaking to and propelled him across the room. "This is my daughter," he told the man, who looked me up and down approvingly. "Jane, I want you to meet someone who is going to make Valentine's chorea a household word."

The man was president of the second-largest advertising agency in New York. His wife's family was at risk for Valentine's, and he had volunteered his services to publicize the disease. "What your organization needs is better PR. You scientists get on TV and what do you do but sling around a lot of big words. A bunch of talking heads. Like I was telling Herb here, we're going to put together a series of public-service spots. With you and your sister, we can't miss."

I saw Willie come in. His mother introduced him to a gaunt blonde in a scarlet sheath, who kissed him. I turned back to the PR man, who was talking about the "spots" my sister and I would appear in. Willie came up to me then. "Hey," he said, "Jane. You look great."

I was confused. Was this the real Willie Land, or the Willie Land about whom I had been dreaming for so many weeks? I blinked and tried to make the two Willies line up. "You do, too," I said. "That's a beautiful tux."

He stroked the lapels. "My dad wore it the year he was nominated for an Oscar. It's been hanging in mothballs for about a century. But it's kind of classy, don't you think?" He turned so I could see the tux from all sides. It fit him perfectly, but I couldn't understand how he could stand to wear it. After my mother died, I couldn't bring myself to put on anything she had ever owned. "I didn't hear from you," he said. "I know you've been busy. That's fantastic, about all those sick people you turned up in Maine. But I thought . . . I sent those cards."

I tried to remember why I hadn't written back.

Honey tapped the microphone. "Everyone?" The amplifier buzzed. "Could we each find our places?"

Willie's place tag was next to mine. A waiter came with wine, and Willie laid his hand across his glass. He rested his arm across my chair, and even though I wasn't sure what this gesture meant—he might not have had anywhere else he could stretch it—I felt wonderfully at ease. I closed my eyes and inhaled the sharp scent of mothballs, then settled against his arm. We sat that way and listened as Honey expressed her wish that the newly reorganized Institute for Valentine's Research and Education wouldn't lose sight of the needs of the average man and woman, "the husband who loves his wife dearly but cannot endure another day of isolation, or the wife who banishes her husband for drinking, only to learn that he was, in reality, a victim of a dreadful disease." I tried to connect what Honey was saying to the Valentine's victims I had met in Maine. But she was one of those people who can't speak of suffering without inflecting her speech like an actor reciting Shakespeare. The microphone's echo made it even harder to believe the suffering was real.

Vic was seated at the opposite end of the dais. The night before, in the lab, he had motioned me into his office. I assumed he was curious about what I intended to say at the benefit. Instead, he sat there toying with a candy bar and asked if I had ever stopped to think that we didn't really know what we were doing with this Valentine's thing. I felt the tears welling in my eyes. If Vic, of all people, didn't believe my experiments would work, then maybe I was deluded to think they would.

He must have seen my distress. "I don't mean we won't find the gene. I mean, what's going to happen when we do find it?" He unwrapped the Baby Ruth and took a bite. "Dianne is pregnant again." I couldn't tell if his tone was rueful or resigned. He finished the candy and wiped his mouth. "I took her for an ultrasound. Don't worry. It's nothing serious. Her OB is just a little worried because she hasn't been gaining weight. But Dianne and I were sitting in the waiting room, and the woman next to us announced that she was there because she wanted to find out her baby's sex while it was still early enough to do something about it. That's how she put it, *do something about it*. I asked if she already had too many girls, and she said no, she and her husband didn't have any kids at all. Having a boy was very important to her husband, and she wanted to make him happy. Then the nurse called her in, and I sat and looked around the room and tried to figure out which other couples were there to find out the gender of their babies before it was too late to 'do something' about it."

I should have guessed that a man who had attended a seminary might find abortion distasteful. Still, I felt betrayed. I excused myself by saying that I had to take my samples from the centrifuge. The lab was like a Laundromat; if you didn't remove your bloods the minute the drum stopped spinning, you would find your test tubes on a shelf with a nasty note informing you of what an inconsiderate douche bag you were. I left Vic without reminding him that he, of all people, shouldn't be trying to prescribe what a scientist should or shouldn't do.

Honey stopped speaking. The audience clapped. I heard Honey introduce me but I remained sitting in my seat, stupidly hoping I might gain some advantage by this delay. I was reluctant to make too many claims for my work, for fear I couldn't keep them.

Finally, I took my place at the podium and thanked everyone for coming. I meant what I said, but the PA system gave my thanks the same tinny ring it had given Honey's. I pulled the rubber band from my notes and began to deliver the explanation of my work I had given Willie. But whenever I said words like "restriction enzymes" or "polymorphisms," the audience squirmed. I was trying to describe how to label a probe with a radioactive tag when Laurel came in. She wore a strapless dress with turquoise sequins. Her companion was a thin, muscular black man with a clipped beard. He was, I saw, the only black person there. I wasn't sure why this upset me. The only black Americans who got the disease were those with white blood. Then it came to me that my father had neglected to invite Rita Nichols. She might not have wanted to leave her sons alone. But she ought to have been invited.

Laurel and her date slipped into two chairs along the back wall. I finished my speech and asked if anyone had any questions. No one did, so I sat back down.

Next up was Paul Minot. He walked to the podium in a ruffled blue tux that he must have rented from the shop that rented tuxes to the New Jerusalem boys who were going to their prom. We would need to excuse him, he said.

He didn't get out into society much. Where he came from, if folks heard you were paying five hundred dollars a plate to eat dinner, they would be awfully disappointed if that plate wasn't gold. Not to mention the food. The audience laughed appreciatively. "And all this talk about enzymes and polywhatsits—I can't pretend that I understood half of what the speaker before me was saying."

I winced. Was he extracting revenge for my refusal to go out with him? I had fixed him up with Maureen. Maybe he was only playing to his audience. That's what politicians did, didn't they? They played to their audience.

"All I can do is tell you about the people I know," he went on. "And try to give you some idea of how much you would be changing their lives if you found a cure for this illness." Miriam dimmed the lights and projected Paul's slides on a screen. There was the Smith family tree, and the Shaker barn in New Jerusalem, and photos of several families from whom we'd drawn blood. All this made me feel like an ambassador soliciting funds for his poverty-stricken tribe, all those pot-bellied children displayed before their huts, the thin-breasted mothers giving suck to lackadaisical infants with flies on their eyes.

Willie squeezed my shoulder. "Don't you just love home movies?" he whispered. The audience applauded with that extra show of force meant to convey more than mere politeness. Paul returned to his seat. Maureen touched his hand.

"And now," Honey said, "I would like you to give your very warmest welcome to the very first recipient of the new Dusty Land Award, honoring, as it does, the individual who has made the greatest contribution to Valentine's research."

Vic shuffled to the podium with the bewildered expression of a beauty queen who doesn't realize how attractive she is. The microphone was low, but rather than lift it he lowered his neck and bent his knees. He thanked Honey and the institute for giving him this award. Then he pulled out a crumpled envelope.

"Let me ask each of you a question," he started. "If this envelope contained a sheet of paper on which was written the day and manner of your death, how many of you would open it?"

This wasn't the speech I had expected, an optimistic prediction of the progress that lay ahead and a plea for more funds.

"For the first time in human history," Vic went on, "we are developing the power to tell a healthy person when and how he will die. But who can predict what anxieties such knowledge might bring? Think of the parent who learns that a child carries a fatal gene but can't inform him and must live with the secret. Think of the young person who gains access to the information that she will never reach middle age."

It was a setup, I thought. A trap. Why hadn't he warned me? Or maybe he had tried to warn me the night before and I hadn't let him. Now, at the benefit, Vic exhorted his listeners to consider all the tests the medical profession might develop. Would parents test a fetus to see if the child would be too ugly, or too short, or not intelligent enough? Would young men demand that their prospective spouses submit to a battery of tests to make certain they didn't carry deleterious genes? He lifted the envelope. "I propose, ladies and gentlemen, that we organize a conference to address issues such as these and safeguard against the careless use of whatever tests we might develop down the road."

My father sprang up. "Yeah, yeah," he said. "But don't forget that while you're debating what to do, my daughters over there could get Valentine's and die."

I looked to Laurel, who sat with her smile rigidly fixed. No wonder she avoided such functions. The Valentine's Poster Kids, that's what we were.

Honey took the microphone. "Everyone?" she said. "I'm sure we've appreciated hearing so many different points of view." She motioned for the waiters to bring dessert. As the guests savored the chocolate mousse ("Chocolate mouse?" Willie joked, which made me laugh), Honey and my father worked their way from table to table, trying to minimize the damage Vic had done. They kept gesturing for Laurel and me to join them.

"I'll be back in a second," Willie said. "I want to tell your boss how much I liked his talk."

I looked around for Maureen, but she must already have left with Paul. I wasn't about to stay on the dais by myself, but I was equally reluctant to let Willie and Vic discuss the dangers of my research when I wasn't there to defend it.

"That was a great speech," Willie was saying. "I've been worrying about that stuff for a long time. But what do I know? You're the expert. I was hoping that if you ever do put that conference together—the one you were talking about—maybe I could wrangle an invitation?"

Vic looked at me then, anxious to convey that he hadn't meant to upset me. I wanted to tell him that he had every right to follow his conscience, but it wasn't fair to expect that the people he hurt wouldn't be upset. Why was he pushing everyone to work so hard on my experiments, believing as he did they were morally wrong?

Vic folded his leg against the wall. "Your father has a point. I suppose we need to find the gene before we decide how to use it. I get so caught up in these grand theological questions I forget how many people might die in the meantime."

He glanced at me to see if this slip about people dying had disturbed me; I gave no indication that it had. Across the room, Laurel and her date stood beside a miniature palm. They both looked so colorful—Laurel in turquoise sequins, her date in blue silk—they reminded me of tropical fish.

Vic's wife came up and tugged his arm. "I'm sorry," he said, "but we have to get back to our hotel room before the babysitter turns into a pumpkin." He shook Willie's hand again before Dianne pulled him away.

"He's a great guy," Willie said. "You're lucky to work for him."

From the speech Vic had given, I didn't think I would be working for him much longer.

"I wouldn't worry," Willie said. "A person can be of two opinions about something. Not everyone is as single-minded as you are."

The pianist started to play "Over the Rainbow," which had been my mother's favorite song. I remembered her standing beside the sink, singing the words in a soft, off-key voice, her sponge circling a soapy plate, over and over.

"What about it?" Willie was saying. "Will you let me come?"

"Where?" I said.

"To that island."

He wanted to come to Spinsters Island? The last thing I needed was another person trying to supervise my work, especially if that person thought what I was trying to do was morally wrong. "There's no hotel there," I said. "The woman who owns the garage is putting us up. But she doesn't have much room."

He could bring a sleeping bag, he said. He could camp out in her yard.

I forced myself to say no a second time.

"Your father already said I could come."

"My father?"

Willie cracked his knuckles. "I told you, I'm thinking about making a donation. One Land Enterprises. We always check out the businesses we intend to invest in."

"Check us out? We're not a business."

"Right," he said. "What I meant is, we need to make sure the money's doing some good. That it's going to help those people."

"Do you think I want to hurt them?"

"Not on purpose. But I told you, Vic's speech . . . I've been worrying about that for a long time."

"So you're going to come up there with me and decide if what I'm doing is wrong?"

"I wouldn't put it that way."

"No," I said. "But that's basically what you'll be doing. I just hope you don't plan on standing there and lecturing everybody on how they shouldn't donate blood until some committee has figured out whether I'm bent on destroying the human race."

"You think I would do that? Like I said, some people aren't as single-minded as you are. Some of us are just a little bit confused."

I might have apologized and said I trusted him, but I saw Laurel walking toward us. Willie seemed to hesitate, then he turned and loped off.

Laurel hugged me. "I'm sorry I missed your talk. Cruz's motorbike broke down and it took us forever to get it fixed." Cruz, it turned out, was the lead choreographer for the Harlem Modern Dance Troupe. "You look stunning," Laurel said. "This must be so exciting for you. Do you really think you'll find the gene? A person would have to give blood, wouldn't she? To take this test?" Laurel shuddered. "You know how much I hate needles. Why don't *you* take the test and let me know the answer."

She wasn't kidding. No matter how many times I explained it, she continued to believe that a fifty-fifty chance of inheriting the gene meant that of any two siblings, one would get Valentine's and the other would not. I was about to tell her yet again that each sibling had a one-in-two chance of getting the disease, independent of the other sibling's chance, but I knew she would protest that she had no head for math.

"Don't look now," she said, "but Dad's headed this way."

He put one arm around each of us. "How are my two girls?" He kissed my cheek, then Laurel's. "No offense, Jane, but this genetics thing is horseshit. How can you explain such beautiful girls inheriting their looks from a *meeskeit* like me?" All three of us stood quietly, thinking of my mother. "She would be proud of you," he said. He rarely called her by her name. *Glori Weiss*, I thought. *My mother, Glori Weiss.*

"Dad," Laurel said, "there's a friend of mine I'd like you to meet." Cruz straightened his cravat, but Honey motioned from across the room with such urgency that my father said, "Sorry, kids, but I'm needed," and off he went, visibly relieved to have this excuse to avoid meeting his daughter's "friend."

Cruz obviously was annoyed that Laurel hadn't managed to complete the introduction. "It's late," he said. "I told everyone we would be at the party by ten."

"Maybe we could all go out somewhere together," I said.

"Oh," Laurel said. "Cruz invited me to meet his friends. They're having a party uptown."

"I could come with you," I said. "I do go to parties now and then."

"Sure," Laurel said. "If you want to."

I could tell she didn't think I would fit in at a party where people drank and smoked pot and didn't talk about genetics. Maybe I wouldn't. Besides, I wanted to spend time with my sister, not with an entire dance troupe.

"We're not going to stay at the party very long anyway," Laurel said. "As soon as the sun's up, we're leaving for Vermont. Cruz is helping me put together this new piece I was telling you about."

"You drove all this way and we don't even get to have breakfast with you? Dad's going to come back here, and I'm going to have to tell him that you left?"

Laurel tossed her hair. "Do you think you're the only one who's busy? I've got a concert coming up. Half the numbers aren't choreographed. We don't have the costumes. We have a new dancer who can't pick someone up without dropping her."

Cruz held up his long, tapered hand. I wanted to say that my sister and I had been arguing for thirty years without the need for a referee. "I know you're busy," I said. "I can't help it if I love you."

"I love you, too," she said. "But I'll see you at the wedding. Honey said the renovations are going more quickly. They've set the date for the first Saturday in November. We can show Cruz the hot spots in Mule's Neck."

I bit my lip and nodded the kind of nod that doesn't indicate assent so much as a reluctance to let the fight escalate to the point where neither side can win. I followed them to the lobby and hugged Laurel good-bye. But I couldn't bring myself to return to the banquet hall. And I certainly didn't want to go up to my room alone.

I went to use the powder room. I had just taken refuge in a stall when the outer doors banged open and two pairs of flat-heeled pumps walked in.

"I only suggested we look into it," Miriam said. "We might as well stop by the agency, as long as we're down here."

"I don't want to 'look into it.'" The voice was Barbara Lewis's. "I like my life the way it is. I don't need a kid. You're enough for me."

"You mean your horses are enough for you. Your mutts."

Barbara Lewis said something I couldn't make out. And, the last thing I heard before the bathroom doors swung shut: "You'll just have to find someone who does."

⫶⫶⫶⫶⫶⫶⫶⫶⫶⫶⫶⫶⫶⫶⫶⫶⫶⫶⫶⫶⫶⫶⫶⫶⫶⫶⫶⫶

Hours later, after I had fallen asleep in my hotel room, I heard a knock and jumped up, dreaming I had dozed off in the powder room and Miriam Burns and Barbara Lewis were rapping at the stall. I stumbled to the door and found Laurel in the harsh light of the corridor, disheveled and pale.

"You don't mind?" she said. "I decided I don't want to spend the night with Cruz."

I was wearing the lacy nightshirt she had brought me from Brussels—I had packed it on the crazy chance I would spend the night with Willie.

"Did I buy you that?" she said. "It's a shame there's no one but me to see it." She took off her dress and climbed beneath the covers. I turned off the lamp and got in the other side. She smelled of cigarette smoke and the balsam shampoo she always used. She lay there, on her back, her arm across my waist. "I wish I remembered more about Mom. From before she was sick."

It ought to have made me happy to be lying there with Laurel, reminiscing about our mother. But that seemed another grudge she held against me, that I had known our mother longer than she had.

"One of the only things I remember is the night she told us she was going to college," Laurel said. "I said—you remember this? I said, 'Why would you want to do that? Your life is over.'" I could feel my sister flinch. "It had nothing to do with Valentine's. It was because she seemed so old. But she wasn't that much older than we are now. Maybe I just wanted to be cruel."

I drew my hand across Laurel's cheek. "Every kid wants her mother to herself."

"That's what's so horrible about someone dying. You don't want to remember the good times, because they're too painful, and you can't help but remember the awful things you said when the person was alive."

I pressed my face to her hair.

"After I'm gone, don't think about all the awful crap I did to you, okay? Jane, promise me. After I'm dead, you'll only remember the times like this, when I was nice."

13

The trip to Spinsters Island had to be delayed. I tried to hurry Miriam, but preparations were slowed because the island wasn't connected to the mainland by phone. When she and Paul took the mail boat over to set up the bloodletting party, the fishermen claimed they couldn't talk. "Too busy." "Don't know nothing about that Valentine's thing." The only islander who was willing to help was Eveline Barter, who owned the island's gas station and, according to Miriam, would have given Paul whatever he asked. "Throw a dance," Eve told Miriam, who conveyed this suggestion to me. If we brought "refreshments" from the mainland and paid the town's musicians to hammer out some tunes, then sat beside the door and collected the islanders' blood as admission, Eve guaranteed they would come.

The only site large enough to hold such a function was the Spinsters Island schoolhouse, whose roof had blown off in a hurricane. While it was being rebuilt, Eve had agreed to post signs in her garage and pass the news to her customers. If they heard we were providing free beer, the only ones who wouldn't show up were the ones too debilitated by the illness to crawl there.

And so, on the last Friday of September, I found myself standing in the cabin of the mail boat halfway between New Jerusalem and Spinsters Island. The pilot, a square, squint-eyed man named Charles Stacks, was telling me that the winters here were so cold the open sea froze. No boats could get through, and the ice was too treacherous to be covered on foot. Whole months might go by in which no communication with the outside world was possible except by shortwave radio and the occasional plane.

One night, Stacks said, a man by the name of Calvary Ross vanished from the island. "Good-looking fella. Brainy. Only one in his family lucky enough he didn't get the disease. Leastwise, it looked like he didn't get it. He was in his fifties by then, still hale. Then one night he opens the door, everybody's still asleep, and off he goes. They found his tracks next day, down to the beach. But couldn't find no sign of him. Not on the ice, nor nowhere else." Stacks had been staring out the windshield, as if the story might be projected on the fog up ahead. Then he turned to me, and his eyes still seemed focused on something far off. He had cataracts, I realized. The lenses of his eyes were as filmy as the boat's salt-encrusted glass.

Peering through that windshield, one hand on the steering wheel and the other on a thermos of coffee, Stacks recounted the suffering "that chorea thing" had caused. There had been Matthias Few, who kept his job at the cannery past the point where he could hold his carving knife steady. And Toddy Van, who lost his balance hauling traps and drowned. Dottie Birch and Blair Martingale were left alone with young kids when their husbands passed on. And then there had been Bird Ransom, who owned the garage on the island before Eve Barter moved out and bought it. Apparently, this Ransom fellow had raped or otherwise impregnated half a dozen girls, most of them younger than fifteen, before the islanders ran him off. Sure, Stacks said, everyone figured the Valentine's sexed him up. But no one else ran around raping little girls, now did they. The SOB was lucky they didn't do worse than run him off. On and on Stacks went; I had the sense he was telling me these stories not to prove what a blessing it might be if we cured this disease, but the futility of even trying.

I stood beside him in the pilothouse, smelling the bitter scent of his coffee and straining to make out whatever he was seeing through the fog. The air was heavy and warm, but I sensed the next storm might bring an autumn chill. Ahead, the land thickened. A wave pitched the boat skyward. A moment later, as we dropped, I couldn't distinguish my excitement from fear. I am not a superstitious person. I knew other people's lives weren't being scripted to play a role in my own. But some power in the universe was trying to control my fate. First, we had lost Vic. Dianne had started spotting, and the obstetrician advised her to stay in bed so she wouldn't lose the pregnancy. Then Maureen heard a rumor that a team of French scientists had stumbled on a family in which everyone with Valentine's had a visible notch in chromosome three. The French scientists were due to fly to California for a gene-mapping conference, and Vic dispatched Yosef to L.A. to find out if the rumor was true. "Don't worry," Yosef told me. "I take these French guys to dinner, buy them a couple bottles of fancy California wine. If they really know something, I get them to spill the beans. We start looking on their chromosome with the bloods we got from Maine, beat them to the shoot-out with their own ammunition."

"Yosef," I said, "we are not shooting anybody. Just ask about their data. If they've got something solid on this family, they'll share the information."

He imitated my voice: "'Ask, Yosef. Share.' Just because you never have any fun, you got to spoil mine?"

"All right," I said, then went out to the drugstore and bought him a rubber dagger and a pair of mirror-lens glasses. "Here," I said. "Enjoy yourself. But if you're captured, we'll say that no one named Yosef Horowitz ever worked in this lab."

He saluted with the dagger. "Don't worry. If I get captured by the enemy, I fall on my sword, tear out my own kishkes. Is Jewish version of seppuku." And so, instead of flying north to Bar Harbor, Yosef, in a flowered shirt and dark glasses, flew west to L.A.

Worst of all, Rita had been forced to stay home. Her older son, Dennis, a brilliant boy who, in seventh grade, had scored nearly 700 on the math SATs, had been on a field trip to the battleground in Lexington. He and his classmates were walking beside the road when a man tossed a brick from a passing car. It struck Dennis on the head and he had yet to regain consciousness. The police were looking for the driver, but the teacher hadn't made a note of the license and the cops weren't convinced the brick had been thrown with malicious intent. "You tell me," Rita said. "Only one black child in that class. What's the chance a big old brick accidentally just *slipped* out of that white man's hand?"

I felt terrible. How could any grown-up throw anything at a child, let alone a brick? Even if Dennis were to come through without any significant brain damage, he would never again feel safe. But for my sake, I wished Rita had been able to come with us. She possessed the same gift as Miriam, the ability to convey that she understood her patients' suffering and would give them credit for it, but only if they agreed to bear their pain with grace and do as they were told.

When the three of us—Sumner, Willie, and I—had arrived in New Jerusalem the evening before, we had found Miriam in such a foul mood that the most innocent question—how could we be sure the donors would show up at this dance we were throwing?—was met by an impatient growl. "They show up, they show up. They don't, they don't. If you think I'm about to beg those ornery sons of bitches to give us what's in their own best interest to give, you got another think coming." There was no sign of Barbara Lewis—no dinner, no Monopoly game, no opening and shutting of doors in the night.

"Your lady friend," Sumner asked. "The veterinarian? She seems a very knowledgeable woman. Do you think she would object if I paid a call?"

"You can do whatever you damn well please," Miriam informed him, which Sumner was used to doing anyway, and did on this occasion, only to learn that Barbara Lewis wasn't home, unless she had declined to open her door to him.

Now, on Stacks's boat, Miriam sat scowling beside the anchor. Sumner was holding back his tie, leaning over the prow, and trying not to throw up. The only passenger who seemed happy was Willie. He stood with his hair whipping in the wind, as excited as a boy who has dreamed his whole life of going to sea.

But when we reached the open water, the waves grew too violent even for him. He ducked his head and came in the cabin. His elbow knocked Stacks's thermos and splashed coffee on his map. Stacks set the thermos upright and resumed staring out the windshield. I waited for Willie to apologize. Maybe Buddhists didn't believe in apologies. He certainly hadn't shown any signs of remorse for bribing my father to let him come on this trip.

"How do you know where the shoals are?" he asked. The boat wove this way and that to avoid the jagged rocks that barely broke the surface. "They look like a herd of whales."

Stacks brushed his hand above the chart, which was stained by rings of coffee as well as the splash from the thermos. Half a hard-boiled egg hid the mainland from view. "Maps," he said. "Try using a map to find your way in and you'll see where you end up." He told us about the poor misguided tourists who had made this trip without him, hapless men with keen eyes, fancy equipment, and elaborate charts who had gored their boats on rocks or lost themselves in the fog.

"Nothing more dangerous than a map," Willie agreed. "A map only fools you into thinking you know where you are."

I wondered what he would have said if I had confided my dream that within our own lifetimes, if we lived normal lives, the entire human genome would be mapped. *Would you know yourself any better than you know yourself now?* The day before, in New Jerusalem, while I had gone to draw blood from a family I had missed on our earlier trip, Willie had explored the ruins of the Shaker village. In some half-hidden cupboard he had found a stack of hymnals and a sheaf of Shaker chants. The lyrics struck me as childish, rhyming "virgin" with "sin," "God above" with "pure love." The melodies, which he had plucked out on Miriam's ancient upright, sounded like nervous variations on "Row, Row, Row Your Boat." They were recorded not with notes but the letters of the alphabet: *c c g b d.* . . . "It's like that genetic code you showed me," Willie said. "The only difference is, this code has seven letters instead of four."

I might have found this statement remarkable, if I hadn't felt the need to stay mad.

"Don't you get it?" He pulled off those dime-store glasses, and I thought he was giving them to me, so I could see what he saw, but he laid them on the keyboard. "Do, fa, fa, mi, do. You can sing a person's chromosomes. Your genetic code is the music that describes who you are."

"Land ho!" Sumner cried.

Stacks cut the motor and sidled toward the dock. He leaned overboard and tossed a noose, which tightened around a post. When he slung down the mail sack, its thud against the pier led me to wonder if the letters held bad news. One by one, we stepped down: Willie's red All-Stars; Miriam's rubber-soled oxfords; Sumner's tasseled loafers; and the hiking boots I had ordered the week before from L.L. Bean. The dock swayed beneath our feet. But then, so did the island. The ground shuddered like an animal shaking off flies.

"Thunder Beach," Stacks explained. "Southeast coast ain't so protected as this one. Those waves, they pick up these giant boulders, and bang, they smack them against the cliffs. You can feel it all the way to here." He dragged the mail sack along the dock. "If I was you, I'd stop out there."

"Jesus," Willie said. "Would you take a look at that guy?" I thought he meant Stacks. Then I saw a skinny man stagger down the street, listing left, right, left, right. No sooner had the man disappeared around a corner than a middle-aged woman tottered across her yard with a huge metal washtub. She hung a shirt on the clothesline. But when she lifted another shirt, she froze, as if she had accidentally pinned her hands to the rope.

"Everyone here's got it," Willie said. "It's as common as the flu."

I forgave him everything then, relieved that he, too, had assumed on some level that getting the disease required some special talent. The truth was, you didn't need to be famous, as Willie's father had been. You didn't need to be beautiful, or tragic, or smart. You got Valentine's because your parents had given you the gene. You got it because you had been born on an island where one in ten people carried the disease.

I looked around and realized I had spent most of my life searching for this island and yet trying to avoid it. As a child, I had overheard my parents' furtive discussions about my mother's older brothers, and I had conflated their illness with a name I kept hearing on the news. *Valentine's Korea* was a dangerous place, I thought. My uncles were soldiers who had been sent there and died. Although what this fighting had to do with love I couldn't say. I wouldn't have been surprised to see my uncles here now, in this strange and isolated world where nothing seemed familiar yet everything did. I imagined Max and Jake lurching along the main thoroughfare of Spinsters Island. My mother, I thought, might be waiting around the next curve.

Six shabby houses stood farther up the hill, their yards strewn with mangled bikes, toilet seats, and clothes wringers. How could anyone live in such a place? Laurel had said she didn't care what she left behind as long as she lived widely while she had the chance. But that seemed impossible here. How could anyone live widely on an island that measured five miles across?

Sumner stooped to disentangle a cradle from a wreath of rusted bedsprings.

"Would you leave that be!" Miriam snapped, and Sumner looked around, puzzled, as if he only now understood that the island was inhabited. Since coming ashore, we had seen only that staggering mute and frozen woman. But I sensed the others watching, like natives who suspect that the invaders bearing gifts have plans to subdue them. Even the deer seemed suspicious, lifting their heads from the geraniums as we passed. (The deer were the size of dogs. Paul Minot had told me that wealthy sportsmen from New York had imported game to Spinsters Island in the late 1800s. With no predators, the deer had overrun the place. They didn't get much food, but even the smallest could survive.)

People here made do with what they had. In Eveline Barter's yard we saw a red Texaco gas pump with a yellow Shell head. We saw the chassis of a thirties Buick with the powder blue hood of what must have been a Cadillac. In the back of a Chevy pickup with a crude wooden bed sat three sacks of groceries. A deer stood on its hind legs, licking a bag of Cheetos.

"Scat!" A woman in pink curlers burst from the house and chased the deer. She wore overalls with nothing underneath. The tops of her breasts were crisscrossed with stretch marks. Her skin was flushed and shining, as if she had just stepped from the bath, but her palms were stained with grease.

"Go on. Scat. Get out of here!" The deer casually stepped down, licking Cheetos dust from its muzzle, then wandered toward Willie and sniffed his duffel bag.

The woman hoisted all three sacks of groceries. "You two," she inclined her head toward Miriam and Sumner, "you can put your stuff in the back room. One bed, one sofa, you figure out between yourselves who gets which. Hell, you can climb in together for all I care. You young ones," her eyes darted from Willie to me, then back to Willie, "you're welcome to the porch. All of you, help yourselves to whatever's in the icebox."

Eve Barter led us to her kitchen, but she didn't set down the sacks. The icebox truly was an icebox. A sampler hung above the stove: THIS IS MY KITCHEN AND I'LL DO WHATEVER I DAMN WELL PLEASE. On the oilcloth-covered table sat three baking tins of blueberry muffins. "Those are strictly off-limits. Made them for the party." She smiled up at Willie, who, I could see, was trying not to look down at her breasts. "Long drink of water, aren't you. None of the pip-squeaks on this island are tall enough to get the decorations stuck to the ceiling of that schoolhouse. You come along and help me get up those balloons and whatnot." She led us back outside, the three sacks of groceries still pinned across her chest. She started up the hill. "Bring the booze!" she called back. "If we get the alcohol set up, the word'll go out. Some of those bloodhounds probably could sniff the stuff clear across to South Point." She walked back a few paces. "You did bring the booze, didn't you?"

"We did," I assured her, then I remembered we had left the crates on Stacks's boat.

"I'll get it," Willie said. He trotted toward the dock, grateful, I thought, to delay his visit to the schoolhouse. I wondered if I ought to leave him with all that beer, but even with his confession that he used to be an alcoholic, I couldn't imagine him drunk.

"I'm going in to lie down." Miriam scowled at Sumner, daring him to say the bed would be his, then stomped into Eve's house. I started to invent my own excuse to slip away,

but Eve had taken the groceries to the schoolhouse, and
Sumner had returned to examining the junk pile in which
he had found the cradle. I walked quickly up the hill, toward the island's center. At one point, I passed through a
field of withered corn. I thought of my mother and how
much time she had spent tending her garden. A shriveled
cob lay beside my boot. I picked it up and squeezed it until the sockets pricked my palm. I felt like sitting in that
cornfield and refusing to go on until my mother came and
found me. We had never discussed her diagnosis. All she
had ever said was, "Your father told you, didn't he." And
when I admitted he had, she had gone out to her garden
and pulled weeds for the rest of the afternoon. It hadn't
occurred to me until now that she had retreated so deeply
into her illness to spare herself the agony of watching her
daughters watch her die.

The path cut across a meadow. The blueberry bushes
blazed a brilliant red. I found a claw-footed tub mired in
the dirt like the skeleton of some beast that had gotten
stuck there and starved. Fifty yards farther, I came upon
a short, spiked fence. The tombstones inside bore blunt
English surnames: Small, Rich, Dodd, Long. There were
three Fews, two Smiths, and half a dozen Martingales.
Carved atop the stone for Bea and Hiram Martingale
were a pair of clasped hands. Several of the dates marked
lives that had lasted nine decades; others, far briefer. *Loving mother of Althea, Obadiah, Bathsheeba, Jericho, and Luke*
read the stone for Lucy Few, who had died at twenty-four.

I had little idea where my own ancestors lay buried. My
mother's father had lived a few miles from Mule's Neck, but

he died before I was born and my mother rarely mentioned him. We never visited his grave. I had been five when my uncle Max died—his Valentine's had struck him young and progressed at such a rate that he was dead before forty—and ten when my uncle Jake had followed him. They had always struck me as old, no doubt because they twitched and seemed peculiar. When my parents thought I wasn't listening, they discussed the checks my father sent my aunts and whether the amounts were large enough, especially for Jake's widow, Yvette, who had been left with three kids. Apparently, to protect my mother and increase her chances of getting married, her parents had lied to her and said that Valentine's struck only men. Who knows if she believed them. Certainly, it seemed to strike the men in my mother's family in ways that seemed even crueler than it might have struck a woman. My uncles had finished years of training for their professions—Uncle Max had been a podiatrist, and Uncle Jake had studied pharmacy—only to find that their hands shook too badly to cut a patient's corns or funnel pills in a jar. A woman could bear children in her twenties and raise them to adolescence. Her death was sad but not wasteful. Her survivors wouldn't starve.

Someone must have been buried earlier that week. I kicked the mound of fresh earth, then watched in terror as the dirt bubbled and heaved. It was only a mole. My heart stilled. The fright passed. Death was what it was. People who were born here must have feared that the larger world held fates more frightening even than Valentine's. If you stayed, you belonged to a sort of aristocracy, like royal Europeans who intermarried despite the risk of bearing heirs with weak chins or weak minds. Within the boundaries of this island, no names could have been more famous than Smith, Martingale, or Few. The names on the tombstones reminded me of the romances my sister used to read, *Wuthering Heights, Jane Eyre,* and *Pride and Prejudice,* novels whose concerns seemed too limited to hold my attention, all those artificial barriers of breeding and wealth. Now it seemed to me those authors had gotten everything right, except that it wasn't bad blood but bad genes that kept lovers apart.

As it turned out, everyone gave blood, even those islanders who weren't at risk. They seemed to find it reasonable that the price of an evening of pleasure be pain. By five, they had lined up beside the schoolhouse, the men in stiff white shirts, the women in flowered dresses with wide cardboard belts. The children kept peeking in to see if balloons truly did hang from the ceiling and a bowl of punch and a case of beer really were sitting on the teacher's desk beneath the letters of the alphabet and the time line that stretched from prehistoric times to the 1950s. Miriam dragged a table beside the threshold and jabbed each person's arm as he or she came in. One old man was pushed to the dance in a homemade cart. Another man made the trek from the east point of the island for the first time in years. "Yow!" he said when Miriam jammed him with her needle. "I'd a-known you was a-going to break my arm, I'd a-thought twice about coming."

After the guests gave blood and let Sumner examine

them, they were allowed to dance and drink. The band was set up beneath a yellowed map of Asia. Eve Barter, on a stool, wore shiny white boots, her beefy legs bare to the hem of her short red skirt. Her sausage curls wobbled as she pumped a spangled blue accordion. "Listen up!" she ordered the musicians. "I don't think we were all playing the same song that time. Ned, I know we been doing a lot of funerals lately, but our audience here is trying to dance." She addressed this to a teenage boy with a pompadour; the mouthpiece of a sax dangled from his lips like a cigarette. Beside him sat a whey-faced guitarist who had been a bishop on the mainland before he lost his church, I never found out why. The pianist wore white gloves and pumped the pedals with such vigor she seemed to be marching, hour after hour, without reaching the end of whatever parade she was in.

Willie had been persuaded to take a turn on someone's guitar. But he was clearly out of practice and couldn't keep up. A string popped. I saw him mouth *shit*. Like me, he rarely cursed. Someday, I would like to take a poll of how many people whose parents died of Valentine's try their very best not to swear.

When the band took a break, Eve offered Willie a beer. He shook his head. She tried again. He paused, then put the bottle to his mouth and drank.

I stepped forward to stop him. It hadn't occurred to me that he might become as unglued by this crazy island as I was. Midway across the room, I was stopped by a man with wind-burned skin and splintery teeth. "Want to dance?" he asked me angrily. The band resumed playing, and my partner pulled me across the floor. I had never danced a polka. I stumbled, but my partner yanked me back up. "You may be smart," he said, "but you're not much of a dancer, are you."

The polka seemed frantic, the way a seizure might be. I thought of primitive tribes who mimed the deaths they feared—to ward them off, to boast: *We are the tribe who lives with such predators baying outside our huts.* At last the song ended. I looked around, but Willie wasn't there. I thought of going to find him, but I needed to help Miriam pack the blood. It was after one thirty. The youngest children dozed on the heaps of coats. A few spun in tired circles. For the first time, I noticed that about a quarter of the children had a dense mask of freckles. Were the freckles linked to Valentine's? *If only,* I thought, then realized that I had condemned those freckled children to death.

I carried the Styrofoam racks to Eve's kitchen and put them in her icebox, then sat on the stoop listening to the smack of riggings against the masts and trying to imagine what Willie would be like after drinking all those beers. I stood and took a step beyond the ring of light from Eve's porch, and he materialized before me, as if he had been standing there all along, waiting until I took that first step.

"I've been a jerk about this whole thing," he said. He took a long swallow from his bottle. "I wanted to come here with you, and I didn't think you would let me, so I gave your dad that check. I shouldn't have done that. But I'm just not sure how I feel about . . . I'm not about to take this test of yours. But you've got all these people out here, living like this. And I do have my son to think about."

He took an even longer swallow. "What I mean to say is, I was hoping you would just sort of walk around with me awhile. Because all of this has me shaken up. Those kids back there? And that young guy who plays the sax? I didn't catch on at first, but then I started looking at how bad his hands shook. And Ted? My son, Ted? I kept thinking about what happens if he has it. I'm in love with you. There's that, too. So maybe you could come?" He took a last swig of beer and sent the bottle flying. An enormous shape flapped furiously above the trees. "If you don't come with me, I'm going to go back to that schoolhouse and finish off every last beer in the joint."

"No," I said. "I'll go with you." He didn't seem drunk as much as he seemed unmoored. I grabbed his hand, and suddenly I felt as if everything had been planned—by whom or what I couldn't say. Willie and I were supposed to end up on this island. He wasn't my worst choice. He was my only choice, really. Who else could understand everything I had been through? With whom else could I strike an equal bargain—*I'll risk caring for you, if you'll take the same risk for me?*

We set off along the cliffs. Willie had borrowed the headlight from someone's bike, and he used it to light the path. Waves smacked the rocks below us. I didn't care where we went or what happened when we got there. Here, on this island, a marriage between two people with Valentine's chorea wasn't absurd. Here, it made sense.

Something speared my leg. I cried out. Willie swung his light and caught the gleam of antlers. The deer was dead, its mouth set in a rubbery grimace. He knelt and touched its head, gently, like a man stroking his wife's brow to keep her mind off her labor. He seemed sober by then.

We walked another mile. The path turned to stone. A wave exploded beneath our feet. We stood there like that. He put his hands around my waist. I leaned against his chest.

"I thought I had it beat," he said. I assumed he meant his drinking, but then he said, "I just wasn't exposed to any of this before. Not so much of it. All at once. When I'm by myself, I can convince myself . . . I guess this is how you've felt all along. And here I was, going on and on about how I wasn't afraid of dying."

"I'm not afraid of dying," I said. "I mean, not the pain. I just can't give it all up. Being alive. Everything. How I feel . . . here, now, with you."

He slid his hands along my ribs. I held my breath, waiting for those hands to move higher.

"But when you die, it's not as if you know you're dead. It's not as if half of you stays behind and hears the other half crying in the dark, crying that you're lost."

If only he would stop talking! If only he would lift his hand another inch!

"Don't you want to give up that other half, the half that keeps watching?"

"I think I would miss it," I said.

"That's only because it's been with you for so long. You're used to driving yourself crazy."

I told him I would stop driving myself crazy if I knew I didn't have it.

Nah, he said, that wasn't true. "Everybody's like that. Everybody except a few Buddhists who've attained satori."

I told him that despite what he might think, I wasn't the type of person who was going to spend her whole life sitting around trying to become perfect. I had too much to get done.

He pulled away. "You think *I'm* trying to lead the perfect life? You don't see me planning who I'm going to fall in love with according to a bunch of statistical formulas and graphs on a place mat. You don't see me spending my life trying to make sure I have this perfect kid."

"He doesn't need to be perfect."

"Yeah? Tell me you wouldn't marry me right now if I could guarantee that I don't have that damn gene. That you don't have it. That we could have ourselves a one hundred percent grade-A certified healthy kid." He pressed his hands against my head. "You know what nirvana is? I'll tell you what nirvana is. It's watching your kid eat Cheerios. You ever seen a kid eat a bowl of Cheerios? The way he dips the spoon in the bowl? The way he brings it up to his mouth and makes sure he gets everything in? The way he chews? He's not thinking about anything except those Cheerios. That's nirvana. And making love is nirvana. Here, on this ledge, on the darkest night you've ever seen, and not thinking about anything else but making love."

He unbuckled my watch. Then he burrowed in my trouser pockets and took out my radiation badge and a calculator marked, though there wasn't enough light to read it, BELONGS TO S. BATE. He made a pile beside the cliff, like a cairn. *Don't think,* I kept thinking. It occurred to me that neither of us had brought a condom. *Don't think*, I thought again. *Put your hand around his neck. Lie back. Don't say no.*

My foot hit a can; it clattered down the cliff. Willie started kissing me, and I couldn't think of anything except how lucky I was, because in the midst of so much nothing I had been allowed to exist, to think everything I had ever thought, learn everything I had ever learned, feel everything I had ever felt. I had seen chicks in their shells. I had seen burning bushes and rotting deer. And I had been allowed to fall in love with someone as completely as I now loved this man.

14

The morning I got home from Spinsters Island, I discovered a Seal-a-Meal bag on my lab bench with a mouse corpse inside. Lew had managed to keep alive a runty mouse we thought might be homozygous for the Valentine's gene, and I had put Maureen in charge of watching him. A note in her meticulous hand was inscribed on the label: "So sorry! Things with Paul got pretty intense. I tried to preserve the remains for dissection." I found myself weeping. It wasn't only that the organs would have deteriorated too badly for an autopsy, or even that the mouse hadn't lived long enough to reproduce. I composed myself enough to slice open the bag. The corpse was oddly mummified. I touched the skin. "Maureen!" I yelled. "Get over here!"

"Just a sec-ond," she sang. I heard the wheelchair whir.

I tossed the mouse in her lap.

"Ew!" she said. "Poor little mousie. Is that any way to show respect for the dead?"

"You creep. I've had it up to here with your jokes."

"How could I resist? Paul and I were at a pet store—he wants to buy a sheepdog to keep him warm when I'm not around." She stroked the body. "Admit it, you were furious. You thought Paul and I were fucking so hard we couldn't be bothered with a mouse."

"I wasn't angry," I lied. Then I saw her disappointment. People never got mad at someone in a wheelchair. "You're right. I was furious. I still am." I twisted my hands around her neck.

"Help!" She crossed her eyes. "Murderer! Help!" She spun out of reach. "We put the toy mouse in the cage with the real homozygous mouse, to see what he would do."

"And?"

"He humped the bejeezus out of the thing. You better put a girl mouse in with that little guy soon. Even cripples have sex drives."

I knew she was dying to tell me about Paul. "All right," I said. "What happened?"

She shut her eyes. "What's to tell? The handsomest, kindest guy in the universe comes to spend the week. An hour after he gets here he's kissing my hands, telling me they're beautiful. He picks me up in his arms like I'm Scarlett O'Hara, we spend ninety-six hours without leaving my apartment, I come every which way, he misses half his conference on fish-meal by-products, and then, before he leaves, he invites me up to his place in Maine for a week." She patted her cheek. "Pinch me."

"Maureen, I don't want to pinch you."

"Pinch me!" she insisted.

I tugged her left earring, which was shaped like Ronald Reagan.

"Ow! Good. Now pull Nancy."

I tugged the other earring.

"Ow! That's great, I'm not dreaming. I mean, Jane, it's not only Paul. I think I have this blindness thing figured out." She indicated I should lean closer. "Snails. It's the snails. Paul and I are making love, and suddenly I'm thinking about this one family I stayed with. I smelled this really vile smell, and I asked the woman what she was cooking. She was too embarrassed to tell me, but then she finally did. She was stewing these snail things. They're supposed to get her pregnant. This woman and her husband were trying to have a baby, so she was cooking up these snails. Lots of people do it, but they don't go around broadcasting the fact. The husbands don't want anybody to think they're having trouble getting their wives knocked up. Nobody wants to be known as a snail eater. But God knows what sorts of parasites those snails they have down there carry."

I saw tiny worms sinking their teeth into an embryo's eye.

"I called the public health team I work with. It's going to take forever—you know how slow these bureaucracies are. But they promised they would go around and get these families to admit they ate snails while they were pregnant. They'll send the little beasties to their lab, and after they've figured out what they're infected with, I'm going to write this paper and send it to *Nature*, and then I'm going to spend a week in Maine, boffing my brains out." She rubbed her eyes with her wrist. "I can't believe it, Jane. After everything I've been through."

I bent down and hugged her. "You deserve it. I'm thrilled for you, Maureen." And really, I was. It's one of the best feelings you can have, to be genuinely happy for someone else.

She wiped her nose. "And you! How was life among the mutants? Did this Willie jerk apologize?"

"As a matter of fact, he did. He said, 'I'm a jerk, and I apologize.'"

"I was only asking." She pouted.

"I'm serious. He apologized. Then we took off our clothes and made love at this place called Thunder Beach." It felt wonderful to say this. I was telling my best friend about having sex with my boyfriend on an island in Maine.

"Right," she said. "You go, like, a couple of eons without so much as kissing a man. Then you take off your clothes and have sex with some guy you barely know at a place called Thunder Beach."

She was talking too loudly. Vic poked his head from his office door. "You're back," he said. "Come in and tell me what's up."

"Wait," Maureen said. "You weren't kidding?"

"I'm coming, Vic," I called. "Pinch me," I told Maureen. The rubber mouse hit my back.

"So how'd it go?" he said. "Sorry I couldn't be there. Dianne's still in the hospital. I've got four kids to keep supplied with jelly and peanut butter." He swung his shoes on the desk. A crescent of hairy skin rose above each sock. "Are you still upset with me? You don't think I'm supporting you enough. But I'm not trying to stop anything. Me, of all people. It's just that there might need to be safeguards."

He was going to offer an analogy. I still couldn't understand why people thought that comparing any two things made either of the two things clearer.

"It's like driving," Vic said. "A society can post speed limits and right-of-way signs without prohibiting cars."

I nodded. But the analogy didn't apply. There was a one-in-two chance I had Valentine's disease, a one-in-two chance my sister had it, and a one-in-two chance the man I loved had it. How could anyone think I would do anything to harm anyone who had the gene?

Vic swung his legs to the floor. "You think of some nice theory, and the next thing you know you're telling people they're going to die without being able to offer them the slightest comfort. If that's what we're doing here, I'll quit and walk away." He looked down at his shoes, as if, at any moment, they might carry him out of the room of their own volition. "I've been thinking about this a lot. Really, Jane, it's been hounding me."

I looked out the window. In the lab across the alley, a woman in a lab coat held a beaker filled with a bright blue liquid above her head. She flicked it with her finger, studied it, then poured the contents down the drain.

Susan Bate stalked in. "He's doing it again. I'll kill him, Vic, I'll kill him!" She wore a leotard, sweatpants, and ballet shoes; three mornings a week, Susan biked to the lab from a predawn ballet class. Sometimes, during group meetings, she sat on the floor with her legs in a *V*, bobbing right, center, left. "Can I talk to you? In private?"

I settled on Vic's desk. When she saw that I wasn't leaving, she began to talk anyway.

"I've been running four blots a day. You know, to test the bloods?" She shot me a glance to let me know how much I owed her. "About half the blots have been coming up blank. It's Yosef and Lew. They're afraid I'll find the marker and get the credit."

Credit? I thought. For what? Susan hadn't conceived the theory or technique behind the experiments. She hadn't collected any blood.

"It took me a while to figure out how they were sabotaging my blots. I keep my reagents locked up. I don't take my eyes off the gels while they're running. Then it came to me. The only time I'm not here is late at night, when the filters are soaking in the water bath. Yosef and Lew must be switching the temperature so the DNA can't hybridize, then switching it back just before I come in." She paced Vic's office, daintily sidestepping stacks of reprints. "I put a hair on the dial last night. It wasn't there this morning."

Vic pressed his fingertips together. "Susan, I can understand your frustration. You've been working hard. All of us feel the pressure to help Jane find her gene."

Susan pirouetted. "*Her* gene? What makes it hers? Who's been running all the blots around here, anyway? I'm the one who's risking my career on this stupid wild-goose chase."

I had been acting before, pretending to strangle Maureen. It frightened me to think I could have done real violence to Susan. Her behavior seemed intended to provoke people to abuse her, as if she were trying to prove it was her fate to be abused.

"This isn't a contest," Vic said. "Do you really think Yosef or Lew would maliciously turn the dial on your water bath? Isn't it more plausible the hair simply slipped off? Or Cesar disturbed it when he was cleaning? Blots go wrong all the time."

Susan wasn't buying Vic's defense. "Are you going to confront them or should I?"

The woman across the alley was filling another flask with solvent. I knew what she was feeling, that irrational assurance that the new experiment would go right, even though she wasn't sure why it had failed the first time. Some experiments took weeks or months to try again. You spent all that time hoping, and sometimes you were rewarded with the result you hoped to find. But if my attempt to find the gene for Valentine's failed, I would never find the courage to start over. If Willie and I broke up, I would never find the strength to start loving someone else.

"I'll speak to them," Vic told Susan. "I'll make sure no one turns the dials on your water bath if I have to sleep here myself."

Susan studied Vic to see if he was saying this to humor her. But his face held no guile. Even Susan could see that. "All right," she said. "But if it happens one more time, I'll take an ax to their benches."

After she had gone, I asked Vic if he ever thought of throwing her out. Just because she had been abused didn't mean she had the right to abuse other people.

"Of course I think about throwing her out. I spend most of my time thinking about doing things I can't do. If you can *do* something, you don't spend much time *thinking* about doing it." His telephone rang. "Yes?" he said. "The conference is when? It meets where? I should speak for how long?"

I went back to my bench. I had been away so long my labmates had piled dirty equipment on every surface. I tossed a half-eaten fig bar and a slice of pizza in the trash. Susan darted by with a rack of bloods. "How nice of you to visit us," she said. "Do you think you'll have a few minutes to run a blot or two before you need to dash out again?"

Yosef slunk through the door in his mirror-lens glasses. Susan hissed at him. Yosef crossed his arms as if warding off a vampire. "What's she been telling you? She doesn't consider maybe her blots are coming out bad because she isn't careful, she hooks electrodes up backward?"

"Vic!" Susan called. "Come out here!"

Vic pointed to the receiver against his ear.

Susan shook a finger at Yosef. "You'll get yours," she said.

"Oh, baby." Yosef kissed me on the cheek. "Why can't every girl be as nice as you?"

"Yosef." I pushed him off.

"I speak this from my heart. You are the only one I think isn't out to get me. You never do anything bad, and what do you get?" He pulled the toy dagger from his coat and dangled it above my head. "You get this terrible sword hanging over you all the time. Is cosmic injustice." He took off his sunglasses and held up his left hand. "I swear, I stop all my other work, even secret project—which, I have got to admit, is going nowhere fast—and I help you look for this gene. No matter how long it takes. And I don't want no credits." He stuck out his bottom lip. "Except maybe I get my name second on your paper."

"Second name!" If all went well, the second authorship would go to Miriam. That was the least I could do, although I doubted she would care about seeing her name on a paper in a journal she never read.

Yosef affected a wounded look. "Hey, who else brings home a top-secret tip about where we should start looking?"

One of the French scientists had told Yosef his lab had found a deletion on the short arm of chromosome three. When Yosef asked why the data weren't being presented at the conference, the scientist confided that he and his colleagues needed to test another family, to be sure the correlation was high enough. For all Yosef's paranoia, he was convinced the French scientist was telling the truth. I wasn't so sure. What if the man was baiting us with false information to make us waste our time? Let Yosef keep trying chromosome three. I would look elsewhere. I had the feeling Valentine's wasn't caused by a deletion, a lack of something, but rather by an excess, of what I didn't know.

"Whhelll, sweetheart," Yosef said, "best we get working. Is like one of those riddles: If four eager beavers chop so much wood, how much wood can eager beavers chop before other eager beavers publish same result first? Or this one: How many days will the turkey need to find the needle in that straw stack?" He tweaked my nose. "It's a joke. We will find the needle. Maybe, if we are lucky, it will only take a few years."

Across the room, Susan turned her miniature TV to a talk show about the sexual misconduct of dentists. Yosef went over to his bench and switched on his boom box; the bottles on my shelf rattled to the beat. I thought of Achiro and how he had managed to work without listening to all this noise. "How can you stand it?" I asked him once. *Only thing distract me is voices from Japan,* he said. At the time, I thought he meant he only paid attention to Japanese words. Now, I wondered if he meant his wife's and his daughters' voices echoed in his ears: *Hurry. Please, come home. If you stay away much longer, when you come home we won't be there.* How long would Willie wait for me? How many times could he and I make love before he asked for something more? I shouldn't sleep with him again. I knew that. But how could I refuse? I couldn't even keep from thinking about having sex with him. I kept telling myself this was different from my mother's Valentine's-induced preoccupation with sex, the way she announced at breakfast one morning that my father wasn't a handsome man but he had a great cock. My own fantasies were normal. Most people had them. Dreaming obsessively about sex wasn't only a symptom of Valentine's disease; it was a symptom of being human. "It's driving me crazy," my mother had once confided. "But God help me, Janie, I like to think about men."

15

Thirty-two degrees, the surface of the road both water and ice. That was the kind of thing I liked to think about, how a substance could be a liquid and a solid simultaneously, not whether I should be in love with the man I was in love with. It was the first Friday in November. Willie and I were driving to Mule's Neck for our parents' wedding. The heater blew stale, gassy air. Passing trucks splattered slush. He rubbed a circle of fog from the windshield, hunched forward, and drove at forty miles an hour. I was glad he had to concentrate. Otherwise he might want to talk, and what was there to talk about, really? After we had gotten back from Spinsters Island, I had waited in the hope he might call or show up. Finally, I called him. The answering machine clicked on. I left a message; he didn't return it. I tried to reach him from the lab, but he was never in his office. Or he guessed who was calling and refused to pick up.

Eventually, I came to think he had slipped on the ice or axed his leg. Maybe he was dying and couldn't crawl to his desk to answer. I was about to borrow Maureen's van and drive to New Hampshire, but I gave him one last try. This time he picked up. I could tell from the way he spoke that he had been drinking.

"Yeah," he mumbled. "I should have called. We shouldn't . . . I mean, I shouldn't have . . ."

If he hadn't been crying, I might have killed him. How could he have fallen in love with me and convinced me not to calculate the risk of loving him back, then decided he was wrong and start drinking again?

"I just had a few beers," he said. His voice sounded as if it had crawled through the wires from New Hampshire. "I've just . . . I've had a lot of thinking to do. Believe me, the last thing you need to worry about is my drinking. I'll be all right for the wedding. I promise."

I had hung up but I hadn't cried. If I had started crying, I might have thrown things. I might have climbed into bed and never climbed out. It was two in the morning, but I strapped on my helmet, wondering why they couldn't manufacture helmets for hearts, then I biked to the lab and ran more gels. In those weeks before the wedding, I barely left my bench. Then Willie called and picked me up. I opened the door to the Jeep and thought: *He isn't even handsome. He's too flabby. Too pale. He's just another person.*

"Hey," he said meekly. The temperature shifted one-tenth of one degree, some bond between us crystallized, and all I wanted to do was lean against him and press my lips to his fleshy neck.

We drove all the way to Lenox without making more than perfunctory comments about the slick roads and strong wind. For our parents' sake, I hoped the next day would be warmer. My father's house was on a hill and if this weather didn't let up, the guests would need to park their cars at the bottom, strap cleats to their shoes, and hike to the top. Honey and my father planned to be married in the house. The reception would follow at King's Hong Kong Chinese. It had the only hall in town that could hold so many guests. But I couldn't figure out why Honey had agreed to hold her reception at a restaurant with red vinyl booths. Maybe the tackiness would be outweighed by the chance this would give her friends to drive by one of the department stores that bore her new name. They would see her new house. "Our country place," she called it.

Not that Honey was a snob. She just couldn't believe that her ability to pay the rent no longer depended on whether she looked good in a skimpy costume and could kick her legs above her head. Her wedding to my father would be a lot more glamorous than her wedding to her first husband. "Oh, Janie," she had confided to me late one night on the phone, "when I married Dusty, he was still something of a cowboy. He absolutely loathed churches. We were married by some awful justice of the peace in Oklahoma. He and Dusty got drunk and took turns shooting chickens from the porch. Who could have imagined that I would have the wedding of my dreams at such a late age?"

A gust of wind hit the Jeep. Willie closed his eyes, and the Jeep spun lazily in a circle. One corner of the hood narrowly missed a trailer in which a horse flicked its tail. Around and around we spun, the seconds moving so slowly that time seemed to be a liquid like water that froze. The Jeep came to rest facing the wrong way on the grass between the lanes. Willie pressed his fists against the roof. I tried to stop trembling. We could have been killed. By a gust of wind. A horse.

"You weren't even trying," I said. "You let the wind take us."

"I got tired," he said. "I haven't had a beer since Tuesday. My mind was on something else. It was on Ted. It would have been a whole lot worse if I'd jumped on the brakes." It turned out that Ted was hitching from Montana, where he had been working on a ranch. He told his father he wanted to "live for a while" before he went to college, as if he equated learning with death.

We got back on the turnpike just long enough to reach the next exit. The town of Malvern Hill was a row of darkened souvenir shops, a taxidermist, a diner, and a movie theater that was closed until the following spring. Willie parked beside the theater. The posters advertised an aging Marilyn Monroe and Clark Gable in *The Misfits* and Dusty Land addressing a mob of disgruntled townspeople from a mule in *Farmer Sinclair*. He was the same age as Willie, with the same cleft chin and broad cheeks. The actor on that mule could have been Willie with a crew cut.

"That's what it's like to be famous," he said. At first, I thought he meant fame kept a person's memory alive. Then I noticed that some wise guy had traced FUCK in the grime across Willie's father's face.

I asked if he ever watched his father's movies.

"I used to," he said. "The late show. Or revivals in theaters like this. After the curtains closed I'd sit there a long time, like maybe he was going to change into regular clothes and come out." He threw his voice so the poster seemed to twang in a musical drawl: *"Hey, kid, how you doin'? Heard you pluckin' that guitar in your room, didn't sound half bad. Now, about that girl in your art class. The one you took a shine to. What's her name? Denise? Here's how you go about gettin' her attention . . ."* Willie snorted. "Then I got older, and all I wanted to do was go up there and punch a hole in the screen. Here I was asking him all this important stuff, and all he could do was say those same lousy lines from *Farmer Sinclair: 'Don't wait up for me, son. I'm goin' down to Washington to fix what needs fixin'.'"* He used his parka to wipe the glass. "This hard for you?" he asked. "Your dad remarrying and all?"

It was. And it wasn't. I was happy that my father would have a new companion. But wives weren't interchangeable. Surely mothers weren't. "She was so beautiful," I said. "People used to think she was an actress." A few dried leaves scraped across the mosaic at our feet. "One time, I went to see this movie at the old Orson Welles Theater. In Cambridge, you know? Before it burned down? Anyway, that woman came on, the woman who holds the torch for Columbia Pictures? That's who my mother reminded me of. She had that faraway look, as if maybe she was thinking . . . I'll never know what she was thinking." My throat knotted. "The woman with the torch never stayed on the screen for very long. You would blink and she'd be gone."

He put his arms around me. The damp feathers in his parka made me think of the poultry farms around Mule's

Neck. "Maybe we shouldn't have stopped here," he said. "Maybe we should get back on the road."

"No," I said. "I'm hungry. I've got to eat." I dried my nose on his sleeve.

"You been skipping meals again?"

"No," I said. And I hadn't. I devoured two-sandwich lunches at the deli, then lingered over rice pudding and hot cocoa to delay returning to the lab. One Saturday, I had cooked a slab of London broil for my weekly dinner with Maureen, only to remember that Maureen had gone to Maine, after which I ate both portions myself.

"We might as well eat an early dinner," he said. "Maybe the sleet will let up."

The Malvern Diner was larger than the Drurys' trailer, although with each gust of wind it threatened to break loose from its foundation. I ordered the chicken parmigiana, salad, and a side dish of macaroni and cheese. Willie ordered a chocolate frappé. For dessert, I ate apple pie with ice cream.

"So." He slurped the frappé. "I'm not sorry about what we did. It's just, when we got back from that place, I couldn't stop thinking about what it would really be like if both of us came down with the disease. Or if we had a kid who was even more likely than Ted to get it."

This was crazy, I thought. He had given me something wonderful, then taken it back, then given it again, then taken it back. And now? What was I supposed to do—turn all his old arguments against him?

"I care about you, Jane. I care about you a lot. But we're going to be part of the same family. We're going to be stepbrother and stepsister. Think of all those times we'll be sitting across from each other at some big table with a turkey on it. My mother didn't even want me to marry Peg. She was furious that we had a kid. She's terrified, just terrified, that Ted's going to come down with it. That he'll have to go through what she watched Dusty go through. So, maybe you could tell me that you won't hold this against me. At least not forever."

I wanted to say I would. But how could I pretend that he was no more to me than a stepbrother when every time I looked at him I would remember what we had done on that island? "I'll forgive you," I said. "Someday. But not right now."

"All right." He slapped the table. "You ready to hit the road?"

⸻⸻⸻

We crossed the Hudson at five. The bridge was narrow and high and glazed with ice. The wind kept threatening to snatch the Jeep and toss it in the river. I thought of Henry Hudson pitching on those waves, sailing up that nameless river without a map.

The directions to Mule's Neck became more complex. *Take that right. Turn left past that barn.* It came to me how easily I could have been born somewhere else, born to other parents. Although, if I had been, I wouldn't have been aware of the fate I had been spared.

"That's the exit," I said, and even at twenty miles an hour, Willie needed to pump the brakes to keep from skidding. I had heard talk that the ramp there curved so sharply because my father had bribed the governor to run the exit past his store. For years, I had been intending to confront my father with this charge, but I had never gotten around to it. I could imagine his defense: the engineers could have found a way to build the ramp safely, or they could have built the ramp farther north. No matter where the exit went, my father would have given money to whatever numskull ran for governor on the Democratic ticket. I told myself that my father's work for the Valentine's foundation would benefit far more people than his road had injured, although it also seemed true that, like most people's children, I would be the only person who would carry out such a detailed accounting of his good and bad deeds.

We pulled into the lot for Weiss's, which seemed fuller than I remembered. Since the early seventies, my father's stores had been losing business to the trendier malls near Albany. He had tried to keep up, but he had never really meant to run that kind of store. When he had come home from the war, it was all he could do to buy the old bait-shop that stood on this site and fill it with watch caps, rubber boots, and knives he bought cheap from Uncle Sam. By the late 1950s, he was able to knock down the bait shop and build this cinder-block bunker with an escalator up, although he never built one down. "Anyone too lazy to walk down a flight of stairs, I can do without their business," he used to say.

I was well past the line of registers before I began to notice all the changes. Someone had put in a new mint-green carpet and chrome-and-glass counters with sliding doors. The clerks stood behind those counters looking stunned by all the light, ill at ease among the mannequins who struck poses on their pedestals with sneering mouths and cocked hips.

"It looks like a whorehouse," I said.

Willie's head brushed an inflatable candy cane that was the closest Weiss's Supply had ever come to Christmas decorations. "It's my mom," he said. "She changes everything she gets her hands on. And if your father knows what's good for him, he'll do what she says to do. If my dad hadn't met her, he'd have ended up a dime-a-dozen alkie cowpoke." Caught by his reflection in a three-way mirror, he bent and tied his shoe. "How do you think I stopped boozing? There I was in that godforsaken cabin, pissing and moaning because my wife went off and took my son, the snow's halfway up the door, and my mom gets through like the friggin' Mounties. She's got on these pointy leather boots, hat not worth a damn, nothing in her purse but an airline ticket with my name on it, one-way to Japan. Why Japan? Who knows. She must have thought Asians don't drink. Which they don't. Much. Or rather they do, but it's hard for a foreigner to figure out how to ask for beer. And that sake stuff—I never was much for drinking my booze warm." All four Willies—the real one and the three reflections—shook their heads. "I'm in this garden in Kyoto, I'm staring at this rock, this little stream, and that's it, I stopped *wanting*. I can't explain it, Jane. You would laugh if I tried. All I'll say is, I knew that if only I would stop worrying about so many things, I wouldn't have anything left to worry about. I spent nine months at that temple. Then I scrounged enough money for a ticket home and never touched another beer. Well, mostly I didn't. Just some nights, when Ted had gone back to Long Island."

I saw him sitting in his cabin, drinking glass after glass of the chocolate milk he had bought for the son who'd just left.

"The long and the short of it is, if she wants you to change, you change."

He made it sound easy. In truth, I had always thought it was difficult to change. My sister used to spend hours practicing new ways to sign her name, *Laurel Weiss, Laurel Weiss,* forcing her hand to crown the *W* and *L* with curly loops. But whenever she grew impatient, she signed her name with the same blocky capital letters she had learned in elementary school.

We walked through Men's Haberdasheries, past ties and suspenders of a quality the store had never carried. I pushed a door with no nameplate and was relieved to see my father's office exactly as it had been. He sat behind his desk, signing checks. "Janie!" He got to his feet and held me at arm's length and inspected me. I began to say *Don't,* then realized I had been inspecting him, too, to see how badly he had aged in the few months since I'd seen him. "I'm sorry to take you away from your work for this silly business. If it was up to me, we'd just go see the rabbi and get this over with. But Honey wants the real thing. And hell, it's the broad's last chance." He cuffed Willie's arm. "No offense, son. Your mother may be a broad, but she's the classiest broad on the planet." He fingered my shirt. "Why don't you run upstairs and pick out something nice." He jerked his thumb toward the ceiling. "You ought to see it. Fancy sofas and chairs. Whatnots on the tables. Honey's still hocking me to redo the fitting room—you know, divide it into stalls. I say, what's the matter with the fitting room the way it is, all one big space? One dame doesn't like to see another dame in her *gatkes*? And she says no, if women see each other trying on clothes they start comparing themselves, each one thinks the other one is skinnier or she's got a bigger bust, and next thing you know, everybody's got their own clothes back on and they're headed out the door." He waited to hear whose side I would take.

"That's okay, Dad," I said. "I already have a dress," and I offered silent thanks to Maureen that I did. I had been avoiding that fitting room for years, as if my mother's reflection might still be flitting from glass to glass, trapped in the room where she had spent so many hours trying on the latest clothes.

"And what about you?" My father jabbed Willie in the ribs. "We've got some irregular suits on special. Not that I would expect you to pay, now you're family."

I needed a moment to understand he meant Willie would be his stepson. Never mind Willie's mother, what would my father think if I dated—or married—Willie?

"Thanks for the offer, Herb." Willie returned my father's jab. "But I've got the clothes situation under control."

I asked if my father wanted us to pick up some groceries on our way through town.

"Ahh," he said, "you didn't shlep all this way to cook for me. Besides, Honey ordered a crate of stuff from New York. She worries I don't eat right when she's not here."

Which he probably didn't. Since my mother's death, he had subsisted largely on sandwiches and hot dogs he brought home from the snack shop at the store.

"I've got to finish these checks. Maybe you could do me a favor. It's her things. Someone needs to get rid of them before Honey moves in."

"Her" meant my mother. But I wasn't sure which "things" he meant me to throw out. A week after my mother's death, my father had given all her clothing to the thrift shop. He had kept only her hairbrush and her cap from graduation.

"The kitchen things," he said. "You know how women are," as if I weren't one myself but had studied them at college. "One woman doesn't want to cook with another woman's things. Your mother's books are in the basement. If you want them, they're yours. If not, just get rid of them."

We left him at the store, doing work he had manufactured so he wouldn't have to watch his daughter throw out his wife's textbooks from college. The Jeep crawled slowly up the hill, Willie peering out the windshield like an elderly woman afraid of breaking a hip. "I'll come in for a while," he offered. "If you want me to come in." But I could tell he was anxious to drive to the motel where his mother and Ted were staying. "He's hitching in," Willie said. "I used to hitch all over. But it's not like it used to be. And Ted, well, he's not much of a fighter. I know it doesn't matter if I wait up for him. But I'd rather be there, in case he calls."

I shook my head to clear the image of my sister driving to Mule's Neck on the back of Cruz's motorbike. That icy ramp, unlit. Cruz, a stranger, unaware of how sharply the exit curved.

"See you at the wedding," Willie said. And he left me standing in front of the house in which my mother had lived and died and in which my father would be getting married to another woman the following day.

I tottered up the walk, balancing my weight between my suitcase in one arm and the mouse cage in the other. For weeks I had been trying to get the homozygous mouse to mate. Despite Maureen's report that he had humped that rubber toy, he had refused to mount a real mate. Maybe the disease had rendered him infertile. Still, I kept hoping. Some mice are just picky. Before leaving Cambridge, I had placed a new female in the cage; I had brought along the pair because I needed to record the exact date they mated— this involved a twice-daily gynecological exam of the girl mouse—so I wouldn't miss the birth.

The dining room had been enlarged and an extension added. The new room looked like a greenhouse, with tropical flowers and potted plants. In the corner stood my globe, so exotic and oversized it might have been a meteor that had landed in the middle of the new Persian rug. I found the spot where Mule's Neck would have been if the mapmaker had marked places that small. Until now, my father had left his hometown only to be a soldier in World War II and to pursue a cure to the disease that killed his wife. I spun the globe, praying that he and Willie's mother would have time to travel everywhere, to make love in strange beds, to eat good meals, to see interesting sights.

The new kitchen was double the size of the old one, all butcher block and tile. Lined up along one wall were my mother's old dishes, which had probably cost twenty dollars for the set when she had bought them at Weiss's. I wrapped the dishes for the thrift shop. In another carton, I packed the glass dessert-bowls in which I had displayed the eggs for my science-fair project. But I kept the Waring blender, which my father had brought home from the store to help my mother make baby food to suit Laurel's finicky taste. I stroked the jar of ribbed glass, the beveled silver base with its four upright prongs. The year I had spent nursing my mother through the last ravages of her illness, I had used this blender to mix chicken for her dinner. I had tied a beautician's smock around her neck, tilted her body forward, and spooned the gruel in her mouth. I had reminded her to swallow, made sure her mouth was clear, then spooned in more gruel, following the method I had read in a pamphlet that began: "So, you got the news, your loved one has Valentine's."

Once, just to hear myself talk, I had explained to my mother that a blender exactly like this one had been used to perform one of modern biology's most famous experiments. The blender was the perfect equipment with which to shake loose the tails of viral phage from the bacteria they had latched on to, allowing scientists to study the DNA with which the virus had infected the cells. I hated that blender, remembering all the times I hadn't run it long enough so the meat was too thick and my mother gagged, or the times I had neglected to strain the puree and my mother had coughed and coughed, spraying pap across the room. Still, this blender had kept her alive a year longer than she might otherwise have lived.

I set aside my mother's tablecloths for Laurel, and the little yellow corn-holders Laurel and I had bought our mother for her birthday one year. It was after eight thirty. My father couldn't invent things to do much longer at the store. I went down to the basement and found the box of books. On top of the stack was a spiral-bound notebook with a psychedelic cover. Given all the money that my mother's parents had wasted on their sons' education, they hadn't been inclined to send her to college, too. She hadn't started school until the 1960s, a middle-aged housewife in tailored suits amid long-haired kids in jeans. Like Laurel, I had resented her new career. I was still at that age when I assumed my mother's attention should be devoted to me. But I couldn't help but feel proud that she was smarter than other mothers. Bored as I was at school, she allowed me to skip my classes and go to hers. We rode back and forth to Albany, chatting about astronomy or math. Once, during lunch, I asked about the smell in the college cafeteria. It was like my father's cigars, only sweeter.

"Oh, it's marijuana," she told me absently. "Some of the boys were smoking it in organic chem the other day." She didn't seem to care what her classmates smoked. She was too intent on making up for all those lost years—after she finished her undergraduate degree, she started taking classes toward her doctorate in biology—to notice that the men wore earrings or the young women went braless or her notebooks were covered with multicolored sequins that changed their patterns when you moved your eyes.

"Biology 212, Introductory Genetics," read the title of one such notebook. My mother had recorded the instructor's lectures in obsessive detail, with meticulous illustrations in colored ink. These were the notes of someone who feared she might forget her own name if she didn't write it down. And this was, in fact, the first information she had lost. "I don't know," she said, studying for the comprehensive exams for her Ph.D., exams she never took because she didn't see the point, she had been diagnosed by then, "it's as if everything I've learned is one of those lazy Susans down at King's, and it's spinning so fast I can't grab the answers I want." The rest of the box was filled with thick texts like *Advanced Neuroanatomy* and *Mammalian Genetics*. On page 467 of this latter text was the information that Valentine's chorea was inherited in a dominant Mendelian fashion. The disease, the text said, had no known treatment or cure. The passage had been highlighted in yellow marker, so I knew that she must have read it.

I set aside *Reproductive Biology*, with its Technicolor photos of fetuses in various stages of development, the first such photos ever taken from inside a human womb. It occurred to me that my mother's years as a parent hadn't been the obstacle to her education I had always assumed they were, but the spur to go to college and study how a child unfolded from an egg and a sperm.

I had just repacked the books when my father came home. He looked around the kitchen to make sure I had done what he had asked. "Come on," he said. "Help me get rid of all this food that Honey sent before it goes bad."

I built us both sandwiches. My father washed down his meal with brandy, then bit off the tip of a cigar and began to smoke.

"So," he said, "what'd you think of the store? I wouldn't have minded retiring. But no one would have bought the chain in the shape those stores were in. I saved enough money for you and Laurel. But now there's Honey to think about, and Ted." His cigar made him cough. I had never heard him cough from smoking. "I'll still be working less. Honey found some smart boychik with a Harvard MBA to oversee the day-to-day operations. I'd rather spend my time running the foundation. Besides, a woman like Honey doesn't marry an old fart like me so she can sit around and twiddle her thumbs. She's got a condo lined up for us in Palm Springs." He peered at me to see if I would object. "You think all your old man's good for is selling pots and pans?" He tapped the ashes from his cigar. The stench of tobacco made my stomach contract. "I'm not quitting the foundation. But Honey's right, a man deserves a few good years before he kicks off."

"Of course you do," I said, although I couldn't imagine my father sunning himself in Palm Springs. Like most daughters, I couldn't imagine my father as anything other than what he had been when I was young. "Dad?" I said. "Did you and Mom ever think you shouldn't have kids?"

"Ahh," he said, "why bring all that up now." He tossed back another shot of brandy. "People didn't think that way back then. Who knew why children got sick? Whooping cough. Polio. If it wasn't a bum heart, it was measles or scar-

let fever. Maybe if you heard some girl's mother had run off
with the milkman, or her uncle liked little boys, you would
have thought twice about marrying into a family like that.
But your mother? She was like any woman. She wanted
babies. She wanted a home. A woman didn't decide not to
have a kid just because her father and brothers had died
of some crazy disease most people hadn't heard of. And
who knows, maybe she believed the cockamamie story your
grandmother told her, that girls couldn't get Valentine's. As
if I was the kind of skunk who would leave a girl high and
dry because of something that ran in her genes."

I supposed he was right. My mother had gotten pregnant with me, then with my sister, because she had hoped
beyond hope that she had been spared the disease that killed
her father and older brothers. Blessed with two daughters,
she had chosen to believe her mother's lie that girls didn't
get Valentine's. After her children were all grown up, she
had allowed herself to plan for a life that extended past her
thirties. She defied her husband's objections about going
back to school, knowing these were only for show (he paid
for her tuition, and bought her a car so she could travel
back and forth to Albany).

Then her memory started failing. Crossing the stage to
receive her diploma, she stumbled and nearly fell. Other
symptoms surfaced. She began to study genetics from ne-
cessity more than from love. She tried before she left to
pass the torch on to me.

My father pointed to the clock. "Think your sister'll get
here tonight? She's coming with that dancer." He tugged at
his cheeks, which were slack and gray as putty. "She thinks

if she comes in late enough, I won't make a fuss about where they sleep. What do I care who she shacks up with. You know what I would give if this could be her wedding? Or yours?" He pulled me close. "That Willie is a mensch. I don't expect you should live like a nun. But use your head, doll. This family doesn't need any more tsuris. We've already got so much tsuris we could run a sale."

After he went to bed, I sat up awhile. Then I put on my hat and coat and went out. I had missed this in Boston, where I rarely found the time—or felt safe enough—to take long walks at night. Clouds swam before the moon like amoebae swimming past the light beneath a microscope. I skated down the hill toward my high school. I circled the building, peering in at windows and straining to make out what was written on the boards. The windows in the gym were laced with wire mesh. Even the clock was protected, as if, should a ball crack its face, time itself might stop. Had I ever been so young as to tumble on those mats? Had I ever been the girl who so anxiously waited beside her science-fair project in this very same gym?

The day of the fair, when the judges had come to examine my display, I could tell they were tired—the exhibits had been arranged in alphabetical order by the students' last names. I also guessed the judges—the vice-principal, Mr. Koots; Mr. Ryback, who taught sophomore chemistry; and Mrs. Scipione, who taught junior high math—thought they knew everything about chickens and eggs. Desperate, I came up with a strategy: I would try to explain what scientists *didn't* understand about eggs and chicks, although I worried the judges might think I was lazy, like a student who writes a composition about not being able to decide what to write.

"Well then," Mrs. Scipione said. "Perhaps in your studies of the chicken and the egg, you've come across the answer to a very vital question." This seemed a setup for my father's favorite joke. But Mrs. Scipione looked too serious for that. She twisted the yarn her glasses hung from. "I was hoping you could tell me at what moment life starts."

I had always supposed that a person's life started when she left for college. Then I saw that the question really meant: At what point does an egg become a chick? I was struck by the importance of this question. From the way Mrs. Scipione tapped her pen against her clipboard, I could tell that she knew the answer. What the men thought was harder to guess. Mr. Koots ground an invisible cigarette-butt into the shiny floor, while Mr. Ryback studied the two-headed fetus I had found in one egg. I was desperate to earn Mrs. Scipione's approval. But the question seemed too hard. Eggs weren't living things. An egg was dairy, not meat. It was a *thing*, like a cabbage. Then again, weren't vegetables and fruits somehow "living"? At what point did an egg become a chick? When the heart started pumping? But didn't a creature need to eat and reproduce? Maybe it became a chick when the brain started growing. But that would have meant that in peeling all those eggs and dissecting all those embryos, I had dissected living things.

I took such a long time thinking that Mrs. Scipione answered the question herself. "At *conception*," she said.

"You mean, right from the start? With the rooster and the hen? But that's crazy," I said. So of course I didn't win.

After the award ceremony, I went out to the playground to figure out if I should care. Mrs. Scipione's question wasn't like other questions. No matter how long you studied when life began, you would never find the answer, because the answer was something you would need to know before you started. Arguing with Mrs. Scipione would be like spinning on the merry-go-round: *I think this; you think that.* I considered asking my mother. But it was my father who picked me up. He didn't seem surprised I hadn't won.

"We could eat the eggs," he joked.

As soon as we got home, I went out to my mother's garden and buried the embryos in the dirt. I stuffed the posters in the trash, then lay in my bunk for hours, listening to Laurel practicing the cello. The music she played that night somehow expressed all the anger and disappointment I couldn't put into words.

Now, on the eve of my father's wedding, I walked back up the hill to our house to wait for her arrival. As a sort of consolation I settled in the easy chair and switched on the TV. *The King and I* was showing; it was Laurel's favorite musical. I remembered one night when I lay reading on the sofa and this song began to play. Laurel pulled me to my feet and swung me around the living room, "One two *three,* one two *three,*" guiding me in a waltz as Anna guided the king. "Won't you *dance,* won't you *dance,* won't you *dance.*"

I slept sitting in the chair. At dawn, I went outside. The wind had blown itself out, and the air had warmed slightly. Ice melted from the trees. I walked around the back. The new conservatory covered most of the land that had been my mother's garden, a plot of ground so large our family couldn't consume all the vegetables. Often, she would become so absorbed in her gardening she would forget Laurel and me. We played hide-and-seek among the cornstalks. Once, when Laurel hid, I couldn't find her. I raced up and down the rows, then walked around the neighborhood calling her name. *Did you think I'd been kidnapped again?* she asked me, laughing. *Were you worried I wouldn't come back?* I didn't ask where she had been. I knew she had run off only because I always made such a point of keeping her in sight.

The rental company arrived, unfolding chairs in the conservatory and unrolling a bolt of white silk down the aisle. The florist brought bird-of-paradise. The ceremony was scheduled to begin at twelve thirty; it was nearly eleven when Cruz and Laurel pulled up. They arrived in a battered red MG. The door opened and out poured excuses. They had been up late the night before, rehearsing. The roads up north were very slick. Still, I couldn't help but think they might have arrived earlier if Laurel hadn't been reluctant to spend the night with me.

She went in to take a shower. Cruz loitered on the lawn as if he wanted to ask me something. But he must have sensed that he, too, ought to hurry in and change. I went up to my room and put on the suit Maureen had picked out. Laurel reappeared, her newly washed hair clinging to her back. Her skin radiated life in a way that made the robe superfluous. I struggled to pull on my panty hose, then smoothed my hair in place and put on the feathered cap Maureen had made me buy, then decided against it and took it off.

"Oh, you have to," Laurel said. "It's perfect." She cocked the brim and stepped back, then threw her arms around me as if I were the one getting married. "Are you happy? You look as if, I don't know, you've got a secret. You're in love with Willie, aren't you. I would be, too." I tried to interrupt. "You've got a wonderful job. You're on the verge of a breakthrough." She spun like a child. "Oh, Jane, I'm on the verge of something, too. Not like you are. I'm not saving any lives. But you can't imagine what Cruz has taught me. About dance. About myself. You're coming, aren't you, to the concert? There'll be a big surprise. Something only you will appreciate."

In the room next door, our father cursed. "Laurel! I need your help!"

She smiled at me and tied the robe tighter. "Just a minute," she called back. The robe had been our mother's. I had my memories of those afternoons driving with my mother back and forth to Albany, discussing evolution, and Laurel had this, the traded clothes, the tips about makeup and hair. How many siblings did this, I wondered, divided up their parents' interests, as if my mother's scientific curiosity and beauty were heirlooms that had to be apportioned, one trait to each child?

We finished getting dressed. Laurel leaned toward the mirror, dabbing on blush and mascara, then glazing her lips with gloss. The clock in the mirror moved backward half an hour. A car honked. I looked out and saw Willie in the back seat of a limousine. A slender young man sat beside him in the back, and Honey in the front. The doorbell rang, announcing the first of Honey's guests from New York. Our neighbors arrived. My mother's friends conveyed with a hug or a pat that they hadn't forgotten my loss but were happy for my father.

"Where's Charlene?" I asked Karl Prince, who was pulling off his overshoes.

He looked inside the empty black rubber skins. "Didn't your father tell you? The doctors removed the other breast. But it didn't matter by then. She passed on at the end of August."

I put my hand to my mouth. I almost believed that if I hadn't asked the question, Charlene Prince wouldn't yet be dead.

"Maybe you could stop by and see Karen?" Karl asked. "She can't seem to get over it." As if grieving for a mother were an exam I could help another daughter pass.

"I'll try," I promised Karl, although I had planned to drive back to Boston with Willie that night. Charlene Prince had been the only woman in Mule's Neck who had volunteered to look after my mother when I needed a break.

Karl honked his nose in his handkerchief. "We're all proud of you, Jane. I used to tell Charlene, 'I gave that girl her start.' You knew more about chickens when you were twelve than I'll ever know, and I been working with them every day of my life." He kicked his rubbers beneath the bench. "Though you never did tell me that secret, how to grow chicks without the rooster."

Why hadn't I said it the first time? What a self-righteous prig I'd been. "You never paid me, Karl," I said.

He laughed and stuffed his handkerchief in his pocket. "Guess the preacher's getting ready. We better go sit down."

The rabbi took his place at the little table they had set up by the arbor, and Willie's cousin Irene started playing her flute. My father limped down the aisle, screwing up his face to signal that he wasn't the reason the audience was there. Then came Willie and his mother. Honey wore an off-white lace dress that hugged her waist, with a slit down the front to show off those magnificent legs. Her crown of gold-white hair didn't seem out of place at a wedding. The veil softened her features and made her appear half her age.

"What a lovely bride," people murmured.

"Such tragedies for them both."

"Thank goodness they met."

I had never been the kind of girl to imagine my wedding, but it was hard not to see myself walking down this same aisle with my arm through my father's. Willie would be standing by the chuppah in that charcoal tux with the black lapels. The reality that this would never happen wrenched a cry from my throat.

The rabbi blessed the wine. My father took a gulp then held the cup to Honey. He was sixty-six years old. His bride wasn't much younger. Were their odds really so much different from Willie's and my own?

My father lifted Honey's veil. She leaned down to him and they kissed. I reached across Cruz and squeezed Laurel's hand.

Willie's son, Ted, let out a cheer. "Way to go, Grandma!" I turned and looked, straining to see if he resembled his father. But Irene had already started playing the recessional and everyone pivoted to watch the bride and groom walk back down the aisle.

Laurel and I made our way through the crowd to offer our good wishes to the newlyweds. Ted sashayed up behind us in the reception line, ducking his head like a cowpoke approaching the new schoolmarm. He wore pointy boots with lassoes etched on the sides, tight black jeans, and a starched white shirt. He slid the turquoise clasp on his string tie up and down, then toyed with the silver loop in one ear. He was rangy, almost frail, half a foot shorter than his father, with close-cropped red hair he must have gotten from his mother and a normal chin with no cleft.

"You're Dad's new girlfriend, aren't you." He winked, and it was a boy's wink, so deliberate I could almost see his brain order his eyelid to shut. Whatever Willie had told him—something scrawled on a postcard the month before—by now was stale news. "That's terrific. He's still a young guy. It's good for him to have a purpose in his life besides making money." His own goal, Ted explained, was to compete in a famous rodeo that spring. Then he would write a book about his adventures. Then he would go to college and earn a degree in environmental law. Or maybe he would start his own recording studio, so he could produce authentic country music. Not the commercial shit the big companies in Nashville put out. He would do this, then he would do that, then he would try something else.

"I guess you two met." Willie slapped his son on the back. "What's this young varmint chewing your ear about?"

I had never seen him so self-conscious, like a bad actor attempting to play someone's dad. In that too-folksy voice, he offered his son advice about never trusting horses enough to walk behind them and the tendency for harmless-looking scrapes to get infected. Like my own father, he kept asking Ted if he needed a few bucks to tide him over. He suggested Ted buy a pickup, so he wouldn't have to hitch. It struck me that this young stranger, with his cowboy boots and earring, was my relative now. My step-nephew, wasn't he? Although if I married Willie, he also would be my son. What if Ted had the gene for Valentine's? What if he and his father *both* had it?

We reached the head of the receiving line, and Laurel took the opportunity to hand Honey her gift. She had bought them tickets to the Follies, and a certificate for dinner at Laurel's favorite Left Bank bistro. I remembered walking Laurel downtown to buy gifts for our parents, Laurel contributing whatever money she had saved from her allowance, which never came to more than a fraction of the cost. This time, we hadn't even considered going in on a gift. Just as well, I thought. We couldn't have agreed on what to get.

"Why, Laurie," Honey said. "What an original, thoughtful present." She pressed her cheek to Laurel's. "I'm sure it will be one of the nicest meals of my life. And I know that your father will enjoy the Follies." She fluffed the carnation on his lapel.

My father grabbed her hand as if he were capturing a bee. "Are these real girls we're talking about? Not boys dressed up as girls? Yeah, sure, I'll enjoy it." He kissed the hand, then tucked it beneath his arm for safekeeping.

"And that globe!" Honey said. "Janie, it must have cost you a fortune."

"Well," I said, "after everything you've both—"

My father cut in. "Two hundred dollars, am I right? If you spent a dime, you spent two hundred dollars." He frowned the kind of frown he put on when workmen gave him an inflated estimate. Honey tugged away her hand. She knew what he was going to say next and hoped that she would have the time to stop him from saying it. "You just find us that gene, doll. There's no present on earth we could appreciate more than that."

I glanced at my sister, thinking of Abel and Cain and how one sibling's gift had been accepted by God and the other sibling's spurned. Here Laurel had gone to all the trouble to come up with a gift our father and Honey might appreciate, and I had won the contest with a mouse.

"Laurel! Sweetie! Over here!" A plump older woman who was wearing enough beaded jewelry to stock a bazaar waved an aerogram above her head. "I've got regards for you from Hank!"

"Excuse me," Laurel said tightly. "I hope you'll both enjoy France." And she went to visit with the mother of her senior-year boyfriend. I moved past my father to the new mahogany table on which the wedding gifts had been piled.

"This sister of yours," Cruz said. "What I want to know is, this business about her genes, it's on the level? It isn't *my* genes that are the problem?"

"Just be nice to her," I said. "All right?"

"I'm asking for a straight answer here. Is anything wrong with your sister? Is she sick?"

No, I said. She wasn't sick. But someday she might be.

"Someday is a long way off. She tells me you're looking for a cure for this Valentine's thing. Just how long's that going to take? We talking months here? Years?"

It wasn't a cure, I said. It was only a test.

Cruz took this in. "To make sure she's all right? And if she's not, what? I'm supposed to say, 'See you later, I'm out of here'? What kind of craziness you cooking up in that lab of yours?"

"I'm just not explaining it very well."

"No explanation is going to make me see why I've got to wait for some test to be sure how I feel about your sister. Do me a favor. Make sure your father knows his daughter is the one who won't let me do the right thing."

Cruz went to find Laurel. I felt tired and old. I wanted to tell everyone: *If you want to get married, get married. If you don't, for Pete's sake, don't.* I started for the door to take a walk and get some air, but Honey wouldn't let me. She handed me a champagne glass. From the way she was tottering on her heels, I had the impression she had already downed several glasses.

I felt the waxy seal of her lipstick on my cheek. "Teddy was so late coming in last night, Willie and I sat up talking until all hours." She motioned to the server, took another fluted glass, and sipped. "Excuse me for prying, but it's very hard . . ." She had a gauzy, wistful look. "You've met my Teddy, haven't you? Teddy's such a sweet boy. A darling. You have no idea what a grandmother feels for a grandchild. And to think he might . . . Jane, it's one thing to take care of a sick husband. To *not* be able to take care of a sick husband. But a child, Jane. A child. To think there's nothing you can do. To think you will need to watch them suffer."

I started to say it wasn't any of her business if I had a child. But then I realized it was. Any child I might have with Willie would be her grandchild. If Willie and I got sick, Honey might end up raising him or her. "I know you mean well," I said. "But really, it's my decision."

"No," she said. "It isn't. It isn't, Jane. Promise me! You really and truly need to promise me that if anything happens between you and my son, you will not have a child!" She took a step to grab my arm. Instead, she lost her balance and tottered backward. She stretched out her arm to grab the globe and sent it toppling. We heard a terrible crack, and it suffered a jagged rift from north to south.

Willie helped her to her feet. My father rushed over and righted the toppled globe.

"Mom," Willie said. "Are you all right? Did you break anything?" He looked at the globe, then at me. "I mean, you didn't hurt yourself, did you?"

"No, no, of course not." She seemed confused. "Janie and I were just talking."

"It's okay, Mom. Whatever it is, you and Jane can talk later. If you and Herb go to the restaurant now, the guests will have to follow."

Tenderly, he took his mother's arm and escorted her from the room. I saw Honey make a detour to the bathroom, where she must have patted cold water on her face, because she came out looking more sober. Then Willie drove his mother and my father to King's in the limousine, while I drove Laurel, Cruz, and Ted in my father's rusted Dodge, trying not to think about Honey's warning that I not marry her son, or at least not have his child. I couldn't help but take the cracked globe as an omen.

The restaurant was overflowing with bouquets; the flowery scent, combined with the smell of all the greasy food, made me feel ill. I was hungry, and I wasn't. I barely had time to grab an egg roll and stuff it in my mouth before the band started playing. My father pulled Honey on the dance floor. Then Willie cut in and danced with his mother, and Laurel danced with our father. I was paired with Cruz.

"Loosen up," he said. "Dancing's what you do when you stop thinking about dancing."

I was relieved when we switched partners.

"Hi, Sis." Willie kissed my ear. "You look terrific."

I shrugged. "Maureen helped me pick out the suit."

"Not much good at taking compliments, are you."

I pulled back to see his face. "Not when I don't know how to take them."

"Okay," he said. "I deserved that. Truth is, when I'm away from you, I think one thing. And then, when I get closer, I start thinking of something else."

"Hey, Dad." Ted tapped his father's shoulder. "Mind if I horn in?"

"As it happens, I do."

"Tough nuts," Ted told him. He ducked beneath his father's arm and pushed me back in a two-step, although the song had three beats. I was glad that he'd cut in. I intended to ignore everything his father said.

"Has he popped the question yet?" Ted asked. "He's kind of goofy, with all that sixties meditation crap. I didn't see him much when I was a kid, but he's been a great dad since then. Mom's never said a bad word against him." Ted let go and stepped back, as if he only then realized his hands were wrapped around his father's girlfriend's waist. "Uh, nice hat," he said.

His bewilderment moved me. He was so young and naive, and so unaware that he was both. "Your father really loves you," I said. "You do know that, don't you? You'll be careful at that rodeo?"

"Oh, go on." He gouged a dragon's eye with his boot. "You sound like my mother."

I *felt* like his mother.

The waiters brought our soup. I found my place and spooned down a bowl of wonton. The fat on Laurel's soup congealed while she performed a jitterbug with Cruz. The dance seemed more like an argument. Back-to-back, they locked elbows. Laurel flung her legs toward the ceiling, her dress fanning to reveal her panties. After the song ended, Cruz held her with her arms pinned behind her back. She pulled away and came to sit by me.

"You keep avoiding me," I said. I hadn't planned to scold her, but losing my father made me all the more frightened of losing my sister, too.

"I am not," she said. Strands of damp hair clung to her temples. She raked them back. "It's just that you always act as if there's something I should be doing that I'm not. Even if this concert comes off the way I hope, you'll be sitting in the audience wondering when I'm going to get on with my real life. You'll ask me what I plan to do when I can't dance anymore."

"I'm your sister. I care what happens to you."

She laid her hand on mine. "I don't think the way you do. I don't like to plan ahead. It makes me crazy."

"Everyone! Please!" Honey, who had changed into a pink suit and pillbox hat, ordered the guests out front. She and my father were driving to LaGuardia, then flying to France. She walked out to the limousine. "Heads up, everyone!" she cried, then hurled her bouquet as far as she could in the direction opposite me. It was caught by Irene, who was Honey's sister's child and therefore had no chance of inheriting the gene for Valentine's.

Later, in that intricate choreography of cars that happens at a wedding, I drove Cruz and Laurel home in my father's Dodge. Laurel and Cruz changed into matching leather pants, then climbed back in the MG. I bit my lip to keep from telling Cruz to drive carefully.

Laurel motioned me to the window. "I'll see you soon. Before the concert."

"So we can go sailing?" I said.

Laurel looked as stricken as I had intended she look. "I did say that, didn't I. Well, I try to honor my promises. Don't I, Cruz, love?" She took his hand and kissed it. "Jane, I'm not ready to tell Dad yet, but Cruz and I decided we might get married. We're thinking of holding the ceremony on the top of Mount Washington." She laughed a high, false laugh. "I'm only joking. We'll hold it somewhere safe."

They roared off down the street. Laurel believed she would marry Cruz, just as she believed she would take me sailing. She said these things in good faith, as she had thanked me for saving our mothers' linens and little yellow corn-holders. Although, when I went inside, I saw that she had left these items on her bed.

Someone rang the doorbell. Ted shambled in.

"Cool," he said, "what's this?" He held up the mouse cage, which was sitting beside the door. "These your pets, or are they an experiment?"

"An experiment." I explained that I was breeding the affected male to see if he might be homozygous for the Valentine's gene.

Ted smacked kisses at the mice. "Which one's the guy and which one's the girl? Both of them look healthy."

It was true; the runt had grown. He rarely slipped into trances, and he only trembled when he was startled. Vic still maintained that the mouse had inherited two doses of the gene, but I was no longer sure. Maybe he had only been malnourished, and with all the food and attention I had lavished on him, he had thrived and caught up.

"Maybe he's just getting better," Ted suggested.

"You don't get better with Valentine's."

"Just because no one's ever recovered in the past doesn't mean no one ever will. It's like the sun coming up. Just because it's come up every morning for the past million years doesn't mean it has to come up again tomorrow."

There was nothing worse than an amateur logician.

"Maybe if a mouse has two doses of the gene, it gives it, you know, immunity? Like getting a shot of the polio virus makes you immune to polio."

"A gene isn't a virus," I said.

"Maybe it's a miracle. God can keep a sparrow from falling, so why can't he cure a mouse?"

"You don't really believe God performs miracles for mice."

"Whew," he said. "Dad was right. You're a pretty serious person."

I said that I guessed I was. "The only miracle I believe in is that the universe got started. It's miracle enough that we're standing here talking."

Ted grinned. "It's like that watchmaker thing."

"Watchmaker?"

"You know, Ike Newton and the Deists."

He made it sound like a rock group. Still, he knew who Newton was. He had heard of the Deists.

"You'll let me know what happens? If he comes down with it or not?" He meant the mouse, not his father. Ted wrote his address on a matchbook. Did he smoke? Please, God, no. "I'm like my dad," he said. "I'm a very curious guy." He told me about this white calf he had seen in South Dakota. Its parents had both been black, and the tribe there believed the calf was a sign from their messiah. When I unraveled the genetics that might have produced a white calf from a black cow and a black bull, I was afraid that Ted would accuse me of spoiling another miracle, but he laughed and said, "Sure, I get it. You're pretty good at ex-plaining all this science stuff."

He helped me carry out my luggage. Ted squeezed into the back seat of the Jeep with the box of my mother's books, squirming like a child who is bored with a journey before he's left home. Willie had convinced him to accept a bus ticket back to Montana, and we were dropping him off at the Greyhound station in Albany. The three of us rode without speaking, but I could tell that Willie's mind was on Ted. The Jeep would drift toward the shoulder, then toward the yellow line, then back toward the shoulder. We pulled into the parking lot behind the buses. Willie unfolded some bills from his wallet. Ted jammed his fists in his jeans and refused to accept the money. His bus snorted into its stall. Ted grabbed his duffel bag and bounded up the steps.

"I'll tell you," Willie said, stabbing the key in the igni-tion, "there aren't too many things you get to do a second time. But I sure wish I could get the chance to be a better dad." We crossed the river at Albany. Three hours later, we pulled up to the tollbooths outside Newton. Willie lifted his haunches to slide his change from his pants. "How do you decide which probe to try next? Is there some kind of order? Or do you guess?"

"Sure, I go in order," I said, neglecting to mention this only meant I tested probes in the order in which we had re-ceived them in the lab. "Yosef got a tip that the gene might be on chromosome three. He's trying probes from there."

"You think he's right?"

"No."

"So, basically it's random."

I admitted it was.

"I thought so. Those blots you showed me that night, all those little lines, they're like the patterns the sticks make when you throw the *I Ching*."

"You're suggesting I use a bunch of sticks to find the gene?"

The Boston skyline rose up before us. The light atop the old Hancock tower blinked red. *Steady blue, clear view. Flashing blue, clouds due. Steady red, rains ahead. Flashing red, snow instead.* I liked knowing the code. I liked thinking of all those satellites and radar devices, all those gauges on top of Mount Washington, all of humankind's accumulated knowledge of the winds and tides reduced to a simple red light flashing *snow snow snow snow.*

"What you're doing is guesswork," Willie said. "Why pretend it isn't? You know how it is—you toss a coin and it comes up tails, but you see you're disappointed that it didn't come up heads, so you forget the dime and do what you wanted to do all along. The *Ching*'s the same way. You interpret the patterns the way your intuition says to interpret them."

"Okay," I said. "Why don't you throw the sticks for me and let me know what they say." I hadn't meant to sound snide; I was only tired. We pulled up to my apartment. "Are you all right driving back to New Hampshire?" I was afraid he would have an accident. With the mood he was in, he might go home and start drinking. "You're welcome to stay on my couch."

There was a moment's delay, in which he seemed to be deciding if he wanted to sleep with me again. "Remember, you were going to let me know about this forgiveness thing."

"Sure," I said. "I'll call you."

But he was the one to call me. I had been dreaming of Ted, who was sitting on that bus, growing older and older the farther west it rolled. I kept yelling, *Turn around and come back home,* but his ears were plugged with earphones and he just waved and smiled that dopey grin.

"Try chromosome thirteen," Willie said.

"Isn't thirteen an unlucky number?"

"Try it, okay? As a favor to me."

"Fine," I said. "I'll try it." Anything to get off the phone and close my eyes.

Looking back, I'm relieved that he wasn't right. I didn't go into the lab the next morning, hybridize a blot with a probe from chromosome thirteen, and find a pattern that revealed the gene. In fact, when I went in, the first thing I did was have a fight with Susan Bate.

"Why, Jane Weiss," she said. "What a pleasant surprise. I think I found what you've been looking for."

"Oh?" I said. "You did?"

"Don't worry, I'll be sure to put your name on the paper. You should thank me. You've been out partying while I've been slaving in this shit hole."

Yosef sidled up between us. "Don't worry," he said. "She didn't find your gene. She is reading the blot upside down. You squint at those little lines long enough, you see what you want to see."

"You can't stand it that a woman found the gene before you did," Susan told him. "Just wait until Vic gets back from D.C. We'll let him be the judge."

I knew she hadn't found the gene. Not a week went by that Susan didn't claim she had made a great discovery. She wasn't that bad a scientist. It was just, as Yosef said, she too often saw what she wanted to see rather than what her experiments really proved. "I'll stop by later," I said. "Just let me set up some gels."

Grumbling, Susan went back to her bench. Yosef blew me a kiss and went back to his.

There was no putting it off. I walked across the hall to the freezer to collect my probes for the day. Shivering, I reached for the Eppendorf tube that was next on my list, a probe from chromosome six. Willie's voice said: *Thirteen.* I stopped and said: *No. It's on chromosome twenty.* I had no real reason to choose that tube. We had received only one probe from that short, misshapen chromosome. But something about the Eppendorf seemed to glow.

I thawed the tube at my bench. I set up a rack of samples from a family in New Jerusalem, cut the DNA with enzymes, and pipetted each person's fragments into a separate lane on a gel. When the gel finished running, I would transfer the fragments to a nitrocellulose blot and hybridize the whole thing with a radioactive probe from chromosome twenty. In the meantime, I set up a second gel, with a different pairing of fragments and probes. A third gel, then a fourth. I got so caught up in the rhythm of the experiment that I was able to ignore everything else—Willie's flip-flop intentions, my sister's reluctance to visit me, my own exhaustion and excessive hunger, the period I had missed, and the fetus that I suspected was growing in my womb.

I worked for six days. Then I sat down at my desk, trying not to listen to Susan's TV battling with Yosef's boom box, and I scrutinized the blots I had developed that week. One line in particular caught my notice, near the bottom of the first blot, the one with the probe from chromosome twenty. Three of the lanes showed a certain pattern of bands. The other lanes didn't. I deciphered the code on the tubes of DNA. The first pattern corresponded to DNA from the three members of the family who shared the disease, while the other lanes belonged to those members who had been given a clean bill of health. It was probably a coincidence. I had tested only twelve samples. Afraid to jinx the result, I said nothing to anyone. Slowly, I poured gels with DNA from two other families and biked home for the night. I tried not to get excited, like someone who has discovered a suitcase full of cash but expects the rightful owner will show up to claim it.

Later that week, I tried to analyze the data from all three families. The computer I was using was little more than a toy. The keys were sticky with Coke and doughnut grease. Vic wandered by the cubicle in which the computer was crammed with reference books, broken cameras, and an IBM Selectric that hadn't worked in years. He paused above my shoulder. Unlike the other postdocs, I never played computer games. *Don't tell him,* I warned myself. If the linkage turned out to be a mirage, Vic would think I was too desperate to judge my results objectively.

He moved on, and I relaxed. The printer squealed and spit out paper, the answer in ink so faint I could barely read it. According to the computer, the odds were fifty to one that the linkage I had discovered between the marker and the gene couldn't be accidental. Good but not great. With such a low score, the "pattern" I had found was most likely a fluke. I needed to test other families. It was even more complex than I had led Willie to believe. To find out if a certain person carried the gene for Valentine's, you needed to test not only that person, but his entire extended family. This was because the marker for Valentine's chorea manifested itself in a slightly different pattern in each family with the gene. It was as if, long ago, God had handed out a set of colored handkerchiefs, two to each person. Some handkerchiefs were red, others were green, or yellow, or blue. In one family, everyone who had inherited a red handkerchief might carry the gene for Valentine's, while those members of the family with other colors did not have the gene. In another family, the green handkerchief might be the lethal marker. In healthy families, a red or green handkerchief meant nothing at all, because no one had the gene.

I tested the DNA from a third family in New Jerusalem, but there seemed to be no correlation between the pattern on the blots and Sumner's judgments as to who did or did not show symptoms of the chorea. I kicked the cabinets beneath my bench, then stomped to the bathroom, punched the stall, and swore. I splashed cold water on my face, kicked the stall, and swore some more. Composed now, resigned, I went back to the lab and cleared the samples from my bench. Glancing at the labels, I saw that I had misread the code on one tube. In Yosef's spidery script, the *N*'s looked like *M*'s. I retested the data. The correlation had shot up to a hundred to one.

Still, that wasn't good enough. You couldn't publish a paper with a correlation of less than one thousand to one. If I tested a family that wasn't related to the family from Maine, and if the test worked for them, I would be sure I had found a pattern. I waited until midnight, when everyone except Achiro's replacement had gone home. I was hybridizing a blot of the Drurys' DNA with the probe from chromosome twenty when someone came in. I turned my head to see who it was and spilled the probe.

"That sucks," Susan said.

I looked down at the puddle.

"Sorry I've been giving you such a hard time. I shouldn't have said I found the gene when I hadn't. Those assholes get me so angry, I forget this is your life we're talking about. It must be awful, having so little chance to find the marker."

I restrained myself from saying: *Oh yeah? You think I have no chance to find the marker?*

"We girls should stick together." Susan sashayed to the water bath and scrutinized the dials. "Maybe you want to come over to my apartment? There's this drink I make with ginger beer and vodka. We could get plastered and talk."

I felt sorry for her then. She was lonely and afraid. I wanted to wrap my arms around her. If only she had tried to make friends earlier. But the last thing I wanted now was to sit in Susan's kitchen, get drunk, and gripe about Lew. "Some other time," I said. "Thanks. I mean it. Really."

"Right. Some other time." She stood there, legs bowed, ballet slippers turned out, and I was seized by the desire to twirl her around the room in a mad pas de deux. Maybe next week, when Maureen and I went dancing, we would ask Susan to go with us.

She dropped her right ear to her shoulder, swung back her head, then pressed her other ear to the other shoulder. "If you want to reject my offer of friendship," she said, working her head the other way, "I won't take it personally. But if I were you, I'd join Workaholics Anonymous. There's a group that meets at the Cambridge Y. If you don't fight these obsessions, they can kill you."

I nodded. "I'll look into it."

"You think I'm being weak for admitting I have a problem. Not all of us can tough it out like you and your bionic friend in the wheelchair. Some of us, the pressure starts to get to us. It squeezes our brains and makes our eyeballs pop. So excuse me for thinking you might need someone to drag you out of this dungeon for a while. It won't happen again." On her way out she kicked a box, which snowed Styrofoam pellets across my bay. They would be squeaking beneath my feet until Cesar swept them up. He would think I had made the mess, but I didn't have time to care. As soon as Susan left, I prepared a new probe and set the Drurys' blot to soak. The telephone rang.

"I've been missing you," Willie said. "Anything special going on? Or is it just another late night?"

Don't tell him, I thought. *Not yet.* "Nothing special," I said. "Just another late night."

"What've you been up to? How many of those little marker things you tried?"

"About nine," I said, trying to keep my heart from beating so loud.

"Nine's not so many. Have you tried chromosome thirteen?"

"No," I said. "I will."

"You do that," he said, although he sounded as if he didn't have much faith that I would. "How's everything else?"

Well, I thought, I'm pregnant. At least, I think I might be pregnant. I haven't had time to buy a test. I might be pregnant with a child who has a horrifying disease for which there is no cure and raising that child with a husband who might also get sick and die. "Fine," I said. "The usual."

"Jane, is something wrong?"

"Wrong? There's nothing wrong."

He tried another tactic. "I got a postcard from the folks. It showed this beautiful full moon over the Eiffel Tower. It's her *Honey moon*. Get it?"

"Sure," I said. "I get it." If I didn't tell anyone about the correlation, it might turn out to be real. If I didn't take the pregnancy test, I might not turn out to be pregnant.

"I wouldn't want you to hurt yourself laughing too hard."

I was startled by his anger. He had just caught me at a bad time, I said. I would call him in a few days. I might have something to tell him then.

"What?" he said. "What is it? Why can't you tell me now?"

"No," I said. "Not now." And I hung up before I could break my promise to myself and blurt out the news that I had found the probe.

At the end of that week, while my labmates were at the deli drinking beer, I developed the blot from the Drurys' DNA. I moved in slow motion, aware of the pull and release of each muscle, the pressure of the linoleum against my feet. I tried not to think my result might be wrong. But I knew it was right. I just knew. Even before I typed the data into the computer, I was able to guess the answer. The printer hummed, the daisy wheel shrieked into place. The odds that the gene for Valentine's chorea was linked to the marker on chromosome twenty were several thousand to one. I ran the data again, and when the answer came out the same as the first time, I pulled a stream of paper from the printer and danced around the cubicle. I thought of calling Maureen so we would go out and get drunk and celebrate.

But I never made that call. How could I explain—to myself, Maureen, or anyone who understood anything about genetics—that I had found the needle in the haystack on, what, my ninth try? Call it luck. Intuition. A miracle. Chance. I was plagued by the possibility this was all a big joke, like the rubber mouse in the Seal-a-Meal bag, or the coal Maureen had once smeared around the eyepiece of my microscope on April Fool's, or the fake bottles of reagents she had arranged on my shelf—"Elixir of Youth," "Cure for

Cancer," "Drink Me." But Maureen didn't have the power to make a marker seem linked to a gene if it wasn't. And she would never be that cruel. Nature wasn't like Willie, changing its mind about whether to bestow its favors or not. But I couldn't help but worry that Someone had this power, some mischievous god who was watching me and laughing, waiting to jump out and reveal his best trick.

16

The reporters, I was sure, would get everything wrong. That's why scientists submitted their results not to newspapers, but to journals. The editors sent the manuscript to a panel of experts for review. They accepted a paper only if its data and conclusions convinced the experts. I wished this same process could have been applied to other questions—for instance, whether you should marry a man whose love might bring you grief. But no one claims to be an expert on such matters, and I wouldn't trust anyone who did. Passion tends to be more persuasive than fact. The way in which you might represent your data to a scientist might not be the way you would represent that same data to yourself.

Vic made everyone in the lab swear not to reveal our findings. We couldn't be certain we were right until our paper was reviewed and accepted for publication, and the editors of *Cell* might retract their acceptance if the results were leaked to the press. Unfortunately, my father didn't know this. When I called to tell him we had found a marker for the gene, he reacted so strongly I forgot most of the things I intended to say. I should have driven out to Mule's Neck to see his face when he learned that all his work had paid off and the longest long shot had come in. But events cascaded too quickly. We needed to repeat my experiments and triple-check the results; it could ruin a career to announce a discovery your colleagues couldn't reproduce. We needed to write the paper and rush it off to *Cell* before some other lab scooped us. I thought of summoning my father to Boston to tell him the good news in person, but he wouldn't have agreed to come unless I told him why.

So I called him that night, the night I found the marker. I heard him chewing on his brisket. "What is it, doll? What's the matter?"

I was about to give him the gift he had always wanted, and even though that gift might save my sister's life, I couldn't bring myself to tell him, to become *the good one* forever, to move so far ahead in whatever race Laurel and I were running she could never catch up.

But of course I did tell him. "We found it, Dad. The marker. We can use it to develop a test for the gene."

The phone clattered and then went dead. Honey said she found him slumped against the counter, beating his forehead with the phone. She assumed one of their children must be sick. Or maybe it was Ted. She snatched away the phone. "Who is this!" she demanded. "Tell me who this is!"

I explained the good news. Then I listened to my father say, "I love you, Janie. I'm prouder than any father has any right to be. Maybe your mother's death wasn't for nothing." And in the midst of all this turmoil, I neglected to warn him that he mustn't release the news until my paper came out in *Cell.* He called the *New York Times,* the *Washington*

Post, the *Wall Street Journal,* and all three major TV stations. Luckily, the discovery was too important for *Cell* to allow it to slip by. The editors rushed our paper into print two weeks ahead of schedule. The press conference was set for December 16.

I had daydreamed for years about writing a paper that would earn the respect of the fifty or so biologists in my field. Those few families at risk for Valentine's would likely care as well. But the prospect of revealing my results to a crowd of reporters was as unsettling as the notion of getting married in Yankee Stadium. Even more disconcerting, Vic informed me that I would need to lead the press conference. He would be up there on the stage, but he planned to use his few minutes in the limelight to make a plea for the NIH to formulate guidelines for genetic testing and to impose a moratorium until those guidelines were in place.

I shouldn't have been surprised. But Vic hadn't said a word about his reservations since his speech in New York. When I had shown him the blots, he assumed the expression of a man who is trying to believe he really has seen an angel. "Jane," he said, and held the X-ray to the light, calling my name to make sure I had seen the visitor, too, and yes, it truly did have a halo and wings.

We sequestered ourselves in Vic's office to write the paper. He rarely went home, although his wife was in the last week of her pregnancy. We lived on food from the vending machines—potato chips and crackers were the only food I could tolerate anyway—and sandwiches Yosef brought us from the deli. I would doze on Vic's couch while he wrote a section of the paper, then he would grab a nap and I would write the next section. It didn't matter who wrote what. Our minds thought the same thoughts, produced the same words, although Vic's talent for understatement was nearly biblical. "It is likely that Valentine's chorea is but the first of many hereditary diseases for which a marker will be found," the first line read.

Finally, we were done. The Federal Express carrier scuffled in, slush on his boots, then scuffled out again with the envelope we gave him. I collapsed in Vic's arms. That was when he said he wouldn't be leading the press conference. "This isn't something new," he said. "I've always had opinions. But I kept them to myself. I thought I could be one person at home and another person in the lab. There's never been a problem with that. Nothing I couldn't reconcile." Amid the clutter on his desk stood a portrait of his wife and four sons, their faces as unremarkable as fingerprints. "Telling a parent that a fetus has a such-and-such chance of inheriting a disease and giving him or her no other choice but to abort that fetus . . . If that's where this has led us . . ."

I wasn't sure what I would do if I found out I was pregnant. But how could anyone oppose a test that would tell me if the fetus was carrying the gene? Anything that gave me more information was a blessing, I thought.

"Jane," Vic said, "I never would have gotten into this if it hadn't been for you. I let my concern for your welfare get the better of my judgment. To be frank, I hadn't thought this out. In my wildest dreams, I couldn't imagine you would be this successful." He patted my arm. "I hope you realize you've accomplished a wonderful thing. I didn't mean to steal your thunder."

"Sure," I said. Whatever thunder he meant, I didn't begrudge it. But whatever I had accomplished didn't seem wonderful. I felt as if I had committed some terrible crime and the punishment would soon come due.

The day of the press conference I spent nearly an hour staring stupidly into my closet, deciding if I should wear the suit I had bought for my medical school interviews twelve years earlier. I wasn't a salesman. My data were right. I didn't need to *sell* them. So what was I so scared of? Still, I put on the suit, and later, when the director of public relations at MIT led my father, Sumner, Vic, and me through the halls to the auditorium, I was glad I had worn it. If anything went wrong, I could go home and take off that suit and pretend that whatever had gone wrong had happened to someone else.

We took our places before the microphones. I felt as if I had been called upon to testify against some powerful wrongdoer, and anything I said would be turned against me. The reporters would try to stump me the way Mrs. Scipione had stumped me at the science fair. They would ask me a question that wasn't relevant and rob me of the prize that by all rights should have been mine.

My father welcomed the reporters, but he didn't understand the science well enough to answer their questions. Vic announced his intention to set up the NIH committee and said he would answer questions later, in the lobby. Then he sat down. This left Sumner to speak for all of us. I expected him to steal credit for the discovery. Instead, he was the most humble of spokesmen, bringing clarity and charm to the chaos, paying proper due to everyone; a collector, after all, doesn't earn credit by pretending he has painted his artwork himself. I never could have kept my answers so brief or caused my voice to rise and fall in just the right spots. I had none of the grace Sumner had perfected in his years of telling patients what was killing them without subjecting them to lectures on base pairs and proteins or the neural gaps in their brains.

The reporters seemed grateful. They raised their hands and waited, as deferential as the undergraduates who usually occupied their seats. Sumner drew diagrams with colored markers on a board. The reporters took notes. Then one reporter stood and said that she had a question for Dr. Weiss. She wore a rumpled brown dress. The dark circles beneath her eyes made her look sad.

"Dr. Weiss," she said, "isn't it true that you might carry the gene for Valentine's? Have you taken the test yet? If you haven't, do you ever intend to do so?"

I was too startled to say a word. Later, I would wonder why I hadn't refused to answer. But then, in that auditorium, I assumed the reporters set the rules. If they asked, I had to answer, the way I'd had to answer Mrs. Scipione's question. Besides, this reporter looked so exhausted I wanted to give her something that would allow her to go home and rest. I would take the test, wouldn't I? What choice did I have? How would it look if a scientist preferred ignorance to fact? But already I had begun to wonder if Willie wasn't right. As crippling as doubt was, to live without hope might be even more paralyzing.

The reporter asked again: "Have you taken the test?"

I tried to say no, but my tongue was too dry. "I haven't taken it yet," I said finally, pleased I had gotten that much out. But the woman kept pressing.

"Why haven't you?" she said. And I didn't know what to say. That I hadn't had the time? That I wanted to enjoy my triumph for at least a few weeks before learning, as I feared, that I had the gene? That I might be pregnant? That I wasn't yet sure whether the fetus could be tested? The equations had too many variables. My father, for one. How would he react if it turned out that one or both of his daughters carried the gene for Valentine's? He hadn't brought that up. Maybe, like me, he had been distracted. Or he was having second thoughts.

Another reporter raised his hand. "Could you tell us what you plan to do about those people who donated blood for your experiments? Specifically, the ones who tested positive for the gene. Have they been informed of this fact?"

Thankfully, this was a question I had considered. Writing our paper, Vic and I had been careful to disguise the donors' identities. The results of all the tests were kept locked in Vic's office. They wouldn't be released to a donor unless he or she consented to receive counseling from Miriam Burns or one of our staff psychologists. Leaning closer to my microphone, I detailed the measures we had taken to protect the donors' privacy. *You're doing fine,* I thought. *Just finish this question and they'll leave you alone.*

Then I stopped in midsentence. In my mind's eye, I saw Rita Nichols holding the blood she had drawn from me in New Jerusalem. What had happened to that sample? Had my own DNA been tested with the rest? I knew I looked absentminded, standing on the stage staring at a pedigree no one else saw, but I needed to figure out if there were enough samples from my family to determine if I had the gene. Several years earlier, when I had begun working on this project, I had driven to Schenectady to see my aunt Yvette and my three adult cousins. Although crazy Aunt Yvette held my family responsible for her husband's early death, my father had convinced her to give a sample of her blood. Maybe it was possible to determine which pattern the marker took in my family with the samples we already had. Did everyone know my result except me? Did Vic know? Did Maureen?

"Dr. Weiss!" The reporters' mouths moved, but they seemed to be speaking underwater. "Do you plan to get married?" "Do you plan to have children?" "What about your sister? Will she agree to have the test?" Reporters lived for this, a *scoop*, the way scientists lived for exciting results. What would happen if they knew that Dusty Land's son was also at risk for Valentine's and I might be carrying his child? Standing there, I realized that I had held a tube of Willie's blood. I had stood watching as he poured that blood out the window. If only I could have tested both samples, Willie's and mine. I wondered if he would let me draw another sample, if doing so meant I might carry our child to term. But of course he would tell me no. Either a person wanted a child or she didn't. A parent shouldn't have the right to test the fetus and choose.

I must have mumbled something. Or maybe I stood there dumb. All I remember is that Sumner raised his hand and thanked everyone for coming. I slipped out a side door.

My family was planning a celebration, but they would have to celebrate without me. Laurel wasn't the only one who could fail to show up at family events.

I spent from five until midnight wandering Harvard Square, sipping cups of cocoa in various cafés and watching the homeless kids in front of the T station, hands jammed in their pockets, bobbing like pigeons for warmth. I read the titles in bookstores, browsing aisles I usually didn't visit. Philosophy. Religion. Child Care. At one in the morning, I went back home, warmed yet another cup of cocoa, then I let it grow cold as I puzzled out what to do. The next day would be Saturday. I didn't need to go into the lab. Even so, the phone in my apartment probably wouldn't stop ringing. My father and Honey would come by. Maureen would call. And Vic. Willie would call, I knew. He had left message after message, which I hadn't returned. I would buy a pregnancy test. If the test turned out positive, and I was certain it would (as a sort of compensation for my unbelievable good luck in finding the probe, I was sure I'd had the unbelievably bad luck to get pregnant the only time I had had sex in three years), I would need to tell the father.

By dawn, I had grown restless. I couldn't keep putting off decisions that couldn't be put off. I walked to Central Square and bought the paper. The morning was overcast. Paul Minot was down from Maine, visiting Maureen, and I didn't want to interrupt them. Besides, I was afraid that Maureen would consider an abortion an affront to anyone whose parents might have judged their child too imperfect to live.

I loitered by the Dunkin' Donuts. The smell of coffee made me queasy, but the bland, cakey crullers seemed just what I needed to make my nausea subside. I bought four crullers and took the bag to a bench by city hall, where I studied that day's *Times*. In the lower-left-hand corner, just beneath a story about the latest cease-fire in Beirut, there was a head shot of Sumner, that sealish face and double chin. RESEARCHERS REPORT GENETIC TEST FOR RARE KILLER, the headline ran. "Scientists at the Massachusetts Institute of Technology have discovered the first genetic test for Valentine's chorea, a fatal disorder that slowly destroys the victim's mind and nervous system. . . ." Sumner described the "emotional relief" the test might bring people at risk for "this scourge." He was cut off by a notice that the article was continued inside, as if my life were a serial whose next installment was delayed to keep the audience coming back.

On the jump page, I found a brief but surprisingly accurate description of the method I had used to locate the marker. A diagram detailed each step, although Willie would have said such illustrations made sense only to those who already knew what they meant. Beneath the photo was a sidebar. The reporter (I guessed the byline belonged to the woman in the brown dress) had done her research thoroughly. "Though apparently healthy, Weiss, 33, lives with the knowledge that she might carry the silent gene for this killer." Dr. Weiss, she went on, was "obviously reluctant" to submit to the test or to divulge her result. The reporter mentioned Willie, although she didn't link him to me and said only that his father, "a popular performer," had died of Valentine's chorea in 1969, which was why the condition was sometimes referred to as "Dusty Land disease," which sounded like something a person might contract by living in a desert. Willie, whom the reporter had reached in New Hampshire, was quoted as saying, "I'm happy for all the folks who want to know if they have it. Me, I think a test that tells you when and how you're going to die is just about the last thing anyone needs."

Thanks a lot, I thought. *Couldn't he have kept his reservations private?* "Willie Land," I kept reading, trying to convince myself this "Willie Land" in the paper was the father of my child.

There was a photo of Dusty lying shriveled in his bed, and another of me, leaning against a wall in Kresge Auditorium, blank eyed, detached. The profile ended with a quote from my father—harmless, thank God—about the need to redouble our fundraising efforts and develop not only a test for Valentine's, but also a cure.

The other newspapers carried similar quotes. The *Post,* in its lead editorial, endorsed Vic's committee. "Human beings," it said, "are the only creatures who seem to be aware they will die. Until now, we have been spared knowing the details. How will seemingly healthy young people react to learning that an agonizing death lies in wait when they reach middle age? Surely this is too important an issue to be left to scientists." The *Journal* debated the ethics of insurance companies refusing coverage to those who tested positive for the gene. The *Globe* ran a picture that my father must have given them—a snapshot of my mother, Laurel, and me taken in the fifties. All three of us wore identical dresses with green leaves, red cherries, and white collars. Laurel and I wore our hair parted down the middle, braided, with bows. Laurel's eyes were more slanted than mine, and my nose was a little longer, but I was surprised by how much we both resembled our mother.

I studied those photos. But it wasn't news of the past I needed. It was news of my future. That's why people read newspapers, I thought. For the horoscopes and the forecasts, the predictions of war and whether the market will go up or down. Everyone pretends to care what happened the day before to strangers, but all we really want to find are clues to our own future.

A man with matted hair settled on my bench. I had seen him often in Central Square, walking with a strange hop-skip-hop-jump to avoid stepping on the cracks, touching every second telephone pole. I held out the crullers.

"Are they poison?" he asked.

No, I said. I had just bought more than I could eat.

"You made an error," he said. He took a cruller, set it on his knees, clapped twice, took a bite, set it down, clapped two more times, took another bite, clapped.

I walked to the drugstore and bought a pregnancy kit. I wanted to take the test right then, but I would need to wait until the next morning, when my urine was fresh. In the meantime, I would go home and grab a glass of milk to wash down the crullers. I would put on a warmer jacket, then bike to the lab and find out if my blood had been tested. If it hadn't, I would start running the gels myself. I was a scientist. I couldn't allow my fear to prevent me from doing what I needed to do. I would get in touch with Laurel and beg her to give me a sample of her blood. When the data were in—Laurel's blot, my own, our cousins', and our aunt's—I would try to figure out which pattern the marker for Valentine's took in our family, and, after that, whether I had the gene. And whether Laurel had it.

I climbed the stairs to my apartment, patting my trousers for the key. I must have left without locking the door, I thought. I went in and found my sister standing before a window. On the floor beside her feet lay a rubber wet suit.

She lifted the newspapers from my arms and dropped them by the trash. "You should never, never read your own reviews. They'll only throw you off. It's like trying to drive while you're looking in the rearview mirror." She smiled the smile that meant she knew how much I loved her. "My brilliant sister, Jane." Lifting the wet suit, she looked like Peter Pan bringing Wendy his shadow. "I know today isn't ideal sailing weather, but this will keep you warm."

I didn't know what to say. Wet suit or not, the last thing I wanted was to spend this miserable afternoon bobbing up and down on the Charles River. "Are people even allowed to go sailing when it's this cold?"

"You think everything is illegal. There's no law against going sailing in December."

"What about you? You don't have a wet suit."

"I haven't capsized a boat in years." Laurel folded the limbs of the suit and tucked the amputated torso in her leather backpack. "You wanted to go sailing so badly . . . that's why I took off a day from rehearsals and drove all the way down from Vermont."

The invitation seemed more like a punishment than a treat, but I couldn't bring myself to turn it down. I asked if I was supposed to change into the wet suit, and if so, what I was meant to wear underneath.

Laurel smiled, exposing the bridge of skin to her gum. "You remember that guy Chuck I went out with? He lent me a key to the Harvard boathouse and forgot to ask for it back. You can put the wet suit on there. You'll want to bring a slicker and rubber boat-shoes."

I owned neither of these items, so I pulled on a nylon windbreaker and a blue woolen cap from Weiss's. We walked down to the street, where Cruz's motorbike was parked. Laurel handed me a helmet, although she didn't have one herself.

"This was the only way I could get down here," she apologized. "It's okay, Cruz taught me how to ride."

I shrugged and climbed on. I didn't care about anything but wrapping my arms around my sister and burying my face in her hair. The boathouse wasn't far. Few cars were on the streets. But I had to use all my self-control not to drag my heels to slow her down.

We parked beside the boathouse. Laurel let us in. The room smelled of damp wood; the river sloshed beneath the floor. Laurel handed me the wet suit. Maybe we could just go for a walk, I suggested. I knew a nice café where we could stop for hot cocoa.

"You keep after me and after me to take you sailing. Then you say no, you don't want to go sailing, you want to drink hot chocolate."

"I didn't mean for you to take me sailing in December! I just wanted to spend time with you. To talk. We do have a lot to talk about."

Laurel glanced around the boathouse. "I could teach you how to row. That would keep you warm. A scull is even less likely than a sailboat to capsize, and you can right it yourself."

There was no point in arguing. It was like the time we were kids and she wrote a play and refused to speak to me until I gave in and agreed to act the role she had assigned. "All right," I said. "I've always thought rowers looked, I don't know, as if they were doing something human beings weren't supposed to be able to do."

"They can. Come on, I'll show you."

I struggled into the wet suit—it was warm but constrictive, like being swallowed by a snake—and helped Laurel slide the scull from its rack. Balancing it above our heads, we maneuvered it to the dock. She fitted it with oars and showed me how to climb in. At first, it was awkward. But I sat behind Laurel and did whatever my sister did, rolling the oars beneath my palms, pushing out, then pulling up, and in no time we were gliding so fast I felt afraid; skimming that close to the surface in such a frail shell was like soaring through the clouds on a paper airplane.

"You're doing great!" Laurel called back to me. "You're a natural!" She began to row faster, as if she were trying to get away from me. Inside the wet suit I was sweating. *Stroke, stroke, stroke, stroke.* We rowed beneath the heavy gray stones of the bridge, which magnified the oars' slap on the water. We would be stopped by the dam eventually. We couldn't keep rowing out to sea.

I opened my mouth to tell Laurel to stop. The wind caught my throat, and I leaned overboard and gagged. The doughnuts came up. I kept retching bile, as if I might vomit out my unborn child.

Laurel looked over her shoulder. "Jane? Are you okay? What's the matter? Jane!"

It scared me that anyone, especially my sister, would regard me with such concern. I swallowed hard and wiped my mouth. "I'm not sick," I said. "I'm pregnant."

Laurel's oars windmilled against the water. The scull spun sideways and rocked. I gripped the sides of the boat. Laurel fumbled with the oars, laying them inside the scull. "You poor thing." She patted my ankle. "How many weeks has it been?"

The river smelled of sewage. "Eleven," I said.

"What are you waiting for? You didn't do it on purpose, did you?"

I asked if she was kidding.

"How do I know? Maybe you found out that you don't have the gene."

"Or maybe I don't plan everything. Maybe I'm not quite as cold-blooded as you've always thought. Maybe I was tired. Maybe the moon was out. Maybe there was no moon. Maybe I was lonely. Maybe I wanted to be in love with someone. Maybe I *was* in love with someone." I started crying harder, the truth coming to me as I said it. "Maybe I really, really wanted to have a kid, and I knew I couldn't bring myself to have one on purpose. Maybe I wanted to trick myself into needing to marry Willie. Maybe I made love to a man without protection because I got tired of thinking so much. Of protecting myself so much. Of protecting all of us so much."

Laurel stared at the shore. "But if he's at risk, and you're at risk . . . Jane, you know I'm no good with statistics. But it's higher, isn't it? The chance? Any baby you might have with Willie would be more likely to get it?"

She sounded jealous, as if I had attempted the most difficult dive in the Olympic event she had been practicing all these years.

"Does Willie know?" she asked. "No, I'll bet you haven't told anyone. But listen, don't try to go through this alone. It's awful. I don't only mean how much an abortion hurts. And believe me, it does hurt. I'm talking about how terrible you feel afterward." She dipped her hand in the river and spread cold water on my forehead, then tapped the remaining drops on my neck, like perfume. "You swear you'll never let it happen again. And the second time . . . The second time, I almost didn't go through with it. I was about to walk out. Then I realized that my kid wouldn't have anyone but me to take care of it. I'm not sure I would be a decent mother even if I weren't at risk. I can't imagine myself staying in one place and being responsible for someone else all the time."

The clouds were suffocatingly low, the same slate gray as the river. I imagined Laurel on her back, knees up, gripping a stranger's hand.

"I'll go with you," she said. "All you have to do is to let me know when."

She was saying this to prove she was less judgmental than I was. Or she found it easier to be with me now that she knew I wasn't perfect. I told her I hadn't decided what to do. Besides, I didn't know her number in Vermont. I didn't even know if she had a phone.

"Let's get you home," she said. "We'll take it as slowly as you need to. If you feel sick again, we'll rest."

It took us twice as long to row back as it had taken us to come. I crawled out of the scull and lay on the swaying dock. I had to close my eyes so I wouldn't see the clouds rushing past.

"I'm sorry," Laurel said. "I can't lift the boat myself."

Somehow I got to my feet. We swung the scull to our shoulders and slid it in its berth. Laurel handed me her jacket. The leather smelled of balsam. "We need to get you home so you can take a hot shower. Then I'll have to start back. There are people I need to see about scenery and costumes. It gets dark so early these days, I would rather drive while it's light."

I clenched my jaw shut to keep my teeth from chattering. "Wait," I said. "I have a favor to ask you."

Laurel climbed on the bike. "It can wait until we get you in a hot bath."

"No," I said. "I have to know what to do."

She looked puzzled. "But it isn't my decision. I can't tell you whether to have a baby." She dropped her hands from the handlebars. "I see. You mean, you want to know if you have it. And you need my blood to find out." Her eyes narrowed. "This isn't a trick, is it? So you can find out if *I* have it?"

I was too tired to launch into an elaborate analogy about colored handkerchiefs. Laurel and I would never speak the same language. Maybe few sisters did. "You'll just have to trust me," I said.

Her foot tapped the kickstand. "I knew you would want something in return."

The accusation felt oddly true. Why else would it feel so satisfying to catch my sister at last, to find the ammunition to force her to *give*? "I don't have to tell you the result. I could use your blood to figure out if I have the marker. But I don't need to tell you if you have it." This was ridiculous, I knew. If Laurel's blood tested positive, how could I hide my grief? "You can refuse. I won't hold it against you."

"Sure you won't." Laurel laughed. "I've always been the selfish one. You and Dad knock yourselves out finding a cure for this thing. What do I do? I dance. I run off to Europe. I let you give up a year of your life looking after Mom." She shook her head. "I said you can have my blood. Do whatever you need to. Just don't tell me anything until after the concert. Not my result. Not yours. I don't even want to see you before then."

I told her she could take more time to think about her decision.

"I know what I owe you." She studied my face. "Your complexion looks green. You're shivering."

I kept thinking she would change her mind. Whatever my sister said now, she would find an excuse to back out later. "There's a shower at the lab," I said. "I'll be fine once I get out of this stupid wet suit."

"You're sure?"

I nodded.

We rode the motorcycle to the lab and took the elevator up. "I shouldn't have rushed you," I said. "There's too much to think about."

Laurel pursed her lips. "Jane, ever since I was a little girl I've known I would die young. If this is bad news, it's just what I expected. Nothing much will change, except I won't take Cruz down with me. And if it's good news, I guess I'll need to change the way I think about my life."

From outside, near the loading dock, came the insistent *beep beep beep* of a truck backing up. I imagined the truck running someone over. It was possible, after all, to hear danger approach and not be able to avoid it. "I shouldn't pressure you into doing this," I said.

"I told you I would help."

I wanted time to think and calm my nerves. "Just wait here. I have to go clean up." I left Laurel at my bench and went to take a shower in the stall beside the mouse room. Beneath the soothing spray I finally stopped shaking. I rinsed out my mouth and spat the sour taste down the drain, put on a pair of sweatpants and a sweatshirt that said MIT BEAVERS.

When I returned to the lab, I was relieved and disappointed to see Laurel wasn't there. I could always drive up to Vermont and draw the blood. Meanwhile, neither of us would have done anything that couldn't be undone.

Then she came back in. I asked what she had been looking for. "A ladies' room," she said. "I got lost in all those corridors." I was about to ask whether she was sure she knew what she was doing when Susan Bate waltzed in. I braced for a tirade. Susan had been furious to learn she wasn't an author on the paper; after much deliberation, Vic had decided her contribution merited only an acknowledgment.

"Why, Dr. Jane Weiss. A celebrity. Here, in our very own lab. It's been quite a little gold mine for you, hasn't it. You'll get your own lab now for sure. Are you here to say good-bye to all the little people you stepped on on the way up?"

I surprised myself by grabbing her arm and digging in my fingers. "I don't know what's bothering you," I said. "But

I've never done anything to hurt you. If you can't think of your own experiments, you should find something else to do."

"Take your hands off me. You're paranoid. You must be getting it already." She bared her small teeth. "I already told Vic I'm leaving. Who needs a life like this, spending all your time studying things you can't see with people you can't trust." She pulled away. "I just came in to get a leotard. I'm not spending another minute in this loony bin." She gave me the finger and left.

"Whew." Laurel whistled. "They say dancers are temperamental."

"She is a dancer. Sort of."

"Isn't that like being 'sort of' a scientist?"

"I don't know," I said. "She takes some kind of dance therapy. For incest survivors. It's supposed to help them to like their bodies."

Laurel turned and looked out the window. Her hips seemed heavier, I thought. We both couldn't be pregnant, could we? No, she was only getting older. Was it possible that my baby sister had just turned thirty? It seemed cruel to prolong her suspense, but I couldn't move. Too many things were happening too quickly.

"If you can handle knowing the truth, I can, too," she said.

The truck beeped again. "I'm not sure I *can* handle it," I told her.

When Laurel smiled she looked fifteen. "Of course you can. Let's just do this. However it turns out, I won't hold anything against you. I need to know. For my own sake."

I nodded. She was right. I found the supplies and pulled on some latex gloves. It was as if I had been told to sit behind the wheel of some destructive machine—a bulldozer, or a tank—and I wanted to protest that just because I had designed the machine, I shouldn't necessarily be allowed to drive it.

"Just remember," Laurel said. "I don't want you to tell me anything about either of us until after the concert."

I tied the tourniquet around her arm, feeling as if I ought to ask permission of someone. But there was no one I could ask.

"Jane. I can't stand here like this forever."

The crook of Laurel's arm was as soft and white as a child's. I swabbed the spot and cocked the needle. How could I explain that I'd had the premonition of hurting her, of causing her pain beyond the needle's prick? She turned to face the calendar from BioGenetics. The page still said September. Maybe none of this had happened. I hadn't yet slept with Willie. I hadn't yet found the probe.

Laurel tensed, the sinew rising from her arm. I slipped in the needle, then drew the plunger back. As the syringe filled with blood it came to me that I had made a mistake, an error of reasoning so unforgivable I ought to relinquish any claim to thinking like a scientist. My certainty that Laurel didn't have the gene was nothing but a hunch, a wishful thought, a suspicion based on little but my long-held belief that I had inherited the gene and my sister hadn't.

17

Laurel didn't stay long enough to watch me run her test. I suppose I understood, although if our positions had been reversed, I would have watched every step.

"You're right," I said. "There's no point in waiting. The results won't be ready for another six or seven days."

She took back her leather jacket, hugged me, and went out, then returned a moment later. "I know I said I didn't want to see you until after the concert, but if you need me to go with you to the clinic . . ." She jotted her telephone number on a pad of graph paper, then added "Laurel" beneath, the L carefully looped, as if I otherwise might have forgotten whose number it was.

It was the first time my sister had given me a gift that wasn't easy to give. "Thanks," I said, still holding the tube of blood. "Have a safe trip." I watched from the window until the toy-size motorcycle crossed the bridge. I pressed the tube against my cheek, as warm as a human mouth would have been. *Don't think,* I thought. *Just pretend it belongs to someone else.* I spun the sample in a centrifuge, then siphoned off the serum and lysed the remaining layer of cells to release Laurel's DNA. I felt like a child mixing food coloring, ink, and her mother's perfume to brew a magic potion, half-believing it might work, all the while knowing she was pretending to powers she did not have.

I set the tube rocking in a water bath. The next morning, I would come in and dip a glass wand in the tube until it touched the tiny clump of *stuff* at the bottom. If all went well, the sticky strands of DNA, like cellophane noodles, would cling to the tip of the wand and unfurl. I would repeat this procedure until Laurel's DNA was pure. Then I would fracture it with enzyme, run the gel, and hybridize the blot with the probe from chromosome twenty. I would carry out this protocol with DNA from my cousins, my aunt, my father, and myself. Finally, I would spread all seven films across the conference-room table and break the code that revealed which members of my family carried the gene. *Please,* I bargained with a God I didn't believe in. *Do anything you want to with my blot. Just don't let Laurel have it.*

Then it was my turn. I went to Vic's office, lifted the ceramic turtle one of his sons had made in art class, and found the key to his desk. In the drawer lay the notebook in which Yosef had recorded the donors' names. I ran my finger down the list: Yoder, Young, Wicks. When I reached the two entries for Weiss, every hair on my body stood up.

Beside my father's name, a check indicated his blood had been immortalized and spun down. The column beside "Weiss, Jane Ellen" was blank. Trying not to think what this omission meant, I memorized the code beside my name and hurried down the hall, repeating the numbers.

I walked inside the cold room and found the Styrofoam rack that ought to have contained my blood. But the slot by my code was empty. I checked the other racks to see if my sample had been misplaced. Maybe someone had taken it. Susan. Or that reporter. No, I thought. The woman in the brown dress might have been smart, but she couldn't hope to run the right gels and interpret the blots. Besides, not even the most diligent reporter would care enough about my fate to risk such theft.

I went back to Vic's office and jotted the codes for my father's DNA, my cousins', and my aunt's. Those tubes were gone, too. I dialed Yosef's number, praying he would be there. When he picked up the phone, I heard a party in the background. He yelled something in Russian. "Yeah." His voice was muffled. "Solzhenitsyn fan club."

I told him who it was. I didn't mean to bother him at home. I just had a quick question.

He yelled again, "Slava, get off her!" Then, his voice brighter: "Sweetheart, is the happiest day of life, seeing your picture in the paper this morning."

He meant the happiest day of *his* life. My success made him happy.

"You want to come to my party? You're the only one I know who has something to drink a toast to."

"Not right now," I said. "I just wanted to find out about that blood Rita took from me that day. Did it ever get tested?"

He rasped a long drag on his cigarette. "I wonder when you are going to remember that." He slowly exhaled. "Don't worry, you've got nothing to be concerned about."

"What do you mean? It tested negative?" I shook the receiver, as if I could shake the answer out of him.

"I wish that is what I meant."

"Yosef! It tested positive?"

"Jane, calm down. It hasn't tested anything. I got to your name in that book, and I thought, *Hooboy, Jane doesn't remember about this.* It is only by luck that I get this blood first. Who knows what that Susan would have done with such information. I don't put it above that woman to play blackmail. I think, *Nobody but Jane is going to do anything with this blood.*"

But the DNA was missing, I said. And the rest of my family's blood wasn't where it was supposed to be.

"Not missing," he said. "Just hidden. Say the word and I tell you where."

Again my eyes brimmed. "You did that for me?"

"Sweetheart," he said, "this is what friends do. They keep out eyes for each other." A woman called something in Russian, and Yosef yelled something back. "You sure you want to know this?"

Yes, I said, I did. He told me where he had hidden it.

"Yosef?" I said. "Don't tell anyone, okay? I won't know my results for another few days, and I don't want everyone looking at me funny in the meantime." The idea of Yosef himself staring at me expectantly was more than I could bear. How could I have thought of subjecting Laurel to that?

"My lips are sealed," he said. "But if you want me to be there when you look at your blot, I will be there. I will do anything you want me to do."

"Thanks. Really." I wiped my eyes with a tissue from Vic's desk.

"It is nothing," Yosef said, although the quaver in his voice betrayed that it was. "Sure you won't come to my party?"

No, I told him. But if there was anything I could do to make this up to him—

"Here's what you can do. You can get my family out of Russia. Find us all a nice big apartment in Boston. Find me a job that makes, oh, sixty grand a year so I can support everyone in the style to which they would like to become accustom."

I stifled my impatience to run the next test. I told Yosef that I was sure he would find a good job. Vic had promised he would help.

"Nice try, but I know real world. What do I have except fifth name on a paper someone else write? Three years as postdoc, and all I got is one paper, and it's not even my own work."

"You're a good scientist," I said. "You just need more time. You need a lucky break, like I had. Otherwise I would still be trying all those probes." The idea that I could have spent the next ten years running all those gels made me slump in Vic's chair. Why had I been granted such supernatural good luck? Because some Omnipotent Being knew my life depended on my experiments in ways Yosef's didn't? No. It was only chance. And the same blind chance that had dealt me such a lucky hand with this gene might deal me an extraordinarily unlucky hand some other time. If it hadn't already. If I hadn't gotten pregnant from one indiscretion. If the fetus Willie and I conceived wasn't carrying the gene for Valentine's.

"Can't be a postdoc forever," Yosef said. "Can't support a mother and father and two sisters on twelve thousand dollars a year." Voices in the background argued in Russian. But Yosef kept talking to me, or maybe to himself, in a blurry voice. "You know what I wish? You laugh, but I wish I could be science teacher. Teach high school biology. Or what you call it here, junior high. Teach biology so the kids don't think it's a boring thing. But you tell me, who in America is going to hire a Russkie to teach science? They think I will teach kids the wrong science so America lose the *Sputnik*. They don't like a teacher who doesn't speak English so good. You think only you and Maureen got these handicap things? Being born in Russia, that's a handicap, too."

How could he compare being born in Russia with living in a wheelchair? "I know it's been hard for you," I said. "But it isn't really the same."

"In Ukraine where I was born, is great handicap to be a Jew. Can't go to university. Can't get a good job. I leave my mother, father, sisters—good sisters, best sisters a man can have. I leave everything, I come to America, and what do I find? Is handicap to be a Russkie. Not so bad if you are a very, very smart Russkie. But a so-so smart Russkie?"

He wasn't giving himself enough credit, I said. He was smarter than I was. It was only that I had been—

"Lucky. I know. But how long can I sit around waiting for some good luck? My sisters stay there much longer, they marry Russkie guys who won't treat them right. They'll get bad veins in their legs, bad teeth, bad everything. Maybe the government will give the girls a visa. But my father, he works at a power plant they got there in Ukraine. *Nuclear* power plant. My father is only minor engineer, more like fancy janitor, but they say he knows secrets. He keeps telling me, 'Yosef, we don't get out, something very bad happens, I feel it in my bone,' and I think, Yeah, and if you do get out, you're going to find out your son isn't a real doctor, doesn't have a big American house you can live in. Doesn't have a small American house. Doesn't have *any* house to live in." A woman's voice moaned in the background. "Okay, okay, I stop crying in beer. You remember, if you need me, I be there in a snap." He crooned a few parodic bars of "You've Got a Friend" and hung up.

I walked back to the cold room, and there, in a box marked YOSEF HOROWITZ, KEEP OUT, I found the Eppendorf tube with my code on the label. I pressed my forehead to the shelf. Yosef had already extracted the DNA from my blood, so I was two steps ahead, which meant that my results would be ready before my sister's.

I worked hour after hour, setting up the gels. By the time I left the lab, it was five on Sunday morning. The temperature had fallen, but if I walked quickly enough I could almost keep warm. Down Main Street and up Massachusetts Avenue, past Central Square toward Harvard. I wondered what it would be like to learn that the illness I had feared for most of my life did in fact lie in wait. I was surprised by how calm this made me. I shouldn't be out walking at this hour, but my fate seemed contained completely in that vial in the lab. Nothing else had the power to hurt me. Down Brattle Street and past the Mount Auburn Cemetery. What unsettled me was the possibility that I didn't have the gene. Something essential would be taken away. I would, at thirty-three, become someone else entirely.

I walked faster, as if my destination lay farther than I had thought. I might live to be ninety. All that extra life to fill up! There would be no reason not to marry. I could conceive another child, this time with a man who wasn't at risk for Valentine's.

But the child in your womb is the child you have been given.

By whom? I thought. In what way was this unborn child "mine"? I saw those chicks in their shells, their hearts beating, their black eyes staring. Who knew when a human life might start? Not, as Mrs. Scipione seemed to think, at the moment it was conceived. Still, I couldn't help but see a fully formed infant inside my womb. If I tested negative for the marker, the fetus would have only a one-in-four chance of inheriting the gene. My result would be ready in five days. In the meantime, I would go home and pee in the little cup. Did it count as "first urine" if I had been working all night? I hated all these tests. If only I could peer up my own vagina and see if there was an embryo in my uterus. If only Valentine's disease had an unmistakable sign—a rash, say, or a lump—rather than hazy "symptoms" like clumsiness or forgetfulness or obsessing about having sex with a man you loved.

I went home and ate some crackers. I was crouching above the toilet, peeing in the cup, when the telephone rang. Laurel, I thought. She might have panicked about the test and needed my reassurance. A memory flashed through my mind of our mother tricking Laurel into going to the doctor for a shot, the nurse sticking Laurel in the arm, Laurel screaming and screaming until she hyperventilated and passed out, as if to demonstrate what happened when you tricked people into doing things that supposedly were for their own good.

I put the cup beside the sink and ran to catch the phone.

"Jane. It's me. Willie. I was just meditating, and all of a sudden it came together. What a dope. I admit it, I've been mad. A guy asks you to forgive him. He calls you and calls you. He wants to congratulate you. For Pete's sake, he's seen your picture in every newspaper in the country. And you can't even pay him the courtesy of calling him back."

I nearly hung up to avoid admitting how much I must have hurt him.

"So, I'm sitting here stewing about it, and wham, out of nowhere, I think: You made love to the woman. The last time you saw her, she was eating like a horse. She won't return your calls. You slept with her, maybe you got her pregnant, and then you said, 'Hey, sorry, it was all a big mistake.' She doesn't want to have anything to do with you. She thinks you've got this killer disease, the kid will have it, she knows you'd be dead set against her getting rid of it."

I loved his voice. I loved *him*. The only way I could bring myself to abort our child was to never see or hear from him again.

"You're not saying anything," he said. "So, am I right? Are you pregnant?"

I nodded yes but couldn't speak.

"You *were* pregnant, but you're not anymore? I won't lecture you. This was my fault. I don't know what I was thinking. It was a power trip, I guess. I was going to get you to make love to me instead of figuring out all those statistics. Talk about statistics! We sleep together once and . . . Never mind. Maybe I thought . . . I don't know what I thought. Only, Jane? You have to tell me now. You can't leave me hanging like this."

"Willie." I meant to say more, but for the fourth time that day I started crying.

"It's okay, Jane. Whatever it is, it's okay. Whatever you decide, I'll see you through it. If you want to have the baby, we'll take care of it. Or I'll raise it myself. If you want to have an abortion, that's not what I would choose, but I'll go there with you. Or maybe you had it done already? You're sitting there feeling miserable, and there's no one you can tell? Whatever it is, I'll be there in two hours."

"I want," I said. "I want . . ."

"Whatever it is, Jane."

"I want you to take the test."

"Whew." The same explosion of breath I had heard from Achiro, like someone being punched in the gut. "Got me there. Suckered me into that one. Should have seen it coming. You've been planning that one a long time."

The truth was, I hadn't planned it at all, any more than I had planned to take advantage of my sister's sympathy. "Will you take the test?"

"I can't. Jane. It would go against everything I believe. Look, I promised you, no lectures. It's okay for you—you want to know. But I don't. How could I kill something just because it has my same genes? That would be like saying I wish they'd killed me. I said I would take care of it. And I don't just mean now."

"What if you're not there? What if neither of us is there to take care of this child? And who's going to take care of *us*?"

"Whoa," he said. "You've already got both of us dead and buried. You've just got to trust that somebody is going to be there to take care of whoever needs taking care of."

"Why? Why do I have to trust that?"

"Because that's what faith is. That's the way human beings are. They take care of each other."

"I can't have a baby knowing that it's going to get sick."

"So you still are pregnant? Jane? What you just said, you're still pregnant?"

I took a breath. "Yes, I'm still pregnant." I knew without seeing him that he had closed his eyes and raised his fist.

"Okay," he said. "Yes. I'd like to come down and talk to you." He was trying not to spook me, like a police officer coaxing a distraught woman from a ledge.

I wanted him to be with me right now. But the decision about the baby needed to be mine. What if he promised he would marry me and raise the child, then changed his mind? I didn't want to see him until I knew my results. It took all my self-control to tell him, "Next weekend. You can come down Saturday, for Laurel's concert. We can talk about it then."

"Won't that be too late?"

"Please."

"But if you need me in the meantime—"

I need you now. Just come. "I'll call you," I said.

"Right," he said. "Jane? What I told you on the island, I still mean it."

I thought of that cup in the bathroom. What if I followed the instructions, mixed all the chemicals, and the little ring that meant you were pregnant didn't appear? "You're lying. You were mad as hell at me for not calling. You didn't love me. You wanted to wring my neck."

"I loved you *and* I wanted to wring your neck." He must have been nervous—his laugh came out that bray. "I meant to ask, what's up with little Mickey?"

"Mickey? The homozygote?"

"Yeah, how's our little homozygote? How's the bugger doing?"

"Well." I drew it out. "I think he's expecting, too."

18

The first thing that Monday morning, I called the clinic in Brookline and arranged an abortion for the following week. I wasn't sure what I would do, but I wanted the appointment, just in case. Then I biked to the lab, hoping Vic would be in Washington. But of course he was there. He wore a suit—not the old one, whose sleeves were too short, but a new gray tweed tailored with a much more substantial person in mind. A new garment bag was hanging from his door. He stood beside his desk, sliding manila folders into an attaché case. I went about my business as unobtrusively as possible, but someone came up behind me—I heard the squeak of new shoes.

"How are you holding up?" Vic asked. Vivian Gold, the lab's technician, scurried in and out with boxes of supplies. I could tell she was trying to overhear our conversation. "That was one rough press conference. I've never known questions to get so personal. I should have guessed. I should have found some way to save you."

I would get over it, I said. I would be more prepared the next time.

"Good," he said. "I'm glad to hear that." He tightened his tie until the knot kissed his Adam's apple. "I have to admit, I was wondering what you would do about the test." He cleared his throat so many times I worried that the tie might be choking him. "You still haven't . . . have you?" He flapped one hand to wave away his question. "You don't have to tell me. But I hope you don't mind if I suggest someone you might talk to." He handed me a card. Helen Bausch-Tannenbaum, M.D., Ph.D. "She's the psychologist who's agreed to serve on our committee. She's on the staff at MacLean. Harvard Medical faculty, top drawer. If you want to talk to her, just say the word. I doubt she would even charge you. We're trying to get a sense of how to go about counseling people in your position."

My position, I thought. Even if I took the trouble to explain *my position* to this Helen Bausch-Tannenbaum, what would she advise that I hadn't yet considered? I told Vic I didn't want to talk to anyone right then, I just needed time to think.

"Of course," he said. "I just didn't want you to feel I was leaving you high and dry. I'll be spending Mondays and Tuesdays in Washington, and the rest of the week up here. I'll do everything in my power to find places for anyone who's not happy with my switching gears this way. Not that you'll have any trouble. Your only problem will be to make the best choice. My advice is, listen to all the offers, then go where you think you'll be able to do the best science."

Already I had been approached by the directors of several labs. The prospect that I might be flown out to the Salk or find myself discussing my requirements for lab space with the director of the Rockefeller Institute, or even here, at MIT, left me short of breath. Although I couldn't help thinking that if I learned I had the gene, I might not want to spend the last years of my life cooped up in a lab, even if it were the Salk.

"At least I don't have to worry about finding someone who's willing to take in Susan," Vic said. "It's best for her, I think." He lowered his voice, although Susan hadn't come in. "Her personality might be an advantage, as a lawyer. With her background in genetics—mark my words, DNA testing for paternity and rape will be the coming thing— she might make quite a career." Vic glanced around the lab. "Where's Yosef? Where's Lew?"

I hadn't seen Lew in days. And it seemed like tattling to reveal that Yosef probably was home with a hangover. I tried changing the subject. "Maureen should be getting a million offers, too, shouldn't she."

"She hasn't told you?"

"Hasn't told me what?"

He lifted his hands. "She got shafted. It's heartbreaking. We got the news Friday. A paper arrived at *Nature* with basically the same results, about the parasites."

"But who—"

"Some Peruvians at the university down there. They claim they came up with the result independently. But that's a lot of . . . It's just not very likely. The paper looks like something someone threw together in one afternoon. Maybe someone at the public health department leaked

Maureen's idea. Maybe they wanted it to be a Peruvian scientist who gets the credit."

"What's she going to do?" The shrillness of my voice set a rack of beakers chattering on their shelf.

"What can she do? It's not as though we have proof of any wrongdoing. I went far enough, telling Matthew Quinburn I thought there had been foul play. He said, 'Oh, tut, tut, that's not a very sporting way to respond to a competitor.'"

It couldn't have happened, could it? Those two trips to Peru, all those hours in the lab, that brilliant intuition . . . "I'll go over there right now," I told Vic.

He seemed relieved. If there was anything he could do to help Maureen feel better, I should let him know. "And, Jane?" he said. "Remember, if you ever want to talk to someone, to Dr. Tannenbaum . . ."

"Doctor who?"

"Dr. Tannenbaum. The psychologist."

"Oh, right. I have her card."

He crossed his arms. "I seem to have started a number of things without thinking how they might turn out. If I've caused you any harm—"

"Vic," I said, "no matter what happens, I won't blame you." I meant what I said. Then why did I assume that if Laurel tested positive, she would blame me?

"Is there anything else wrong? You seem, well, I can't quite put my finger on it." He lowered his gaze to my waist.

"I'd better go," I said. "I'm worried about Maureen."

He rummaged through his pockets as if he had left his talent for giving comfort in that other suit back home. "I'll

see you later in the week. There's a number on my desk . . .
it's where I'll be in Washington, in case anyone needs me."
But he sounded as if he guessed that no one would.

Maureen lived in a dorm for MIT students a decade
younger than she was, but the apartment lay within wheelchair distance of the lab and was built to be accessible. I
took the elevator to the seventeenth floor and walked down
a cinder-block hall carpeted with what appeared to be As-
troturf. When I knocked, no one answered. Maureen had
given me a key for emergencies. I knocked again and then
went in.

The air inside was rank. Scattered around the living
room were cardboard plates, white cartons oozing oily
sauce, chewed samosas, and wads of rice. Maureen's collection of shoes lay strewn about the floor, as were her un-
derpants and her leggings. "Maureen?" I called. "It's me."
I drew back the bilious orange drapes that came with the
apartment. In the bedroom off the living room I found
the empty wheelchair. A lump Maureen's size lay beneath
the red silk quilt. I sat on the mattress. "Vic told me what
happened. God, I don't know how they could do that to
you. Maybe you could prove they stole the idea. Maybe you
could get someone down there in the public health department to admit they sold you out."

Maureen groaned and rolled over. Spikes of yellow hair
were matted to her skull. She smelled like spoiled cheese.
"It's not just that. It's everything." I reached out, but she
thrashed away. "He won't come! He won't come!"

"But I thought he was coming down here this weekend. He couldn't make it?"

"The asshole won't live here. He came to visit me so we could work things out. I just assumed . . . There are thousands of jobs here for someone with his qualifications. He could find a job in government. Or as a lobbyist. Or he could work for some kind of fish business. There are a lot more things he can do down here than I can do up there!" She snapped her head back and forth. "But he won't. He says he can't leave that stinking little fishing town of his." Her voice curdled into something ugly. "'*They're my people. They depend on me. My roots are there.*' Christ, when I hear people talk about their roots, I want to vomit."

"He expects you to move up there? What does he think you'll do, become a lobsterman?"

She pulled herself up. She wore a black bra and black panties. I could see the way arthritis had twisted her hips, as if someone had wrung her pelvis. "One minute he's saying he can't live without me. The next, I'm not worth giving up that stupid mayor's job or that stupid job at that stupid library."

Maybe she could get a job at the Jackson Lab, I said. Bar Harbor wasn't far from New Jerusalem. Maybe Paul just assumed she could work there.

"An hour's drive on those windy little roads? What am I going to do if I get stuck in the snow? Besides, why would I want to work in a mouse lab? I'm a molecular biologist. I don't like working with anything whose cage you have to clean." She clawed at her scalp. Several spikes came uprooted. I had always thought this was a figure of speech;

no one would actually tear out her hair. "How the hell would I even get around that town? There isn't a decent sidewalk. If you want anything, you have to get in the van and drive."

I reminded her that she would have someone to help her.

"I don't know what I would have!" She started crying again. "I don't know if he really cares where he lives, or he's just using this as an excuse."

I told her she was wrong. Paul was the one who had proposed to her, hadn't he?

"Sure he proposed. He's probably one of these guys who gets off on the idea of fucking a crip. Don't look so shocked. There are plenty of guys like that. It's exotic. It makes them think they're great guys—hey, they don't mind if their girlfriend's in a wheelchair. Then they start to think what it would really be like to have to deal with the wheelchair all the time, and, like, if they had a kid, they might have to do a lot of the day-to-day taking care of it."

Paul wasn't that kind of guy, I said.

"You don't think so?" She wiped her eyes, leaving mascara on the sheet. "I don't know what to think anymore. Like Yosef says, it's a cosmic plot. Who do you know who's had more rotten luck than me?" She slapped the headboard. "How could so many shitty things happen to one person?"

I shrank back, as if my own good fortune had come at her expense. "Come on, we'll go to the lab and call what's-his-name, in Lima, the one who runs all those free clinics. He's a good guy, and he loves to gossip. He probably knows what happened. And if he doesn't, he'll help us find out."

"Never mind that. It would have been nice. Really nice. But that's not what I was in it for. We found the parasite.

No one else is going to go blind. The people whose opinions count know I did the work. But, Jane, the whole reason I didn't take the time to fly down there and find those parasites myself was Paul. If I don't end up with him, after all of this, I swear . . ."

"All right, so there must be something you can do about him. If he loves you, there ought to be a way."

"You sound like a cue for a song-and-dance number."

"It beats lying around this pigsty in your underwear."

"What, singing?"

"No, doing something."

She ran the edge of the quilt between her knuckles. "Fine. I'll *do* something. I'll drive up there. What that will accomplish I don't know. But if you think I should *do* something, I'll hang out around town and see if I can imagine spending the rest of my life there. I'll ask him straight out why he's gotten cold feet, and I'll be able to see his face when he answers me. Only, you're going to have to drive up there with me, Miss Do-Something, because I don't have money to take the plane and I can't drive eight hours by myself."

Sure, I thought, why not. If we drove up to New Jerusalem, Maureen would know she had done everything she could to convince Paul to marry her. As for me, I was too scattered to do anything much in the lab. And there was something up there, in New Jerusalem, or maybe on the island, some information I lacked, an important piece of data. One of the samples didn't fit.

I asked Maureen when she wanted to leave. She fluffed her hair. "I'll need a few hours to put myself together. I ought to call him and let him know we're coming. But he'll only talk me out of it. Let's just go. We'll leave this afternoon. About one?" She swung herself into her chair, then rolled across the putrid shag to the bathroom. I gathered up her shoes and tossed them in the closet. I threw away the cartons of rancid food, stuffed the dirty clothes in the hamper. "Need anything at the store?" I called. "Or at the lab? You okay in there?" Steam swirled about the bathroom. In the shower stall, Maureen was slumped on her plastic chair, water beating against her shoulders. "Maureen?" I said. "I know things seem bad now. But you're attractive. You're smart. You're funny. If worse comes to worst, you'll find someone else."

She spoke without lifting her head—I barely could distinguish her voice from the shower's hiss. "Yeah. I'm smart. I'm funny. And I don't have itty-bitty flippers instead of arms. I should be happy to be alive. I'm lucky to have a career. I'm lucky not to be sitting on a street corner in a little wooden cart begging for change. I'm greedy to want a kid. I'm greedy to want a nice guy to love me and cuddle up with me at night and make sure I don't fry if there's a fire."

I was ashamed to admit I had been thinking just that: my friend ought to be grateful for everything she had. As I ought to have been grateful for everything *I* had. As any of us ought to be grateful. As so few of us ever are.

||||||||||||||||||||||||||||||||||||||

I called Yosef at his apartment. When no one answered, I wrote him a note asking him to perform the next few steps on my test, and on Laurel's test, and to keep an eye on the pregnant mouse. I was licking the envelope shut when he came in. I asked if he was all right; he certainly didn't look it.

He took out a comb and studied his reflection in the autoclave door. "This morning I remember how, when you call, I talk too much and wallowed in pity for myself. Don't take any of what I said so serious."

"You said we were friends. You said you would do anything for me. You were sweet."

"I was? Okay, that part you can take serious."

I handed him the note, which he read, squinting at the paper.

"Sure you don't want I should go with you? Just say the word and I break this guy's legs. Ha! It's only a way of talking, but it would be some kind of justice, I put this guy in a wheelchair and let someone dump *him*."

"I'll be glad if you just do the tests and take care of the mouse. And listen. I know this is going to come out wrong, but if I do get my own lab and you ever need a job—"

"You let me be flunky? Sure, every lab needs a centrifuge, a microscope, a Japanese postdoc, and a Russian flunky."

"Come on. You'd be more like a research fellow. An associate. Until you get your own lab."

"You don't hurt my feelings. But I can't afford this fooling around no more. Today I set up an interview with, what you call them—cannibal? headhunter?" He tossed a handful of pill-shaped mints in his mouth. "I'll stop complaining. How do you say in America, at least I have my health? I have my mother, even if she lives in a terrible place, can't buy any soap, my sisters can't buy sanitary napkins, I have to mail all of this in a big box from America. For them, I can do something. For Maureen, this guy doesn't marry her, I break his legs. For you? If your test doesn't turn out so good, what can I do for you?" He put his arm around me. "All I can say is, if this news isn't so good, I will take care of you. You understand? I will take care of you."

I wanted to ask him, *Why? Why would you take care of me? We're not even related. You barely know me.* "I'll be back in a few days," I said. "Don't say anything to anyone. And don't let that headhunter talk you into anything you don't want to do."

"'Want.' This is an American option. You have a daddy with a trust fund, you can do what you want." He pinched his tongue in contrition. "Sorry, sweetheart. I guess even having a father with a trust fund doesn't always mean you get to do what you want to do."

〰〰〰〰〰〰〰〰〰〰〰〰

I walked back to the dorm. Maureen, who usually arrived an hour late for everything, sat beside her van. Her hair rose from her scalp, clean and freshly spiked. She wore plain silver earrings and no makeup except for some shadow to camouflage the pink rims of her eyes.

"I'm still too upset to drive. Here, lift me into the passenger seat. Then you can clamp my wheelchair in the empty space behind the wheel and sit in that."

I did as she instructed. I settled in the wheelchair and tested the levers that had been installed to allow Maureen to control the pedals by hand. *It's okay,* I told myself. *You don't really need a wheelchair. This is only temporary.* The day was sunny but cold. Few cars were driving north this week before Christmas, so I didn't need to concentrate. I pictured the test that Yosef was carrying out on Laurel's DNA. I imagined myself reading the blot and not seeing the marker for the gene, telling Laurel the good news, Laurel throwing out her arms and clutching me with relief. And then, as if performing some act of mental self-sacrifice, I leaped ahead to the scene in which my own blot revealed a smear of radiation where the marker should be. I would keep my appointment at the clinic. I would tell Willie that I was sorry but we could only be friends. He would have to accept this. I was accepting it myself.

I touched Maureen's hand. "It's going to be fine," I said.

She sniffed. "Sure." Then she turned to face the window and didn't say another word until I pulled into the parking lot of an orange-roofed Howard Johnson's, the kind with Simple Simon and the Pie Man on top. I ordered the turkey dinner—stuffing, mashed potatoes, succotash, stewed tomatoes, peach pie. "I'll have toast and coffee," Maureen told the waitress, then left the toast on her plate.

We arrived at Paul's house at nine. While I zipped my parka, Maureen scowled into the side mirror, checking her hair.

"Do you want me to stick around?" I had planned to spend the night with Miriam, or, if she was busy, at the boardinghouse on Front Street. The next morning, I would take the boat to Spinsters Island.

"Thanks," Maureen said. "This is just between the mayor and me."

"Well, if you need a place to stay, drive down to Miriam's and honk."

She pushed the button on her wheelchair and crunched along the damp gravel to the porch. I climbed the steps, rang the bell, gave Maureen a quick kiss, and hurried off. I glanced back and saw Paul open the door and look down. From the dismay on his face, before he managed to hide it, I knew we shouldn't have come.

<hr />

I headed toward the town, walking along the bay in the moonlit dark. It seemed appropriate that I come by stealth. I had stolen information. If the inhabitants of New Jerusalem saw me now, they would demand to know the answers. Saying *you're fine* would be easy. But how could I tell anyone that he or she would die?

I reached the two-porched Victorian. A child inside shrieked. I assumed a frantic mother had brought an infant to the house. But when Miriam opened the door, I saw a child but no parent. The baby couldn't have been more than six months old. Dark skinned, with large eyes and a silky fringe of black hair. He dangled from a harness suspended from the ceiling by a hook, kicking his legs so furiously that his rage propelled him back and forth. I barely could hear Miriam above the child's screams and the howling of a dog on the other side of the wall.

"I'm afraid you haven't picked a very good time." Miriam wore a corduroy shirt with an epaulet of spit-up across the shoulder. She looked more anxious than usual but less dour. "He has a hard time falling asleep. His digestion, I

think it is. A pediatrician friend swears by this contraption."
Miriam unbuckled the baby from the swing and walked
him around the parlor. The child wailed like a tortured cat,
which set the dog howling louder. Someone pounded on
the wall. "Just ignore her. I've been listening to those damn
dogs of hers for years." Miriam found a pacifier beneath a
chair, wiped it on her sleeve, and plugged it in the baby's
mouth. The pacifier muted the baby's cries but didn't stop
them. "You hold him, and we'll try something else." She
handed me the baby and started toward the kitchen. "His
name is Raphael."

"Raphael," I said, rubbing his back and pacing about
the room with the same bouncy step I had seen Miriam
use. He kept crying but less forlornly. His head smelled
like bananas and vanilla. I inhaled the scent so deeply I
nearly reeled. Miriam came back with a bottle of formula.
Collapsing in a rocker, she took the baby in her lap. He
stopped crying and made a noise—*ah-ah-ah*—that seemed
an answer to the rocker's squeak. But he wouldn't close his
eyes. I bet myself that Miriam would drop to sleep before
the baby.

"There's a woman who comes in to look after him while
I'm seeing patients," she said drowsily. "But the way he cries
all the time, I end up coming up here to look after him
anyway. Or else I keep him in the room with me while
I'm examining someone, which isn't exactly ideal." The
townspeople, she said, had been remarkably understanding.
"Not a single one of them has asked where he came from.
Maybe they think I had an affair with a passing Portuguese
sailor. Or they think lesbians can have babies by immac-

ulate conception. Or maybe they're afraid if they ask too many questions, I'll pack him up and leave." She folded her arms across the baby. "Barbara hasn't been quite so tolerant. We're not on speaking terms right now."

If Miriam had seemed fated to share her life with anyone, it had to be Barbara Lewis. It seemed impossible that she would sacrifice her love life with her soul mate to raise someone else's child.

"I don't mean to be rude." Miriam kept rocking so as not to wake the baby. "And you're certainly welcome to stay as long as you like. But do you mind if I ask why you're here?"

I said I didn't know. I wanted to come. I had to.

Would I be going to the island? she asked.

First thing the next day.

She affected a shudder. "I wouldn't ride out with that Charlie Stacks if he was piloting the only boat to heaven. Stubborn SOB. I've offered a dozen times to drive him down to Portland to get those cataracts lasered off. 'The gods wanted me to see, I'd be seein',' he says. I say to him, 'Charlie, your heart's not ticking right, I'll drive you down to Portland, get one of those pacemakers put in.' He tells me, 'The gods wanted my heart tickin' any faster or slower, they'd a' set it that way.' Fine for him, throwing away his life. But there's no reason he has to endanger innocent people. I've been trying to get your friend the mayor to find a replacement. But Paul Minot is too good for his own good, if you know what I mean."

Our voices woke the baby. He stiffened in Miriam's arms and spit up a milky curd. He started shrieking again.

Barbara pounded the wall. The dog barked. Miriam and I were up much of the night, taking turns with Raphael, walking him around the living room. Barbara kept pounding. The phone rang. *If "that kid" didn't stop making such a racket . . .*

At least they were speaking again, I thought. All that thumping on the walls reminded me of two prisoners sending messages to each other. Eventually they would find a way to tunnel through the wall.

At three, Raphael fell asleep. I slumped across the sofa and dozed until the post-office clock struck seven fifteen. The boat left at seven thirty. I brushed my teeth, changed my shirt, and scrawled "Thanks" on a pad of prescription forms by Miriam's telephone.

When I reached the boat, Stacks was coiling a line and pushing off. I stepped aboard and said my name.

"Come back again, have you. Paying her a return call."

I didn't ask if he meant Eve Barter. After handing him the fare, I went to sit in the stern. The waves kept flinging up the boat, then letting it drop with a smack. My stomach lifted and fell, lifted and fell. I gagged and retched but managed not to throw up. The ride took forever, whether because the waves kept pushing us back or the absence of landmarks made progress seem slow. I joined Stacks in the cabin.

"Rough enough for you?"

I didn't want to give him the satisfaction of saying it was.

"Think a sharp pair of eyes would do me any better on a day like this? Now, my *ears*. Wouldn't want to lose those.

Ears is how I know half what's out there." He blew a blast on his horn. The echo came back delayed, as if another ship had moaned in the fog to our left. "'Blind as a bat,' is it? Bat wouldn't have no trouble hearing its way in." He squeezed the horn, tilted his head to hear the echo, turned the steering wheel a few degrees to the right. In this way, we drew close to Spinsters Island, the dock looming from the fog an instant before we would have hit it. He tossed the rope, missed, tugged it back, tossed it again. This time the loop caught. He jumped off the boat and set the ladder. "Just don't you go around expecting no hero's welcome," he told me.

I didn't expect anything, I said.

"Person's made a certain way, that's the way he's meant to be made. Gets time for him to pass over, he passes over. You go around taking away the things make a person who he is, he ends up not being anyone."

The road shook beneath my feet. I had intended to walk to Thunder Beach, but the thought of the icy spray made me reconsider. I followed Stacks up the road. The windows of the houses had been blinded with plywood boards and foil. The town had turned its hindquarters to the world and curled up for the winter; disturbed in hibernation, it might gnash its teeth and strike out.

Stacks asked if I was planning on staying or going back.

Of course I was going back.

"See that you're on time then. There'll be a storm to-night for sure."

I walked to Eve Barter's garage. A light flickered in the kitchen.

"Door's unlatched!" she called. "Just about finished, Rudy. Come in."

I went in and found Eve working at a table covered with the parts of a dismantled engine. On a corner of the red-and-white-checked oilcloth sat two baking tins of popovers, a kettle, and a cup. Eve's hair, curled in rollers, was hidden beneath a scarf. Her breasts swelled from her robe. She wiped the carburetor with a rag, then held it up and peered inside. "I thought you were Rudy Sugar, come to get his DeSoto."

I asked how she had learned to work on cars.

She wrenched free a spark plug. "Always liked working with my hands." She blew inside the carburetor and wiped it with her rag. "Sewing seemed just about the most boring thing a person could do. Came time for the boys and girls to split up in seventh grade, I said I wanted to take shop. The principal didn't have any objections, so long as I agreed to take home ec, too. Which I'm glad I did, because it turned out I liked the baking part just fine. Stuck out my chest and talked sweet to the shop teacher, he didn't object either. Opportunity to buy this garage came along, I was ready to take advantage."

"How did you come to buy the garage? May I ask?"

Eve set down the carburetor and picked up a screwdriver. "You come all the way from Boston to ask me that? Is this a business call? Pleasure? Isn't exactly the best season for a visit."

"It's a business call. Mostly."

"Need some more blood?" There was a catch in Eve's laugh, like an engine misfiring.

"That's part of it. There were some discrepancies."

"Yeah?" she said. "What sorts of discrepancies?"

"I was wondering if you might be related to someone on the island. I know you said you weren't, but maybe you forgot. Maybe it's someone who's only distantly related."

"I got it, don't I." She stabbed the table with her screwdriver. "Didn't ruin enough lives. Must be laughing in his grave, the cunt-sucking son of a bitch. What'd he ever give me? I ask you. What'd that miserable fucker ever give me except this garage and his filthy blood?" She raised her arm to sweep the engine parts to the floor, then reconsidered. "Bad enough what he did to all those young girls here. He gets run off to the mainland and messes up my mom. Fifteen years old and pregnant by a man she doesn't even know."

I moved a step closer.

"That cock-fucking mothersucker. Must have had some fit of repentance. Lawyer we never heard of tells us this Ransom guy left Mom his garage. As if she might say, 'Oh, fine, he left me a garage on some shitty island, that makes amends for what he done.'" Eve yanked off her kerchief and began pulling out her curlers. "But me, I was a kid. Didn't have much prospects. Sort of curious, owning something and not knowing what it looked like. Mom said to come out and sell it, but I decided to stick around." She yanked the screwdriver from the table, then jammed it in again. "Son of a cock-sucking, bitch-fucking bastard."

I lifted Eve's hands. The back of each was hatched by burns. "My mother had these, too," I said. "She used to reach in the oven to get out a pan, and her arms would jerk, and she'd burn the backs of her hands on the top rack."

Eve put her arms around my waist and leaned her head against me. I stroked her damp hair. After a few minutes, she sat up straight and wiped her eyes on the greasy rag. "Don't feel bad for telling me. Not like I didn't guess. I just needed a kick in the pants is what I needed. Last thing I want to do is to hang around and end up like the rest of these sorry so-and-sos. I'll sell the place and get out while I can. Just don't spread the news. I'd rather not anyone put two and two together and figure out who my dad was."

I promised I would keep the diagnosis to myself.

"I suppose that was the business part. You want some hot popovers? Sit down and I'll make us a fresh pot of tea."

I said no, but she kept insisting. Still wearing my parka, I sat. Eve poured us both tea from the china pot. We ate three popovers apiece. And it came to me that this must have been part of why I'd come, to drink tea with Eve Barter and so be forgiven for the unforgivable message I had brought.

After I left Eve's kitchen, I wandered back to the dock. Charlie Stacks stood at the prow of his boat, sniffing the air. It was only four thirty, but the sun was going down. I could smell the storm coming, although I couldn't have told you what it smelled like. I stared across the water. I didn't look forward to consoling Maureen. And I was even less eager to get back to the lab. Maybe it would be better to let Yosef read the results. Would it be less excruciating to hold the gun myself, or ask someone else to hold it? I had to laugh. If I let Yosef read the blot, would I be playing *Russian roulette?*

We were halfway across the bay when Stacks clasped a hand to his chest as if he were pledging allegiance. "I'm not feeling so well," he said. "Town's that way. Stay this course, but keep an eye out for rocks."

He waited until I had taken the wheel then staggered out of the cabin. Maybe he was trying to prove that my eyes, though younger than his, were less useful than his ears. I saw nothing but the horizon, the sun resting on the land like a note on a stave. I craned my head out the door. "Mr. Stacks? Are you all right?"

I should have shut the engine and gone to see if he needed first aid. But I didn't know how to restart the boat. I looked for a way to make the engine go faster, but neither lever produced this result. I twisted the dials on the radio but heard only static. If I headed straight for the setting sun I would be sure to reach the mainland. But what about the rocks? I glanced at the coffee-stained map. Wasn't that guppyish shape the island? I was afraid to take my eyes from the sea, but every now and then I tried squinting at the map, and I grew more confident I could steer my way in, avoiding the giant sandbar lurking to my left, the shoals off to starboard.

After what seemed forever, a steeple pricked the sky. Lumpy buildings. Faint lights. I steered clear of a rock on which a gull sat flapping its wings and laughing. Then I passed a buoy whose bell clamored in our wake. I was congratulating myself on having navigated my way to the shore when I realized that the map I had been using was upside down.

I approached the dock sideways but cut the motor too late. A knot of fishermen on the wharf watched the boat drift by. "Get a doctor!" I shouted as I ran the boat aground.

"What the hell you doing!" Stacks called.

Two fishermen sauntered toward the ferry. The shorter and less attractive—he reminded me of a hedgehog— reached up and swung me down. I ran to find Miriam. Halfway along Front Street, my body seemed too heavy to move. I gulped air to keep from vomiting, then forced myself to run the rest of the way. The three women in Miriam's waiting room studied me as if they could guess I was pregnant and expected me to miscarry right there. I brushed past the receptionist, through the frosted door, and choked out an explanation.

"Damn him," Miriam said. She asked the woman on her examining table to watch Raphael, who was chewing on a rusk. She called the nearest hospital and demanded an ambulance, then gathered a stethoscope, an oxygen tank, and some drugs and stuffed these in her bag. Raphael started crying. "I'll kill that selfish old coot," Miriam grumbled.

When we got back to the beach, Stacks was slumped against an oil barrel like something that had washed ashore and nobody cared to salvage. "Ain't going to that hospital," he told Miriam.

"Yes you damn well are. And you're going to let them put that pacemaker in. I won't have you calling me out at all hours and disturbing my child."

The ambulance came. The EMTs ignored Stacks's protests and shoved him in the van. Miriam grumbled goodbye to me and hurried back to her office. The fishermen stared at me as if they expected me to do something with the boat. I backed away, as if this were a conspiracy to lure some unsuspecting passenger into taking Stacks's place and ferrying the mail back and forth to Spinsters Island forever.

I kept walking out of town. I was nearly to Paul's house when he rode up behind me.

"Where did you leave her?" I said.

"You sound as if you think I did away with her. I had a board meeting. It wasn't as if I knew she was coming."

I had forgotten how attractive he was. Poor Maureen.

"It's not what you're thinking. It just came to me, after I proposed, that I would be wrong to leave here. It would sound more admirable to claim the people here need me. But it's the reverse that's true. What would I be in Boston? I'm sure I could manufacture a cause. But I wouldn't be as valuable there as I am here. I've told her straight out, if she decides to move up here, we'll get married anytime. I know the sacrifice she would be making. I'll understand if she chooses not to make it. But I'm not a coward. I'm not a hypocrite."

"You're a bureaucrat," I said. "She keeps getting screwed by bureaucrats."

We climbed the steps to Paul's house. "Thank God," Maureen said. "If I had to sit here another minute . . ."

He carried her to the van. I clamped the wheelchair behind the steering wheel, settled in the chair, and turned the key. Paul stood beside Maureen's window, but she wouldn't look his way, as if her neck had lost its last degree of mobility.

"I'll write you," he said. "We can still be friends, can't we?"

"No," Maureen said. "I don't think we can."

When we reached the main road, she blew her nose. "I can't believe I have to start over. From scratch. I was tempted to pitch it all and stay. But I would go nuts here, Jane. I would go absolutely nuts, cooped up in that house. I love him. But since when has loving someone ever been enough?"

19

Neither of us was in a rush to get back. After an hour on the road I told Maureen I was too tired to keep driving. We checked into a bed and breakfast. The bathroom was too small for Maureen's chair; I helped her hobble to the toilet, then turned and waited until she was ready to hobble back. There was only one bed. We stripped to our underwear and settled on opposite sides of the mattress.

Maybe we should stay awhile, I said.

Maureen asked for how long.

I don't know, I said. An extra day. Maybe two.

Sure, Maureen said.

I told her that I was pregnant.

"Oh, sweetie." She sighed. She held my hand and sympathized but didn't offer advice, whether because she was too tired and depressed or because she knew I wouldn't listen. It came to me again that if we had grown up in a society in which pregnant couples were able to test their fetus to make sure it didn't carry the genes for any serious disease, Maureen probably wouldn't have been alive.

We slept hours past breakfast. The day was brilliant but cold, even for December. Huddled inside our jackets we scurried from shop to shop, browsing through shelves of plastic lobsters and picturesque postcards of the islands offshore. I thought of sending one to Willie, but what would I have written? *I'm having your child, let's get married.* Or: *I've decided to abort it.* I wondered if I would ever lead a life in which I could drop a postcard to my boyfriend with a simple "I miss you."

We slept twelve hours that night, ate our breakfast with the other guests, then tried to stroll the boardwalk, but we couldn't withstand the wind.

"We might as well go home," Maureen said.

We might as well, I said.

We expected the weather would turn warmer farther south, but the wind grew more bitter. The heater whimpered and squealed, then stopped working. Rather than wait in a grimy service station for some mechanic to repair it, we sat rigid with cold, breath clouding our faces, all the way back to Boston. It was a Thursday afternoon. Most people were at work. The Charles was filmed with ice.

I parked the van and helped Maureen get out. She poked around in the depths of her overnight bag, then pulled out a tissue. "On top of everything, I'm coming down with a cold." She blew her nose. "Let me know what you decide. I'll shake myself out of this."

"Don't worry about me," I said. "You've got your own problems."

I walked home and spooned a jar of peanut butter onto stale rye bread for dinner. Around eight, I wrapped a scarf around my face and biked to the lab. Going up in the elevator, I wiped my nose on my scarf; I was getting Maureen's cold.

"Homozygous mouse is fine," Yosef said. "I just came back from checking. As for the test, all you got to do on your own DNA is develop the blot. Other gel is hybridizing, it should be ready tomorrow. You want me to stay? I don't like to think you're here all by yourself."

I thanked him but said I didn't want anyone around when I read it. He understood, didn't he?

"No," he said. "If it's me, I want friend around to help take bad news. Or help enjoy good news." He put his lips to my ear. "I'll be praying," he whispered.

I took the cassette—a piece of X-ray film clamped between cardboard sheets—and spun the darkroom door. I flicked on the red light, and, hands moving by rote, slid the film from its sheath. I set the timer for a few seconds longer than required. I wasn't in any hurry. I shook off the extra drops of fixer from the film. I tried to calm my thoughts, but my heart beat as wildly as a Geiger counter. I turned on the white light and found the lane I wanted. The heavy smudge, here, and the empty space, there, meant I had inherited one good gene from my father and another good gene from my mother.

I went limp. My legs buckled. I sank to the floor. "Thank you," I kept saying, although I wasn't sure whom I was thanking. God wouldn't use a person's health to punish or reward her, would he? Still, I found myself bargaining: *Don't let Laurel have it. Let both of us be okay.*

I plunged my X-ray in the fixer for another five minutes. Later, carrying my film down the hall, I stared at the empty space where the marker should have been but wasn't. I clipped the film above my bench, then sat and watched it dry. Yosef came in. I looked up at him and smiled.

"Thank God," he said quietly.

"I already thanked him."

He laughed. "Two Jewish atheists thanking God, is funny." He kissed my hair. His lips lingered. "You come over. I'll get some champagne. We'll make a very big celebration."

I almost said yes. But that wasn't what I wanted, getting drunk with Yosef. We would end up in bed, and everything between us, all this tenderness, would be ruined. I would need to see him in the lab the next day and pretend we hadn't had sex.

"Not tonight," I said. "Maybe tomorrow."

He jabbed a Camel in his mouth. Usually, he obeyed the rule about not smoking in the lab, but he lit the cigarette and inhaled, and when he let out that breath, all his hope and animation seemed to go with it. "Sure," he said. "You change your mind later, you call me at home, no matter what the time."

I would do that, I said. He made the thumbs-up sign, hugged me again, and went out. I didn't want to leave the film hanging where anyone could see it, so I pressed it in Saran Wrap, slipped it inside my parka, and biked home. I hung the film from the Venetian blinds in the kitchen and then paced the living room. "I'm lucky," I said aloud.

"I don't have it. I won't die." But how could I believe that? How could a smudge on a piece of film reveal anything so private and essential about me? How could it make me another Jane Weiss?

I dialed my father's number, but before anyone could answer I hung up. *What about Laurel?* he would ask. He would be in Boston that weekend for her concert. If my sister's test, like mine, turned out to be negative, I could see the happiness on his face when I told him that both his daughters were fine. And if Laurel's test turned out positive, maybe my own good news would temper his grief.

I phoned Maureen instead.

"That's wonderful," she croaked. "I'm so happy for you. That's terrific." But nothing she said seemed ecstatic enough. Maybe, deep inside, she envied my good luck. Or maybe nothing anyone could say would satisfy a person who had learned she wouldn't die.

"We'll go dancing," Maureen promised.

"Great," I said. "We'll do that."

I looked for Willie's number in New Hampshire. It was past ten. I imagined the phone ringing in his shack with no one there to hear. I was trying to figure out what message I would leave when Willie said, "Hey." For a moment I couldn't answer. "Anyone there?" he asked.

"It's me," I said. "It's Jane."

"Jane," he said. "Hey. How are you? Are you all right? Is something wrong?"

"I thought maybe you could come down here tomorrow instead of Saturday." *Go ahead, you can say it.* "I need to talk to you. I need to see you."

He told me he could come right then, if I wanted.

I looked around at the threadbare couch that had come with the apartment and the empty beakers in which I had arranged Laurel's bouquets. Yes, I said. I wouldn't mind if he came. I would be grateful. *Please, come.*

"I'll be there in two hours. Is that okay? I could drive faster, if I needed to drive faster."

"No," I said. "Two hours. That's fine."

He took an hour and forty-five minutes to drive down from New Hampshire. In the meantime, I unpacked my mother's books and found a photo of a fetus at twelve weeks' gestation, the face featureless except for those darkly lidded eyes. The gelatinous arms and fingers hung poised like those of a pianist preparing to play. In the center of the chest, a crimson blob beat 150 times a minute—even faster than my own heart had chattered in the darkroom a few hours earlier, when I was being reborn. It wasn't a question of when life started, I thought. It wasn't a question of whether I would care for a child who had been born with an illness that couldn't be foreseen. Like any mother, I would do everything possible to save my child's life. But wasn't it wrong to knowingly give birth to a child who would suffer? And what if the child had a one-in-two chance? Or less, a one-in-four chance. Was that half a sin? One quarter?

I heard someone on the stairs. Willie's hair was a mess. He stepped into the living room and stood awaiting my instructions.

"I don't have it," I said.

"You don't have what?" he said. "The baby?"

"The test . . . I don't have Valentine's."

I watched the news travel from his brain to his heart. He kissed me on the mouth, then crushed me to his parka and swung me around the living room, whooping so loudly I was afraid he would wake the landlord. "This is great!" he said. "Don't shush me!" He whooped again. "Jesus, if you can't make noise at a time like this!" He whooped a third time, spinning me until we sprawled awkwardly across the couch. I wanted to say: *If my result makes you so happy, why don't you take the test?* But I knew this made sense only if I could promise that he, too, would have a negative result. How could all three of us be so lucky? All four.

We talked about the baby. Again I brought up the possibility that Willie let himself be tested. When he repeated his refusal, I had to sit on my hands to keep from hitting him. "I'm kind of thirsty," he said.

I didn't have any chocolate milk, but I offered to make him some hot cocoa. I spooned powder in two cups and boiled water in a pan. Bringing the cups to the living room, I stumbled. Chocolate sloshed to the rug. The old fear surged back. Then I thought: *I'm just clumsy.* Most people were. Not those few graceful human beings like Cruz and my sister, but everyone else. "Should I go?" Willie asked. "I could find a room at a hotel."

I panicked. "No. Stay."

He thumped the cushion he was sitting on; dust rose about our heads. "On this ratty thing?"

We put down our cocoa and I led him to my room, to the single bed covered with the daisy-print comforter my mother had picked out from Weiss's linen department the week I left for college.

"You sure about this?" he asked.

"No," I said. "But I want to do it anyway."

"What guy could refuse an invitation like that?" He unbuttoned his shirt, unlaced his red sneakers, and lay down in his jeans. I stretched out beside him. The bed was barely wide enough for him, let alone for both of us. I put my head on his chest, which was hairy and soft and smelled like the woods on a rainy day. I had missed this the most without knowing it, lying with my cheek against a man's chest, hearing his heart. He rubbed my back. He lifted off my shirt and kissed my neck, then kissed each swollen breast and tender nipple. I wrapped my arms around his back and squeezed until his spine cracked. We made love, long, slow love, every second stretching out longer than a normal second. Exhausted, we slept. A car alarm went off. I leaped up, looked around the room, took a breath, and relaxed. We made love a second time. In the morning, when we awoke, he reached for me again, but this time I pulled back. In a little while I would be developing Laurel's blot. If her test turned out badly, I would never forgive myself for making love with him that day.

We ate, washed, and dressed, then walked to the lab holding gloved hands. When Yosef saw me, he grinned and presented me with a rose. Then he noticed Willie. I could hear Yosef think: *Sure, Russkie can't compete with American cowboy looks like John Wayne.* Well, I thought, he would need to get used to Willie's presence. Everyone would.

I went into Vic's office. He was talking on the phone. I waited until he set down the receiver. "My blot turned out negative. I don't have the gene."

He bowed his head and twined his fingers. When he looked up again, his face was wet. "This is what it was all about, wasn't it. Jane, I think that half the reason I wanted this moratorium was because I was so sure you had it. I thought I could prevent you from finding out. Wasn't that crazy? But there's this side of it, this blessing. People finding out they've got their whole lives ahead of them." He stared up at the ceiling. "And your sister? Here I've been acting as if . . . Have you done her test yet? Does she . . . Well, does she?"

I felt a pressure behind my eyes. "I'm about to find out. Wish us luck, okay?"

"I do." He swiped his cheeks with his knuckles. "Believe me, I do."

I took Laurel's blot to the darkroom. Willie followed me through the door. I stood there a while, the undeveloped blot pressed between my hands as if my sister's fate would remain blank until someone read the dashes and dots on this X-ray. How long had it been since I had thought like a scientist? I turned on the red light and slipped the film from its jacket. Dipped it in the developer. Set the timer for two minutes, then started counting to one hundred and twenty myself. I did the same for the fixative. When the timer rang, I jerked the film from the tank and held it to the light. A few drops of fixative drizzled on my face.

"So?" Willie said. "So, so, so?"

I looked twice, then a third time, and then a fourth. My breath escaped in a rush. "She doesn't have it either. Look, there, that empty spot. She doesn't have it! She doesn't have it!" I was trembling so hard I would have been sure I had Valentine's, except I knew the real reason: I was trembling from joy.

⁓⁓⁓⁓⁓⁓⁓⁓⁓⁓⁓⁓⁓⁓⁓⁓⁓⁓⁓⁓⁓

To pass the thirty-six hours until Laurel's concert would be over and I could tell her the good news (as if "good" were an adequate word to describe the news I was bringing), Willie and I went back to my apartment, did crosswords, and cooked our lunch. Every few minutes the reality of Laurel's reprieve gripped my heart. I leaped up and started dancing. I hugged myself, or hugged him. I sighed or started laughing. I was nagged by the sense that I ought to be doing something more important than sitting on the sofa feeling happy. Then Willie asked if I knew a nine-letter word meaning "related to the lungs," and I told him "pulmonary," which I knew he knew himself, and he thanked me and kissed me, and I reminded myself that there wasn't any point to giving someone back her life if she didn't know how to use it. When Willie sat on the floor with his eyes shut and meditated, I spent the same hour meditating on him—the deep vertical crease that divided his face, branched above his throat, and rejoined to meet his sternum, that line of bushy hair that descended to his navel, and on below that. I delighted in the details that kept him from being symmetrical: the tornadoes of hair that swirled across each shoulder, but in opposite directions; the brown mole above one elbow; the jagged scar along one hirsute shin, like a road hacked by a machete. I watched the fans of hair open beneath his arms, the creamy skin rippling down his ribs. I was so glad he was there, sitting on my floor in his boxer shorts and socks, I had to go touch him. I sank to his lap and ran my hands across the skin and hair I had just studied. We made love yet again, and I wondered if I would ever take making love for granted. And later, when we were cooking, I wondered if I would ever chop meat without watching my hands, without thinking of Valentine's, even to think that I was free, that I didn't have it.

I took a second helping of chili. I hadn't thrown up since that afternoon with Laurel, rowing too hard, although my breasts often ached. Willie asked if I wanted to go out and see a movie. In the middle of the day? I said.

"It's not illegal," he pointed out.

Laurel, too, had accused me of thinking everything except work was illegal. The concert wouldn't begin for another six hours. A movie would pass the time. We studied the listings.

"Anything but *Sophie's Choice*," I said.

We ended up seeing *E.T.* When we came emerged from the theater the sun was still out, and I felt as disoriented as if I were an alien. We walked arm in arm around Harvard Square, among the other young couples, and I thought: *No, not an alien. I was an alien before. Now I'm a human being.* We passed a furniture store with a display of futon beds in the window.

"What if we decided to live together?" I asked. "I couldn't move to New Hampshire."

"Of course you couldn't," he said. "I can do my stuff

anywhere. All I need is a telephone. We could find a place here and use the cabin weekends."

In another store, we saw a brightly patterned yellow dress.

"That would look great on you," he said. "Come on, I want to buy it." He asked the clerk to get the dress, shoved me in a fitting room, and handed it in. I pulled it on. He was right, the dress had been designed for someone like me, with an olive complexion, no hips and no bust. Although even on me the bodice felt snug. And it might only grow snugger. *That doesn't matter,* I thought. I still had my appointment at the clinic.

"We'll take it," Willie said. "Keep it on, you can wear it to the concert." He bought a new pair of khaki pants and a flannel shirt for himself. We went back to my apartment to grab a bite and rest. At five o'clock, Honey called from New York to say she and my father had decided not to drive to Boston for the concert. They didn't want to disappoint Laurel, but Herb was coming down with the flu, and with the weather so brutal . . .

Honey must have heard Willie's voice in the background. "Janie," she said, "don't you dare let him drive back to that awful cabin tonight. They're expecting snow. Tell him I'll pay for a hotel," and I wondered if she was afraid for her son's safety, or afraid that he would otherwise spend the night in my bed.

We took the Jeep into town. The moon threw eerie shadows of the bridge across the ice. I could think of nothing except the gift I was bringing Laurel. The concert stretched ahead, a two-hour desert I needed to cross.

The performance would be held in a small brick firehouse that had been gutted and rebuilt as an avant-garde theater. An usher with a ring through his nose showed us to our seats. The chairs reserved for our parents sat empty until a boy and girl so thin they could have shared a single seat asked if they could sit there.

I barely noticed the three women who performed the first dance. Laurel wasn't among them, although, according to the program, Laurel Weiss and Cruz Martin had choreographed the piece. One dancer was black, another Hispanic, the third woman was Chinese, but each of the three wore a peach-colored leotard and a lacquered blond wig; with no pubic hair or nipples, they seemed like plastic dolls. They danced on high heels, arms and legs working with mechanical stiffness. The accompaniment consisted of popular love songs from the past several decades. I recognized the songs from the sixties and early seventies, but few from the eighties. If Willie moved in, we could buy a stereo. Maybe he could teach me to play the guitar.

Then the music stopped, and the doll-women snapped in two and flopped forward. The audience applauded. I glanced at the program. The next number, which Laurel had choreographed herself, was called "*Myxomycetes.*" I assumed myself to be the only member of the audience who knew this to be the name of the group to which the slime molds belong. I sat up and waited. The light turned blue-green. A convoluted ball of dancers in many-colored leotards rolled out onstage. To a drumbeat, the ball split down the middle, and these halves split again, again and again, until the floor writhed with cells, each a different color, flowing like amoebae on their bellies or on their backs, scraping food bits in their mouths.

Then the drumbeat grew faint. The cells twisted in hunger. A violin shrieked. The amoebae stopped writhing and began to grope toward one another. As the violin played—I recognized the melody but couldn't think where I had heard it—the dancers linked themselves like the segments of a caterpillar, the legs of the first looped about the shoulders and neck of the second, as Laurel and I had once played on our parents' lawn; "inchworm," we called the game. Now, with fifteen people, the worm inched across the stage toward the one patch of floor on which the spotlight glowed red. The dancers at the rear formed a base while the others climbed atop them, higher and higher, a slender stalk, a filament. This wasn't the same species of slime mold I had shown Laurel that day, walking in the woods, but another, more common species—*Dicto-something*, I thought. I imagined my sister in some library in Vermont, poring over biology texts until she found the slime mold whose reproductive cycle would provide the best dance.

The pillar grew tall enough to reach the colored lights above the stage. The woman on top curled herself tightly, then burst into space. The next dancer did this, then the next below, until fifteen spores lay scattered about the bare floor. They remained dormant, then began to writhe and feed. The violin shrieked. The cells came streaming together as the violin played the melody Laurel had practiced on her cello all those evenings years before, in Mule's Neck, when we both were young girls. Four times the slime mold went through its cycle, the lights fading as the fifth stalk of spores reached full height.

The applause for this piece was stronger and more approving. Pride clotted my chest. Maybe my sister would go on to accomplish great things.

"That was pretty good," Willie said. "What was it supposed to be? Was it some kind of mushroom?"

I had just enough time to read the name of the next piece on the program—"Valentine's Dance"—before the theater went dark. The sort of discordant modern music I had never liked squalled from the speakers. Laurel came on. She was dressed in a flowered shift and the white shawl she had worn to our brunch at the Ritz. She darted this way, then that, hurried and confused and overwhelmed by the tasks she needed to accomplish, all the choices she faced, around and around in ever-tighter circles, until, like a skater, she drew in her arms and spun so quickly she blurred. There was scattered applause, but the dance wasn't over. Laurel started to dance in circles so small her feet barely moved. I saw our mother trapped in that spotlight, shaking so furiously no body could bear the stress.

She erupted in a seizure, eyes rolled back in her head. If she had acted that way three centuries earlier, she would have been taken for a witch. "Shit!" she screamed. "Fuck you! Up! Your dirty! Arsehole!" Since she didn't name a target, she seemed to be cursing everyone around her, or cursing life itself. I thought I couldn't force myself to sit still another moment, but just then, Laurel froze with her arms extended straight out, hands cupped, head thrown back in an attitude the Shakers would have interpreted as: *I accept whatever gifts the Lord chooses to give.*

Then the music started again. Other dancers appeared, the original members of Six Left Feet. Each dancer performed his or her own imitation of a Valentine's victim, although with so many people performing the dance it became something everyone was prey to, the way the king of Sweden had put on a yellow star and so protected the Jews.

"I'm not sure she should have done that," Willie said. The audience whistled and clapped. They seemed to feel Laurel's frenzy as their own, although few of them could have known much about Valentine's chorea, if they even knew what it was. "She shouldn't have made it so pretty."

I was surprised to understand something he didn't. I would explain all that later, after I talked to Laurel. The usher led us to a shabby brick room with flaking pipes. I pushed my way between bodies still slippery with sweat.

"What did you think?" Laurel asked. She swabbed her neck. Her lipstick had bled in tiny lines around her mouth.

I told her I loved it. "Laurel, really, I've never . . . The one about the slime mold!"

"You knew? You remembered?"

"Of course! I didn't think you were paying attention."

"And the one about . . . you know." Laurel flinched and closed her eyes. "I wasn't sure what you would think about that last one."

I wanted to tell her how affected I had been, how moved. But Laurel's friends and fellow dancers were talking too loudly and crushing too close.

"You didn't like it?" She seemed ready to cry.

"No. It isn't that. I have something else to tell you."

Her smile dissolved.

"You don't have it," I said. "Your test turned out negative. You're all right. You'll never get it." I meant to add: *I won't either. We'll both live long lives. Let's take that trip to Europe.* But Cruz came between us. He grasped me by both shoulders and demanded to know why Laurel was so upset. He let me go and shepherded her to a corner of the dressing room. He gestured to her angrily, pointing to his palm as if some rule she had sworn to abide by was written there. Laurel's friends crowded in. I pushed my way toward her, but Cruz kept himself between us.

"Cruz, darling," Laurel said, "could you find my shawl? Please? I'm very cold."

He dodged sideways to Laurel's dressing table, one eye trained on me. Laurel gnawed at the skin around her thumbnail, a habit I thought she had broken in grade school. "Jane, I can barely . . . Does this mean? I can't even get the words out."

"No," I said. "I don't have it either. Neither of us has it. I swear, we're both fine. Neither of us is going to get Valentine's. Ever."

She pulled back to see my face. The ragged sound she uttered was part sob, part laugh. "Jane! I can't believe it. Jane!" Still crying, she laughed and laughed and clutched me to her chest. I knew I couldn't keep holding her forever, but I intended to hold on to her as long as I could. This was the moment everything had led to, the moment I thought I would remember for the rest of my life.

"Jane, it's all so . . ." She drew away abruptly. "I don't know what to think."

She didn't know what to think? She wouldn't die. She wouldn't get sick.

"This was going to be my last dance. I was going to retire. I couldn't have done that piece if I didn't think I . . ." Laurel rubbed her own bare shoulders. "I couldn't have been a dancer in the first place. It was all because I didn't care. All my energy . . . If I'd thought any of it mattered, if I'd had to be careful, you know what I would be?" She fluttered her hand like a movie star dismissing her hairdresser. "I would be someone's spoiled wife."

"Baby," Cruz said. He wrapped the shawl around her. "Whatever she's been telling you, don't pay attention. You can do anything you set your mind to. Isn't that what all this proved? You're free now. Hear me, free?"

"Free?" Laurel said.

A bony Asian woman in a black silk dress nudged me aside. She introduced herself as the *Herald*'s arts reporter. "If you aren't too busy now?" she said to Laurel.

Laurel reached to take my hand, but we were already too far apart. "It's too crazy," she said. Another surge of well-wishers backed me toward the door. "I'll see you later!" Laurel called across the room. "I'll stop by at your apartment!"

I held up two fingers in a *V*. I wanted to tell her how important it was, what she had done, all those years she had spent dancing. But she was too far away, and I was too self-conscious to shout.

Willie and I left the theater. The wind bit our faces. Christmas decorations bobbed from the trees on the Common. I felt deflated and wrung out. I hadn't expected Laurel to kiss my hand with gratitude. But to be blamed? To be told that I had robbed her of the inspiration that allowed her to work?

Willie coughed, and I turned to study his profile. How would he react if he learned he didn't have it? And Ted, I thought. Wouldn't Willie be grateful if I told him that his son didn't have the marker? But what if Ted did have it? What would Willie do if I tested his son and brought home such bad news? The Jeep's heater huffed noisily. I slid closer to his side.

"You know," he said, "something this big is never going to turn out quite the way you imagine it should." He put his arm around me. "For what it's worth, I love you. I love you so much, I'm going to spend the rest of my life with you."

And then, unexpectedly, I was overcome with happiness. It traveled up my legs like the warmth from the heater, so relaxing that it induced something like sleep. What I was feeling was *bliss*, I decided. We passed the point on the bridge where Willie had stopped the Jeep the night I first met him. *Just be happy*, I thought, as if joy were a bridge you could only cross running, without looking back.

I reached in my pocket and found a quarter. *Oh, go on*, I thought. I flipped the coin and slapped it against my hand. Then I held it to the windshield. When I saw that the coin said heads, I was so disappointed I willfully changed the no to *yes*.

We parked. Snow was falling. A few flakes wafted here and there in Brownian arcs. I let them fall on my upraised face like drops of fixer from the X-ray.

We went up to my apartment and drank more hot cocoa. I meant to call Honey and Herb, but Willie took away my cup and pulled me to the floor. As I lay there beneath him, wrapped inside my comforter, I could swear I felt our baby somersault inside. That, too, would be fine. We would manage somehow. All three of us would manage, though I couldn't have said how.

20

The next morning, when I finally called my father, Honey refused to wake him. "Janie," she said, "I've never seen him this sick. It's a terrible flu. He can barely stand up." But I insisted that she put him on.

He made an inhuman hacking sound. "What?" he wheezed. "Hello?"

"Neither of us has it," I said. And, as had happened when I told him about finding the marker, I didn't hear anything in reply until Honey snatched away the phone and demanded that she be told what awful news I had given him. Herb was crying, she said. And when I told Honey the same news I had told my father, Honey cried, too.

Eventually, he got back on the line and said that he and Honey were driving up to Boston, while Honey tried to convince him to put off the celebration until he was over the flu.

We ended up at Tommie's, at a table set for five but with one empty chair. Laurel had gone home to Vermont. When I reached the number she had left, she said she was too worn out to drive all the way back to Boston and needed "time to settle down." My father was so disappointed I blurted out that I was pregnant, as if the embryo could fill the fifth seat. "We're having a baby," I announced, then realized I had forgotten to consult the child's father.

Honey choked on a scallop. "Planning to—?"

I was already three months pregnant, I said.

My father jumped up, as if he didn't know whom to fight. But he wasn't about to let the fate of a grandchild who didn't yet exist steal the relief he had bought so dearly. He slapped Willie on the back, sneezed, crushed my shoulders, and didn't even ask if we intended to get married. Honey sipped water and smiled a stiff smile until her son reminded her that congratulations were in order.

She choked out a word that might have been "Congratulations," or it might have been "I can't." I could tell she was thinking about the members of the family who hadn't yet received a clean bill of health. She put her face in her hands and started sobbing. I leaned over and tried to comfort her. She stood. Her chair fell backward. "I'm sorry," she said. "Janie, I'm very happy for you. And for Laurel, too, of course. I'm very relieved for you both. I'm grateful for all you've done. But I can't . . . You can't expect me to . . ." Willie came up behind her and wrapped her in his arms, as he had wrapped Flora Drury in his arms. My father went over and did the same. It was hardly the celebration for which I had hoped. But I finally got up and joined them.

ııııııııııııııııııııııııı

In the three weeks that followed, I received dozens of inquiries from universities offering me my own lab. Reporters kept calling. I was interviewed for *Nova* and a television program in Japan. (I couldn't help but wonder if Achiro would watch the show, if news of my success would please him.) What I wanted most was to see Laurel. I longed for her embrace, for the sense that we had overcome the long rivalry between us. I dialed her apartment in Vermont, imagining a day when I would have that number memorized. I tried again the next morning, and the next, until, in frustration, I let the phone keep ringing until someone picked up, revealing herself to be one of Laurel's neighbors who had stopped by to feed the cat. Laurel, the woman said, had gone to New York to see her boyfriend and wouldn't be back until the end of that week.

And so, a few days later, when the phone started ringing in the middle of the night, I had some idea who it might be. I untangled myself from Willie, thinking we would need to buy a double bed, soon, and grabbed the phone before it woke him.

"I'm downtown," Laurel said. "I'm in the lobby at South Station." She had taken the train up from Manhattan and missed the last bus to Vermont. She had only enough money to make this call.

I told her to take a cab and I would pay the driver.

"It's such a beautiful night," she said. "I would rather walk."

"At this hour? Are you nuts?"

"I shouldn't be bothering you," she said. "You need your sleep. What was I thinking? I *wasn't* thinking. I can't seem to hold a thought in my head. Don't worry about me, Jane. I'll spend the night here."

I started to tell her to wait and I would come get her, but she already had hung up. Was she in her right mind? She almost sounded drunk, although she rarely drank anything stronger than tea.

I told Willie I needed to take the Jeep, but my voice didn't seem to reach him. He slept heavily, as if such a large body sunk him deeper into sleep. I usually got up every few hours to take antacids or pee, but this didn't disturb his rest. What would happen when our baby woke crying in the night? Would I need to clobber him to get up, or would it be less bother to change the diaper myself? Would we fight about things like that? How could I get angry at someone who might become ill at any time?

"I need to go rescue Laurel," I said. I expected no response. But as I reached across his chest to grab the keys, he asked if he should come. "No," I said. "There's no reason both of us need to freeze." I would have felt easier with his company. And now, of course, I regret more than anything that I didn't beg him to come. But I suspected then that my sister wouldn't reveal what was really troubling her unless we were alone.

I pulled on tights beneath my jeans, although I could barely zip shut the zipper. A scarf pulled high, a hat pulled low. The frigid air stung my sinuses. The Jeep door whined; the seat complained beneath my weight. I was afraid the engine wouldn't turn over, but it did. The streets were so quiet I hoped Laurel might be safe; even a mugger wouldn't be out on such a cold night. The moon was so brilliantly full, it looked like a hole in the sky through which white paint was pouring down to glaze the Charles. The scene was even more surreal because a wooden desk was sitting on the ice about twenty yards from the Cambridge shore, with a chair and a pole lamp. I could make out a pile of textbooks on the desk, a typewriter, and a telephone. MIT students were given to playing pranks. Not long before, they had stolen a statue of a cow from a steak house on Route 1 and hoisted it to the dome on the main building. But hauling a desk on thin ice? Someone's roommates had risked their lives to play this joke.

South Station, which was being remodeled, was a mess of scaffolding, plywood tunnels, and plastic tarp. I checked the waiting room, the bathrooms, the luggage room, the platforms, then got back in the Jeep and navigated the tangle of one-way streets that surrounded the station. In a few minutes, I would pull over, find a phone, and call home. Maybe my sister had come to her senses and taken a cab.

But no, there she was, walking toward the Common. I could just make out her shawl. That couldn't be all she was wearing, could it? Worse, when I drove up, she shook her head like a little girl refusing a ride from a stranger—although, as a little girl, Laurel had several times accepted rides from people she didn't know. She didn't smell of alcohol, but there was a frantic look in her eyes. She left the sidewalk and veered across the Common. I parked the Jeep, then raced across the snow, praying I had been right and it was too cold for criminals.

"If we have to take a walk," I said, "can we take it somewhere besides the park?"

She looked around as if she were only now realizing where we were. "I don't want to go to your place."

I followed her back along the path, across Beacon toward Charles Street. I felt safer there, as if all the fancy shops, deserted at this hour, would somehow protect us. Then she took off across Storrow Drive to the river. Her hands must have been freezing—she worked them into the rear pockets of her jeans.

"I saw Cruz," she said. "I knew it would be ugly, but it was worse than ugly. I don't ever want to go back."

Well, I said, no one was forcing her to live in New York.

She shook her head. "Vermont. Not New York. I bought a round-trip ticket, but there's no reason for me to go back there." She pulled a hand from her jeans and brought out a ticket, which she tossed in the snow. I had to remove my own gloves to pick it up.

What about her dance troupe? I asked. The reviews had been terrific. Or hadn't she read them? I had memorized the quotes: *Explores interesting new ground . . . often compelling . . . original . . . deeply felt.*

"What do my reviews have to do with anything? I couldn't do that again."

"Of course you could!" I had meant to be encouraging, but my voice came out sharp. "Think of all the years—"

"That's exactly what I am thinking about. What am I going to do with all those years? I was a good enough dancer—for someone who was going to die soon. But for an ordinary person . . . And without Valentine's, I am pretty ordinary. Jane, I don't know how to *be* ordinary. And even if I were good enough, how much longer could I keep at it? My knees are shot—all that skiing, a bad landing I took skydiving. Do you think I would have taken all those chances with my legs if I had thought any of it mattered?" She tossed her hair; the strands crackled and threw off a spark. "And don't talk to me about choreography. That was Cruz. Well, no. The idea about the slime mold was mine. But what to do with it, how to turn it into art . . ."

"So why don't you marry him?"

"Because you have to be able to imagine spending your life with someone. Getting old with him. I don't love him. It didn't matter before. If he wanted to marry me, fine. We would work together a few years, have some fun, and as soon as I got sick he would run away. But all those years and years together . . . And kids. He wanted to have kids."

"But you can!" I said. "You *can* have kids. Don't you see? You won't get Valentine's, and any kid you might ever have won't get it either."

She slumped against my chest. "I have no excuse for it now, do I. I have nothing to live for. Or not to live for."

"Stop feeling sorry for yourself," I said. She was prettier than anyone else I knew. She was talented and smart. How dare she talk as if she had nothing left to live for?

"I can't do it," she said. "I was never scared of anything before. Because none of it mattered. 'Creative terror,' that's what I used to call it. What am I supposed to do now? Even giving you that blood—it was my chance to be a heroine. I was sure it would show that I had the gene and you didn't. So what can I do now? You get to work on the cure. You'll have your kid. You have Willie. Dad, he's got the foundation. Your lives are still wrapped up in it." She laughed a laugh that sounded like the ice on the river cracking. "You were smart to get attached to a man who's still at risk."

I had to crumple Laurel's shawl in my fist to keep from wrapping it around her neck. "How can you say that?"

She hid her face. "I don't know what I'm saying. I know how hard you've worked. I know how happy you are for me. And I was, too. At first. Those first few days I was euphoric. How could I not be? Then I got back to Vermont and had time to think. Cruz kept calling and demanding I go down there. And I did. But he wants kids. I don't love him. I told you that already. But even if I did, I can't have a kid."

"Of course you can have a kid. Laurel, you're only thirty!"

"You don't know the truth. No one knows. It was that summer in Alaska. With that guy Spence? Remember him? The lumberjack?"

He had hardly been a lumberjack; his father owned half the timber in the state.

"I got pregnant. For the third time. I told you about the first two times. But there was a third time. It was terrible. I convinced some doctor to tie my tubes. He didn't want to, at first, because I was only in my twenties. But he was some old guy in the middle of Alaska, I'm not sure he even had a license, and I convinced him I had Valentine's disease. It wasn't such a lie. I believed it. Every time I missed a dance step, every time I forgot something, or my moods changed, I knew I had it. I can't have kids, Jane. I dropped out of school. I aborted three pregnancies. I had my tubes tied. I don't know how to earn a living. All I can do is to spend other people's money. Do you know how much I owe? I owe eighty-five thousand dollars. I would get an offer for a credit card, and I would think, sure, why not, run it to the limit. Where do you think Cruz and I got the money to put on that show? I don't know how to live within a budget. I don't know how to be a sister, or a lover, or a friend. I don't know how to be a grown-up. I don't even know who I am without it. Do you understand? I don't know."

We were in the shadowy nowhere beneath the T. The trains had stopped running. If I climbed the bridge, Laurel might follow me. We would be safer up there. Even at this hour there was an occasional car. But once we reached Cambridge, we would have to walk past the projects, the construction sites, all the bars. We could go up to my lab, but what would we do there? Laurel wouldn't want to be reminded of the day she had given blood.

"What's that?" she asked. She pointed across the ice. From this distance, the desk might have been anything. I told her what it was. And for the first time that night, my sister smiled. She looked beautiful again. "I'm going out there," she said. "Didn't you always want me to finish college? I'm going to sit at that desk."

I grabbed her shawl—but I was too late, that's all I was left with. She spun away from me and hurried across the ice. She couldn't be serious, I thought. The Charles never froze completely, not even during a prolonged cold spell. The ice supported the desk, but that was near the far shore and who knew what lay between. I wanted to run and drag her back, but she was halfway across the ice. Besides, she was stronger than I was. What if we both fell in? What would happen to my baby? Better if I ran for help.

I glanced back toward the brownstones, not one of which was lit. Oh, what did that matter, disturbing someone's sleep! Still, it might be quicker if I flagged down a cab. The driver could radio in for help. Storrow Drive was deserted, but there was traffic on the bridge. At the very least, I could keep an eye on Laurel.

I started running up the steps to the pedestrian overpass. I took the stairs two at a time. It occurred to me that my sister was mentally ill. A scene flashed through my mind—it was from that musical, *The King and I*. The king's unhappy concubine, Tuptim, choreographs her version of *Uncle Tom's Cabin*. The slave girl, Eliza, escapes across the ice. When Simon Legree tries to cross the same river, the Buddha calls out the sun so the wicked slavedriver falls through the ice and drowns. Was Laurel thinking about Eliza's dance across the ice? Did she think she had to make good on her promise to die young? None of this made sense, and the thought that my sister truly had suffered a breakdown frightened me as much as the probability of her plunging through the Charles.

I reached the bridge and stood there panting. I looked down. Laurel was three-quarters of the way between the Boston side of the river and the desk. The moon had disappeared, but the ice glowed pure white, as if it were lit from underneath, and the mere fact that it seemed possible to walk across something you usually couldn't walk across made me understand why my sister wanted to try. "Laurel!" I called down, but she was too far away to hear.

I don't have any memory of what happened next. I only know that I saw my sister vanish. I remember waving the shawl—I must have flagged down a cab. But by the time the driver had managed to call the police, by the time the divers got there, by the time they fished my sister's body from the Charles, it was far too late for any of us to save her.

21

I slept to avoid grieving for my sister. I slept to keep from thinking I was responsible for her death. If I had never developed a test for Valentine's, she wouldn't have learned she didn't have it. She might have kept living her reckless life forever, assuming she would come down with Valentine's but never developing the disease or dying. I allowed Willie to rouse me from my bed and nearly carry me to her funeral, then I crawled back in that same bed to avoid the memory of watching Willie and Ted and Karl Prince and Cruz lower Laurel's casket into its yawning grave, then watching my own hands as they helped the rabbi shovel some dirt on top.

I slept to avoid answering my father's calls and listening to him cry and rant and take the blame on himself when it should have remained mine alone. I slept as a reward for all the sleep I had given up working in the lab, and to forestall the overwhelming task of zeroing in on the gene, figuring out which protein it coded for, and trying to undo whatever damage that protein wreaked. Most of all, I slept to keep from fretting about the child inside my womb and what I would do if I found out it was carrying the gene for Valentine's. The blessings of ordinary life seemed as fragile as the bones of that fetus inside me. Maybe, like Laurel, I had found the stamina and courage to work so hard for so long because I assumed I would die young and rest forever in the grave.

I went into the lab only when I could no longer force myself to sleep. I used the sun's glare as an excuse to shut the shade and block my view of the Charles. The river terrified me now. I kept imagining Laurel plunging through the ice, myself leaping in, some unnameable force dragging both of us down. I crossed the river only when Willie persuaded me to keep my appointment with the obstetrician Honey had picked out in Boston. As the Jeep neared the bridge—not the Longfellow, which I no longer could bear to cross, but the bridge near BU—I shut my eyes and counted. My throat tightened. I shook. Of all the rotten luck, traffic slowed to a stop and we sat on that bridge for so long I finally felt compelled to open my eyes and look down.

The water was no longer frozen, but I could somehow tell how very cold it still must be. A long-necked black bird I took to be a cormorant dove underwater. I tried to predict when and where it might surface, but the bird seemed to stay submerged too long for any creature to survive. I imagined Laurel's body among the weeds. I saw my mother's skeleton in a rotted dress from Weiss's. Why had they died and I hadn't? And my mother's brothers. And my grandfather. And those sufferers up in Maine. Why was I healthy and they were not? And what about the children who had tested positive for the gene, and for whom, as Vic said, nothing could be done?

"I don't want to be here," I said. "I don't want to be here!"

Willie thought I didn't want to stay on the bridge, so he honked his horn and swerved among all the stalled cars. I made it through the checkup. Then we returned to Cambridge by way of a third bridge, near Newton. He gunned the Jeep; I closed my eyes and hummed until we reached the other side. For the next several months, whenever I was scheduled for a checkup, this was the bridge we crossed and the method we used to cross it.

Willie worried about me, of course. But he had the sense not to say much. The night Laurel went through the ice, I called him from the police station and he hurried down to drive me back to my apartment, where I registered that he had stayed up for us, waiting, with a pan of cinnamon buns he had baked from scratch. When he understood what had happened, he wrapped the comforter around my shoulders and led me to bed. Then he moved in and took care of me. When I berated myself for not calling Laurel more often, not truly understanding what she was going through, he reminded me that my sister had been responsible for her own life. It wasn't my test that killed her. It was the way she had chosen to respond to the same genetic hand that fate had dealt me. He kept our refrigerator stocked with nutritious foods, cooked me breakfast and dinner, and used the blender to mix me frappés. When I cried, he rubbed my back. He made sure I took my iron pills. Only once did he lose his patience, when the doctor put his stethoscope to my belly and I didn't seem to care.

"That's our child," he said. "That's its heart, Jane. You've got to snap out of this."

I promised him I would.

"When? When the kid's twenty? When you've missed the whole thing?"

My father seemed to suffer the same loss of zeal that I did. He surprised me by relinquishing the presidency of the foundation. He wanted, he said, to spend more time with Honey. But I suspected that, like me, he was giving in to grief and self-reproach. "My job's over now," he said, a victory that entailed pretending that his son-in-law and Ted and his own unborn grandchild weren't still at risk.

Only Vic didn't stop work. One afternoon—I was in my fifth month—he called to tell me that he would be spending the next several weeks in Washington, setting up a committee to formulate guidelines for genetic testing, not only for Valentine's, but for all the diseases for which tests might be developed. This much I had predicted. But he shocked me by accepting Honey's request that he take over the Valentine's foundation until my father found the heart to resume his old post. Instead of switching to a line of research whose morality was unassailable, Vic was doubling down on his efforts to find the gene for Valentine's. There was no going back now, he said. The only solution lay in getting past this hopeless limbo we were in.

Vic's energy, his unwillingness to be crippled by the same doubt that had crippled me, made me all the more tired. I couldn't bear his solicitude. He seemed to think I had gotten pregnant on purpose, in response to finding out that I didn't have the gene. Every time he saw me, he described another reward of giving birth. "It's a miracle," he said portentously. "A child is the very definition of grace."

I went in to the lab as infrequently as I could. Not that anyone I knew was there. Yosef had accepted a position as a salesman for a biological supply house. Susan was staying home, cramming for her LSATs. Lew was at McLean, recovering from another bout of manic depression. And Maureen was flying around the country giving seminars in the hope of landing a job. When I did go in, I spent my time complying with requests from other biologists that I send them copies of the probe. Everyone was racing to clone the gene. While the test for the marker required DNA from the patient's entire family, a test for the gene itself could be accomplished with blood from the patient alone. Even if I hadn't felt so sluggish, I would have needed years to achieve this.

My due date came and went. I began to think of my pregnancy as an experiment that had failed. I napped on the couch while Willie sat in the kitchen studying the annual reports of companies he might invest in. But my languor unnerved him. "We could drive to New Hampshire," he said, an offer I declined, not wanting to give birth in a cabin in the woods with no running water.

"Babies have their own clocks," Honey assured me. I could guess what it was costing her not to point out that she had begged me not to have a child with her son. "Willie came two months ahead of schedule. He was the teensiest thing. The doctors told me he might not pull through. And now, well, just look at him—six feet four inches, and so healthy I can't think of the last time he had a sniffle."

Healthy, I thought. In the heartbeat of silence that followed, Honey, I was sure, was thinking the same thing.

My father was less optimistic. "Something's wrong," he kept mumbling. "The kid's getting too big," although I had put on less than twenty pounds. "Tell that doctor of yours to make the kid come out now."

As it happened, my contractions started the day my regular obstetrician left town for Nantucket. The OB on call was a stern older woman with a face like a pie plate and a watch hanging around her neck upside down, so only she could read it. She was semiretired, and my regular obstetrician had warned us that Dr. Krook had "antiquated ideas."

"You going to do the right thing by this gal?" she asked Willie, and even though we were planning on getting married, I was glad he didn't volunteer this information. A wave of cramps wrung my womb. I reached for his hand, panting, not to any rhythm—I hadn't had the heart to take the class—but in response to the ebb and flow of pain. The contraction subsided. Through blurry eyes I saw the obstetrician studying my chart. "Both of you have a history of Valentine's chorea in your families?"

I struggled to sit up, but Willie was already answering. "What do you propose we do about it now?"

The next contraction clenched my uterus. I gasped and leaned back. The obstetrician clocked the time. The fact that her watch was hanging upside down upset me terribly.

"All I meant was that two educated people such as yourselves ought to know better."

And I thought as I lay there that it isn't always possible to know what "better" might mean. Maybe I had had a child because I had grown so tired of weighing the pros and cons of each option. Maybe I had had a child because, by the time my head was clear enough to reach a decision, the pregnancy seemed too complex an experiment to destroy. Or maybe I had had a child because I was sick to death of death and wanted to give my father something to live for. Or maybe I had had a child because tossing a coin had revealed what I wanted to do all along.

"Now push," the doctor ordered. I didn't need to be told. I had no other desire but to push. Still, I held back. I would never have a child in my body again, never share this sensation so many women before me had known. "They wanted to put me under," my mother said. "That's what they did back then. They put the mother to sleep so she wouldn't make any trouble. But I raised a fuss and told them, 'Don't you dare. This is one moment I am not about to sleep through.'" My mother, Glori Weiss, had felt this same pain, this same suspense and exaltation, and perhaps this same worry that the child she already loved, the child she would undergo any torture to spare, might someday fall ill.

Then I couldn't keep from pushing and out my baby rushed on a wave of warmth.

"A girl," the obstetrician announced. "Small. But she seems to be fine."

One of the residents held her up. Her face was round and red, with a tuft of wet hair peaking from the crown. She looked like a beet from my mother's garden.

"And what's the baby's name?" the resident asked.

"Lila," I said. "Lila Weiss Land." I had intended to name her for my mother, but I was afraid of cursing her with my mother's bad luck. Besides, "Glori Land" sounded like some dopey doublespeak for heaven. No other member of our family had been blessed with both good health and a euphonious name. My father's father had run off when he was a boy, and his mother had been a shrew. That left only my mother's mother, Lillian, but "Lillie Land" sounded ridiculous. Then Willie took me for a walk through the Arnold Arboretum. The lilacs were in bloom. Lilac? I thought. No. *Lila*. Lila Weiss Land. Then I realized that "Lila" sounded like Laurel.

"But that's what she wanted," Willie said. "Remember the day we all had brunch? Remember how Laurel whispered something? Well, what she said was, 'Make my sister happy. And if you ever have a kid, name the baby for me.'"

That was just like my sister, to strike the tragic aunt's pose. I was nearly as afraid that Lila would take on my sister's personality as that she might inherit her grandfather's faulty gene. But it was a nice name. *Lila Land*.

"She's too, too precious," Maureen cooed. "What a peanut! Look at those tiny hands! And that mouth! Have you ever seen anything so kissable?" She produced a heart-shaped box wrapped in shiny paper. "Why are baby clothes all so boring? It took me hours to find these." In the box lay a pair of red-and-white-striped booties to which she had applied silver sequins and scarlet bows.

Yosef came next, clean-shaven and newly coiffed. "I make more in my first week as a salesman than in two month as a postdoc. If my family gets visas, I will meet them at the airport driving a long black Lincoln Town Car," although I could tell he was saying this to keep up his spirits; he hated his job, selling water baths, autoclaves, and spectrophotometers. "Best part is I finally got money to buy nice things for my friends." He produced a giant stuffed mouse whose fur was so soft I couldn't help but stroke it, and six smaller stuffed babies, imitations of the litter that had been born to the runt I was more than certain than ever must be a homozygote: all six of its pups seemed to be afflicted with the heterozygous form of Valentine's.

On the morning I was discharged, Willie packed the stuffed mice in a box, then went to bring the Jeep. An orderly came in to get me.

"I don't need a wheelchair," I said.

"Rules, rules, rules," the young man sang. "You trip and fall with that baby, we're all in deep shit."

I had just settled in the chair and accepted Lila in my arms when Rita Nichols appeared in running shoes and her nurse's uniform. I hadn't seen Rita since our trip to New Jerusalem. She had resigned from the project to devote more attention to her sons, especially Dennis, who had emerged from his coma but still seemed to be suffering some mental impairment; the boy who had scored nearly 700 on his math SATs now had trouble adding. "At least with Valentine's, you got fifty-fifty odds," Rita told me when I visited. "A black boy in Boston, he's lucky he sees twenty without getting killed or messed up in his head."

She had just finished her shift on the neurological ward. "Been meaning to come to see you, but you know how it is." She lifted Lila's arm and let it drop. "Thin as a chicken bone." She tsk-tsked. "Not an ounce of extra meat on her. Just like my James at that age."

I told her again how sorry I was about what had happened.

She shook her head, which to me, in the wheelchair, seemed seven feet high. "Dr. Butterworth, he says Dennis probably will get back most of what he's lost. Thank Jesus for that man, all he's done for my boy. It's James I'm keeping my eye on now. Better he ends up a momma's boy than he ends up like his brother." She turned to leave. Her sneakers squeaked. "Whatever happened to that woman? What's her name, Dreary? Drury?"

My sorrow was made even more pronounced by the hormones. "She died," I said, tears rising to my eyes. I hadn't wanted to attend Flora's funeral; it was too soon after we had buried Laurel. But Willie came with me. There was a brief service in an evangelical church near Pittsfield. Willie and I sat near the back, and no one seemed to notice us. Only when the dozen or so mourners moved outside for the burial did Flora's husband register that we had come. He strode over to me then, and I drew back, as if I were afraid he might strike me for torturing his wife without doing anything to relieve her suffering. Instead, he embraced me in a grip so strong I could feel my child kick to free itself from being smothered.

"You tried," he said. "You're the only goddamn person who gave a fuck about my wife." Then he broke down and sobbed. His friends, huge men who seemed ill at ease in suits that barely concealed their tattoos, their thick gray beards and long gray hair showing signs of having been trimmed for this occasion, needed to support Mac through the remainder of the funeral. The ones who hadn't arrived on motorcycles herded him and his kids to their trucks and cars.

One of the women who remained behind came over and tried to comfort me. "Don't feel bad," she said. "Death was a release for that poor woman. She finally found her peace with Jesus." Which, I suppose, she had.

"Social Services ought to check on that family," Rita told me in the hospital. "I never was too sure what I thought about the father."

"He's all right," I said. "He loves those kids. Maybe it'll be easier for him now that Flora's gone." Except that I knew it wouldn't be. Mac might be able to derive some comfort in finding out that three of his four children didn't have the gene that had killed their mother. But his youngest child, Annette, the one who had stayed home from school to watch *Gilligan's Island* with her mother—Annette had tested positive.

I stroked my baby's head. "I'll try to remember to visit them and see how they're getting on."

"You do that," Rita said. "Maybe, if you want some company, I'll come along for the ride."

The orderly pushed my wheelchair down the corridor.

"Thanks for sending me that magazine," Rita called after us. "Didn't understand most of what you and Dr. O'Connell wrote, except the part with my name in it. But it sure looks nice on the coffee table. Something to pass on to the boys."

||||||||||||||||||||||||||||||||||||

After we brought Lila home, Honey and my father drove to Boston to help us. I tried to persuade them to rent a condo nearby. My father seemed to derive some small comfort from holding Lila. But Honey wouldn't hear of it. "You two are on your own now. There's a company from Toronto that's interested in buying the stores. We've got to make everything shipshape for when we show the big shots around."

Sell the stores? It was one thing for my father to take a rest from the foundation, but to give up his stores? He was only sixty-eight. What would he do to keep his mind occupied? Honey, I guessed, was trying to distance them from the possibility that Willie or Ted might come down with Valentine's, which would mean that Lila would be at risk. But the baby started crying right then, and I never got the chance to ask.

In fact, Lila cried and screamed for hours.

"Here," Willie said. "You hold her. I've got one last trick up my sleeve."

I tried everything I could think of, but Lila kept wailing the same one-syllable sound over and over, as if she were crying out for something, or issuing a warning—

"Food!" perhaps, or "Fire!"—in a language none of us understood. Willie, in the meantime, had gotten his guitar. He had taken lessons as a kid, but after his father got sick, he gave it up. To stop Lila crying, he played the few songs he knew. I knew infants couldn't focus, but she seemed to be watching her father's hands. She held her fingers poised exactly like the fetus in my mother's copy of *Reproductive Biology*. Her father strummed the strings, and she laughed and drew back her lips, exposing that tiny bridge of flesh that was so like her aunt's. I couldn't help but wonder if, as Willie had said, a person's DNA could be written out and played like a musical score, what our daughter's genetic code might sound like.

He played "The Water Is Wide" and "Twinkle, Twinkle Little Star," then some Spanish bolero thing that involved a trill, at which Lila flapped her arms. Her father trilled again, and I saw the repetition of notes in my head, a stutter in the code, *CGC CGC CGC*. The Valentine's mutation was a stutter like this trill. A genetic trill, I thought. A multiplication of DNA triplets where there should have been only one. The triplets might code for too much of some protein, some neurotransmitter that flooded the brain's synapses and wouldn't let them relax, or some chemical that ate away those nerves. The more repetitions a person's gene suffered, the more severe the disease. Or the earlier the onset. I promised I would allow myself three more months of rest, of grieving for my sister, of caring for my daughter, before I began the arduous task of setting up my own lab and finding some way to sequence the gene and prove that this vision I had been granted was true.

22

For the past fifteen years, I have managed not to show concern when Lila tripped on the stairs, spilled her orange juice, or appeared not to hear my request that she take out the trash. This past winter, when she spent hours staring into space instead of doing her homework, I managed to smile, knowing this to be the symptom of her crush on Robbie Koch, whose knowledge of the classics astounds even me. Whole weeks have gone by in which I never once thought about the odds that Lila's father inherited the gene for Valentine's and passed it to her.

Willie, after all, turned fifty-five last month without showing the slightest sign of being ill. As he blew out the candles on the German chocolate cake Lila and I had baked, I found myself marveling at how lucky we have been and how I ended up with so much more than I could have hoped. I have a husband. I have a daughter. I have a lab of my own, in the same building in Harvard Yard where I did my dissertation (I turned down an offer from Mass. General because my office would have overlooked the Charles). We own this triple-decker in Somerville, and Willie's cabin in New Hampshire—some of my happiest memories are of the weekends the three of us have spent there, the walks we have taken in those woods. Maybe Sumner was right. Collecting things does give your life more dimensions. It makes you feel richer, more real. Then again, the more you own, the more vulnerable you are to loss.

A few hours ago, Lila's stepbrother, Ted, called unexpectedly from Texas. I put Willie on the phone, then went up to my office to do some work. Lila was in her room, mooning about Rob, no doubt. But I couldn't concentrate on the paper I was supposed to write. The instant I heard Willie sob, I jumped up and raced down the stairs and found him in the kitchen, inspecting an arty portrait of Lila in the leotard she wore to her first ballet class. From that moment, I knew I would think of Lila's chances again and again. And the more I tried to stifle it, the more uncontrollably the thought would spring to mind. Would Lila think about it, too? How often do adolescents think about death? More likely, she would brood on her father's fate rather than her own. I wished we could keep the news to ourselves. But Lila has always been able to sense when either of us is upset.

Besides, we have made a point of telling her the truth. If we didn't, Willie said, she would only imagine worse. If she doesn't hear about Ted's diagnosis from us, she might hear the news from him. Having reached his midthirties and become, of all things, a federal marshal, Ted seems to view the truth as something for a posse to pursue and bring back, a philosophy apparently shared by the female Texas Ranger to whom he has proposed. According to this woman, the results of the test she asked Ted to take wouldn't affect her commitment to marry him. She just wanted to know "what she was getting into," so there "wouldn't be any surprises," as if marriage were an ambush she hoped to pull off with as few casualties as possible.

The test is now available at centers around the country, as long as the client agrees to submit to the counseling procedures Vic's committee devised. Since the gene itself is known, the test can be done with nothing but the patient's DNA. "It's, like, a formality," Ted told Willie, the test no more threatening than the FDA's inspection of a prime cut of beef. But when his result came back positive, Ted's fiancée said she would need another few months "to think things over." I wanted to demand that Ted call off the engagement, but I couldn't interfere. Ted is a grown-up. He needs to make his own decisions.

After Willie told me all this, he went out to take a walk while I sat in the kitchen brooding. Next week, when Honey and my father fly east from Palm Springs, I will break the news to them. I envy their ignorance. For them, Lila, Willie, and Ted are still free of the gene. The only benefit is that my father might rouse himself from the despondency in which he has been mired for so long. After he sold his stores, he went back to helping Vic supervise the foundation, but only in the most perfunctory way. Perhaps that will change. My father would stay alive and keep running the foundation forever if it might save his granddaughter a moment's illness.

I hate to say this, but I have often thought about waiting until Lila is asleep, then sneaking into her room and stealing enough blood to run the test. But I don't have a vampire's stealth. It would violate Vic's protocol to run the test on a minor. And this, the strongest argument: instead of lowering my daughter's risk from 0.5 to 0, the test might raise that chance to 1.

The tumbler on the front door clicks. I jump up, not wanting Willie to figure out that I have been sitting in this chair the entire time, thinking about our lives, justifying the decisions we both made, or put off making. I boil some water to cook lasagna. Willie goes to the refrigerator and unclips the report card from the hand-painted swan magnet Lila brought home in third grade: A's in music and art, an A+ in biology, A's in English and math. "This means I have it, too, doesn't it?" he asks, as offhandedly as if he were asking a question about whether I have remembered to turn off the stove.

I catch my breath and tell him, "Yes, sweetheart, it does." Although I am very quick to add that in cases like his, in which the onset is so late, the disease progresses slowly. He might live a relatively unfettered life through his fifties and early sixties.

"Thank you," he says, as if I were a judge who has handed down a sentence far more lenient than the evidence might allow.

He kisses me, then wanders to the living room, where he searches for a book about Buddhist philosophy he hasn't touched in years. He takes it from the shelf and sits in a chair to read it. For a minute, I see him as he might look ten or fifteen years in the future, slumped in that same chair, shaking for most of any given day, no longer able to swallow solid food, so I have to spoon pap in his mouth, the way I once fed my mother. For all I know, all three of them will end up sick, maybe at the same time. If Willie is incapacitated by Valentine's, I will be left to care for Ted.

I go to him and take away the book. I climb in his lap and lay my head against his chest.

"Would you have wanted to know?" he asks. "All those years ago . . . Would you have married me if you had known?" There is a bitter twist to his voice. "Both of us, we thought we could outguess this thing."

He doesn't finish the thought. If he ever does, I will counter with the charge that my test isn't what is causing him this pain; it's his stubborn insistence on our having a child. But even if I had known, would I have not married Willie? Do I wish my darling Lila had never been born? I hope neither of us will ever make any such accusations. The mutual deterrence of knowing each of us possesses such a catastrophic weapon will help enforce the peace.

"I have to go up there now," I say. "I have to go tell her."

"What?" he says. "Oh, Jesus. I haven't thought any of this through."

"She'll figure it out," I say. "She'll know something's wrong the minute we sit down to dinner."

He nods. "Thanks," he says. "It's not fair to you to have to do it. But I'm just not ready."

"I know." I squeeze his hand, then start the long climb up those stairs. I knock at Lila's door. She is lying across her bed, reading a book about Greek gods and goddesses.

"Hi, Mom," she says, not because she is particularly glad to see me, but because her love for Robbie has flooded her brain with excess love for everything on the planet. "Sweetheart," I say, "there's something you need to know."

She listens. She pays attention. But I know none of this is sinking in. She is only fifteen. She doesn't want anything to spoil the pleasure of being in love. Besides, we have shielded her too well. She has never seen anyone with full-blown Valentine's. I assure her that her father and stepbrother are fine for now, that it will be years before either one shows signs of the condition. Like most kids, she trusts medicine to cure even the worst disease. As for herself, maybe she believes, as her aunt and I once did, that being at risk for a malady with the misleadingly romantic name of Valentine's disease is somehow exciting.

"Thanks for telling me, Mom." She gives me a hug, as if I am the one who needs consoling. "Is Dad here? I just have two chapters left in my book. Do you mind if I finish before I come down for dinner?"

I kiss her and go downstairs, sick with relief at having told her, unsettled by how well she took the news. "She seems okay with it," I tell Willie. "At least for now."

I put dinner on the table. When Lila comes down, she gives her dad a hug. "I love you," she says.

"I love you, too," he tells her back.

But that's all any of us say right then. We eat the lasagna in silence, except when Lila blurts out that Robbie has written an updated version of a play called *Lysistrata*. "We're putting it on at school," she says. "Is it okay if I play one of the women who won't let their husbands have sex until they end some war? The guys are supposed to wear these big, you know, versions of their, you know, their *pe-*

nises, and we aren't sure if the principal will let us use the props or not. But even if she does, I think everyone in the cast will need permission."

We tell her she can be in the play no matter what. She thanks us, then runs back up to her room, no doubt so she can phone Robbie with the news. I scrape the leftovers in the trash—all three of us have left most of the lasagna on our plates—and wash the pan. Willie pours himself some chocolate milk and goes back in the living room to read his book. After I finish cleaning up, I go upstairs and take a bath. It's barely nine, but I get in bed. That's when Lila appears at my door. She's wearing the lacy nightshirt her aunt Laurel once brought me from Brussels. It bothers me that Lila thinks her aunt's life as a dancer was far more glamorous than my hours in the lab or her father's visits to the companies he invests in. What if her response to learning she's at risk for Valentine's mimics my sister's? The thought of Lila breaking up with Robbie—or any other boy—makes my heart ache so badly that I would betroth her right now, if such things were still done. All her complaints about the fun she's had to miss, practicing Laurel's cello . . . *Keep playing*, I want to say. *Play the best you can, for as long as you're able. Don't you dare give it up!*

"Mom?" Lila asks. "Do you mind if I sleep in your bed tonight?"

She is carrying the battered stuffed mouse she put away the day she started kindergarten. In her room lives a real mouse, a distant descendant of the mouse I had predicted had a rodent variation of Valentine's disease, but which lived a long life—for a mouse, that is—and died of old age. In homozygotes, we think now, the two faulty chromosomes cancel each other out. Some overload is reached, and the brain finds a way to compensate for the damage. If the same is true for humans, then Lila might stand a better chance if I carried the gene for Valentine's and she got a copy of the bad gene from me as well as from her dad.

Then again, that's only a conjecture. There's so much we still don't know. My theory about the mutation being a triplet repeat turned out to be true, but I haven't been able to isolate the protein for which the gene codes. And the gene's effects on the nervous system have proven to be much more obscure than anyone could have predicted. I disagree with Sumner about how to spend our grants, whether at the level of molecules and genes, or the gross anatomy of the brain. But I can't afford to push our disagreements too far. Who knows but that Sumner might find the cure first. And he's still the best clinician in the country when it comes to treating Valentine's.

"It's not fair," Lila complains, then climbs on her father's side of the bed. She doesn't ask where he is. Maybe she has seen him reading in the living room. Or she already has become reluctant to bring her troubles to him. She snuggles closer and pounds the mattress. "Why Dad?" she sobs. "Why Ted?"

I refuse to talk statistics. I simply nuzzle her hair, which is soft but unwashed—it's as if she is two people, the girl who can go weeks without washing her hair, and that other girl, the one who washes her hair every night with lemon juice and applies to her face whatever beauty treatment the teen journals advise; the girl who says she wants to be a marine biologist, and some other girl who says she will *kill* herself if she doesn't get the lead in some ninth-grade production of *The Wizard of Oz*.

"What if I pray?" she asks. "There has to be *something* I can do."

"No, there isn't," I tell her furiously. "You mustn't ever think there is." And then, although I know it is exactly the wrong thing to say, "I won't let anything bad happen. To any of us. Lila, I promise."

That's when I decide I will get up even earlier the next morning than I usually do. I have so few years to save my husband. To save his son. To allow my daughter to have a child without being afraid she might pass on this curse to yet another generation. Surely, by the first or second decade of the twenty-first century, someone will have found a cure for Valentine's. But who can I rely on to be as devoted and obsessed as I am? So yes, I will get up even earlier. I will go into the lab and work harder than ever, become even more efficient. I will fiddle with the budget to find the money to hire more postdocs—sometimes, my father's lessons in accounting come in handier than anything I learned in grad school. And I will need to call Vic, who, in addition to running his lab and sitting on the board of the Valentine's foundation, holds an appointment with the NIH, an organization that is currently considering two of my grants. I will cancel my vacation to New York, although Maureen will be hurt—we were supposed to go shopping for her wedding dress.

I *will* attend Maureen's wedding. How could I disappoint not only my oldest and dearest friend, but also my daughter? When Lila heard the news that her auntie Maureen was engaged to the man who runs the lab across the hall from her own lab at Columbia—a lab Maureen was offered after twelve years in exile in Salt Lake City—she was so excited she danced around the kitchen. "That is *so* romantic! She just met the guy, like, two months ago! Does that count as love at first sight?" A beat later, more sober, she asked if her aunt Maureen was too old to have kids. I nodded; she was. Her fiancé was even older, and they both were too busy to have a child. I presented Lila with all the same excuses Maureen had given me to hide her disappointment that she would never have a daughter like mine.

So the three of us will go to Manhattan for the wedding. We will buy tickets to a ballet at Lincoln Center, tour the Museum of Natural History, take in MoMA and the Met. Yosef will steal an afternoon from work and treat us all to lunch. "Only not Russian Tea Room," he will joke. "I've got more than enough Russkies at home." Yosef finally managed to bring his family to New York. He married a girl he only half loved to help him care for his parents, and they now have three kids. Yosef hates his job—I often find brochures from his company in my mailbox, the ads for enzymes and gels and new biotechnological gizmos overlaid with Yosef's handwritten claims: "Puts hair on chest!" or, "Shines shoes and cures female complaint!" But he loves the money it allows him to lavish on his kids, on his parents, and on us. Once, he took Lila on a spree to FAO Schwarz. If I tell him she might have the gene for Valentine's, he will want to take her on a spree to Bloomingdale's. Then again, what harm could that do? Why should I deny Lila any-

Acknowledgments

This book was inspired by the dedication and brilliance of the men and women who found the marker for Huntington's chorea, a story wonderfully told by Alice Wexler in her memoir, *Mapping Fate*. Readers may notice certain parallels between the histories of Jane Weiss and the neurobiologist Nancy Wexler, or between Arlo Guthrie and Willie Land. That said, *A Perfect Life* is entirely a work of fiction, and no resemblance is intended between the occurrences and characters portrayed in this book and any actual events or people.

I am deeply grateful to those who provided me with advice and encouragement while I was researching, writing, and editing this novel: Charles Baxter, Suzanne Berne, Nicholas Delbanco, Tom Glaser, Linda Gregerson, Sharon Greytak, David Housman, Marcie Hershman, Maria Massie, Maxine Rodburg, Adam Schwartz, and Therese Stanton. Most of all, I want to thank my agent, Jenni Ferrari-Adler; my editor, Megan Lynch; and everyone at Ecco Press who has helped to give life to this book.

thing she might enjoy? Although I would hate to treat her as if she were one of those kids who gets to go to Disney World because she has only a few months to live. For all we know, she's perfectly healthy.

I pull her closer to my chest, then find myself thinking of the very first time I ever nursed her. That awful obstetrician had instructed me to allow my daughter no more than five minutes on each side. I debated going back to my room to get a watch, but Lila was already batting a breast as if it were a vending machine that wouldn't give her what she paid for. I squeezed the swollen nipple and helped her latch on. She closed her eyes to concentrate. I felt a stab of pain, then a surge of relief as she started to drain my milk. I had nothing to do but study her face, mouth working, eyes shut. I watched that face for so long, I had the sensation that Lila and I were one. And I drew as much contentment from watching that face as Lila seemed to draw from sucking at my nipple. Not a single clock marked those minutes. Time hadn't merely stopped. It had ceased to exist.